THIEF OF TIME

A Discworld® Novel

www.**booksattransworld**.co.uk

Also by Terry Pratchett

THE CARPET PEOPLE*
THE DARK SIDE OF THE SUN
STRATA · TRUCKERS* · DIGGERS* · WINGS*
ONLY YOU CAN SAVE MANKIND*
JOHNNY AND THE DEAD* · JOHNNY AND THE BOMB*
THE UNADULTERATED CAT†
(with Gray Jolliffe)
GOOD OMENS
(with Neil Gaiman)
THE DISCWORLD COMPANION†
(with Stephen Briggs)
THE PRATCHETT PORTFOLIO†
(with Paul Kidby)

The Discworld® series:
THE COLOUR OF MAGIC*
THE LIGHT FANTASTIC*
EQUAL RITES* · MORT* · SOURCERY*
WYRD SISTERS* · PYRAMIDS* · GUARDS! GUARDS!*
ERIC* (with Josh Kirby)†
MOVING PICTURES* · REAPER MAN*
WITCHES ABROAD* · SMALL GODS*
LORDS AND LADIES*
MEN AT ARMS* · SOUL MUSIC*
INTERESTING TIMES* · MASKERADE*
FEET OF CLAY* · HOGFATHER*
JINGO*
THE LAST CONTINENT*
CARPE JUGULUM*
THE FIFTH ELEPHANT*
THE TRUTH*

THE COLOUR OF MAGIC (graphic novel)
THE LIGHT FANTASTIC (graphic novel)
MORT: A DISCWORLD BIG COMIC (with Graham Higgins)†

SOUL MUSIC: The Illustrated Screenplay
WYRD SISTERS: The Illustrated Screenplay
MORT – THE PLAY (adapted by Stephen Briggs)
WYRD SISTERS – THE PLAY (adapted by Stephen Briggs)
GUARDS! GUARDS! – THE PLAY (adapted by Stephen Briggs)
MEN AT ARMS – THE PLAY (adapted by Stephen Briggs)

THE STREETS OF ANKH-MORPORK (with Stephen Briggs)
THE DISCWORLD MAPP (with Stephen Briggs)
A TOURIST GUIDE TO LANCRE a Discworld Mapp
(with Stephen Briggs and Paul Kidby)
DEATH'S DOMAIN (with Paul Kidby)
NANNY OGG'S COOKBOOK

* available in audio
† published by Victor Gollancz

THIEF OF TIME

Terry Pratchett

Doubleday

LONDON · NEW YORK · TORONTO · SYDNEY · AUCKLAND

TRANSWORLD PUBLISHERS
61–63 Uxbridge Road, London W5 5SA
a division of The Random House Group Ltd

RANDOM HOUSE AUSTRALIA (PTY) LTD
20 Alfred Street, Milsons Point, Sydney
New South Wales 2061, Australia

RANDOM HOUSE NEW ZEALAND
Poland Road, Glenfield, Auckland 10, New Zealand

RANDOM HOUSE SOUTH AFRICA (PTY) LTD
Endulini, 5a Jubilee Road, Parktown 2193, South Africa

Published 2001 by Doubleday
a division of Transworld Publishers

A catalogue record for this book is available from the British Library.
ISBN 0385 601883

Typeset in 10½/14½pt Meridien by Falcon Oast Graphic Art

Printed in Great Britain
by Clays Ltd, St Ives plc

1 3 5 7 9 10 8 6 4 2

According to the First Scroll of Wen the Eternally Surprised, Wen stepped out of the cave where he had received enlightenment and into the dawning light of the first day of the rest of his life. He stared at the rising sun for some time, because he had never seen it before.

He prodded with a sandal the dozing form of Clodpool the apprentice, and said: 'I have seen. Now I understand.'

Then he stopped, and looked at the thing next to Clodpool.

'What is that amazing thing?' he said.

'Er ... er ... it's a tree, master,' said Clodpool, still not quite awake. 'Remember? It was there yesterday.'

'There was no yesterday.'

'Er ... er ... I think there *was*, master,' said Clodpool, struggling to his feet. 'Remember? We came up here and I cooked a meal, and had the rind off your *sklang* because you didn't want it.'

'I *remember* yesterday,' said Wen thoughtfully. 'But the memory is in my head *now*. Was yesterday real? Or is it only the memory that is real? Truly, yesterday I was not born.'

Clodpool's face became a mask of agonized incomprehension.

'Dear stupid Clodpool, I have learned everything,' said Wen. 'In the cup of the hand there is no past, no future. There is only now. There is no time but the present. We have a great deal to do.'

Clodpool hesitated. There was something new about his master. There was a glow in his eyes and, when he moved, there were strange silvery-blue lights in the air, like reflections from liquid mirrors.

'She has told me everything,' Wen went on. 'I know that time was made for men, not the other way round. I have learned how to shape it and bend it. I know how to make a moment last for ever, because it already has. And I can teach these skills even to you, Clodpool. I have heard the heartbeat of the universe. I know the answers to many questions. Ask me.'

The apprentice gave him a bleary look. It was too early in the morning for it to be early in the morning. That was the only thing that he currently knew for sure.

'Er . . . what does master want for breakfast?' he said.

Wen looked down from their camp and across the snowfields and purple mountains to the golden daylight creating the world, and mused upon certain aspects of humanity.

'Ah,' he said. 'One of the *difficult* ones.'

For something to exist, it has to be observed.

For something to exist, it has to have a position in time and space.

And this explains why nine-tenths of the mass of the universe is unaccounted for.

Nine-tenths of the universe is the knowledge of the position and direction of everything in the other tenth. Every atom has its biography, every star its file, every chemical exchange its equivalent of the inspector with a clipboard. It is unaccounted for because it is doing the accounting for the rest of it, and you cannot see the back of your own head.*

Nine-tenths of the universe, in fact, is the paperwork.

And if you want the story, then remember that a story does not unwind. It weaves. Events that start in different places and different times all bear down on that one tiny point in space-time, which is the perfect moment.

Supposing an emperor was persuaded to wear a new suit of clothes whose material was so fine that, to the common eye, the

* Except in very *small* universes

clothes weren't there. And suppose a little boy pointed out this fact in a loud, clear voice . . .

Then you have The Story of the Emperor Who Had No Clothes.

But if you knew a bit more, it would be The Story of the Boy Who Got a Well-Deserved Thrashing from His Dad for Being Rude to Royalty, and Was Locked Up.

Or The Story of the Whole Crowd Who Were Rounded Up by the Guards and Told 'This Didn't Happen, Okay? Does Anyone Want to Argue?'

Or it could be a story of how a whole kingdom suddenly saw the benefits of the 'new clothes', and developed an enthusiasm for healthy sports* in a lively and refreshing atmosphere which got many new adherents every year, and lcd to a recession caused by the collapse of the conventional clothing industry.

It could even be a story about The Great Pneumonia Epidemic of '09.

It all depends on how much you know.

Supposing you'd watched the slow accretion of snow over thousands of years as it was compressed and pushed over the deep rock until the glacier calved its icebergs into the sea, and you watched an iceberg drift out through the chilly waters, and you got to know its cargo of happy polar bears and seals as they looked forward to a brave new life in the other hemisphere where they say the icc floes are lined with crunchy penguins, and then *wham*! Tragedy loomed in the shape of thousands of tons of unaccountably floating iron and an exciting soundtrack . . .

. . . you'd want to know the *whole* story.

And this one starts with desks.

This is the desk of a professional. It is clear that their job is their life. There are . . . human touches, but these are the human touches that strict usage allows in a chilly world of duty and routine.

Mostly they're on the only piece of real colour in this picture of blacks and greys. It's a coffee mug. Someone somewhere wanted to

* Mostly involving big, big beachballs.

7

make it a *jolly* mug. It bears a rather unconvincing picture of a teddy bear, and the legend 'To The World's Greatest Grandad' and the slight change in the style of lettering on the word 'Grandad' makes it clear that this has come from one of those stalls that have *hundreds* of mugs like this, declaring that they're for the world's greatest Grandad/Dad/Mum/Granny/Uncle/Aunt/Blank. Only someone whose life contains very little else, one feels, would treasure a piece of gimcrackery like this.

It currently holds tea, with a slice of lemon.

The bleak desktop also contains a paperknife in the shape of a scythe and a number of hourglasses.

Death picks up the mug in a skeletal hand . . .

. . . and took a sip, pausing only to look again at the wording he'd read thousands of times before, and then put it down.

VERY WELL, he said, in tones of funeral bells. SHOW ME.

The last item on the desktop was a mechanical contrivance. 'Contrivance' was exactly the right kind of word for it. Most of it was two discs. One was horizontal and contained a circlet of very small squares of what would prove to be carpet. The other was set vertically and had a large number of arms, each one of which held a very small slice of buttered toast. Each slice was set so that it could spin freely as the turning of the wheel brought it down towards the carpet disc.

I BELIEVE I AM BEGINNING TO GET THE IDEA, said Death.

The small figure by the machine saluted smartly and beamed, if a rat skull could beam. It pulled a pair of goggles over its eye sockets, hitched up its robe and clambered into the machine.

Death was never quite sure why he allowed the Death of Rats to have an independent existence. After all, being Death meant being the Death of *everything*, including rodents of all descriptions. But perhaps everyone needs a tiny part of themselves that can, metaphorically, be allowed to run naked in the rain*, to think the unthinkable thoughts, to hide in corners and spy on the world, to do the forbidden but enjoyable deeds.

* Quite an overrated activity.

Slowly, the Death of Rats pushed the treadles. The wheels began to spin.

'Exciting, eh?' said a hoarse voice by Death's ear. It belonged to Quoth, the raven, who had attached himself to the household as the Death of Rats' personal transport and crony. He was, he always said, only in it for the eyeballs.

The carpets began to turn. The tiny toasties slapped down randomly, sometimes with a buttery squelch, sometimes without. Quoth watched carefully, in case any eyeballs were involved.

Death saw that some time and effort had been spent devising a mechanism to rebutter each returning slice. An even more complex one measured the number of buttered carpets.

After a couple of complete turns the lever of the buttered carpet ratio device had moved to 60 per cent, and the wheels stopped.

WELL? said Death. IF YOU DID IT AGAIN, IT COULD WELL BE THAT—

The Death of Rats shifted a gear lever and began to pedal again.

SQUEAK, it commanded. Death obediently leaned closer.

This time the needle went only as high as 40 per cent.

Death leaned closer still.

The eight pieces of carpet that had been buttered this time were, in their entirety, the pieces that had been missed first time round.

Spidery cogwheels whirred in the machine. A sign emerged, rather shakily, on springs, with an effect that was the visual equivalent of the word 'boing'.

A moment later two sparklers spluttered fitfully into life and sizzled away on either side of the word: MALIGNITY.

Death nodded. It was just as he'd suspected.

He crossed his study, the Death of Rats scampering ahead of him, and reached a full-length mirror. It was dark, like the bottom of a well. There was a pattern of skulls and bones around the frame, for the sake of appearances; Death could not look himself in the skull in a mirror with cherubs and roses around it.

The Death of Rats climbed the frame in a scrabble of claws and looked at Death expectantly from the top. Quoth fluttered over and pecked briefly at his own reflection, on the basis that anything was worth a try.

SHOW ME, said Death. SHOW ME . . . MY THOUGHTS.

A chessboard appeared, but it was triangular, and so big that only the nearest point could be seen. Right on this point was the world – turtle, elephants, the little orbiting sun and all. It was the Discworld, which existed only just this side of total improbability and, therefore, in border country. In border country the border gets crossed, and sometimes things creep into the universe that have rather more on their mind than a better life for their children and a wonderful future in the fruit-picking and domestic service industries.

On every other black or white triangle of the chessboard, all the way to infinity, was a small grey shape, rather like an empty hooded robe.

Why now? thought Death.

He recognized them. They were not life forms. They were . . . non-life forms. They were the observers of the operation of the universe, its clerks, its *auditors*. They saw to it that things spun and rocks fell.

And they believed that for a thing to exist it had to have a position in time and space. Humanity had arrived as a nasty shock. Humanity practically *was* things that didn't have a position in time and space, such as imagination, pity, hope, history and belief. Take those away and all you had was an ape that fell out of trees a lot.

Intelligent life was, therefore, an anomaly. It made the filing untidy. The Auditors *hated* things like that. Periodically, they tried to tidy things up a little.

The year before, astronomers across the Discworld had been puzzled to see the stars wheel gently across the sky as the world-turtle executed a roll. The thickness of the world never allowed them to see why, but Great A'Tuin's ancient head had snaked out and down and had snapped right out of the sky the speeding asteroid that would, had it hit, have meant that no one would have needed to buy a diary ever again.

No, the world could take care of obvious threats like that. So now the grey robes preferred more subtle, cowardly skirmishes in their endless desire for a universe where nothing happened that was not completely predictable.

The butter-side-down effect was only a trivial but telling indicator. It showed an increase in activity. Give up, was their eternal message. Go back to being blobs in the ocean. Blobs are easy.

But the great game went on at many levels, Death knew. And often it was hard to know who was playing.

EVERY CAUSE HAS ITS EFFECT, he said aloud. SO EVERY EFFECT HAS ITS CAUSE.

He nodded at the Death of Rats. SHOW ME, said Death. SHOW ME . . . A BEGINNING.

Tick

It was a bitter winter's night. The man hammered on the back door, sending snow sliding off the roof.

The girl, who had been admiring her new hat in the mirror, tweaked the already low neckline of her dress for slightly more exposure, just in case the caller was male, and went and opened the door.

A figure was outlined against the freezing starlight. Flakes were already building up on his cloak.

'Mrs Ogg? The midwife?' he said.

'It's Miss, actually,' she said proudly. 'And witch, too, o'course.' She indicated her new black pointy hat. She was still at the stage of wearing it in the house.

'You must come at once. It's very urgent.'

The girl looked suddenly panic-stricken. 'Is it Mrs Weaver? I didn't reckon she was due for another couple of we—'

'I have come a long way,' said the figure. 'They say you are the best in the world.'

'What? Me? I've only delivered one!' said Miss Ogg, now looking hunted. 'Biddy Spective is a lot more experienced than me! And old Minnie Forthwright! Mrs Weaver was going to be my first solo, 'cos she's built like a wardro—'

'I do beg your pardon. I will not trespass further on your time.'

11

The stranger retreated into the flake-speckled shadows.

'Hello?' said Miss Ogg. 'Hello?'

But there was nothing there, except footprints. Which stopped in the middle of the snow-covered path . . .

Tick

There was a hammering on the door. Mrs Ogg put down the child that had been sitting on her knee and went and raised the latch.

A dark figure stood outlined against the warm summer evening sky, and there was something strange about its shoulders.

'Mrs Ogg? You are married now?'

'Yep. Twice,' said Mrs Ogg cheerfully. 'What can I do for y—'

'You must come at once. It's very urgent.'

'I didn't know anyone was—'

'I have come a long way,' said the figure.

Mrs Ogg paused. There was something in the way he had pronounced *long*. And now she could see that the whiteness on the cloak was snow, melting fast. Faint memory stirred.

'Well, now,' she said, because she'd learned a lot in the last twenty years or so, 'that's as may be, and I'll always do the best I can, ask anyone. But I wouldn't say I'm *the* best. Always learnin' something new, that's me.'

'Oh. In that case I will call at a more convenient . . . moment.'

'Why've you got snow on—?'

But, without ever quite vanishing, the stranger was no longer present . . .

Tick

There was a hammering on the door. Nanny Ogg carefully put down her brandy nightcap and stared at the wall for a moment. Now a lifetime of edge witchery* had honed senses that most

---

* An edge witch is one who makes her living on the edges, in that moment when boundary conditions apply – between life and death, light and dark, good and evil and, most dangerously of all, today and tomorrow.

people never really knew they had, and something in her head went 'click'.

On the hob the kettle for her hot-water bottle was just coming to the boil.

She laid down her pipe, got up and opened the door on this springtime midnight.

'You've come a long way, I'm thinking,' she said, showing no surprise at the dark figure.

'That is true, Mrs Ogg.'

'Everyone who knows me calls me Nanny.'

She looked down at the melting snow dripping off the cloak. It hadn't snowed up here for a month.

'And it's urgent, I expect?' she said, as memory unrolled.

'Indeed.'

'And now you got to say, "You must come at once."'

'You *must* come at once.'

'Well, now,' she said. 'I'd say, *yes*, I'm a pretty good midwife, though I do say it myself. I've seen hundreds into the world. Even trolls, which is no errand for the inexperienced. I know birthing backwards and forwards and damn near sideways at times. Always been ready to learn something new, though.' She looked down modestly. 'I wouldn't say I'm the best,' she said, 'but I can't think of anyone better, I have to say.'

'You must leave with me now.'

'Oh, I must, must I?' said Nanny Ogg.

'Yes!'

An edge witch thinks fast, because edges can shift so quickly. And she learns to tell when a mythology is unfolding, and when the best you can do is put yourself in its path and run to keep up.

'I'll just go and get—'

'There is *no time.*'

'But I can't just walk right out and—'

'*Now.*'

Nanny reached behind the door for her birthing bag, always kept there for just such occasions as this, full of the things she knew she'd want and a few of the things she always prayed she'd never need.

'Right,' she said.

She left.

Tick

The kettle was just boiling when Nanny walked back into her kitchen. She stared at it for a moment and then moved it off the fire.

There was still a drop of brandy left in the glass by her chair. She drained that, then refilled the glass to the brim from the bottle.

She picked up her pipe. The bowl was still warm. She pulled on it, and the coals crackled.

Then she took something out of her bag, which was now a good deal emptier, and, brandy glass in her hand, sat down to look at it.

'Well,' she said at last. 'That was . . . very unusual . . .'

Tick

Death watched the image fade. A few flakes of snow that had blown out of the mirror had already melted on the floor, but there was still a whiff of pipe smoke in the air.

AH, I SEE, he said. A BIRTHING, IN STRANGE CIRCUMSTANCES. BUT IS THAT WHAT THE PROBLEM WAS OR WAS THAT WHAT THE SOLUTION WILL BE?

SQUEAK, said the Death of Rats.

QUITE SO, said Death. YOU MAY VERY WELL BE RIGHT. I DO KNOW THAT THE MIDWIFE WILL NEVER TELL ME.

The Death of Rats looked surprised. SQUEAK?

Death smiled. DEATH? ASKING AFTER THE LIFE OF A CHILD? NO. SHE WOULD NOT.

' 'scuse me,' said the raven, 'but how come Miss Ogg became Mrs Ogg? Sounds like a bit of a rural arrangement, if you catch my meaning.'

WITCHES ARE MATRILINEAL, said Death. THEY FIND IT MUCH EASIER TO CHANGE MEN THAN TO CHANGE NAMES.

He went back to his desk and opened a drawer.

There was a thick book there, bound in night. On the cover,

14

where a book like this might otherwise say 'Our Wedding' or 'Acme Photo Album', it said 'MEMORIES'.

Death turned the heavy pages carefully. Some of the memories escaped as he did so, forming brief pictures in the air before the page turned, and they went flying and fading into the distant, dark corners of the room. There were snatches of sound, too, of laughter, tears, screams and for some reason a brief burst of xylophone music, which caused him to pause for a moment.

An immortal has a great deal to remember. Sometimes it's better to put things where they will be safe.

One ancient memory, brown and cracking round the edges, lingered in the air over the desk. It showed five figures, four on horseback, one in a chariot, all apparently riding out of a thunderstorm. The horses were at a flat gallop. There was a lot of smoke and flame and general excitement.

AH, THE OLD DAYS, said Death. BEFORE THERE WAS THIS FASHION FOR HAVING A SOLO CAREER.

SQUEAK? the Death of Rats enquired.

OH, YES, said Death. ONCE THERE WERE FIVE OF US. *FIVE* HORSEMEN. BUT YOU KNOW HOW THINGS ARE. THERE'S ALWAYS A ROW. CREATIVE DISAGREEMENTS, ROOMS BEING TRASHED, THAT SORT OF THING. He sighed. AND THINGS SAID THAT PERHAPS SHOULD NOT HAVE BEEN SAID.

He turned a few more pages and sighed again. When you needed an ally, and you were Death, on whom could you absolutely rely?

His thoughtful gaze fell on the teddy bear mug.

Of course, there was always family. Yes. He'd promised not to do this again, but he'd never got the hang of promises.

He got up and went back to the mirror. There was not a lot of time. Things in the mirror were closer than they appeared.

There was a slithering noise, a breathless moment of silence, and a crash like a bag of skittles being dropped.

The Death of Rats winced. The raven took off hurriedly.

HELP ME UP, PLEASE, said a voice from the shadows. AND THEN PLEASE CLEAN UP THE DAMN BUTTER.

Tick

This desk was a field of galaxies.

Things twinkled. There were complex wheels and spirals, brilliant against the blackness . . .

Jeremy always liked the moment when he had a clock in pieces, with every wheel and spring carefully laid out on the black velvet cloth in front of him. It was like looking at Time, dismantled, controllable, every part of it understood . . .

He wished his life was like that. It would be nice to reduce it to bits, spread them all out on the table, clean and oil them properly and put them together so that they coiled and spun as they ought to. But sometimes it seemed that the life of Jeremy had been assembled by a not very competent craftsman, who had allowed a number of small but important things to go *ping* into the corners of the room.

He wished he liked people more, but somehow he could never get on with them. He never knew what to say. If life was a party, he wasn't even in the kitchen. He envied the people who made it as far as the kitchen. There would probably be the remains of the dip to eat, and a bottle or two of cheap wine that someone had brought along that'd probably be okay if you took out the drowned cigarette stubs. There might even be a girl in the kitchen, although Jeremy knew the limits of his imagination.

But Jeremy never even got an invitation.

Clocks, now . . . clocks were different. He knew what made clocks tick.

His full name was Jeremy Clockson, and that was no accident. He'd been a member of the Guild of Clockmakers since he was a few days old, and everyone knew what *that* meant. It meant his life had begun in a basket, on a doorstep. Everyone knew how it worked. All the Guilds took in the foundlings that arrived with the morning milk. It was an ancient form of charity, and there were far worse fates. The orphans got a life, and an upbringing of a sort, and a trade, and a future, and a name. Many a fine lady or master craftsman or city dignitary had a telltale surname like Ludd or Doughy or Pune or Clockson. They'd been named after trade heroes or patron deities, and this turned them into a family, of a

16

sort. The older ones remembered where they came from, and at Hogswatch they were free with donations of food and clothing to the various younger brothers and sisters of the basket. It wasn't perfect, but, then, what is?

So Jeremy had grown up healthy, and rather strange, and with a gift for his adoptive craft that almost made up for every other personal endowment that he did not possess.

The shop bell rang. He sighed and put down his eyeglass. He didn't rush, though. There was a lot to look at in the shop. Sometimes he even had to cough to attract the customer's attention. That being said, sometimes Jeremy had to cough to attract the attention of his reflection when he was shaving.

Jeremy *tried* to be an interesting person. The trouble was that he was the kind of person who, having decided to be an interesting person, would first of all try to find a book called *How to Be An Interesting Person* and then see whether there were any courses available. He was puzzled that people seemed to think he was a boring conversationalist. Why, he could talk about all *kinds* of clock. Mechanical clocks, magical clocks, water clocks, fire clocks, floral clocks, candle clocks, sand clocks, cuckoo clocks, the rare Hershebian beetle clocks . . . But for some reason he always ran out of listeners before he ran out of clocks.

He stepped out into his shop, and stopped.

'Oh . . . I'm so sorry to have kept you,' he said. It was a *woman*. And two trolls had taken up positions just inside the door. Their dark glasses and huge ill-fitting black suits put them down as people who put people down. One of them cracked his knuckles when he saw Jeremy looking at him.

The woman was wrapped in an enormous and expensive white fur coat, which might have explained the trolls. Long black hair cascaded over her shoulders, and her face was made up so pale that it was almost the shade of the coat. She was . . . quite attractive, thought Jeremy, who was admittedly no judge whatsoever, but it was a monochromatic beauty. He wondered if she was a zombie. There were quite a few in the city now, and the prudent ones *had* taken it with them when they died, and probably could afford a coat like that.

17

'A *beetle* clock?' she said. She had turned away from the glass dome.

'Oh, er, yes . . . The Hershebian lawyer beetle has a very consistent daily routine,' said Jeremy. 'I, er, only keep it for, um, interest.'

'How very . . . organic,' said the woman. She stared at him as if he was another kind of beetle. 'We are Myria LeJean. *Lady* Myria LeJean.'

Jeremy obediently held out a hand. Patient men at the Clockmakers' Guild had spent a long time teaching him how to Relate to People before giving it up in despair, but some things had stuck.

Her ladyship looked at the waiting hand. Finally, one of the trolls lumbered over.

'Der lady does not shake hands,' it said, in a reverberating whisper. 'She are not a tactile kinda person.'

'Oh?' said Jeremy.

'But enough of this, perhaps,' said Lady LeJean, stepping back. 'You make clocks, and we—'

There was a jingling noise from Jeremy's shirt pocket. He pulled out a large watch.

'If that was chiming the hour, you are fast,' said the woman.

'Er . . . um . . . no . . . you might find it a good idea to, um, put your hands over your ears . . .'

It was three o'clock. And every clock struck it at once. Cuckoos cuckooed, the hour pins fell out of the candle clock, the water clocks gurgled and seesawed as the buckets emptied, bells clanged, gongs banged, chimes tinkled and the Hershebian lawyer beetle turned a somersault.

The trolls had clapped their huge hands over their ears, but Lady LeJean merely stood with her hands on her hips, head on one side, until the last echo died away.

'All correct, we see,' she said.

'What?' said Jeremy. He'd been thinking: perhaps a vampire, then?

'You keep all your clocks at the right time,' said Lady LeJean. 'You're very *particular* about that, Mr Jeremy?'

'A clock that doesn't tell the right time is ... wrong,' said Jeremy. Now he was wishing she'd go away. Her eyes were worrying him. He'd heard about people having grey eyes, and her eyes *were* grey, like the eyes of a blind person, but she was clearly looking at him and through him.

'Yes, there was a little bit of trouble over that, wasn't there?' said Lady LeJean.

'I ... I don't ... I don't ... don't know what you're—'

'At the Clockmakers' Guild? Williamson, who kept his clock five minutes fast? And you—'

'I am much better now,' said Jeremy stiffly. 'I have medicine. The Guild was very kind. Now please go away.'

'Mr Jeremy, we want you to build us a clock that is accurate.'

'All my clocks are accurate,' said Jeremy, staring at his feet. He wasn't due to take his medicine for another five hours and seventeen minutes, but he was feeling the need for it now. 'And now I must ask—'

'How accurate are your clocks?'

'Better than a second in eleven months,' said Jeremy promptly.

'That is very good?'

'Yes.' It had been *very* good. That was why the Guild had been so understanding. Genius is always allowed some leeway, once the hammer has been pried from its hands and the blood has been cleaned up.

'We want much better accuracy than that.'

'It can't be done.'

'Oh? You mean that you can't do it?'

'No, I can't. And if I can't, then neither can any other clockmaker in the city. I'd know about it if they could!'

'So proud? Are you sure?'

'I'd know.' And he would. He'd know for certain. The candle clocks and the water clocks ... they were toys, which he kept out of a sort of respect for the early days of timekeeping, and even then he'd spent weeks experimenting with waxes and buckets and had turned out primitive clocks that you could, well, very nearly set your watch by. It was okay that they couldn't be *that* accurate. They

19

were simple, organic things, parodies of time. They didn't grind across his nerves. But a real clock . . . well, that was a mechanism, a thing of numbers, and numbers had to be perfect.

She put her head on one side again. 'How do you *test* to that accuracy?' she said.

They'd often asked him that in the Guild, once his talent had revealed itself. He hadn't been able to answer the question then, either, because it didn't make *sense*. You built a clock to be accurate. A portrait painter painted a picture. If it looked like the subject, then it was an accurate picture. If you built the clock right, it would be accurate. You didn't have to test it. You'd *know*.

'I'd know,' he said.

'*We* want you to build a clock that is *very* accurate.'

'How accurate?'

'*Accurate.*'

'But I can only build to the limit of my materials,' said Jeremy. 'I have . . . developed certain techniques, but there are things like . . . the vibration of the traffic in the street, little changes in temperature, that sort of thing.'

Lady LeJean was now inspecting a range of fat imp-powered watches. She picked one up and opened the back. There was the tiny saddle, and the pedals, but they were forlorn and empty.

'No imps?' she said.

'I keep them for historical interest,' said Jeremy. 'They were barely accurate to a few seconds a minute, and they'd stop completely overnight. They were only any good if your idea of accuracy was "around two-ish".' He grimaced when he used the term. It felt like hearing fingernails on a blackboard.

'How about invar?' said the lady, still apparently inspecting the museum of clocks.

Jeremy looked shocked. 'The alloy? I didn't think anyone outside the Guild knew about that. And it is *very* expensive. Worth a lot more than its weight in gold.'

Lady LeJean straightened up. 'Money is no object,' she said. 'Would invar allow you to reach total accuracy?'

'No. I already use it. It's true that it is not affected by temperature, but there are always . . . *barriers*. Smaller and smaller interferences become bigger and bigger problems. It's Xeno's Paradox.'

'Ah, yes. He was the Ephebian philosopher who said you couldn't hit a running man with an arrow, wasn't he?' said the lady.

'In theory, because—'

'But Xeno came up with four paradoxes, I believe,' said Lady LeJean. 'They involved the idea that there is such a thing as the smallest possible unit of time. And it must exist, mustn't it? Consider the present. It must have a length, because one end of it is connected to the past and the other is connected to the future, and if it *didn't* have a length then the present couldn't exist at all. There would be no *time* for it to be the present in.'

Jeremy was suddenly in love. He hadn't felt like this since he'd taken the back off the nursery clock when he was fourteen months old.

'Then you're talking about . . . the famous "tick of the universe",' he said. 'And no gear cutter could possibly make gears that small . . .'

'It depends on what you would call a gear. Have you read this?'

Lady LeJean waved a hand at one of the trolls, who lumbered over and dropped an oblong package on the counter.

Jeremy undid it. It contained a small book. '*Grim Fairy Tales*?' he said.

'Read the story about the glass clock of Bad Schüschein,' said Lady LeJean.

'Children's stories?' said Jeremy. 'What can they tell me?'

'Who knows? We will call again tomorrow,' said Lady LeJean, 'to hear about your plans. In the meantime, here is a little token of our good faith.'

The troll laid a large leather bag on the counter. It clinked with the heavy, rich clink of gold. Jeremy didn't pay it a great deal of attention. He had quite a lot of gold. Even skilled clockmakers came to buy his clocks. Gold was useful because it gave him the time to work on more clocks. These earned him more gold. Gold was, more or less, something that occupied the space between clocks.

21

'I can also obtain invar for you, in large quantities,' she said. 'That will be part of your payment, although I agree that even invar will not serve your purpose. Mr Jeremy, both you and I know that your payment for making the first truly accurate clock *will be* the opportunity to make the first truly accurate clock, yes?'

He smiled nervously. 'It would be . . . wonderful, if it could be done,' he said. 'Really, it would . . . be the end of clockmaking.'

'Yes,' said Lady LeJean. 'No one would ever have to make a clock again.'

Tick

This desk is neat.

There is a pile of books on it, and a ruler.

There is also, at the moment, a clock made out of cardboard.

Miss picked it up.

The other teachers in the school were known as Stephanie and Joan and so on, but to her class she was very strictly *Miss* Susan. 'Strict', in fact, was a word that seemed to cover everything about Miss Susan and, in the classroom, she insisted on the *Miss* in the same way that a king insists upon *Your Majesty*, and for pretty much the same reason.

Miss Susan wore black, which the headmistress disapproved of but could do nothing about because black *was*, well, a respectable colour. She was young, but with an indefinable air of age about her. She wore her hair, which was blond-white with one black streak, in a tight bun. The headmistress disapproved of that, too – it suggested an Archaic Image of Teaching, she said, with the assurance of someone who could pronounce a capital letter. But she didn't ever dare disapprove of the way Miss Susan moved, because Miss Susan moved like a tiger.

It was in fact always very hard to disapprove of Miss Susan in her presence, because if you did she gave you a Look. It was not in any way a threatening look. It was cool and calm. You just didn't want to see it again.

The Look worked in the classroom, too. Take homework,

another Archaic Practice the headmistress was ineffectually Against. No dog ever ate the homework of one of Miss Susan's students, because there was something about Miss Susan that went home with them; instead the dog brought them a pen and watched imploringly while they finished it. Miss Susan seemed to have an unerring instinct for spotting laziness and effort, too. Contrary to the headmistress's instructions, Miss Susan did not let the children do what they liked. She let them do what she liked. It had turned out to be a lot more interesting for everyone.

Miss Susan held up the cardboard clock and said: 'Who can tell me what this is?'

A forest of hands shot up.

'Yes, Miranda?'

'It's a clock, miss.'

Miss Susan smiled, carefully avoided the hand that was being waved by a boy called Vincent, who was also making frantically keen 'ooo, ooo, ooo' noises, and chose the one behind him.

'Nearly right,' she said. 'Yes, Samuel?'

'It's all cardboard made to *look* like a clock,' said the boy.

'Correct. Always see what's really there. And I'm supposed to teach you to tell the time with this.' Miss Susan gave it a sneer and tossed it away.

'Shall we try a different way?' she said, and snapped her fingers.

'Yes!' the class chorused, and then it went 'Aah!' as the walls, floor and ceiling dropped away and the desks hovered high over the city.

A few feet away was the huge cracked face of the tower clock of Unseen University.

The children nudged one another excitedly. The fact that their boots were over three hundred feet of fresh air didn't seem to bother them. Oddly, too, they did not seem *surprised*. This was just an interesting thing. They acted like connoisseurs who had seen other interesting things. You did, when you were in Miss Susan's class.

'Now, Melanie,' said Miss Susan, as a pigeon landed on her desk. 'The big hand is on the twelve and the *enormous* hand is nearly on the ten, so it's . . .'

Vincent's hand shot up. 'Ooo, miss, ooo, ooo . . .'

'Nearly twelve o'clock,' Melanie managed.

'Well done. But *here* . . .'

The air blurred. Now the desks, still in perfect formation, were firmly on the cobbles of a plaza in a different city. So was most of the classroom. There were the cupboards, and the Nature Table, and the blackboard. But the walls still lagged behind.

No one in the plaza paid the visitors any attention but, oddly, no one tried to walk into them either. The air was warmer, and smelled of sea and swamp.

'Anyone know where this is?' said Miss Susan.

'Ooo, me, miss, ooo,ooo . . .' Vincent could only stretch his body taller if his feet left the ground.

'How about you, Penelope?' said Miss Susan.

'Oh, *miss*,' said a deflated Vincent.

Penelope, who was beautiful, docile and frankly dim, looked around at the thronged square and the whitewashed, awning-hung buildings with an expression close to panic.

'We came here in geography last week,' said Miss Susan. 'City surrounded by swamps. On the Vieux river. Famous cookery. Lots of seafood . . . ?'

Penelope's exquisite brow creased. The pigeon on Miss Susan's desk fluttered down and joined the pigeon flock prospecting for scraps among the flagstones, cooing gently to the others in pidgin pigeon.

Aware that a lot could happen while people waited for Penelope to complete a thought process, Miss Susan waved at a clock on a shop across the square and said: 'And who can tell me the time here in Genua, please?'

'Ooo, miss, *miss*, ooo . . .'

A boy called Gordon cautiously admitted that it might be three o'clock, to the audible disappointment of the inflatable Vincent.

'That's right,' said Miss Susan. 'Can anyone tell me why it's three o'clock in Genua while it's twelve o'clock in Ankh-Morpork?'

There was no avoiding it this time. If Vincent's hand had gone up any faster it would have fried by air friction. '*Yes*, Vincent?'

'Ooo miss speed of light miss it goes at six hundred miles an hour and at the moment the sun's rising on the Rim near Genua so twelve o'clock takes three hours to get to us miss!'

Miss Susan sighed. 'Very good, Vincent,' she said, and stood up. Every eye in the room watched her as she crossed over to the Stationery Cupboard. It seemed to have travelled with them and now, if there had been anyone to note such things, they might have seen faint lines in the air that denoted walls and windows and doors. And if they were intelligent observers, they'd have said: so . . . this classroom is in some way still in Ankh-Morpork *and also* in Genua, is it? Is this a trick? Is this real? Is it imagination? Or is it that, to this particular teacher, there is not much of a difference?

The *inside* of the cupboard was also present, and it was in that shadowy, paper-smelling recess that she kept *the stars*.

There were gold stars and silver stars. One gold star was worth three silver ones.

The headmistress disapproved of these, as well. She said they encouraged Competitiveness. Miss Susan said that was the point, and the headmistress scuttled away before she got a Look.

Silver stars weren't awarded frequently and gold stars happened less than once a fortnight, and were vied for accordingly. Right now Miss Susan selected a silver star. Pretty soon Vincent the Keen would have a galaxy of his very own. To give him his due, he was quite uninterested in which kind of star he got. Quantity, that was what he liked. Miss Susan had privately marked him down as Boy Most Likely to Be Killed One Day By His Wife.

She walked back to her desk and laid the star, tantalizingly, in front of her.

'And an *extra-special* question,' she said, with a hint of malice. 'Does that mean it's "then" there when it's "now" here?'

The hand slowed halfway in its rise.

'Ooo . . .' Vincent began, and then stopped. 'Doesn't make sense, miss . . .'

'Questions don't have to make sense, Vincent,' said Miss Susan. 'But answers do.'

There was a kind of sigh from Penelope. To Miss Susan's surprise the face that one day would surely cause her father to have to hire bodyguards was emerging from its normal happy daydream and wrapping itself around an answer. Her alabaster hand was rising, too.

The class watched expectantly.

'Yes, Penelope?'

'It's . . .'

'Yes?'

'It's always now everywhere, miss?'

'Exactly right. Well done! All right, Vincent, you can have the silver star. And for you, Penelope . . .'

Miss Susan went back to the cupboard of stars. Getting Penelope to step off her cloud long enough even to answer a question was worth a star, but a deep philosophical statement like that had to make it a gold one.

'I want you all to open your notebooks and write down what Penelope just told us,' she said brightly as she sat down.

And then she saw the inkwell on her desk beginning to rise like Penelope's hand. It was a ceramic pot, made to drop neatly into a round hole in the woodwork. It came up smoothly, and turned out to be balanced on the cheerful skull of the Death of Rats.

It winked one blue-glowing eye socket at Miss Susan.

With quick little movements, not even looking down, she whisked the inkwell aside with one hand and reached for a thick volume of stories with the other. She brought it down so hard on the hole that blue-black ink splashed onto the cobbles.

Then she raised the desk lid and peeped inside.

There was, of course, nothing there. At least, nothing macabre . . .

. . . unless you counted the piece of chocolate half gnawed by rat teeth and a note in heavy gothic lettering saying:

SEE ME

and signed by a very familiar alpha-and-omega symbol and the word

Grandfather.

Susan picked up the note and screwed it into a ball, aware that she was trembling with rage. How *dare* he? And to send the rat, too!

She tossed the ball into the wastepaper basket. She never missed. Sometimes the basket moved in order to ensure that this was the case.

'And now we'll go and see what the time is in Klatch,' she told the watching children.

On the desk, the book had fallen open at a certain page. And, later on, it would be story time. And Miss Susan would wonder, too late, why the book had been on her desk when she had never even seen it before.

And a splash of blue-black ink would stay on the cobbles of the square in Genua, until the evening rainstorm washed it away.

Tick

The first words that are read by seekers of enlightenment in the secret, gong-banging, yeti-haunted valleys near the hub of the world, are when they look into *The Life of Wen the Eternally Surprised*.

The first question they ask is: 'Why was he eternally surprised?'

And they are told: 'Wen considered the nature of time and understood that the universe is, instant by instant, recreated anew. Therefore, he understood, there is in truth no past, only a memory of the past. Blink your eyes, and the world you see next did not exist when you closed them. Therefore, he said, the only appropriate state of the mind is surprise. The only appropriate state of the heart is joy. The sky you see now, you have never seen before. The perfect moment is now. Be glad of it.'

The first words read by the young Lu-Tze when he sought perplexity in the dark, teeming, rain-soaked city of Ankh-Morpork were: 'Rooms For Rent, Very Reasonable'. And he was glad of it.

Tick

Where there is suitable country for grain, people farm. They know the taste of good soil. They grow grain.

Where there is good steel country, furnaces turn the sky to sunset red all night. The hammers never stop. People make steel.

There is coal country, and beef country, and grass country. The world is full of countries where one thing shapes the land and the people. And up here in the high valleys around the hub of the world, where the snow is never far away, this is enlightenment country.

Here are people who know that there *is* no steel, only the idea of steel.* They give names to new things, and to things that don't exist. They seek the essence of being and the nature of the soul. They make wisdom.

Temples command every glacier-headed valley, where there are particles of ice in the wind, even at the height of summer.

There are the Listening Monks, seeking to discern within the hubbub of the world the faint echoes of the sounds that set the universe in motion.

There are the Brothers of Cool, a reserved and secretive sect which believes that only through ultimate coolness can the universe be comprehended, and that black works with everything, and that chrome will never truly go out of style.

In their vertiginous temple criss-crossed with tightropes, the Balancing Monks test the tension of the world and then set out on long, perilous journeys to restore its equilibrium. Their work may be seen on high mountains and isolated islets. They use small brass weights, none of them bigger than a fist. They work. Well, *obviously* they work. The world has not tipped up yet.

And in the highest, greenest, airiest valley of all, where apricots are grown and the streams have floating ice in them even on the hottest day, is the monastery of Oi Dong and the fighting monks of the Order of Wen. The other sects call them the History Monks. Not much is known about what they do, although some have remarked

---

* But they still use forks, or, at least, the *idea* of forks. There may, as the philosopher says, be no spoon, although this begs the question of why there is the idea of soup.

28

on the strange fact that it is *always* a wonderful spring day in the little valley and that the cherry trees are always in bloom.

The rumour is that the monks have some kind of duty to see that tomorrow happens according to some mystic plan devised by some man who kept on being surprised.

In fact, for some time now, and it would be impossible and ridiculous to say how long, the truth has been stranger and more dangerous.

The job of the History Monks is to see that tomorrow happens at all.

The Master of Novices met with Rinpo, chief acolyte to the abbot. At the moment, at least, the position of chief acolyte was a very important post. In his current condition the abbot needed many things done for him, and his attention span was low. In circumstances like this, there is always someone willing to carry the load. There are Rinpos everywhere.

'It's Ludd again,' said the Master of Novices.

'Oh, dear. Surely one naughty child can't trouble you?'

'One *ordinary* naughty child, no. Where is this one from?'

'Master Soto sent him. You know? Of our Ankh-Morpork section? He found him in the city. The boy has a natural talent, I understand,' said Rinpo.

The Master of Novices looked shocked. 'Talent! He is a wicked thief! He'd been apprenticed to the Guild of Thieves!' he said.

'Well? Children sometimes steal. Beat them a little, and they stop stealing. Basic education,' said Rinpo.

'Ah. There *is* a problem.'

'Yes?'

'He is very, very fast. Around him, things go missing. Little things. Unimportant things. But even when he is watched closely, he is never seen to take them.'

'Then perhaps he does not?'

'He walks through a room and things vanish!' said the Master of Novices.

'He's *that* fast? It's just as well Soto *did* find him, then. But a thief is—'

29

'They turn up later, in odd places,' said the Master of Novices, apparently grudging the admission. 'He does it out of mischief, I'm sure.'

The breeze blew the scent of cherry blossom across the terrace.

'Look, I am used to disobedience,' said the Master of Novices. 'That is part of a novice's life. But he is also tardy.'

'Tardy?'

'He turns up late for his lessons.'

'How can a pupil be tardy *here*?'

'Mr Ludd doesn't seem to care. Mr Ludd seems to think he can do as he pleases. He is also . . . smart.'

The acolyte nodded. Ah. Smart. The word had a very specific meaning here in the valley. A smart boy thought he knew more than his tutors, and answered back, and interrupted. A smart boy was worse than a stupid one.

'He does not accept discipline?' said the acolyte.

'Yesterday, when I was taking the class for Temporal Theory in the Stone Room, I caught him just staring at the wall. *Clearly* not paying attention. But when I called out to him to answer the problem I'd chalked on the blackboard, knowing full well that he could not, he did so. Instantly. And correctly.'

'Well? You did say he was a smart boy.'

The Master of Novices looked embarrassed. 'Except . . . it was not the right problem. I had been instructing the Fifth Djim field agents earlier and had left part of the test on the board. An *extremely* complex phase-space problem involving residual harmonics in n histories. None of *them* got it right. To be honest, even I had to look up the answer.'

'So I take it you punished him for not answering the right question?'

'Obviously. But that sort of behaviour is disruptive. Most of the time I think he's not all there. He never pays attention, he always knows the answers, and he can never tell you how he knows. We can't *keep* thrashing him. He is a bad example to the other pupils. There's no educating a smart boy.'

The acolyte thoughtfully watched a flight of white doves circle the monastery roofs. 'We cannot send him away now,' he said at last. 'Soto said he saw him perform the Stance of the Coyote! That's how he was found! Can you *imagine* that? He'd had no training at all! Can you *imagine* what would happen if someone with that kind of skill ran around loose? Thank goodness Soto was alert.'

'But he has turned him into my problem. The boy disrupts tranquillity.'

Rinpo sighed. The Master of Novices was a good and conscientious man, he knew, but it had been a long time since he'd been out in the world. People like Soto spent every day in the world of time. They learned flexibility, because if you were stiff out there you were dead. People like Soto . . . now, *there* was an idea . . .

He looked towards the other end of the terrace, where a couple of servants were sweeping up the fallen cherry blossom.

'I see a harmonious solution,' he said.

'Oh, yes?'

'An unusually talented boy like Ludd needs a master, not the discipline of the schoolroom.'

'Possibly, but—'

The Master of Novices followed Rinpo's gaze.

'Oh,' he said, and he smiled in a way that was not entirely nice. It contained a certain anticipatory element, a hint that trouble might be in store for someone who, in his opinion, richly deserved it.

'A name occurs,' said Rinpo.

'To me also,' said the Master of Novices.

'A name I've heard too often,' Rinpo went on.

'I suppose that either he will break the boy, or the boy will break him, or it is always possible that they will break each other . . .' the Master mused.

'So, in the patois of the world,' said Rinpo, 'there is no actual *downside*.'

'Would the abbot approve, though?' said the Master, testing a welcome idea for any weak points. 'He has always had a certain rather tiresome regard for . . . the sweeper.'

'The abbot is a dear kind man but at the moment his teeth are giving him trouble and he is not walking at all well,' said Rinpo. 'And these are difficult times. I'm sure he will be pleased to accept our joint recommendation. Why, it's practically a minor matter of day-to-day affairs.'

And thus the future was decided.

They were not bad men. They had worked hard on behalf of the valley for hundreds of years. But it is possible, after a while, to develop certain dangerous habits of thought. One is that, while all important enterprises need careful organization, it is the organization that needs organizing, rather than the enterprise. And another is that tranquillity is always a good thing.

Tick

There was a row of alarm clocks on the table by Jeremy's bed. He did not need them, because he woke up when he wanted to. They were there for testing. He set them for seven, and woke up at 6.59 to check that they went off on time.

Tonight he went to bed early, with a drink of water and the *Grim Fairy Tales*.

He had never been interested in stories, at any age, and had never quite understood the basic concept. He'd never read a work of fiction all the way through. He did remember, as a small boy, being really annoyed at the depiction of Hickory Dickory Dock in a rag book of nursery rhymes, because the clock in the drawing was completely wrong for the period.

He tried to read *Grim Fairy Tales*. They had titles like 'How the Wicked Queen Danced in Red Hot Shoes!' and 'The Old Lady in the Oven'. There was simply no mention of clocks of any sort in *any* of them. Their authors seemed to have a thing about not mentioning clocks.

'The Glass Clock of Bad Schüschein', on the other hand, *did* have a clock. Of a sort. And it was . . . odd. A wicked man – readers could see he was wicked because it *said* he was wicked, right there on the page – built a clock of glass in which he captured Time herself, but things went wrong because there was one part of the clock, a spring, that he couldn't make out of glass, and it broke under the strain. Time was set free and the man aged ten thousand years in a second and crumbled to dust and – not surprisingly, in Jeremy's opinion – was never seen again. The story ended with a moral: Large Enterprises Depend upon Small Details. Jeremy couldn't see why it couldn't just as well have been It's Wrong to Trap Non-Existent Women in Clocks, or, It Would Have Worked with a Glass Spring.

But even to Jeremy's inexperienced eye, there was something wrong with the whole story. It read as though the writer was trying to make sense of something he'd seen, or been told, and had misunderstood. And – hah! – although it was set hundreds of years ago when even in Uberwald there were only natural cuckoo clocks, the artist had drawn a long-case clock of the sort that wasn't around even fifteen years ago. The stupidity of some people! You'd laugh if it wasn't so tragic!

He put the book aside and spent the rest of the evening doing a little design work for the Guild. They paid him handsomely for this, provided he promised never to turn up in person.

Then he put the work on the bedside table by the clocks. He blew out the candle. He went to sleep. He dreamed.

The glass clock ticked. It stood in the middle of the workshop's wooden floor, giving off a silvery light. Jeremy walked around it, or perhaps it spun gently around him.

It was taller than a man. Within the transparent case red and blue lights twinkled like stars. The air smelled of acid.

Now his point of view dived into the thing, the crystalline thing, plunging down through the layers of glass and quartz. They rose past him, their smoothness becoming walls hundreds of miles high, and still he fell between slabs that were becoming rough, grainy . . .

. . . full of holes. The blue and red light was here too, pouring past him.

And only now was there sound. It came from the darkness ahead, a slow beat that was ridiculously familiar, a heartbeat magnified a million times . . .

. . . tchum . . . tchum . . .

. . . each beat slower than mountains and bigger than worlds, dark and blood red. He heard a few more and then his fall slowed, stopped, and he began to soar back up through the sleeting light until a brightness ahead became a room.

He had to remember all this! It was all so clear, once you saw it! So simple! So easy! He could see every part, how they interlocked, how they were made.

And now it began to fade.

Of course it was only a dream. He told himself that and was comforted by it. But he had gone to some lengths with this one, he had to admit. For example, there was a mug of tea steaming on the nearby workbench, and the sound of voices on the other side of the door . . .

There was a knocking at the door. Jeremy wondered if the dream would end when the door was opened, and then the door disappeared and the knocking went on. It was coming from downstairs.

The time was 6.47. Jeremy glanced at the alarm clocks to make sure they were right, then pulled his dressing gown around him and hurried downstairs. He opened the front door a crack. There was no one there.

'Nah, dahn 'ere, mister.'

Someone lower down was a dwarf.

'Name of Clockson?' it said.

'Yes?'

A clipboard was thrust through the gap.

'Sign 'ere, where it says "Sign 'Ere". Thank you. Okay, lads . . .'

Behind him, a couple of trolls tipped up a handcart. A large wooden crate crashed onto the cobbles.

'What *is* this?' said Jeremy.

'Express package,' said the dwarf, taking the clipboard. 'Come all the way from Uberwald. Must've cost someone a packet. Look at all them seals and stickers on it.'

'Can't you bring it in—?' Jeremy began, but the cart was already moving off, with the merry jingle and tinkle of fragile items.

It started to rain. Jeremy peered at the label on the crate. It was certainly addressed to him, in a neat round hand, and just above it was the seal with the double-headed bat of Uberwald. There was no other marking except, near the bottom, the words:

THIS SIDE UP

Then the crate started to swear. It was muffled, and in a foreign language, but all swearing has a certain international content.

'Er . . . hello?' said Jeremy.

The crate rocked, and landed on one of the long sides, with extra cursing. There was some thumping from inside, some *louder* swearing, and the crate teetered upright again with the alleged top the right way up.

A piece of board slid aside and a crowbar dropped out and onto the street with a clang. The voice that had lately been swearing said, 'If you would be tho good?'

Jeremy inserted the bar into a likely-looking crack, and pulled.

The crate sprang apart. He dropped the bar. There was a . . . a *creature* inside.

'I don't know,' it said, pulling bits of packing material off itself. 'Eight bloody dayth with no problemth, and thothe idiotth get it wrong on the doorthtep.' It nodded at Jeremy. 'Good morning, thur. I thuppothe you *are* Mithter Jeremy?'

'Yes, but—'

'My name ith Igor, thur. My credentialth, thur.'

A hand like an industrial accident held together with stitches thrust a sheaf of papers towards Jeremy. He recoiled instinctively, and then felt embarrassed and took them.

'I think there has been a mistake,' he said.

'No, no mithtake,' said Igor, pulling a carpet bag out of the ruins of the crate. 'You need an athithtant. And when it cometh to athith-tantth, you cannot go wrong with an Igor. Everyone knowth that. Could we go in out of the rain, thur? It maketh my kneeth rutht.'

'But I don't *need* an assist—' Jeremy began, but that was wrong, wasn't it? He just couldn't *keep* assistants. They always left within a week.

'Morning, sir!' said a cheery voice.

Another cart had pulled up. This one was painted a gleaming, hygienic white and was full of milk churns, and had 'Ronald Soak, Dairyman' painted on the side. Distracted, Jeremy looked up at the beaming face of Mr Soak, who was holding a bottle of milk in each hand.

'One pint, squire, as per usual. And perhaps another one if you've got company?'

'Er, er, er . . . yes, thank you.'

'And the yoghurt is particularly fine this week, squire,' said Mr Soak encouragingly.

'Er, er, I think not, Mr Soak.'

'Need any eggs, cream, butter, buttermilk or cheese?'

'Not as such, Mr Soak.'

'Right you are, then,' said Mr Soak, unabashed. 'See you to-morrow, then.'

'Er, yes,' said Jeremy, as the cart moved on. Mr Soak was a friend, which in Jeremy's limited social vocabulary meant 'someone I speak to once or twice a week'. He approved of the milkman, because he was regular and punctual and had the bottles at the doorstep every morning on the stroke of 7a.m. 'Er, er . . . goodbye,' he said.

He turned to Igor.

'How did you *know* I needed—' he tried. But the strange man had gone indoors, and a frantic Jeremy tracked him down in the workshop.

'Oh *yeth*, very nithe,' said Igor, who was taking it all in with the air of a connoisseur. 'That'th a Turnball Mk3 micro-lathe, ithn't it? I thaw it in their catalogue. Very nithe indee—'

'I didn't ask anyone for an assistant!' said Jeremy. 'Who sent you?'

'We are Igorth, thur.'

'Yes, you said! Look, I don't—'

'No, thur. "We R Igorth", thur. The *organithathion*, thur.'

'What organization?'

'For *plathementth*, thur. You thee, thur, the thing ith . . . an Igor

36

often findth himthelf between marthterth through no fault of hith own, you thee. And on the other hand—'

'—you have two thumbs,' breathed Jeremy, who had just noticed and couldn't stop himself. 'Two on each hand!'

'Oh, yeth thur, very handy,' said Igor, not even glancing down. 'On the *other* hand there ith no thortage of people wanting an Igor. Tho my Aunt Igorina runth our thelect little agenthy.'

'For . . . *lots* of Igors?' said Jeremy.

'Oh, there'th a fair number of uth. We're a big family.' Igor handed Jeremy a card.

He read:

We R Igors
'A Spare Hand When Needed'

The Old Rathaus
Bad Schüschein
c-mail: Yethmarthter Uberwald

Jeremy stared at the semaphore address. His normal ignorance of anything that wasn't to do with clocks did not apply here. He'd been quite interested in the new cross-continent semaphore system after hearing that it made quite a lot of use of clockwork mechanisms to speed up the message flow. So you could send a clacks message to hire an Igor? Well, that explained the speed, at least.

'Rathaus,' he said. 'That means something like a council hall, doesn't it?'

'Normally, thur . . . *normally*,' said Igor reassuringly.

'Do you really have semaphore addresses in Uberwald?'

'Oh, yeth. We are ready to grathp the future with both handth, thur.'

'—and four thumbs—'

'Yeth, thur. We can grathp like *anything*.'

'And then you *mailed* yourself here?'

'Thertainly, thur. We Igorth are no thtrangerth to dithcomfort.'

37

Jeremy looked down at the paperwork he'd been handed, and a name caught his eye.

The top paper was signed. In a way, at least. There was a message in neat capitals, as neat as printing, and a name at the end.

HE WILL BE USEFUL
LEJEAN

He remembered. 'Oh, Lady LeJean is behind this. She had you sent to me?'

'That'th correct, thur.'

Feeling that Igor was expecting more of him, Jeremy made a show of reading through the rest of what turned out to be references. Some of them were written in what he could only hope was dried brown ink, one was in crayon, and several were singed around the edges. They were all fulsome. After a while, though, a certain tendency could be noted amongst the signatories.

'This one is signed by someone called Mad Doctor Scoop,' he said.

'Oh, he wathn't actually *named* mad, thur. It wath more like a nickname, ath it were.'

'Was he mad, then?'

'Who can thay, thur?' said Igor calmly.

'And Crazed Baron Haha? It says under Reason for Leaving that he was crushed by a burning windmill.'

'Cathe of mithtaken identity, thur.'

'Really?'

'Yeth, thur. I underthtand the mob mithtook him for Thcreaming Doctor Bertherk, thur.'

'Oh. Ah, yes.' Jeremy glanced down. 'Who you also worked for, I see.'

'Yeth, thur.'

'And who died of blood poisoning?'

'Yeth, thur. Cauthed by a dirty pitchfork.'

'And . . . Nipsie the Impaler?'

'Er, would you believe he ran a kebab thop, thur?'

'Did he?'

'Not *conventhionally* tho, thur.'

'You mean he was mad too?'

'Ah. Well, he did have hith little wayth, I mutht admit, but an Igor never patheth judgement on hith marthter or mithtreth, thur. That ith the Code of the Igorth, thur,' he added patiently. 'It would be a funny old world if we were all alike, thur.'

Jeremy was completely baffled as to his next move. He'd never been very good at talking to people, and this, apart from Lady LeJean and a wrangle with Mr Soak over an unwanted cheese, was the longest conversation he'd had for a year. Perhaps it was because it was hard to think of Igor as coming under the heading of people. Until now, Jeremy's definition of 'people' had not included anyone with more stitches than a handbag.

'I'm not *sure* I've got any work for you, though,' he said. 'I've got a new commission, but I'm not sure how . . . anyway, *I'm* not insane!'

'That'th not compulthory, thur.'

'I've actually got a piece of paper that *says* I'm not, you know.'

'Well *done*, thur.'

'Not many people have one of those!'

'Very true, thur.'

'I take medicine, you know.'

'Well done, thur,' said Igor. 'I'll jutht go and make thome break-fatht, thall I? While you get drethed . . . marthter.'

Jeremy clutched at his damp dressing gown. 'I'll be down shortly,' he said, and hurried up the stairs.

Igor's gaze took in the racks of tools. There was not a speck of dust on them; the files, hammers and pliers were ranged according to size, and the items on the work bench were positioned with geometrical exactitude.

He pulled open a drawer. Screws were laid in perfect rows.

He looked around at the walls. They were bare, except for the shelves of clocks. This was surprising – even Dribbling Doctor Vibes had had a calendar on the wall, which added a splash of colour. Admittedly it was from the Acid Bath and Restraint Co., in Ugli, and the colour it splashed was mostly red, but at least it showed some recognition of a world outside the four walls.

Igor was puzzled. Igor had never worked for a sane person before. He'd worked for a number of . . . well, the world called them madmen, and he'd worked for several *normal* people, in that they only indulged in minor and socially acceptable insanities, but he couldn't recall ever working for a completely sane person.

Obviously, he reasoned, if sticking screws up your nose was madness, then numbering them and keeping them in careful compartments was sanity, which was the opposite—

Ah. No. It wasn't, was it . . . ?

He smiled. He was beginning to feel quite at home already.

Tick

Lu-Tze the sweeper was in his Garden of Five Surprises, carefully cultivating his mountains. His broom leaned against the hedge.

Above him, looming over the temple gardens, the big stone statue of Wen the Eternally Surprised sat with its face locked in its permanent wide-eyed expression of, yes, pleasant surprise.

As a hobby, mountains appeal to those people who in normal circumstances are said to have a great deal of time on their hands. Lu-Tze had no time at all. Time was something that largely happened to other people; he viewed it in the same way that people on the shore viewed the sea. It was big and it was out there, and sometimes it was an invigorating thing to dip a toe into, but you couldn't live in it all the time. Besides, it always made his skin wrinkle.

At the moment, in the never-ending, ever-recreated moment of this peaceful, sunlit little valley, he was fiddling with the little mirrors and shovels and morphic resonators and even stranger devices required to make a mountain grow to no more than six inches high.

The cherry trees were still in bloom. They always were in bloom, here. A gong rang, somewhere back in the temple. A flock of white doves took off from the monastery roof.

A shadow fell over the mountain.

Lu-Tze glanced at the person who had entered the garden. He made the perfunctory symbol of servitude to the rather annoyed-looking boy in novice's robes.

40

'Yes, master?' he said.

'I am looking for the one they call Lu-Tze,' said the boy. 'Personally, I don't think he really exists.'

'I've got glaciation,' said Lu-Tze, ignoring this. 'At last. See, master? It's only an inch long, but already it's carving its own little valley. Magnificent, isn't it?'

'Yes, yes, very good,' said the novice, being kind to an underling. 'Isn't this the garden of Lu-Tze?'

'You mean, Lu-Tze who is famous for his bonsai mountains?'

The novice looked from the line of plates to the little wrinkled smiling man.

'*You* are Lu-Tze? But you're just a sweeper! I've *seen* you cleaning out the dormitories! I've seen people kick you!'

Lu-Tze, apparently not hearing this, picked up a plate about a foot across on which a small cinder cone was smoking.

'What do you think of this, master?' he said. 'Volcanic. And it is bloody hard to do, excuse my Klatchian.'

The novice took a step forward, and leaned down and looked directly into the sweeper's eyes.

Lu-Tze was not often disconcerted, but he was now.

'You *are* Lu-Tze?'

'Yes, lad. I am Lu-Tze.'

The novice took a deep breath and thrust out a skinny arm. It was holding a small scroll.

'From the abbot . . . er, venerable one!'

The scroll wobbled in the nervous hand.

'Most people call me Lu-Tze, lad. Or "Sweeper". Until they get to know me better, some call me "Get out of the way",' said Lu-Tze, carefully wrapping up his tools. 'I've never been very venerable, except in cases of bad spelling.'

He looked around the saucers for the miniature shovel he used for glacial work, and couldn't see it anywhere. Surely he'd put it down just a moment ago?

The novice was watching him with an expression of awe mixed with residual suspicion. A reputation like Lu-Tze's got around. This was the man who had – well, who had done practically *everything*,

41

if you listened to the rumours. But he didn't *look* as though he had. He was just a little bald man with a wispy beard and a faint, amiable smile.

Lu-Tze patted the young man on the shoulder in an effort to put him at his ease.

'Let us see what the abbot wants,' he said, unrolling the rice paper. 'Oh. You are to take me to see him, it says here.'

A look of panic froze the novice's face. 'What? How can I do that? Novices aren't allowed inside the Inner Temple!'

'Really? In that case, let me take *you*, to take *me*, to see *him*,' said Lu-Tze.

'You are allowed into the Inner Temple?' said the novice, and then put his hand over his mouth. 'But you're just a swee— Oh . . .'

'That's right! Not even a proper monk, let alone a *dong*,' said the sweeper cheerfully. 'Amazing, isn't it?'

'But people *talk* about you as if you were as high as the abbot!'

'Oh, dear me, no,' said Lu-Tze. 'I'm nothing like as holy. Never really got a grip on the cosmic harmony.'

'But you've done all those incredible—'

'Oh, I didn't say I'm not good at what I do,' said Lu-Tze, ambling away with his broom over his shoulder. 'Just not holy. Shall we go?'

'Er . . . Lu-Tze?' said the novice, as they walked along the ancient brick path.

'Yes?'

'Why is this called the Garden of Five Surprises?'

'What was your name back in the world, hasty young man?' said Lu-Tze.

'Newgate. Newgate Ludd, ven—'

Lu-Tze held up a warning finger. 'Ah?'

'Sweeper, I mean.'

'Ludd, eh? Ankh-Morpork lad?'

'Yes, Sweeper,' said the boy. The suddenly dejected tones suggested he knew what was coming next.

'Raised by the Thieves' Guild? One of "Ludd's Lads"?'

The boy formerly known as Newgate looked the old man in the

eye and, when he replied, it was in the singsong voice of someone who'd answered the question too many times. 'Yes, Sweeper. Yes, I was a foundling. Yes, we get called Ludd's Lads and Lasses after one of the founders of the Guild. Yes, that's my *adopted* surname. Yes, it was a good life and sometimes I wish I still had it.'

Lu-Tze appeared not to hear this. 'Who sent you here?'

'A monk called Soto discovered me. He said I had talent.'

'Marco? The one with all the hair?'

'That's right. Only I thought the rule was that all monks were shaved.'

'Oh, Soto says he *is* bald under the hair,' said Lu-Tze. 'He says the hair is a separate creature that just happens to live on him. They gave him a field posting really *quickly* after he came up with that one. Hard-working fellow, mark you, and friendly as anything provided you don't touch his hair. Important lesson there: you don't survive in the field by obeying *all* the rules, including those relating to mental processes. And what name were you given when you were enrolled?'

'Lobsang, ven— uh, Sweeper.'

'Lobsang Ludd?'

'Er . . . yes, Sweeper.'

'Amazing. So, Lobsang Ludd, you tried to count my surprises, did you? Everybody does. Surprise is the nature of Time, and five is the number of Surprise.'

'Yes, Sweeper. I found the little bridge that tilts and throws you into the carp pool . . .'

'Good. Good.'

'. . . and I have found the bronze sculpture of a butterfly that flaps its wings when you breathe on it . . .'

'That's two.'

'There's the surprising way those little daisies spray you with venomous pollen . . .'

'Ah, yes. Many people find them extremely surprising.'

'And I believe the fourth surprise is the yodelling stick insect.'

'Well done,' said Lu-Tze, beaming. 'It's very good, isn't it?'

'But I can't find the fifth surprise.'

'Really? Let me know when you find it,' said Lu-Tze.

Lobsang Ludd thought about this as he trailed after the sweeper. 'The Garden of Five Surprises is a test,' he said, at last.

'Oh, yes. Nearly everything is.'

Lobsang nodded. It was like the Garden of the Four Elements. Every novice found the bronze symbols of three of them – in the carp pond, under a rock, painted on a kite – but none of Lobsang's classmates found Fire. There didn't appear to be a fire anywhere in the garden.

After a while Lobsang had reasoned thus: there were in fact five elements, as they had been taught. Four made up the universe, and the fifth, Surprise, allowed it to keep on happening. No one had *said* that the four in the garden were the *material* four, so the fourth element in the Garden could be Surprise at the fact that Fire wasn't there. Besides, fire was not generally found in a garden, and the other signs were, truly, in their element. So he'd gone down to the bakeries and opened one of the ovens, and there, glowing red hot below the loaves, was Fire.

'Then . . . I expect that the fifth surprise is: there is no fifth surprise,' he said.

'Nice try, but no cylindrical smoking thing,' said Lu-Tze. 'And is it not written, "Oo, you are so sharp you'll cut yourself one of these days"?'

'Um, I haven't read that in the sacred texts yet, Sweeper,' said Lobsang uncertainly.

'No, you wouldn't have,' said Lu-Tze.

They stepped out of the brittle sunlight into the deep cold of the temple, and walked on through ancient halls and down stairways cut into the rock. The sound of distant chanting followed them. Lu-Tze, who was not holy and therefore could think unholy thoughts, occasionally wondered whether the chanting monks were chanting *anything*, or were just going 'aahaaahahah'. You could never tell with all that echo.

He turned off the main passage and reached for the handles of a pair of large, red-lacquered doors. Then he looked behind him. Lobsang had stopped dead, some yards away.

'Coming?'

'But not even *dongs* are allowed in there!' said Lobsang. 'You have to be a Third Djim *ting* at least!'

'Yeah, right. It's a short-cut. Come on, it's draughty out here.'

With extreme reluctance, expecting at any moment the outraged scream of authority, Lobsang trailed after the sweeper.

And he was just a sweeper! One of the people who swept the floors and washed the clothes and cleaned the privies! No one had ever mentioned it! Novices heard about Lu-Tze from their very first day – how he'd gone into some of the most tangled knots of time and unravelled them, how he'd constantly dodged the traffic on the crossroads of history, how he could divert time with a word and used this to develop the most subtle arts of battle . . .

. . . and here was a skinny little man who was sort of generically ethnic, so that he looked as if he could have come from anywhere, in a robe that had once been white before it fell to all those stains and patches, and the sandals repaired with string. And the friendly grin, as if he was constantly waiting for something amusing to happen. And *no belt at all*, just another piece of string to hold his robe closed. Even some novices got to the level of grey *dong* in their first year!

The dojo was busy with senior monks at practice. Lobsang had to dodge aside as a pair of fighters whirled past, arms and legs blurring as each sought an opening, paring time into thinner and thinner slivers—

'You! Sweeper!'

Lobsang looked round, but the shout had been directed at Lu-Tze. A *ting*, only just elevated to the Third Djim by the fresh look of his belt, was advancing on the little man, his face red with fury.

'What for are you coming in here, cleaner of filth? This is forbidden!'

Lu-Tze's little smile didn't change. But he reached in his robe and brought out a small bag.

' 's a short-cut,' he said. He pulled a pinch of tobacco and, while the *ting* loomed over him, began to roll a cigarette. 'And there's dirt

45

everywhere, too. I'll certainly have a word with the man who does this floor.'

'How dare you insult!' screamed the monk. 'Back to the kitchens with you, sweeper!'

Cowering behind Lu-Tze, Lobsang realized that the entire dojo had stopped to watch this. One or two of the monks were whispering to one another. The man in the brown robe of the dojo master was watching impassively from his chair, with his chin on his hand.

With great and patient and infuriating delicacy, like a samurai arranging flowers, Lu-Tze marshalled the shreds of tobacco in the flimsy cigarette paper.

'No, I reckon I'll go out of that door over there, if you don't mind,' he said.

'Impudence! Then you are ready to fight, enemy of dust?' The man leapt back and raised his hands to form the Combat of the Hake. He spun round and planted a kick on a heavy leather sack, hitting it so hard that its supporting chain broke. Then he was back to face Lu-Tze, hands held in the Advancement of the Snake.

'Ai! Shao! Hai-eee—' he began.

The dojo master stood up. 'Hold!' he commanded. 'Do you not want to know the name of the man you are about to destroy?'

The fighter held his stance, glaring at Lu-Tze. 'I don't need to know name of sweeper,' he said.

Lu-Tze rolled the cigarette into a skinny cylinder and winked at the angry man, which only stoked the anger.

'It is always wise to know the name of a sweeper, boy,' said the dojo master. 'And my question was not addressed to you.'

Tick

Jeremy stared at his bed sheets.

They were covered in writing. His *own* writing.

It trailed across the pillow and onto the wall. There were sketches, too, scored deeply into the plaster.

He found his pencil under the bed. He'd even sharpened it. In his sleep, he'd *sharpened* a pencil! And by the look of it he'd been writing and drawing for hours. Trying to draw a dream.

With, down one side of his eiderdown, a list of parts.

It had all made absolute sense when he'd seen it, like a hammer or a stick or Wheelbright's Gravity Escapement. It had been like meeting an old friend. And now . . . He stared at the scrawled lines. He had been writing so fast he'd ignored punctuation and some of the letters, too. But he could see some sense in there.

He'd heard of this sort of thing. Great inventions sometimes *did* arise from dreams and daydreams. Didn't Hepzibah Whitlow have the idea of the adjustable pendulum clock as a result of his work as the public hangman? Didn't Wilframe Balderton always say that the idea for the Fish Tail Escapement came after he'd eaten too much lobster?

Yes, it had all been so clear in the dream. By daylight, it needed a bit more work.

There was a clatter of dishes from the little kitchen behind his workshop. He hurried down, dragging the sheet behind him.

'I usually have—' he began.

'Toatht, thur,' said Igor, turning away from the range. 'Lightly browned, I thuthpect.'

'How did you know that?'

'An Igor learnth to antithipate, thur,' said Igor. 'What a wonder-ful little kitchen, thur. I've never theen a drawer marked 'Thpoonth' which jutht hath thpoonth in it.'

'Are you any good at working with glass, Igor?' said Jeremy, ignoring this.

'No, thur,' said Igor, buttering the toast.

'You're not?'

'No, thur. I am bloody *amathing* at it, thur. Many of my marthterth have needed . . . *thpethial* apparatuth not readily obtainable elthewhere, thur. What wath it you wanted?'

'How would we go about building *this*?' Jeremy spread the sheet on the table.

The slice of toast dropped from Igor's black-nailed fingers.

'Is there something wrong?' said Jeremy.

'I thought thomeone wath walking over my grave, thur,' said Igor, still looking shocked.

'Er, you haven't actually ever *had* a grave, have you?' said Jeremy.

'Jutht a figure of thpeech, thur, jutht a figure of thpeech,' said Igor, looking hurt.

'This is an idea I've . . . I've had for a clock . . .'

'The Glath Clock,' said Igor. 'Yeth. I know about it. My grandfather Igor helped build the firtht one.'

'The first one? But it's just a story for children! And I dreamed about it, and—'

'Grandfather Igor alwayth thaid there wath thomething very thtrange about all that,' said Igor. 'The ecthplothion and everything.'

'It exploded? Because of the metal spring?'

'Not ecthactly an ecthplothion,' said Igor. 'We're no thtrangerth to ecthplothionth, uth Igorth. It wath . . . *very odd*. And we're no thtrangerth to odd, either.'

'Are you telling me it really existed?'

Igor seemed embarrassed about this. 'Yeth,' he said, 'and then again, no.'

'Things either exist or they don't,' said Jeremy. 'I am very clear about that. I have medicine.'

'It ecthithted,' said Igor, 'and then, after it did, it never had. Thith ith what my grandfather told me, and he built that clock with thethe very handth!'

Jeremy looked down. Igor's hands were gnarled, and, now he came to look at them, had a lot of scar tissue around the wrists.

'We really *believe* in heirloomth in our family,' said Igor, catching his gaze.

'Sort of . . . hand-me-downs, ahahaha,' said Jeremy. He wondered where his medicine was.

'Very droll, thur,' said Igor. 'But Grandfather Igor alwayth thaid that afterwardth it wath like . . . a dream, thur.'

'A dream . . .'

'The workthop wath different. The clock wathn't there. Demented Doctor Wingle, that wath hith marthter at the time, wathn't working on the glath clock at all but on a way of ecthtracting thunthine from orangeth. Thingth were different and they alwayth had been, thur. Like it had never happened.'

'But it turned up in a book for children!'

'Yeth, thur. Bit of a conundrum, thur.'

Jeremy stared at the sheet with its burden of scribbles. An accurate clock. That's all it was. A clock that'd make all other clocks unnecessary, Lady LeJean had said. Building a clock like that would mean the clockmaker went down in timekeeping history. True, the book had said that Time had got trapped in the clock, but Jeremy had no interest whatsoever in things that were Made Up. Anyway, a clock just *measured*. Distance didn't get tangled up in a tape measure. All a clock did was count teeth on a wheel. Or . . . light . . .

Light with teeth. He'd seen that in the dream. Light not as something bright in the sky, but as an excited line, going up and down like a wave.

'Could *you* . . . build something like this?' he said.

Igor looked at the drawings again. 'Yeth,' he said, nodding. Then he pointed to several large glass containers around the drawing of the central column of the clock. 'And I know what thethe are,' he said.

'In my dr— I mean, I imagined them as fizzing,' said Jeremy.

'Very, very thecret knowledge, thothe jarth,' said Igor, carefully ignoring the question. 'Can you get copper rodth here, thur?'

'In Ankh-Morpork? Easily.'

'And thinc?'

'Lots of it, yes.'

'Thulphuric athid?'

'By the carboy, yes.'

'I mutht have died and gone to heaven,' said Igor. 'Jutht put me near enough copper and thinc and athid, thur,' he said, 'and then we thall thee *thparkth*.'

Tick

'My name,' said Lu-Tze, leaning on his broom as the irate *ting* raised a hand, 'is Lu-Tze.'

The dojo went silent. The attacker paused in mid-bellow.

'—Ai! Hao-*gng! Gnh? Ohsheeeeeeohsheeeeeee* . . .'

The man did not move but seemed instead to turn in on himself, sagging from the martial stance into a kind of horrified, penitent crouch.

Lu-Tze bent over and struck a match on his unprotesting chin.

'What's *your* name, lad?' he said, lighting his ragged cigarette.

'His name is mud, Lu-Tze,' said the dojo master, striding forward. He gave the unmoving challenger a kick. 'Well, Mud, you *know* the rules. Face the man you have challenged, or give up the belt.'

The figure remained very still for a moment, and then cautiously, in a manner almost theatrically designed not to give offence, started to fumble with his belt.

'No, no, we don't need that,' said Lu-Tze kindly. 'It was a good challenge. A decent "Ai!" and a very passable "Hai-eee!", I thought. Good martial gibberish all round, such as you don't often hear these days. And we would not want his trousers falling down at a time like this, would we?' He sniffed and added, '*Especially* at a time like this.'

He patted the shrinking man on the shoulder. 'Just you recall the rule your teacher here taught you on day one, eh? And . . . why don't you go and clean yourself up? I mean, some of us have to tidy up in here.'

Then he turned and nodded to the dojo master.

'While I am here, master, I should like to show young Lobsang the Device of Erratic Balls.'

The dojo master bowed deeply. 'It is yours, Lu-Tze the Sweeper.'

As Lobsang followed the ambling Lu-Tze he heard the dojo master, who like all teachers never missed an opportunity to drive home a lesson, say: 'Dojo! What is Rule One?'

Even the cowering challenger mumbled along to the chorus:

'Do not act incautiously when confronting little bald wrinkly smiling men!'

'Good rule, Rule One,' said Lu-Tze, leading his new acolyte into the next room. 'I have met many people who could have heeded it to good advantage.'

He stopped, without looking at Lobsang Ludd, and held out his hand.

'And now, if you please, you will return the little shovel you stole from me when first we met.'

'But I came nowhere near you, master!'

Lu-Tze's smile did not flicker. 'Oh. Yes. That is true. My apologies. The ramblings of an old man. Is it not written, "I'd forget my own head if it wasn't nailed on"? Let us proceed.'

The floor in here was wood, but the walls were high and padded. There were reddish-brown stains here and there.

'Er, we have one of these in the novices' dojo, Sweeper,' said Lobsang.

'But the balls in that are made of soft leather, yes?' said the old man, approaching a tall wooden cube. A row of holes ran halfway up the side that faced down the length of the room. 'And they travel quite slowly, I recall.'

'Er, yes,' said Lobsang, watching him pull on a very large lever. Down below there was the sound of metal on metal, and then of urgent gushing water. Air began to wheeze from joints in the box.

'These are wooden,' said Lu-Tze calmly. 'Catch one.'

Something touched Lobsang's ear and behind him the padding shook as a ball buried itself deeply and then dropped to the floor.

'Perhaps a *shade* slower . . .' said Lu-Tze, turning a knob.

After fifteen random balls, Lobsang caught one in his stomach. Lu-Tze sighed and pushed the big lever back.

'Well done,' he said.

'Sweeper, I'm not used to—' said the boy, picking himself up.

'Oh, I knew you wouldn't *catch* one,' said Lu-Tze. 'Even our boisterous friend out there in the dojo wouldn't catch one at that speed.'

'But you said you had slowed it down!'

'Only so that it wouldn't kill you. Just a test, see. Everything's a test. Let's go, lad. Can't keep the abbot waiting.'

Trailing cigarette smoke, Lu-Tze ambled away.

Lobsang followed, getting more and more nervous. This *was* Lu-Tze, the dojo had proved that. And he knew it, anyway. He'd looked at the little round face as it gazed amicably at the angry fighter and *known* it. But . . . just a sweeper? No insignia? No status? Well, obviously status, because the dojo master couldn't have bowed lower for the abbot, but . . .

And now he was following the man along passages where even a monk was not allowed to go, on pain of death. Sooner or later, there was surely going to be trouble.

'Sweeper, I really ought to be back at my duties in the kitchens—' he began.

'Oh, yes. Kitchen duties,' said Lu-Tze. 'To teach you the virtues of obedience and hard work, right?'

'Yes, Sweeper.'

'Are they working?'

'Oh, yes.'

'Really?'

'Well, no.'

'They're not all they're cracked up to be, I have to tell you,' said Lu-Tze. 'Whereas, my lad, what we have here' – he stepped through an archway – 'is an education!'

It was the biggest room Lobsang had ever seen. Shafts of light speared down from glazed holes in the roof. And below, more than a hundred yards across, and tended by senior monks who walked above it on delicate wire walkways, was . . .

Lobsang had heard about the Mandala.

It was as if someone had taken tons of coloured sands and thrown them across the floor in a great swirl of coloured chaos. But there was order fighting for survival in the chaos, rising and falling and spreading. Millions of randomly tumbling sand grains would nevertheless make a piece of pattern, which would replicate and spread across the circle, rebounding or merging with other patterns and eventually dissolving into the general disorder. It happened again and again, turning the Mandala into a silent raging war of colour.

Lu-Tze stepped out onto a frail-looking wood and rope bridge.

'Well?' he said. 'What d'you think?'

Lobsang took a deep breath. He felt that if he fell off the bridge he'd drop into the surging colours and never, ever hit the floor. He blinked and rubbed his forehead.

'It's . . . evil,' he said.

'Really?' said Lu-Tze. 'Not many people say that the first time. They use words like "wonderful".'

'It's going wrong!'

'What?'

Lobsang clutched the rope railing. 'The patterns—' he began.

'History repeating,' said Lu-Tze. 'They're always there.'

'No, they're—' Lobsang tried to take it all in. There were patterns *under* the patterns, disguised as part of the chaos. 'I mean . . . the *other* patterns . . .'

He slumped forward.

The air was cold, the world was spinning, and the ground rushed up to enfold him.

And stopped, a few inches away.

The air around him sizzled, as though it was being gently fried.

'Newgate Ludd?'

'Lu-Tze?' he said. 'The Mandala is . . .'

But where were the colours? Why was the air wet and smelling of the city? And then the ghost memories faded away. As they disappeared, they said: How can we be memories, when we have yet to happen? Surely what you *remember* is climbing all the way up onto the roof of the Bakers' Guild and finding that some-one had loosened all the capping stones, because *that* just happened?

And a last dying memory said, Hey, that was *months* ago . . .

'No, we're not Lu-Tze, mysterious falling kid,' said the voice that had addressed him. 'Can you turn round?'

Newgate managed, with great difficulty, to move his head. It felt as though he was stuck in tar.

A heavy young man in a grubby yellow robe was sitting on an upturned box a few feet away. He looked a bit like a monk, except for his hair, because his hair looked a bit like an entirely separate organism. To say that it was black and bound up in a ponytail is to miss the opportunity of using the term 'elephantine'. It was hair with personality.

'Mostly my name's Soto,' said the man underneath. 'Marco Soto. I won't bother memorizing yours until we know if you're going to live or not, eh? So tell me, have you ever considered the rewards of the spiritual life?'

'Right now? Certainly!' said . . . yes, Newgate, he thought, that's my name, yes? So why do I remember Lobsang? 'Er, I was thinking about the possibility of taking up a new line of work!'

'Good career move,' said Soto.

'Is this some kind of magic?' Newgate tried to move but hung, turning gently, in the air just above the waiting ground.

'Not exactly. You seem to have shaped time.'

'Me? How did I do that?'

'You don't know?'

'No!'

'Hah, will you listen to him?' said Soto, as if talking to a genial companion. 'There's probably the spin time of a whole Procrastinator being used up to prevent your little trick causing untold harm to the entire world, and you don't know how you did it?'

'No!'

'Then we'll train you. It's a good life, and it offers excellent prospects. At least,' he added, sniffing, 'better than those that confront you now.'

Newgate strained to turn his head further. 'Train me in what, exactly?'

The man sighed. 'Still asking questions, kid? Are you coming or not?'

'How—?'

'Look, I'm offering you the opportunity of a lifetime, do you understand?'

'Why is it the opportunity of a lifetime, Mr Soto?'

'No, you misunderstand me. *You*, that is Newgate Ludd, are being offered, that is by *me*, the opportunity of *having* a lifetime. Which is more than you will have shortly.'

Newgate hesitated. He was aware of a tingling in his body. In a sense, it was still falling. He didn't know *how* he knew this, but the knowledge was as real as the cobbles just below him. If he made the wrong choice the fall would simply continue. It had been easy so far. The last few inches would be terminally hard.

'I must admit I don't like the way my life is going at the moment,' he said. 'It may be advantageous to find a new direction.'

'Good.' The be-haired man pulled something out of his robe. It looked like a folded abacus, but when he opened it up parts of it vanished with little flashes of light, as if they'd moved somewhere where they could not be seen.

'What are you doing?'

'Do you know what kinetic energy is?'

'No.'

'It's what you have far too much of.' Soto's fingers danced on the beads, sometimes disappearing and reappearing. 'I imagine you weigh about a hundred and ten pounds, yes?'

He pocketed the little device and strolled off to a nearby cart. He did something that Newgate couldn't see, and came back.

'In a few seconds you will complete your fall,' he said, reaching under him to place something on the ground. 'Try to think of it as a new start in life.'

Newgate fell. He hit the ground. The air flashed purple and the laden cart across the street jerked a foot into the air and collapsed heavily. One wheel bounced away.

Soto leaned down and shook Newgate's unresisting hand.

'How do you do?' he said. 'Any bruises?'

'It does hurt a bit,' said the shaken Newgate.

'Maybe you're a bit heavier than you look. Allow me . . .'

Soto grabbed Newgate under the shoulders and began to tug him off into the mists.

'Can I go and—?'

'No.'

'But the Guild—'

'You don't exist at the Guild.'

'That's stupid, I'm in the Guild records.'

'No, you're not. We'll see to that.'

'How? You can't rewrite history!'

'Bet you a dollar?'

'What have I joined?'

'We're the most secret society that you can imagine.'

'Really? Who are you, then?'

'The Monks of History.'

'Huh? I've never heard of you!'

'See? That's how good we are.'

And that was how good they were.

And then the time had just flown past.

And now the present came back.

'Are you all right, lad?'

Lobsang opened his eyes. His arm felt as though it was being wrenched off his body.

He looked up along the length of the arm to Lu-Tze, who was lying flat on the swaying bridge, holding him.

'What happened?'

'I think maybe you were overcome with the excitement, lad. Or vertigo, maybe. Just don't look down.'

There was a roaring below Lobsang, like a swarm of very angry bees. Automatically, he began to turn his head.

'*I said don't look down!* Just relax.'

Lu-Tze got to his feet. He raised Lobsang, at arm's length, as though he was a feather, until the boy's sandals were over the wood of the bridge. Below, monks were running along the walkways and shouting.

'Now, keep your eyes shut . . . *don't look down!* . . . and I'll just walk us both to the far side, all right?'

'I, er, I remembered . . . back in the city, when Soto found me . . . I remembered . . .' said Lobsang weakly, tottering along behind the monk.

'Only to be expected,' said Lu-Tze, 'in the circumstances.'

'But, but I remember that back then I remembered about being here. You and the Mandala!'

'Is it not written in the sacred text, "There's a lot goes on we don't know about, in my opinion"?' said Lu-Tze.

'I . . . have not yet come across that one either, Sweeper,' said Lobsang. He felt cooler air around him, which suggested they had reached the rock tunnel on the far side of the room.

'Sadly, in the writings they have here you probably won't,' said Lu-Tze. 'Ah, you can open your eyes now.'

They walked on, with Lobsang rubbing his head to take away the strangeness of his thoughts.

Behind them the livid swirls in the wheel of colour, which had centred on the spot where Lobsang would have fallen, gradually faded and healed.

According to the First Scroll of Wen the Eternally Surprised, **Wen and Clodpool reached the green valley between the towering mountains and Wen said: 'This is the place. Here there will be a temple dedicated to the folding and unfolding of time. I can see it.'**

'I can't, master,' said Clodpool.

Wen said, 'It's over there.' He pointed, and his arm vanished.

'Ah,' said Clodpool. 'Over *there*.'

A few cherry blossom petals drifted down onto Wen's head from one of the trees that grew wild along the streamlets.

'And this perfect day will last for ever,' he said. 'The air is crisp, the sun is bright, there is ice in the streams. Every day in this valley will be *this* perfect day.'

'Could get a bit repetitive, master,' said Clodpool.

'That is because you don't yet know how to deal with time,' said Wen. 'But I will teach you to deal with time as you would deal with a coat, to be worn when necessary and discarded when not.'

'Will I have to wash it?' said Clodpool.

Wen gave him a long, slow look. 'That was either a very complex piece of thinking on your part, Clodpool, or you

57

were just trying to overextend a metaphor in a rather stupid way. Which do you think it was?'

Clodpool looked at his feet. Then he looked at the sky. Then he looked at Wen.

'I think I am stupid, master.'

'Good,' said Wen. 'It is fortuitous that you are my apprentice at this time, because if I can teach you, Clodpool, I can teach *anyone*.'

Clodpool looked relieved, and bowed. 'You do me too much honour, master.'

'And there is a second part to my plan,' said Wen.

'Ah,' said Clodpool, with an expression that he thought made him look wise, although in reality it made him look like someone remembering a painful bowel movement. 'A plan with a second part is always a good plan, master.'

'Find me sands of all colours, and a flat rock. I will show you a way to make the currents of time visible.'

'Oh, right.'

'And there is a third part to my plan.'

'A *third* part, eh?'

'I can teach a gifted few to control their time, to slow it and speed it up and store it and direct it like the water in these streams. But most people will not, I fear, let themselves become able to do this. We have to help them. We will have to build . . . devices that will store and release time to where it is needed, because men cannot progress if they are carried like leaves on a stream. People need to be able to waste time, make time, lose time and buy time. This will be our major task.'

Clodpool's face twisted with the effort of understanding. Then he slowly raised a hand.

Wen sighed.

'You're going to ask what happened to the coat, aren't you?' he said.

Clodpool nodded.

'Forget about the coat, Clodpool. The coat is not

important. Just remember that you are the blank paper on which I will write—' Wen held up a hand as Clodpool opened his mouth. 'Just another metaphor, just another metaphor. And now, please make some lunch.'

'Metaphorically or really, master?'

'Both.'

A flight of white birds burst out of the trees and wheeled overhead before swooping off across the valley.

'There will be doves,' said Wen, as Clodpool hurried off to light a fire. 'Every day, there will be doves.'

Lu-Tze left the novice in the anteroom. It might have surprised those who disliked him that he took a moment to straighten his robe before he entered the presence of the abbot, but Lu-Tze at least cared for people even if he did not care for rules. He pinched out his cigarette and stuck it behind his ear, too. He had known the abbot for almost six hundred years, and respected him. There weren't many people Lu-Tze respected. Mostly, they just got tolerated.

Usually, the sweeper got on with people in inverse proportion to their local importance, and the reverse was true. The senior monks . . . well, there could be no such thing as bad thoughts amongst people so enlightened, but it is true that the sight of Lu-Tze ambling insolently through the temple did tarnish a few karmas. To a certain type of thinker the sweeper was a personal insult, with his lack of any formal education or official status and his silly little Way and his incredible successes. So it was surprising that the abbot liked him, because never had there been an inhabitant of the valley so unlike the sweeper, so learned, so impractical and so frail. But then, surprise is the nature of the universe.

Lu-Tze nodded to the minor acolytes who opened the big varnished doors.

'How is his reverence today?' he said.

'The teeth are still giving him trouble, O Lu-Tze, but he is maintaining continuity and has just taken his first steps in a very satisfactory manner.'

'Yes, I thought I heard the gongs.'

The group of monks clustered in the centre of the room stepped aside as Lu-Tze approached the playpen. It was, unfortunately, necessary. The abbot had never mastered the art of circular ageing. He had therefore been forced to achieve longevity in a more traditional way, via serial reincarnation.

'Ah, Sweeper,' he burbled, awkwardly tossing aside a yellow ball and brightening up. 'And how are the mountains? *Wanna bikkit wanna bikkit!*'

'I'm definitely getting vulcanism, reverend one. It's very encouraging.'

'And you are in persistent good health?' said the abbot, while his pudgy little hand banged a wooden giraffe against the bars.

'Yes, your reverence. It's good to see you up and about again.'

'Only for a few steps so far, alas *bikkit bikkit wanna bikkit*. Unfortunately, young bodies have a mind of their own *BIKKIT!*'

'You sent me a message, your reverence? It said, "Put this one to the test."'

'And what did you think of our *want bikkit want bikkit want bikkit NOW* young Lobsang Ludd?' An acolyte hurried forward with a plate of rusks. 'Would you care for a rusk, by the way?' the abbot added. '*Mmmm nicey bikkit!*'

'No, reverend one, I have all the teeth I need,' said the sweeper.

'Ludd is a puzzle, is he not? His tutors have *nicey bikkit mmm mmm bikkit* told me he is very talented but somehow not all there. But you have never met him and don't know his history and so *mmm bikkit* and so I would value your uninfluenced observations *mmm BIKKIT.*'

'He is beyond fast,' said Lu-Tze. 'I think he may begin to react to things before they happen.'

'How can anyone tell that? *Want teddy want teddy wanna wanna TEDDY!*'

'I put him in front of the Device of Erratic Balls in the senior dojo and he was moving towards the right hole fractionally before the ball came out.'

'Some kind of *gurgle* telepathy, then?'

60

'If a simple machine has a mind of its own I think we're in really big trouble,' said Lu-Tze. He took a deep breath. 'And in the hall of the Mandala he saw the patterns in the chaos.'

'You let a neophyte see the *Mandala*?' said chief acolyte Rinpo, horrified.

'If you want to see if someone can swim, push him in the river,' said Lu-Tze, shrugging. 'What other way is there?'

'But to look at it without the proper training—'

'He saw the patterns,' said Lu-Tze. 'And *reacted* to the Mandala.' He did not add: and the Mandala reacted to him. He wanted to think about that. When you look into the abyss, it's not supposed to wave back.

'It was *teddyteddyteddywahwah* strictly forbidden, even so,' said the abbot. Clumsily, he fumbled among the toys on his mat and picked up a large wooden brick with a jolly blue elephant printed on it and hurled it clumsily at Rinpo. 'Sometimes you presume too much, Sweeper *lookit 'lephant!'*

There was some applause from the acolytes at the abbot's prowess in animal recognition. 'He saw the patterns. He *knows* what is happening. He just doesn't know *what* he knows,' said Lu-Tze doggedly. 'And within a few seconds of meeting me he stole a small object of value, and I'm still wondering how he did it. Can he really be as fast as that without training? Who is this boy?'

Tick

Who *is* this girl?

Madam Frout, headmistress of the Frout Academy and pioneer of the Frout Method of Learning Through Fun, often found herself thinking that when she had to interview Miss Susan. Of course, the girl was an employee, but . . . well, Madam Frout wasn't very good at discipline, which was possibly why she'd invented the Method, which didn't require any. She generally relied on talking to people in a jolly tone of voice until they gave in out of sheer embarrassment on her behalf.

Miss Susan didn't appear ever to be embarrassed about *anything*.

'The reason I've called you here, Susan, is that, er, the reason is—' Madam Frout faltered.

'There have been complaints?' said Miss Susan.

'Er, no . . . er . . . although Miss Smith has told me that the children coming up from your class are, er, restless. Their reading ability is, she says, rather unfortunately advanced . . .'

'Miss Smith thinks a good book is about a boy and his dog chasing a big red ball,' said Miss Susan. 'My children have learned to expect a plot. No wonder they get impatient. We're reading *Grim Fairy Tales* at the moment.'

'That is rather rude of you, Susan.'

'No, madam. That is rather polite of me. It would have been *rude* of me to say that there is a circle of Hell reserved for teachers like Miss Smith.'

'But that's a dreadf—' Madam Frout stopped, and began again. 'You should not be teaching them to read at all yet!' she snapped. But it was the snap of a soggy twig. Madam Frout cringed back in her chair when Miss Susan looked up. The girl had this terrible ability to give you *her full attention*. You had to be a better person than Madam Frout to survive in the intensity of that attention. It inspected your soul, putting little red circles around the bits it didn't like. When Miss Susan looked at you, it was as if she was giving you *marks*.

'I mean,' the headmistress mumbled, 'childhood is a time for play and—'

'Learning,' said Miss Susan.

'Learning *through play*,' said Madam Frout, grateful to find familiar territory. 'After all, kittens and puppies—'

'—grow up to be cats and dogs, which are even less interesting,' said Miss Susan, 'whereas children should grow up to be adults.'

Madam Frout sighed. There was no way she was going to make any progress. It was always like this. She knew she was powerless. News about Miss Susan had got around. Worried parents who'd turned to Learning Through Play because they despaired of their offspring ever Learning By Paying Attention to What Anyone Said were finding them coming home a little quieter, a little more thoughtful and with a pile of homework which, amazingly, they did without prompting and even with the dog helping them. And they came home with stories about Miss Susan.

Miss Susan spoke all languages. Miss Susan knew everything about everything. Miss Susan had wonderful ideas for school trips . . .

. . . and that was particularly puzzling, because as far as Madam Frout knew, none had been officially organized. There was invariably a busy silence from Miss Susan's classroom when she went past. This annoyed her. It harked back to the bad old days when children were Regimented in classrooms that were no better than Torture Chambers for Little Minds. But other teachers said that there *were* noises. Sometimes there was the faint sound of waves, or a jungle. Just once, Madam Frout could have sworn, if she was the sort to swear, that as she passed there was a full-scale battle going on. This had often been the case with Learning Through Play, but this time the addition of trumpets, the swish of arrows and the screams of the fallen seemed to be going *too* far.

She'd thrown open the door and felt something hiss through the air above her head. Miss Susan had been sitting on a stool, reading from a book, with the class cross-legged in a quiet and fascinated semicircle around her. It was the sort of old-fashioned image Madam Frout hated, as if the children were Supplicants around some sort of Altar of Knowledge.

No one had said anything. All the watching children, and Miss Susan, made it clear in polite silence that they were waiting for her to go away.

She'd flounced back into the corridor and the door had clicked shut behind her. Then she noticed the long, crude arrow that was still vibrating in the opposite wall.

Madam Frout had looked at the door, with its familiar green paint, and then back at the arrow.

Which had gone.

She transferred Jason to Miss Susan's class. It had been a cruel thing to do, but Madam Frout considered that there was now some kind of undeclared war going on.

If children were weapons, Jason would have been banned by international treaty. Jason had doting parents and an attention

63

span of minus several seconds, except when it came to inventive cruelty to small furry animals, when he could be quite patient. Jason kicked, punched, bit and spat. His artwork had even frightened the life out of Miss Smith, who could generally find something nice to say about any child. He was definitely a boy with special needs. In the view of the staffroom, these began with an exorcism.

Madam Frout had stooped to listening at the keyhole. She had heard Jason's first tantrum of the day, and then silence. She couldn't quite make out what Miss Susan said next.

When she found an excuse to venture into the classroom half an hour later, Jason was helping two little girls to make a cardboard rabbit.

Later his parents said they were amazed at the change, although apparently now he would only go to sleep with the light on.

Madam Frout tried to question her newest teacher. After all, glowing references were all very well, but she was an *employee*, after all. The trouble was, Susan had a way of saying things to her, Madam Frout had found, so that she went away feeling quite satisfied and only realized that she hadn't really had a proper answer at all when she was back in her office, by which time it was always too late.

And it continued to be too late because suddenly the school had a waiting list. Parents were fighting to get their children enrolled in Miss Susan's class. As for some of the stories they brought home . . . well, everyone knew children had such vivid imaginations, didn't they?

Even so, there was this essay by Richenda Higgs. Madam Frout fumbled for her glasses, which she was too vain to wear all the time and kept on a string around her neck, and looked at it again. In its entirety, it read:

A man with all bones came to talk to us he was not scarey at all, he had a big white hors. We pated the hors. He had a sighyve. He told us interesting things and to be careful when crosing the road.

Madam Frout handed the paper across the desk to Miss

Susan, who looked at it gravely. She pulled out a red pencil, made a few little alterations, then handed it back.

'Well?' said Madam Frout.

'Yes, she's not very good at punctuation, I'm afraid. A good attempt at "scythe", though.'

'Who . . . What's this about a big white horse in the classroom?' Madam Frout managed.

Miss Susan looked at her pityingly and said, 'Madam, who could *possibly* bring a *horse* into a classroom? We're up two flights of stairs here.'

Madam Frout was not going to be deterred this time. She held up another short essay.

> *Today we were talked at by Mr Slumph who he is a bogeyman but he is nice now. He tole us what to do abot the other kind. You can put the blanket ove your head but it is bettr if you put it ove the bogeymans head then he think he do not exist and he is vanishs. He tole us lots of stores abot people he jump out on and he said sins Miss is our teachr he think no bogeymen will be in our houses bcos one thing a bogey dos not like is Miss finding him.*

'Bogeymen, Susan?' said Madam Frout.

'What imaginations children have,' said Miss Susan, with a straight face.

'Are you introducing young children to the occult?' said Madam Frout suspiciously. This sort of thing caused a lot of trouble with parents, she was well aware.

'Oh, yes.'

'*What?* Why?'

'So that it doesn't come as a shock,' said Miss Susan calmly.

'But Mrs Robertson told me that her Emma was going round the house looking for monsters in the cupboards! And up until now she's always been afraid of them!'

'Did she have a stick?' said Susan.

'She had her father's sword!'

'Good for her.'

'Look, Susan . . . I think I see what you're trying to do,' said Madam Frout, who didn't really, 'but parents do not understand this sort of thing.'

'Yes,' said Miss Susan. 'Sometimes I really think people ought to have to pass a *proper* exam before they're allowed to be parents. Not just the practical, I mean.'

'Nevertheless, we must respect their views,' said Madam Frout, but rather weakly because occasionally she'd thought the same thing.

There had been the matter of Parents' Evening. Madam had been too tense to pay much attention to what her newest teacher was doing. All she'd been aware of was Miss Susan sitting and talking quietly to the couples, right up to the point where Jason's mother had picked up her chair and chased Jason's father out of the room. Next day a huge bunch of flowers had arrived for Susan from Jason's mother, and an even bigger bunch from Jason's father.

Quite a few other couples had also come away from Miss Susan's desk looking worried or harassed. Certainly Madam Frout, when the time came for next term's fees to be paid, had never known people cough up so readily.

And there it was again. Madam Frout the headmistress, who had to worry about reputations and costs and fees, just occasionally heard the distant voice of Miss Frout who had been quite a good if rather shy teacher, and it was whistling and cheering Susan on.

Susan looked concerned. 'You are not satisfied with my work, madam?'

Madam Frout was stuck. No, she wasn't satisfied, but for all the wrong reasons. And it was dawning on her as this interview progressed that she didn't dare sack Miss Susan or, worse, let her leave of her own accord. If *she* set up a school and news got round, the Learning Through Play School would simply haemorrhage pupils and, importantly, fees.

'Well, of course . . . no, not . . . in many ways . . .' she began, and became aware that Miss Susan was staring past her.

There was . . . Madam Frout groped for her glasses, and found their string had got tangled with the buttons of her blouse. She peered at the mantelpiece and tried to make sense of the blur.

'Why, it looks like a . . . a white rat, in a little black robe,' she said. 'And walking on its hind legs, too! Can you see it?'

'I can't imagine how a rat could wear a robe,' said Miss Susan. Then she sighed, and snapped her fingers. The finger-snapping wasn't essential, but time stopped.

At least, it stopped for everyone but Miss Susan.

And for the rat on the mantelpiece.

Which was in fact the *skeleton* of a rat, although this was not preventing it from trying to steal Madam Frout's jar of boiled sweets for Good Children.

Susan strode over and grasped the collar of the tiny robe.

SQUEAK? said the Death of Rats.

'I *thought* it was you!' snapped Susan. 'How dare you come here again! I thought you'd got the message the other day. *And* don't think I didn't see you when you turned up to collect Henry the Hamster last month! Do you know how hard it is to teach geography when you can see someone kicking the poo out of a treadmill?'

The rat sniggered: SNH. SNH. SNH.

'And you're eating a sweet! Put it in the bin right now!'

Susan dropped the rat onto the desk in front of the temporally frozen Madam Frout, and paused.

She'd always tried to be good about this sort of thing, but sometimes you just had to acknowledge who you were. So she pulled open the bottom drawer to check the level in the bottle that was Madam's shield and comforter in the wonderful world that was education, and was pleased to see that the old girl was going a bit easier on the stuff these days. Most people have some means of filling up the gap between perception and reality, and, after all, in those circumstances there are far worse things than gin.

She also spent a little while going through Madam's private papers, and this has to be said about Susan: it did not occur to her that there was anything *wrong* about this, although she'd quite understand that it was probably wrong if you weren't Susan Sto Helit, of course. The papers were in quite a good safe that would have occupied a competent thief for at least twenty minutes. The fact that the door swung open at her touch suggested that special rules applied here.

No door was closed to Miss Susan. It ran in the family. Some genetics are passed on via the soul.

When she'd brought herself up to date on the school's affairs, mostly to indicate to the rat that she wasn't just someone who could be summoned at a moment's notice, she stood up.

'All right,' she said wearily. 'You're just going to pester me, aren't you? For ever and ever and ever.'

The Death of Rats looked at her with its skull on one side.

SQUEAK, it said winsomely.

'Well, yes, I like him,' she said. 'In a way. But, I mean, you know, it's not *right*. Why does he need *me*? He's Death! He's not exactly powerless! I'm just human!'

The rat squeaked again, jumped down onto the floor and ran through the closed door. It reappeared for a moment and beckoned to her.

'Oh, all right,' said Susan to herself. 'Make that *mostly* human.'

Tick

And who is this Lu-Tze?

Sooner or later every novice had to ask this rather complex question. Sometimes it would be years before they found out that the little man who swept their floors and uncomplainingly carted away the contents of the dormitory cesspit and occasionally came out with outlandish foreign sayings was the legendary hero they'd been told they would meet one day. And then, when they'd confronted him, the brightest of them confronted themselves.

Mostly sweepers came from the villages in the valley. They were part of the staff of the monastery but they had no status. They did all the tedious, unregarded jobs. They were . . . figures in the background, pruning the cherry trees, washing the floors, cleaning out the carp pools and, always, sweeping. They had no names. That is, a thoughtful novice would understand that the sweepers *must* have names, some form by which they were known to other sweepers, but within the temple grounds at least they had no names, only instructions. No one knew where they went at night. They were just sweepers. But so was Lu-Tze.

One day a group of senior novices, for mischief, kicked over the little shrine that Lu-Tze kept beside his sleeping mat.

Next morning, no sweepers turned up for work. They stayed in their huts, with the doors barred. After making inquiries, the abbot, who at that time was fifty years old again, summoned the three novices to his room. There were three brooms leaning against the wall. He spoke as follows:

'You know that the dreadful Battle of Five Cities did not happen because the messenger got there in time?'

They did. They learned this early in their studies. And they bowed nervously, because this was the abbot, after all.

'And you know, then, that when the messenger's horse threw a shoe he espied a man trudging beside the road carrying a small portable forge and pushing an anvil on a barrow?'

They knew.

'And you know that man was Lu-Tze?'

They did.

'You surely know that Janda Trapp, Grand Master of *okidoki*, *toro-fu* and *chang-fu*, has only ever yielded to one man?'

They knew.

'And you know that man is Lu-Tze?'

They did.

'You know the little shrine you kicked over last night?'

They knew.

'You know it had an owner?'

There was silence. Then the brightest of the novices looked up at the abbot in horror, swallowed, picked up one of the three brooms and walked out of the room.

The other two were slower of brain and had to follow the story all the way through to the end.

Then one of them said, 'But it was only a sweeper's shrine!'

'You will take up the brooms and sweep,' said the abbot, 'and you will sweep every day, and you will sweep until the day you find Lu-Tze and dare to say "Sweeper, it was I who knocked over and scattered your shrine and now I will in humility accompany you to the dojo of the Tenth Djim, in order to learn the Right Way." Only then, if you are still able, may you resume your studies here. Understood?'*

Older monks sometimes complained, but someone would always say, 'Remember that Lu-Tze's Way is not our Way. Remember he learned everything by sweeping unheeded while students were being educated. Remember, he has been everywhere and done many things. Perhaps he is a little . . . strange, but remember that he walked into a citadel full of armed men and traps and nevertheless saw to it that the Pash of Muntab choked innocently on a fish bone. No monk is better than Lu-Tze at finding the Time and the Place.'

Some, who did not know, might say: 'What is this Way that gives him so much power?'

And they would be told: 'It is the Way of Mrs Marietta Cosmopilite, 3 Quirm Street, Ankh-Morpork, Rooms For Rent, Very Reasonable. No, we don't understand it, either. Some sub-sendential rubbish, apparently.'

Tick

Lu-Tze listened to the senior monks, while leaning on his broom. Listening was an art he had developed over the years, having learned that if you listened hard and long enough people would tell you more than they thought they knew.

---

* And the story continues: The novice who had protested that it was only the shrine of a sweeper ran away from the temple, the student who said nothing remained a sweeper for the rest of his life, and the student who had seen the inevitable shape of the story went, after much agonizing and several months of meticulous sweeping, to Lu-Tze and knelt and asked to be shown the Right Way. Whereupon the Sweeper took him to the dojo of the Tenth Djim, with its terrible multi-bladed fighting machines and its fearsome serrated weapons such as the *clong-clong* and the *uppsi*. The story runs that the Sweeper then opened a cupboard at the back of the dojo and produced a broom and spake thusly: 'One hand *here* and the other *here*, understand? People never get it right. Use good, even strokes and let the broom do most of the work. Never try to sweep up a big pile, you'll end up sweeping every bit of dust twice. Use your dustpan wisely, and remember: a small brush for the corners.'

'Soto is a good field operative,' he said at last. 'Weird but good.'

'The fall even showed up on the Mandala,' said Rinpo. 'The boy *knew* none of the appropriate actions. Soto said he'd done it reflexively. He said he thought the boy was as close to null as he has ever witnessed. He had him put on a cart for the mountains within the hour. He then spent three whole days performing the Closing of the Flower at the Guild of Thieves, where the boy had apparently been left as a baby.'

'The closure was successful?'

'We authorized the run time of two Procrastinators. Perhaps a few people will have faint memories, but the Guild is a large and busy place.'

'No brothers, no sisters. No love of parents. Just the brotherhood of thieves,' said Lu-Tze sadly.

'He was, however, a *good* thief.'

'I'll bet. How old is he?'

'Sixteen or seventeen, it appears.'

'Too old to teach, then.'

The senior monks exchanged glances.

'We cannot teach him anything,' said the Master of Novices. 'He—'

Lu-Tze held up a skinny hand. 'Let me guess. He knows it already?'

'It's as though he's being told something that had momentarily slipped his memory,' said Rinpo. 'And then he gets bored and angry. He's not all there, in my opinion.'

Lu-Tze scratched in his stained beard. 'Mystery boy,' he said thoughtfully. 'Naturally talented.'

'And we ask ourselves *wanna potty wanna potty poo* why now, why at this time?' said the abbot, chewing the foot of a toy yak.

'Ah, but is it not said, "There is a Time and a Place for Everything"?' said Lu-Tze. 'Anyway, reverend sirs, you have taught pupils for hundreds of years. I am but a sweeper.' Absent-mindedly, he stuck out his hand just as the yak left the fumbling fingers of the abbot, and caught it in mid-air.

71

'Lu-Tze,' said the Master of Novices, 'to be brief, we were unable to teach you. Remember?'

'But then I found my Way,' said Lu-Tze.

'Will you teach him?' said the abbot. 'The boy needs to *mmm brmmm* find himself.'

'Is it not written, "I have only one pair of hands"?' said Lu-Tze.

Rinpo looked at the Master of Novices. 'I don't know,' he said. 'None of us ever sees this stuff you quote.'

Still looking thoughtful, as if his mind were busy elsewhere, Lu-Tze said, 'It could only be here and now. For it is written: "It never rains but it pours."'

Rinpo looked puzzled, and then enlightenment dawned. 'A jug,' he said, looking pleased. 'A jug never rains, but it pours!'

Lu-Tze shook his head sadly. 'And the sound of one hand clapping is a "cl",' he said. 'Very well, your reverence. I will help him to find a Way. Will there be anything else, reverend sirs?'

Tick

Lobsang stood up when Lu-Tze returned to the anteroom, but he did it hesitantly, embarrassed at appearing to show respect.

'Okay, here are the rules,' said Lu-Tze, walking straight past. 'Word one is, you don't call me "master" and I don't name you after some damn insect. It's not my job to discipline you, it's yours. For it is written, "I can't be having with that kind of thing." Do what I tell you and we'll get along fine. All right?'

'What? You want me as an *apprentice*?' said Lobsang, running to keep up.

'No, I don't want you as an apprentice, not at my age, but you're going to be so we'd both better make the best of it, okay?'

'And you will teach me *everything*?'

'I don't know about "everything". I mean, I don't know much forensic mineralogy. But I will teach you all that I know that is useful for you to know, yes.'

'When?'

'It's getting late—'

'At dawn tomorrow?'

'Oh, before dawn. I'll wake you.'

Tick

Some distance away from Madam Frout's Academy, in Esoteric Street, were a number of gentlemen's clubs. It would be far too cynical to say that here the term 'gentleman' was simply defined as 'someone who can afford five hundred dollars a year'; they *also* had to be approved of by a great many other gentlemen who could afford the same fee.

And they didn't much like the company of ladies. This was not to say that they were *that* kind of gentlemen, who had their own, rather better-decorated clubs in another part of town, where there was generally a lot more going on. *These* gentlemen were gentlemen of a class who were, on the whole, bullied by ladies from an early age. Their lives were steered by nurses, governesses, matrons, mothers and wives, and after four or five decades of that the average mild-mannered gentleman gave up and escaped as politely as possible to one of these clubs, where he could snooze the afternoon away in a leather armchair with the top button of his trousers undone.*

The most select of these clubs was Fidgett's, and it operated like this: Susan didn't need to make herself invisible, because she knew that the members of Fidgett's would simply not see her, or believe that she really existed even if they did. Women weren't allowed in the club at all except under Rule 34b, which grudgingly allowed for female members of the family or respectable married ladies over thirty to be entertained to tea in the Green Drawing Room between 3.15 and 4.30p.m., provided at least one member of staff was present at all times. This had been the case for so long that many members now interpreted it as being the only seventy-five minutes

---

* One reason for this was the club food. At his club, a gentleman could find the kind of food he'd got used to at school, like spotted dick, jam roly-poly and that perennial favourite, stodge and custard. Vitamins are eaten by wives.

in the day when women were actually allowed to exist and, therefore, any women seen in the club at any other time were a figment
of their imagination.

In the case of Susan, in her rather strict black schoolteaching
outfit and button boots that somehow appeared to have higher
heels when she was being Death's granddaughter, this might well
have been true.

The boots echoed on the marble floor as she made her way to the
library.

It was a mystery to her why Death had started using the place.
Of course, he did have many of the qualities of a gentleman: he had
a place in the country – a far, dark country – was unfailingly
punctual, was courteous to all those he met – and sooner or later
he met *everyone* – was well if soberly dressed, at home in any
company and, proverbially, a good horseman.

The fact that he was the Grim Reaper was the only bit that didn't
quite fit.

Most of the overstuffed chairs in the library were occupied by
contented lunchers dozing happily under tented copies of the
Ankh-Morpork Times. Susan looked around until she found the copy
from which projected the bottom half of a black robe and two bony
feet. There was also a scythe leaning against the back of the armchair. She raised the paper.

GOOD AFTERNOON, said Death. HAVE YOU HAD LUNCH? IT WAS JAM
ROLY-POLY.

'Why do you do this, Grandfather? You know you don't sleep.'

I FIND IT RESTFUL. ARE YOU WELL?

'I was until the rat arrived.'

YOUR CAREER PROGRESSES? YOU KNOW I CARE FOR YOU.

'Thank you,' said Susan shortly. 'Now, why did—'

WOULD A LITTLE SMALL TALK HURT?

Susan sighed. She knew what was behind that, and it wasn't
a happy thought. It was a small, sad and wobbly little thought,
and it ran: each of them had no one else but the other. There. It
was a thought that sobbed into its own handkerchief, but it was
true.

Oh, Death had his manservant, Albert, and of course there was the Death of Rats, if you could call that company.

And as far as Susan was concerned . . .

Well, she was partly immortal, and that was all there was to it. She could see things that were really there,* she could put time on and off like an overcoat. Rules that applied to everyone else, like gravity, applied to her only when she let them. And, however hard you tried, this sort of thing did tend to get in the way of relationships. It was hard to deal with people when a tiny part of you saw them as a temporary collection of atoms that would not be around in another few decades.

And there she met the tiny part of Death that found it hard to deal with people when it thought of them as real.

Not a day went past but she regretted her curious ancestry. And then she'd wonder what it could possibly be like to walk the world unaware at every step of the rocks beneath your feet and the stars overhead, to have a mere five senses, to be almost blind and nearly deaf . . .

THE CHILDREN ARE WELL? I LIKED THEIR PAINTINGS OF ME.

'Yes. How is Albert?'

HE IS WELL.

. . . and not really *have* any small talk, Susan added to herself. There wasn't room for small talk in a big universe.

THE WORLD IS COMING TO AN END.

Well, that was *big* talk. 'When?'

NEXT WEDNESDAY.

'Why?'

THE AUDITORS ARE BACK, said Death.

'Those evil little things?'

YES.

'I hate them.'

I, OF COURSE, DO NOT HAVE ANY EMOTIONS, said Death, poker-faced as only a skull can be.

'What are they up to this time?'

* Which is much harder than seeing things that *aren't* there. *Everyone* does that.

75

I CANNOT SAY.

'I thought you could remember the future!'

YES. BUT SOMETHING HAS CHANGED. AFTER WEDNESDAY, THERE IS NO FUTURE.

'There must be something, even if it's only debris!'

NO. AFTER ONE O'CLOCK NEXT WEDNESDAY THERE IS NOTHING. JUST ONE O'CLOCK NEXT WEDNESDAY, FOR EVER AND EVER. NO ONE WILL LIVE. NO ONE WILL DIE. THAT IS WHAT I NOW SEE. THE FUTURE HAS CHANGED. DO YOU UNDERSTAND?

'And what has this got to do with me?' Susan knew this would sound stupid to anyone else.

I WOULD HAVE THOUGHT THE END OF THE WORLD IS EVERYONE'S RESPONSIBILITY, WOULDN'T YOU?

'*You* know what I mean!'

I BELIEVE THIS HAS TO DO WITH THE NATURE OF TIME, WHICH IS BOTH IMMORTAL AND HUMAN. THERE HAVE BEEN CERTAIN . . . RIPPLES.

'They're going to do something to Time? I thought they weren't allowed to do things like that.'

NO. BUT HUMANS CAN. IT HAS BEEN DONE ONCE BEFORE.

'No one would be that stu—'

Susan stopped. Of course someone would be that stupid. Some humans would do anything to see if it was possible to do it. If you put a large switch in some cave somewhere, with a sign on it saying 'End-of-the-World Switch. PLEASE DO NOT TOUCH', the paint wouldn't even have time to dry.

She thought some more. Death was watching her intently.

Then she said, 'Funnily enough, there is this book I've been reading to the class. I found it on my desk one day. It's called *Grim Fairy Tales* . . .'

AH, HAPPY TALES FOR LITTLE FOLK, said Death, without a trace of irony.

'. . . which is mostly about wicked people dying in horrible ways. It's strange, really. The children seem quite happy with the idea. It doesn't seem to worry them.'

Death said nothing.

'. . . except in the case of the Glass Clock of Bad Schüschein,' said

76

Susan, watching his skull. 'They found that quite upsetting, even though it's got a kind of happy ending.'

IT MAY BE BECAUSE THE STORY IS TRUE.

Susan had known Death long enough not to argue.

'I think I understand,' she said. 'You made sure the book was there.'

YES. OH, THE RUBBISH ABOUT THE HANDSOME PRINCE AND SO ON IS AN OBVIOUS ADDITION. THE AUDITORS DID NOT INVENT THE CLOCK, OF COURSE. THAT WAS THE WORK OF A MADMAN. BUT THEY ARE GOOD AT ADAPTING. THEY CANNOT CREATE, BUT THEY CAN ADAPT. AND THE CLOCK IS BEING REBUILT.

'Was time really stopped?'

TRAPPED. ONLY FOR A MOMENT, BUT THE RESULTS STILL LIE ALL AROUND US. HISTORY WAS SHATTERED, FRAGMENTED. PASTS WERE NO LONGER LINKED TO FUTURES. THE HISTORY MONKS HAD TO REBUILD IT PRACTICALLY FROM SCRATCH.

Susan did not waste breath saying things like, 'That's impossible,' at a time like this. Only people who believed that they lived in the real world said things like that.

'That must have taken some . . . time,' she said.

TIME, OF COURSE, WAS NOT THE ISSUE. THEY USE A FORM OF YEARS BASED ON THE HUMAN PULSE RATE. OF THOSE YEARS, IT TOOK ABOUT FIVE HUNDRED.

'But if history was shattered, where did they get—'

Death steepled his fingers.

THINK TEMPORALLY, SUSAN. I BELIEVE THEY STOLE SOME TIME FROM SOME EARLIER AGE OF THE WORLD, WHERE IT WAS BEING WASTED ON A LOT OF REPTILES. WHAT IS TIME TO A BIG LIZARD, AFTER ALL? HAVE YOU SEEN THOSE PROCRASTINATORS THE MONKS USE? WONDERFUL THINGS. THEY CAN MOVE TIME, STORE IT, STRETCH IT . . . QUITE INGENIOUS. AS FOR *WHEN* THIS HAPPENED, THE QUESTION ALSO MAKES NO SENSE. WHEN THE BOTTLE IS BROKEN, DOES IT MATTER WHERE THE GLASS WAS HIT? THE SHARDS OF THE EVENT ITSELF NO LONGER EXIST IN THIS REBUILT HISTORY, IN ANY CASE.

'Hold on, hold on . . . How can you take a piece of, oh, some old century, and *stitch* it into a modern one? Wouldn't people notice that . . .' Susan flailed a bit, 'oh, that people have got the wrong armour and the buildings are all wrong and they're still in the middle of wars that happened centuries ago?'

IN MY EXPERIENCE, SUSAN, WITHIN THEIR HEADS TOO MANY HUMANS SPEND A LOT OF TIME IN THE MIDDLE OF WARS THAT HAPPENED CENTURIES AGO.

'Very insightful, but what I *meant* was—'

YOU MUST NOT CONFUSE THE CONTENT WITH THE CONTAINER. Death sighed. YOU ARE MOSTLY HUMAN. YOU NEED A METAPHOR. AN OBJECT LESSON IS CLEARLY IN ORDER. COME.

He stood up and stalked into the dining room across the hall. There were still a few late lunchers frozen in their work, napkins tucked under their chins, in an atmosphere of happy carbohydrates.

Death walked up to a table that had been laid for dinner, and gripped a corner of the tablecloth.

TIME IS THE CLOTH, he said. THE CUTLERY AND PLATES ARE THE EVENTS THAT TAKE PLACE WITHIN TIME—

There was a drum roll. Susan glanced down. The Death of Rats was seated in front of a tiny drum kit.

OBSERVE.

Death pulled the cloth away. There was a rattle of cutlery and a moment of uncertainty regarding a vase of flowers, but almost all the tableware remained in place.

'I see,' said Susan.

THE TABLE REMAINS LAID, BUT THE CLOTH CAN NOW BE USED FOR ANOTHER MEAL.

'However, you knocked the salt over,' said Susan.

THE TECHNIQUE IS NOT PERFECT.

'And there are stains on the cloth from the previous meal, Grandfather.'

Death beamed. YES, he said. AS METAPHORS GO IT IS RATHER GOOD, DON'T YOU THINK?

'People would notice!'

REALLY? HUMANS ARE THE MOST UNOBSERVANT CREATURES IN THE UNIVERSE. OH, THERE ARE LOTS OF ANOMALIES, OF COURSE, A CERTAIN AMOUNT OF SPILLED SALT, BUT HISTORIANS EXPLAIN THEM AWAY. THEY ARE SO VERY USEFUL IN THAT RESPECT.

There was something called the Rules, Susan knew. They weren't written down, in the same way that mountains weren't written down. They were far more fundamental to the operation of the universe than mere mechanical things like gravity. The Auditors might hate the untidiness caused by the emergence of life, but the Rules did not allow them to do anything about it. The ascent of mankind must have been a boon to them. At last there was a species that could be *persuaded* to shoot itself in the foot.

'I don't know what you expect me to do about it,' she said.

EVERYTHING THAT YOU CAN, said Death. I, BY CUSTOM AND PRACTICE, HAVE OTHER DUTIES AT THIS TIME.

'Such as?'

IMPORTANT MATTERS.

'That you can't tell me about?'

THAT I DO NOT INTEND TO TELL YOU ABOUT. BUT THEY ARE IMPORTANT. IN ANY CASE, YOUR INSIGHT IS VALUABLE. YOU HAVE WAYS OF THINKING THAT WILL BE USEFUL. YOU CAN GO WHERE I CANNOT. I HAVE ONLY *SEEN* THE FUTURE. BUT YOU CAN CHANGE IT.

'Where *is* this clock being rebuilt?'

I CANNOT TELL. I HAVE DONE WELL TO DEDUCE WHAT I HAVE. THE ISSUE IS CLOUDED FROM ME.

'Why?'

BECAUSE THINGS HAVE BEEN HIDDEN. SOMEONE IS INVOLVED . . . WHO IS NOT SUBJECT TO ME. Death looked awkward.

'An immortal?'

SOMEONE SUBJECT TO . . . SOMEONE ELSE.

'You're going to have to be a lot clearer than that.'

SUSAN . . . YOU KNOW THAT I ADOPTED AND RAISED YOUR MOTHER, AND FOUND A SUITABLE HUSBAND FOR HER—

'Yes, yes,' snapped Susan. 'How could I forget? I look in my mirror every day.'

THIS IS . . . DIFFICULT FOR ME. THE TRUTH IS, I WAS NOT THE ONLY ONE TO INVOLVE MYSELF LIKE THAT. WHY LOOK SURPRISED? IS IT NOT WELL KNOWN THAT GODS DO THIS SORT OF THING ALL THE TIME?

'Gods, yes, but people like you—'

PEOPLE LIKE US ARE STILL LIKE PEOPLE . . .

Susan did an unusual thing, and listened. That's not an easy task for a teacher.

SUSAN, YOU WILL KNOW THAT WE WHO ARE . . . OUTSIDE HUMANITY—

'I'm not outside humanity,' said Susan sharply. 'I just have a few . . . extra talents.'

I DID NOT MEAN YOU, OF COURSE. I MEANT THE OTHERS WHO ARE NOT HUMAN AND YET PART OF HUMANITY'S UNIVERSE — WAR AND DESTINY AND PESTILENCE AND THE REST OF US — WE ARE ENVISAGED AS HUMAN BY HUMANS AND THUS, IN VARIOUS FASHIONS, WE TAKE ON SOME ASPECTS OF HUMANITY. IT CAN BE NO OTHER WAY. EVEN THE VERY BODY SHAPE FORCES UPON OUR MINDS A CERTAIN WAY OF OBSERVING THE UNIVERSE. WE PICK UP HUMAN TRAITS . . . CURIOSITY, ANGER, RESTLESSNESS . . .

'This is basic stuff, Grandfather.'

YES. AND YOU KNOW, THEREFORE, THAT SOME OF US . . . TAKE AN INTEREST IN HUMANITY.

'I *know*. I am one of the *results*.'

YES. ER . . . AND SOME OF US TAKE AN INTEREST WHICH IS, ER, MORE . . .

'Interesting?'

. . . PERSONAL. AND YOU HAVE HEARD ME SPEAK OF THE . . . PERSONIFICATION OF TIME . . .

'You didn't tell me much. She lives in a palace of glass, you once said.' Susan felt a small, shameful and yet curiously satisfying sensation in seeing Death discomfited. He looked like someone who was being forced to reveal a skeleton in the closet.

YES. ER . . . SHE FELL IN LOVE WITH A HUMAN . . .

'How very roman*tick*,' said Susan, inserting the k. Now she was being childishly perverse, she knew, but life as Death's granddaughter was not easy, and just occasionally she had the irresistible urge to annoy.

AH. A PUN, OR PLAY ON WORDS, said Death wearily, ALTHOUGH I SUSPECT YOU WERE MERELY TRYING TO BE TIRESOME.

'Well, that sort of thing used to happen a lot in antiquity, didn't it?' said Susan. 'Poets were always falling in love with moonlight or hyacinths or something, and goddesses were forever—'

BUT THIS WAS REAL, said Death.

'How real do you mean?'

TIME HAD A SON.

'How could—'

TIME HAD A SON. SOMEONE MOSTLY MORTAL. SOMEONE LIKE YOU.

Tick

A member of the Clockmakers' Guild called on Jeremy once a week. It was nothing formal. In any case there was often some work for him to do, or some results to be collected, because whatever else you might say about him, the boy had a genius for clocks.

Informally, the visit was also a delicate way to make sure that the lad was taking his medicine and wasn't noticeably crazy.

The clockmakers were well aware that the intricate mechanisms of the human brain could occasionally throw a screw. The Guild's members tended to be meticulous people, always in pursuit of an inhuman accuracy, and this took its toll. It could cause problems. Springs were not the only things that got wound up. The Guild committee were, by and large, kind and understanding men. They were not, on the whole, men accustomed to guile.

Dr Hopkins, the Guild's secretary, was surprised when the door of Jeremy's shop was opened by a man who appeared to have survived a very serious accident.

'Er, I'm here to see Mr Jeremy,' he managed.

'Yeth, thir. The marthter ith in, thur.'

'And you, mm, are . . . ?'

'Igor, thur. Mr Jeremy wath kind enough to take me on, thur.'

'You work for him?' said Dr Hopkins, looking Igor up and down.

'Yeth, thur.'

'Mm . . . Have you been standing too close to some dangerous machinery?'

'*No*, thur. He ith in the workthop, thur.'

'Mr Igor,' said Dr Hopkins, as he was ushered into the shop, 'you do know that Mr Jeremy has to take medicine, don't you?'

'Yeth, thur. He mentionth it often.'

'And he, mm, his general health is . . . ?'

81

'Good, thur. He ith enthuthiathtic for hith work, thur. Bright-eyed and buthy-tailed.'

'Buthy-tailed, eh?' said Dr Hopkins weakly. 'Mm . . . Mr Jeremy doesn't usually keep servants. I'm afraid he threw a clock at the head of the last assistant he had.'

'Really, thur?'

'Mm, he hasn't thrown a clock at your head, has he?'

'No, thur. He actth quite normally,' said Igor, a man with four thumbs and stitches all around his neck. He opened the door into the workshop. 'Dr Hopkinth, Mr Jeremy. I will make thome tea, thur.'

Jeremy was sitting bolt upright at the table, his eyes gleaming.

'Ah, doctor,' he said. 'How kind of you to come.'

Dr Hopkins took in the workshop.

There had been changes. Quite a large piece of lath-and-plaster wall, covered in pencilled sketches, had been removed from some-where and stood on an easel on one side of the room. The benches, usually the resting places of clocks in various stages of assembly, were covered with lumps of crystal and slabs of glass. And there was a strong smell of acid.

'Mm . . . something new?' Dr Hopkins ventured.

'Yes, doctor. I've been examining the properties of certain super-dense crystals,' said Jeremy.

Dr Hopkins took a deep breath of relief. 'Ah, geology. A wonderful hobby! I'm so glad. It's not good to think about clocks *all* the time, you know!' he added, jovially, and with a soupçon of hope.

Jeremy's brow wrinkled, as if the brain behind it was trying to fit around an unfamiliar concept.

'Yes,' he said at last. 'Did you know, doctor, that copper octirate vibrates exactly two million, four hundred thousand and seventy-eight times a second?'

'As much as that, eh?' said Dr Hopkins. 'My word.'

'Indeed. And light shone through a natural prism of octivium quartz splits into only three colours?'

'Fascinating,' said Dr Hopkins, reflecting that it could be worse. 'Mm . . . is it me, or is there a rather . . . *sharp* smell in the air?'

'Drains,' said Jeremy. 'We've been cleaning them. With acid.

Which is what we needed the acid for. For cleaning the drains.'

'Drains, eh?' Dr Hopkins blinked. He wasn't at home in the world of drains. There was a crackling sound and blue light flickered under the door of the kitchen.

'Your, mm, man Igor,' he said. 'All right, is he?'

'Yes, thank you, doctor. He's from Uberwald, you know.'

'Oh. Very . . . big, Uberwald. Very big country.' That was one of only two things Dr Hopkins knew about Uberwald. He coughed nervously, and mentioned the other one. 'People there can be a bit strange, I've heard.'

'Igor says he's never had anything to do with that kind of person,' said Jeremy calmly.

'Good. Good. That *is* good,' said the doctor. Jeremy's fixed smile was beginning to unnerve him. 'He, mm, seems to have a lot of scars and stitches.'

'Yes. It's cultural.'

'Cultural, is it?' Dr Hopkins looked relieved. He was a man who tried to see the best in everybody, but the city had got rather complicated since he was a boy, with dwarfs and trolls and golems and even zombies. He wasn't sure he liked everything that was happening, but a lot of it was 'cultural', apparently, and you couldn't object to that, so he didn't. 'Cultural' sort of solved problems by explaining that they weren't really there.

The light under the door went out. A moment later Igor came in with two cups of tea on a tray.

It was good tea, the doctor had to admit, but the acid in the air was making his eyes water.

'So, mm, how is the work on the new navigation tables going?' he said.

'Ginger bithcuit, thur?' said Igor, by his ear.

'Oh, er, yes . . . Oh, I say, these are rather good, Mr Igor.'

'Take two, thur.'

'Thank you.' Now Dr Hopkins sprayed crumbs as he spoke. 'The navigation tables—' he repeated.

'I am afraid I have not been able to make very much progress,' said Jeremy. 'I have been engaged on the properties of crystals.'

'Oh. Yes. You said. Well, of course we are very grateful for any time that you feel you can spare,' said Dr Hopkins. 'And if I may say so, mm, it is good to see you with a new interest. Too much concentration on one thing is, mm, conducive to ill humours of the brain.'

'I have medicine,' said Jeremy.

'Yes, of course. Er, as a matter of fact, since I happened to be going past the apothecary today . . .' Dr Hopkins pulled a large, paper-wrapped bottle out of his pocket.

'Thank you.' Jeremy indicated the shelf behind him. 'As you can see, I have nearly run out.'

'Yes, I thought you might,' said Dr Hopkins, as if the level of the bottle on Jeremy's shelf wasn't something the clockmakers kept a very careful eye on. 'Well, I shall be going, then. Well done with the crystals. I used to collect butterflies when I was a boy. Wonderful things, hobbies. Give me a killing jar and a net and I was as happy as a little lark.'

Jeremy still smiled at him. There was something glassy about the smile.

Dr Hopkins swallowed the remainder of his tea and put the cup back in the saucer.

'And now I really must be on my way,' he mumbled. 'So much to do. Don't wish to keep you from your work. Crystals, eh? Wonderful things. So pretty.'

'Are they?' said Jeremy. He hesitated, as though he was trying to solve a minor problem. 'Oh, yes. Patterns of light.'

'Twinkly,' said Dr Hopkins.

Igor was waiting by the street door when Dr Hopkins reached it. He nodded.

'Mm . . . you are sure about the medicine?' the doctor said quietly.

'Oh yeth, thur. Twithe a day I watch him pour out a thpoonful.'

'Oh, good. He can be a little, er, sometimes he doesn't get on well with people.'

'Yeth, thur?'

'Very, um, very *particular* about accuracy . . .'

'Yeth, thur.'

'. . . which is a good thing, of course. Wonderful thing, accuracy,' said Dr Hopkins, and sniffed. 'Up to a point, of course. Well, good day to you.'

'Good day, thur.'

When Igor returned to the workshop Jeremy was carefully pouring the blue medicine into a spoon. When the spoon was exactly full, he tipped it into the sink. 'They check, you know,' he said. 'They think I don't notice.'

'I'm thure they mean well, thur.'

'I'm afraid I can't think so well when I take the medicine,' he said. 'In fact I think I'm getting on a lot better without it, don't you? It slows me down.'

Igor took refuge in silence. In his experience, many of the world's greatest discoveries were made by men who would be considered mad by conventional standards. Insanity depended on your point of view, he always said, and if it was the view through your own underpants then everything looked fine.

But young Master Jeremy was beginning to worry him. He never laughed, and Igor liked a good maniacal laugh. You could trust it.

Since giving up the medicine, Jeremy had not, as Igor had expected, begun to gibber and shout things like 'Mad! They said I was mad! But I shall show them all! Ahahahaha!' He'd simply become more – focused.

Then there was that smile. Igor was not easily frightened, because otherwise he wouldn't be able to look in a mirror, but he *was* becoming a little troubled.

'Now, where were we . . . ?' said Jeremy. 'Oh, yes, give me a hand here.'

Together they moved the table aside. Under it, dozens of glass jars hissed.

'Not enough power,' said Igor. 'Altho, we have not got the mirrorth right yet, thur.'

Jeremy pulled the cloth off the device on the workbench. Glass and crystal glittered, and in some cases glittered very strangely. As Jeremy had remarked yesterday, in the clarity that was returning now that he was carefully pouring one spoonful of his medicine down the sink twice a day, some of the angles looked wrong. One crystal had disappeared when he'd locked it into place, but it was clearly still there because he could see the light reflecting off it.

'And we've thtill got too much metal in it, thur,' Igor grumbled. 'It wath the thpring that did for the latht one.'

'We'll find a way,' said Jeremy.

'Home-made lightning ith never ath good ath the real thort,' said Igor.

'Good enough to test the principle,' said Jeremy.

'Tetht the printhiple, tetht the printhiple,' muttered Igor. 'Thorry, thur, but Igorth do not "tetht the printhiple". Thtrap it to the bench and put a good thick bolt of lightning through it, that'th our motto. That'th how you *tetht* thomething.'

'You seem ill at ease, Igor.'

'Well, I'm thorry, thur,' said Igor. 'It'th the climate dithagreeing with me. I'm uthed to regular thunderthtormth.'

'I've heard that some people really seem to come alive in thunderstorms,' said Jeremy, carefully adjusting the angle of a crystal.

'Ah, that wath when I worked for Baron Finklethtein,' said Igor.

Jeremy stood back. This wasn't the clock, of course. There was still a lot more work to do (but he could see it in front of him, if he closed his eyes) before they had a clock. This was just an essay, to see if he was on the right lines.

He *was* on the right lines. He knew it.

Tick

Susan walked back through the motionless streets, sat down in Madam Frout's office and let herself sink back into the stream of time.

She had never found out how this worked. It just did. Time didn't stop for the rest of the world, and it didn't stop for her – it was just that she entered a kind of loop of time, and everything else stayed exactly as it was until she'd finished what she needed to do.

86

It was another inherited family trait. It worked best if you didn't think about it, just like tightrope walking. Anyway, now she had *other* things to think about.

Madam Frout turned her gaze back from the rat-free mantelpiece.

'Oh,' she said. 'It seems to have gone.'

'It was probably a trick of the light, madam,' said Susan. *Mostly human. Someone like me*, she thought.

'Yes, er, of course . . .' Madam Frout managed to get her glasses on, despite the fact that the string was still tangled with the button. It meant that she'd moored herself to her own chest, but she was damned if she was going to do anything about it now.

Susan could unnerve a glacier. All she had to do was sit quietly, looking polite and alert.

'What precisely was it you wanted, madam?' she said. 'It's just that I've left the class doing algebra, and they get restless when they've finished.'

'Algebra?' said Madam Frout, perforce staring at her own bosom, which no one else had ever done. 'But that's far too difficult for seven-year-olds!'

'Yes, but I didn't tell them that and so far they haven't found out,' said Susan. It was time to move things along. 'I expect you wanted to see me about my letter, madam?' she said.

Madam Frout looked blank. 'Wh—' she began.

Susan sighed and snapped her fingers.

She walked round and opened a drawer by the motionless Madam Frout, removed a sheet of paper and spent some time carefully writing a letter. She let the ink dry, rustled the paper a bit to make it look slightly second-hand, and then put it just under the top of the pile of paperwork beside Madam Frout, with enough of it peeking out so that it would be easy to see.

She returned to her seat. She snapped her fingers again.

'—at letter?' said Madam Frout. And then she looked down at her desk. 'Oh.'

It was a cruel thing to do, Susan knew. But while Madam Frout was not by any means a bad person and was quite kind to children, in a haphazard way, she was silly. And Susan did not have a lot of time for silly.

'Yes, I asked if I might have a few days' leave,' said Susan. 'Pressing family matters, I'm afraid. I have prepared some work for the children to get on with, of course.'

Madam Frout hesitated. Susan didn't have time for this, either. She snapped her fingers.

'MY GOODNESS, THAT'D BE A RELIEF,' she said, in a voice whose harmonics went all the way into the subconscious. 'IF WE DON'T SLOW HER DOWN WE'LL RUN OUT OF THINGS TO TEACH THEM! SHE HAS BEEN PERFORMING SMALL MIRACLES ON A DAILY BASIS AND DESERVES A RAISE.'

Then she sat back, snapped her fingers again, and *watched* the words settle into the forefront of Madam Frout's mind. The woman's lips actually moved.

'Why, yes, of course,' she murmured at last. 'You have been working very hard . . . and . . . and,' and since there are things even a voice of eldritch command can't achieve and one of them is to get extra money out of a head teacher, 'we shall have to think about a little increment for you one of these days.'

Susan returned to the classroom and spent the rest of the day performing small miracles, which included removing the glue from Richenda's hair, emptying the wee out of Billy's shoes and treating the class to a short visit to the continent of Fourecks.

When their parents came to pick them up they were all waving crayoned pictures of kangaroos, and Susan had to hope that the red dust on their shoes – red mud in the case of Billy's, whose sense of timing had not improved – would pass unnoticed. It probably would. Fidgett's was not the only place where adults didn't see what couldn't possibly be true.

Now she sat back.

There was something pleasant about an empty classroom. Of course, as any teacher would point out, one nice thing was that there were no children in it, and particularly no Jason.

But the tables and shelves around the room showed evidence of a term well spent. Paintings lined the walls, and displayed good use of perspective and colour. The class had built a full-size white horse out of cardboard boxes, during which time they'd learned a lot about horses and Susan learned about Jason's remarkably accurate powers of observation. She'd had to take the cardboard tube away from him and explain that this was a *polite* horse.

It had been a long day. She raised the lid of her desk and took out *Grim Fairy Tales*. This dislodged some paperwork, which in turn revealed a small cardboard box decorated in black and gold.

It had been a little present from Vincent's parents.

She stared at the box.

Every day she had to go through this. It was ridiculous. It wasn't even as if Higgs & Meakins did *good* chocolates. They were just butter and sugar and—

She scrabbled amongst the sad little scraps of brown paper inside the box and pulled out a chocolate. No one could be expected not to have just *one* chocolate, after all.

She put it in her mouth.

Damn*damn*damn*damn*! It was *nougat* inside! Her one chocolate today and it was damn artificial damn pink-and-white damn sickly damn stupid *nougat*!

Well, no one could be expected to believe *that* counted.* She was entitled to another—

The teacher part of her, which had eyes in the back of its head, caught the blur of movement. She spun round.

'No running with scythes!'

The Death of Rats stopped jogging along the Nature Table and gave her a guilty look.

SQUEAK?

'And no going into the Stationery Cupboard, either,' said Susan, automatically. She slammed the desk lid shut.

SQUEAK!

'Yes, you were. I could hear you *thinking* about it.' It was possible to deal with the Death of Rats provided you thought of him as a very small Jason.

---

* This is true. A chocolate you did not want to eat does not count as chocolate. This discovery is from the same branch of culinary physics that determined that food eaten while walking contains no calories.

The Stationery Cupboard! That was one of the great battle-grounds of classroom history, that and the playhouse. But the ownership of the playhouse usually sorted itself out without Susan's intervention, so that all she had to do was be ready with ointment, a nose-blow and mild sympathy for the losers, whereas the Stationery Cupboard was a war of attrition. It contained pots of powder paint and reams of paper and boxes of crayons and more idiosyncratic items like a spare pair of pants for Billy, who did his best. It also contained The Scissors, which under classroom rules were treated as some kind of Doomsday Machine, and, of course, the boxes of stars. The only people allowed in the cupboard were Susan and, usually, Vincent. Despite everything Susan had tried, short of actual deception, he was always the official 'best at every-thing' and won the coveted honour every day, which was to go into the Stationery Cupboard and fetch the pencils and hand them out. For the rest of the class, and especially Jason, the Stationery Cupboard was some mystic magic realm to be entered whenever possible.

Honestly, thought Susan, once you learn the arts of defending the Stationery Cupboard, outwitting Jason and keeping the class pet alive until the end of term, you've mastered at least half of teaching.

She signed the register, watered the sad plants on the window-sill, went and fetched some fresh privet from the hedge for the stick insects that were the successor to Henry the Hamster (chosen on the basis that it was quite hard to tell when they were dead), tidied a few errant crayons away and looked around the classroom at all those little chairs. It sometimes worried her that nearly everyone she knew well was three feet high.

She was never certain that she trusted her grandfather at times like this. It was all to do with the Rules. He couldn't interfere, but he knew her weaknesses and he could wind her up and send her out into the world . . .

Someone like me. Yes, he'd known how to engage her interest.

Someone like me. Suddenly there's some dangerous clock some-where in the world, and suddenly I'm told that there's *someone like me.*

Someone like me. Except not like me. At least I knew my parents. And she'd listened to Death's account of the tall dark woman wandering from room to room in the endless castle of glass, weeping for the child she'd given birth to and could see every day but could never touch . . .

Where do I even *begin*?

Tick

Lobsang learned a lot. He learned that every room has at least four corners. He learned that the sweepers started work when the sky was light enough to see the dust, and continued until sunset.

As a master, Lu-Tze was kind enough. He would always point out those bits that Lobsang had not done properly.

After the initial anger, and the taunting of his former classmates, Lobsang found that the work had a certain charm. Days drifted past under his broom . . .

. . . until, almost with an audible click in his brain, he decided that enough was enough. He finished his section of passageway, and found Lu-Tze dreamily pushing his brush along a terrace.

'Sweeper?'

'Yes, lad?'

'What is it you are trying to tell me?'

'I'm sorry?'

'I didn't expect to become a . . . a sweeper! You're Lu-Tze! I expected to be apprentice to . . . well, to the hero!'

'You did?' Lu-Tze scratched his beard. 'Oh, dear. Damn. Yes, I can see the problem. You should've said. Why didn't you say? I don't really do that sort of thing any more.'

'You *don't*?'

'All that playing with history, running about, unsettling people . . . No, not really. I was never quite certain we should be doing it, to be honest. No, sweeping is good enough for me. There's something . . . *real* about a nice clean floor.'

'This is a test, isn't it?' said Lobsang coldly.

'Oh, yes.'

'I mean, I understand how it works. The master makes the pupil do all the menial jobs, and then it turns out that really the pupil is learning things of great value . . . and I don't think I'm learning *anything*, really, except that people are pretty messy and inconsiderate.'

'Not a bad lesson, all the same,' said Lu-Tze. 'Is it not written, "Hard work never did anybody any harm"?'

'*Where* is this written, Lu-Tze?' said Lobsang, thoroughly exasperated.

The sweeper brightened up. 'Ah,' he said. 'Perhaps the pupil *is* ready to learn. Is it that you don't wish to know the Way of the Sweeper, you wish to learn instead the Way of Mrs Cosmopilite?'

'*Who?*'

'We have swept well. Let's go to the gardens. For is it not written, "It does you good to get out in the fresh air"?'

'Is it?' said Lobsang, still bewildered.

Lu-Tze pulled a small tattered notebook out of his pocket.

'In here, it is,' he said. 'I should know.'

Tick

Lu-Tze patiently adjusted a tiny mirror to redirect sunlight more favourably on one of the bonsai mountains. He hummed tunelessly under his breath.

Lobsang, sitting cross-legged on the stones, carefully turned the yellowing pages of the ancient notebook on which was written, in faded ink, 'The Way of Mrs Cosmopilite'.

'Well?' said Lu-Tze.

'The Way has an answer for everything, does it?'

'Yes.'

'Then . . .' Lobsang nodded at the little volcano, which was gently smoking, 'how does that work? It's on a saucer!'

Lu-Tze stared straight ahead, his lips moving. 'Page seventy-six, I think,' he said.

Lobsang turned to the page. ' "Because," ' he read.

'Good answer,' said Lu-Tze, gently caressing a minute crag with a camel-hair brush.

'Just "Because", Sweeper? No *reason*?'

'Reason? What reason can a mountain have? And, as you accumulate years, you will learn that most answers boil down, eventually, to "Because".'

Lobsang said nothing. The Book of the Way was giving him problems. What he wanted to say was this: Lu-Tze, this reads like a book of the sayings of an old lady. It's the sort of thing old ladies *say*. What kind of *koan* is 'It won't get better if you pick at it,' or 'Eat it up, it'll make your hair curly,' or 'Everything comes to he who waits'? This is stuff you get in Hogswatch crackers!

'Really?' said Lu-Tze, still apparently engrossed in a mountain.

'I didn't say anything.'

'Oh. I thought you did. Do you miss Ankh-Morpork?'

'Yes. I didn't have to sweep floors there.'

'Were you a good thief?'

'I was a fantastic thief.'

A breeze blew the scent of cherry blossom. Just once, thought Lu-Tze, it would be nice to pick cherries.

'I have been to Ankh-Morpork,' he said, straightening up and moving on to the next mountain. 'You have seen the visitors we get here?'

'Yes,' said Lobsang. 'Everyone laughs at them.'

'Really?' Lu-Tze raised his eyebrows. 'When they have trekked thousands of miles seeking the truth?'

'But did not Wen say that if the truth is anywhere, it is everywhere?' said Lobsang.

'Well done. I see you've learned *something*, at least. But one day it seemed to me that everyone else had decided that wisdom can only be found a long way off. So I went to Ankh-Morpork. They were all coming here, so it seemed only fair.'

'Seeking *enlightenment*?'

'No. The wise man does not seek enlightenment, he waits for it. So while I was waiting it occurred to me that seeking perplexity might be more fun,' said Lu-Tze. 'After all, enlightenment begins where perplexity ends. And I found perplexity. And a kind of enlightenment, too. I had not been there five minutes, for example, when some men in an alley tried to enlighten me of what little I possessed, giving me a valuable lesson in the ridiculousness of material things.'

'But *why* Ankh-Morpork?' said Lobsang.

'Look in the back of the book,' said Lu-Tze.

There was a yellow, crackling scrap of paper tucked in there. The boy unfolded it.

'Oh, this is just a bit of the *Almanack*,' he said. 'It's very popular there.'

'Yes. A seeker after wisdom left it here.'

'Er . . . it's just got the Phases of the Moon on this page.'

'Other side,' said the sweeper.

Lobsang turned the paper over. 'It's just an advert from the Ankh-Morpork Guild of Merchants,' he said. ' "Ankh-Morpork Has Everything!"' He stared at the smiling Lu-Tze. 'And . . . you thought that—'

'Ah, I am old and simple and understand,' said the sweeper. 'Whereas you are young and complicated. Didn't Wen see portents in the swirl of gruel in his bowl, and in the flight of birds? This was actually *written*. I mean, flights of birds are quite complex, but these were *words*. And, after a lifetime of searching, I saw at last the opening of the Way. *My* Way.'

'And you went all the way to Ankh-Morpork . . .' said Lobsang weakly.

'And I fetched up, calm of mind but empty of pocket, in Quirm Street,' said the sweeper, smiling serenely at the recollection, 'and espied a sign in a window saying "Rooms For Rent". Thus I met Mrs Cosmopilite, who opened the door when I knocked and then when I hesitated, not being sure of the language, she said, "I haven't got all day, you know." Almost to a word, one of the sayings of Wen! Instantly I knew that I had found what I was seeking! During the days I washed dishes in an eating house for twenty pence a day and all the scraps I could take away, and in the evenings I helped Mrs Cosmopilite clean the house and listened carefully to her conversation. She was a natural sweeper with a good rhythmical motion and had bottomless wisdom. Within the first two days she uttered to me the actual words said by Wen upon understanding the true nature of Time! It was when I asked for a reduced rate because of course I did not sleep in a bed, and she said *"I was not born yesterday, Mr Tze!"* Astonishing! And she could never have seen the Sacred Texts!'

Lobsang's face was a carefully drawn picture. '"I was not born yesterday"?' he said.

'Ah, yes, of course, as a novice you would not have got that far,' said Lu-Tze. 'It was when he fell asleep in a cave and in a dream saw Time appear to him and show him that the universe is re-created from second to second, endlessly, with the past just a memory. And he stepped out from the cave into the truly new world and said, "I was not born – yesterday"!'

'Oh, yes,' said Lobsang. 'But—'

'Ah, Mrs Cosmopilite,' said Lu-Tze, his eyes misting over. 'What a woman for keeping things clean! If she were a sweeper here, no one would be allowed to walk on the floor! Her house! So amazing! A palace! New sheets every other week! And cook? Just to *taste* her Beans Baked Upon the Toast a man would give up a cycle of the universe!'

'Um,' said Lobsang.

'I stayed for three months, sweeping her house as is fitting for the pupil, and then I returned here, my Way clear before me.'

'And, er, these stories about you . . .'

'Oh, all true. Most of them. A bit of exaggeration, but mostly true.'

'The one about the citadel in Muntab and the Pash and the fish bone?'

'Oh, yes.'

'But how did you get in where half a dozen trained and armed men couldn't even—?'

'I'm a little man and I carry a broom,' said Lu-Tze simply. 'Everyone has some mess that needs clearing up. What harm is a man with a broom?'

'What? And that was *it*?'

'Well, the rest was a matter of cookery, really. The Pash was not a good man, but he was a glutton for his fish pie.'

'No martial arts?' said Lobsang.

'Oh, always a last resort. History needs shepherds, not butchers.'

'Do you know *okidoki*?'

'Just a lot of bunny-hops.'

'*Shiitake*?'

'If I wanted to thrust my hand into hot sand I would go to the seaside.'

'*Upsidazi*?'

'A waste of good bricks.'

'*No kando*?'

'You made that one up.'

'*Tung-pi*?'

'Bad-tempered flower-arranging.'

"*Déjà-fu*?" That got a reaction. Lu Tze's eyebrows raised.

"*Déjà-fu*?" You heard that rumour? Ha! None of the monks here knows *déjà-fu*," he said. "I'd soon know about it if they did. Look, boy, violence is the resort of the violent. In most tight corners a broomstick suffices."

'Only most, eh?' said Lobsang, not trying to hide the sarcasm.

'Oh, I *see*. You wish to face me in the dojo? For it's a very old truth: when the pupil can beat the master, there is nothing the master cannot tell him, because the apprenticeship is ended. You want to learn?'

'Ah! I *knew* there was something to learn!'

Lu-Tze stood up. 'Why you?' he said. 'Why here? Why now? "There is a time and a place for everything." Why this time and this place? If I take you to the dojo, you will return what you stole from me! Now!'

He looked down at the teak table where he worked on his mountains.

The little shovel was there.

A few cherry blossom petals fluttered to the ground.

'I see,' he said. 'You are that fast? I did not see you.'

Lobsang said nothing.

'It is a small and worthless thing,' said Lu-Tze. 'Why did you take it, please?'

'To see if I could. I was bored.'

'Ah. We shall see if we can make life more interesting for you, then. No wonder you are bored, when you can already slice time like that.'

Lu-Tze turned the little shovel over and over in his hand.

'Very fast,' he said. He leaned down and blew the petals away from a tiny glacier. 'You slice time as fast as a Tenth Djim. And as yet barely trained. You must have been a great thief! And now . . . Oh dear, I shall have to face you in the dojo . . .'

'No, there is no need!' said Lobsang, because now Lu-Tze looked frightened and humiliated and, somehow, smaller and brittle-boned.

'I insist,' said the old man. 'Let us get it done now. For it is written, "There is no time like the present", which is Mrs Cosmopilite's most profound understanding.' He sighed and looked up at the giant statue of Wen.

'Look at him,' he said. 'He was a lad, eh? Completely blissed out on the universe. Saw the past and future as one living *person*, and wrote the *Books of History* to tell how the story should go. We can't imagine what those eyes saw. And he never raised a hand to any man in his life.'

'Look, I really didn't want to—'

'And you've looked at the other statues?' said Lu-Tze, as if he'd completely forgotten about the dojo.

Distractedly, Lobsang followed his gaze. Up on the raised stone platform that ran the whole length of the gardens were hundreds of smaller statues, mostly carved of wood, all of them painted in garish colours. Figures with more eyes than legs, more tails than teeth, monstrous amalgamations of fish and squid and tiger and parsnip, things put together as if the creator of the universe had tipped out his box of spare parts and stuck them together, things painted pink and orange and purple and gold, looked down over the valley.

'Oh, the *dhlang*—' Lobsang began.

'Demons? That's one word for them,' said the sweeper. 'The abbot called them the Enemies of Mind. Wen wrote a scroll about them, you know. And he said *that* was the worst.'

He pointed to a little hooded grey shape, which looked out of place among the festival of wild extremities.

'Doesn't look very dangerous,' said Lobsang. 'Look, Sweeper, I don't want to—'

'They can be very dangerous, things that don't look dangerous,' said Lu-Tze. 'Not looking dangerous is what *makes* them dangerous. For it is written, "You can't tell a book by its cover." '

'Lu-Tze, I really *don't* want to fight you—'

'Oh, your tutors will tell you that the discipline of a martial art enables you to slice time, and that's true as far as it goes,' said Lu-Tze, apparently not listening. 'But so can sweeping, as perhaps you have found. Always find the perfect moment, Wen said. People just seem so keen on using it to kick other people on the back of the neck.'

'But it wasn't a challenge, I just wanted you to show me—'

'And I shall. Come on. I made a bargain. I must keep it, old fool that I am.'

The nearest dojo was the dojo of the Tenth Djim. It was empty except for two monks blurring as they danced across the mat and wrapped time around themselves.

Lu-Tze had been right, Lobsang knew. Time was a resource. You could learn to let it move fast or slow, so that a monk could walk easily through a crowd and yet be moving so fast that no one could see him. Or he could stand still for a few seconds, and watch the sun and moon chase one another across a flickering sky. He could meditate for a day in a minute. Here, in the valley, a day lasted for ever. Blossom never became cherries.

The blurred fighters became a couple of hesitant monks when they saw Lu-Tze. He bowed.

'I beg the use of this dojo for a short period while my apprentice teaches me the folly of old age,' he said.

'I really didn't mean—' Lobsang began, but Lu-Tze elbowed him in the ribs. The monks gave the old man a nervous look.

'It's yours, Lu-Tze,' said one of them. They hurried out, almost tripping over their own feet as they looked back.

'Time and its control is what we should teach here,' said Lu-Tze, watching them go. 'The martial arts are an aid. That is all they are. At least, that's all they were meant to be. Even out in the world a well-trained person may perceive, in the fray, how flexible time may be. Here, we can build on that. Compress time. Stretch time. Hold the moment. Punching people's kidneys out through their nose is only a foolish by-product.'

Lu-Tze took down a razor-edged *pika* sword from the rack and handed it to the shocked boy.

'You've seen one of these before? They're not really for novices, but you show promise.'

'Yes, Sweeper, but—'

'Know how to use it?'

'I'm good with the practice ones, but they're just made of—'

'Take it, then, and attack me.'

There was a rustling noise above them. Lobsang looked up and saw monks pouring into the observation gallery above the dojo. There were some very senior ones among them. News gets around quickly in a little world.

'Rule Two,' said Lu-Tze, 'is never refuse a weapon.' He took a few steps back. 'In your own time, boy.'

Lobsang wielded the curved sword uncertainly.

'Well?' said Lu-Tze.

'I can't just—'

'Is this the dojo of the Tenth Djim?' said Lu-Tze. 'Why, mercy me, I do believe it is. That means there are no rules, doesn't it? Any weapon, any strategy . . . anything is allowed. Do you understand? Are you stupid?'

'But I can't just kill someone because they've *asked* me to!'

'Why not? What happened to Mr Manners?'

'But—'

'You are holding a deadly weapon! You are facing an unarmed man in a pose of submission! Are you frightened?'

99

'Yes! Yes, I am!'

'Good. That's the Third Rule,' said Lu-Tze quietly. 'See how much you're learning already? Wiped the smile off your face, have I? All right, put the sword on the rack and take— Yes, take a *dakka* stick. The most you can do with that is bruise my old bones.'

'I would prefer it if you wore the protective padding—'

'You're that good with the stick, are you?'

'I'm very fast—'

'Then if you don't fight right now I shall wrest it from you and break it over your head,' said Lu-Tze, drawing back. 'Ready? The only defence is to attack well, I'm told.'

Lobsang tilted the stick in reluctant salute.

Lu-Tze folded his hands and, as Lobsang danced towards him, closed his eyes and smiled to himself.

Lobsang raised the stick again.

And hesitated.

Lu-Tze was grinning.

Rule Two, Rule Three . . . What had been Rule One?

Always remember Rule One . . .

'Lu-Tze!'

The abbot's chief acolyte arrived panting in the doorway, waving urgently.

Lu-Tze opened one eye, and then the other one, and then winked at Lobsang.

'Narrow escape there, eh?' he said. He turned to the acolyte. 'Yes, exalted sir?'

'You must come immediately! And all monks who are cleared for a tour in the world! To the Mandala Hall! Now!'

There was a scuffling in the gallery and several monks pushed their way out through the crowd.

'Ah, excitement,' said Lu-Tze, taking the stick from Lobsang's unresisting hands and putting it back into the rack. The hall was emptying fast. Around the whole of Oi Dong, gongs were being banged frantically.

'What's happening?' said Lobsang, as the last of the monks surged past.

'I daresay we shall soon be told,' said Lu-Tze, starting to roll himself a cigarette.

'Hadn't we better hurry? Everyone's going!' The sound of flapping sandals died away in the distance.

'Nothing seems to be on fire,' said Lu-Tze calmly. 'Besides, if we wait a little then by the time we get there everyone will have stopped shouting and perhaps they will be making some sense. Let us take the Clock Path. The display is particularly fine at this time of day.'

'But . . . but . . .'

'It is written "You've got to learn to walk before you can run,"' said Lu-Tze, putting his broom over his shoulder.

'Mrs Cosmopilite again?'

'Amazing woman. Dusted like a demon, too.'

The Clock Path wound out from the main complex, up through the terraced gardens, and then rejoined the wider path as it tunnelled into the cliff wall. Novices always asked why it was called the Clock Path, since there was no sign of a clock anywhere.

More gongs started to bang, but they were muffled by the greenery. Lobsang heard running feet up on the main path. Down here, humming birds flickered from flower to flower, oblivious of any excitement.

'I wonder what time it is,' said Lu-Tze, who was walking ahead.

Everything is a test. Lobsang glanced around at the flowerbed.

'A quarter past nine,' he said.

'Oh? And how do you know that?'

'The field marigold is open, the red sandwort is opening, the purple bindweed is closed, and the yellow goat's beard is closing,' said Lobsang.

'You worked out the floral clock all by yourself?'

'Yes. It's obvious.'

'Really? What time is it when the white waterlily opens?'

'Six in the morning.'

'You came to look?'

'Yes. You planted this garden, did you?'

'One of my little . . . efforts.'

'It's beautiful.'

'It's not very accurate in the small hours. There aren't too many night-blooming plants that grow well up here. They open for the moths, you know—'

'It's how time wants to be measured,' said Lobsang.

'Really? Of course I'm not an expert,' said Lu-Tze. He pinched out the end of his cigarette and stuck it behind his ear. 'Oh well, let's keep going. Everyone may have stopped arguing at cross purposes by now. How do you feel about going through the Mandala Hall again?'

'Oh, I'll be fine, I'd just . . . forgotten about it, that's all.'

'Really? And you'd never seen it before, too. But time plays funny tricks on us all. Why, I once—' Lu-Tze stopped, and stared at the apprentice.

'Are you all right?' he said. 'You've gone pale.'

Lobsang grimaced and shook his head.

'Something . . . felt odd,' he said. He waved a hand vaguely in the direction of the lowlands, spread out in a blue and grey pattern on the horizon. 'Something over there . . .'

The glass clock. The great glass house and here, where it shouldn't be, the glass clock. It was barely *here: it showed up as shimmering lines in the air, as if it was possible to capture the sparkle of light off a shiny surface without the surface itself.*

Everything here was transparent – delicate chairs, tables, vases of flowers. And now he realized that glass was not a word to use here. Crystal might be better, or ice – the thin, flawless ice you sometimes got after a sharp frost. Everything was visible only by its edges.

He could make out staircases through distant walls. Above and below and to every side, the glass rooms went on for ever.

And yet it was all familiar. It felt like home.

Sound filled the glass rooms. It streamed away in clear sharp notes, like the tones made by a wet finger around a wineglass rim. There was move-ment, too – a haze in the air beyond the transparent walls, shifting and wavering and . . . watching him . . .

'How can it come from over there? And how do you mean, odd?' said the voice of Lu-Tze.

Lobsang blinked. *This* was the odd place, the one right here, the rigid and unbending world . . .

And then the feeling passed, and faded.

'Just odd. For a moment,' he mumbled. There was dampness on his cheek. He raised his hand, and touched wetness.

'It's that rancid yak butter they put in the tea, I've always said so,' said Lu-Tze. 'Mrs Cosmopilite never— Now *that* is unusual,' he said, looking up.

'What? What?' said Lobsang, looking blankly at his wet finger-tips and then up at the cloudless sky.

'A Procrastinator going overspeed.' He shifted position. 'Can't you feel it?'

'I can't hear anything!' said Lobsang.

'Not hear, *feel*. Coming up through your sandals? Oops, there goes another one . . . and another. You *can't* feel it? That one's . . . that's old Sixty-Six, they've never got it properly balanced. We'll hear them in a minute . . . Oh dear. Look at the flowers. Do look at the flowers!'

Lobsang turned.

The ice plants were opening. The field sowthistle was closing.

'Time-leak,' said Lu-Tze. 'Hark at that! You can hear them now, eh? They're dumping time randomly! Come on!'

According to the Second Scroll of Wen the Eternally Surprised, **Wen the Eternally Surprised sawed the first Procrastinator from the trunk of a wamwam tree, carved certain symbols on it, fitted it with a bronze spindle and summoned the apprentice, Clodpool.**

'Ah. Very nice, master,' said Clodpool. 'A prayer wheel, yes?'

'No, this is nothing like as complex,' said Wen. 'It merely stores and moves time.'

'That simple, eh?'

'And now I shall test it,' said Wen. He gave it a half-turn with his hand.

'Ah. Very nice, master,' said Clodpool. 'A prayer wheel, yes?'

'No, this is nothing like as complex,' said Wen. 'It merely stores and moves time.'

'That simple, eh?'

'And now I shall test it,' said Wen. He moved it a little less this time.

'That simple, eh?'

'And now I shall test it,' said Wen. This time he twisted it gently to and fro.

'That si-si-si That simple-ple, eh eheh simple, eh?' said Clodpool.

'And I have tested it,' said Wen.

'It worked, master?'

'Yes, I think so.' Wen stood up. 'Give me the rope that you used to carry the firewood. And . . . yes, a pit from one of those cherries you picked yesterday.'

He wound the frayed rope around the cylinder and tossed the pit onto a patch of mud. Clodpool jumped out of the way.

'See those mountains?' said Wen, tugging the rope. The cylinder spun and balanced there, humming gently.

'Oh yes, master,' said Clodpool obediently. There was practically nothing up here *but* mountains; there were so many that sometimes they were impossible to see, because they got in the way.

'How much time does stone need?' said Wen. 'Or the deep sea? We shall move it' – he placed his left hand just above the spinning blur – 'to where it is needed.'

He looked down at the cherry pit. His lips moved silently, as though he was working through some complex puzzle. Then he pointed his right hand at the pit.

'Stand back,' he said, and gently let a finger touch the cylinder.

There was no sound except the crack of the air as it moved aside, and a hiss of steam from the mud.

Wen looked up at the new tree, and smiled. 'I did *say* you should stand back,' he said.

'I, er, I shall get down now, then, shall I?' said a voice among the blossom-laden branches.

'But carefully,' said Wen, and sighed as Clodpool crashed down in a shower of petals.

'There will always be cherry blossom here,' he said.

Lu-Tze hitched up his robe and scurried back down the path. Lobsang ran after him. A high-pitched whine seemed to be coming out of the rocks. The sweeper skidded at the carp pond, which was now erupting in strange waves, and headed down a shady track alongside a stream. Red ibises erupted into flight—

He stopped, and threw himself flat on the paving slabs.

'Get down *now*!'

But Lobsang was already headlong. He heard something pass overhead with a plangent sound. He looked back and saw the last ibis tumbling in the air, shrinking, shedding feathers, surrounded by a halo of pale blue light. It squawked and vanished with a 'pop'.

Not vanished *entirely*. An egg followed the same trajectory for a few seconds, and then smashed on the stones.

'Random time! Come on, come on!' shouted Lu-Tze. He scrambled to his feet again, headed towards an ornamental grille in the cliff face ahead of them, and with surprising strength wrenched it out of the wall.

'It's a bit of a drop but if you roll when you land you'll be okay,' he said, lowering himself into the hole.

'Where does it go to?'

'The Procrastinators, of course!'

'But novices aren't allowed in there on pain of death!'

'That's a coincidence,' said Lu-Tze, lowering himself to the tips of his fingers. 'Because death is what awaits you if you stay out there, too.'

He dropped into the darkness. A moment later there was an unenlightened curse from below.

Lobsang climbed in, hung by his fingertips, dropped and rolled when he hit the floor.

'Well done,' said Lu-Tze in the gloom. 'When in doubt, choose to live. This way!'

The passageway opened into a wide corridor. The noise here was shattering. Something mechanical was in agony.

There was a 'crump' and, a few moments later, a babble of voices.

Several dozen monks, wearing thick cork hats as well as their traditional robes, came running round the corner. Most of them were yelling. A few of the brighter ones were saving their breath in order to cover the ground more quickly. Lu-Tze grabbed one of them, who tried to struggle free.

'Let me go!'

'What's happening?'

'Just get out of here before they *all* go!'

The monk shook himself free and sped after the rest of them.

Lu-Tze bent down, picked up a fallen cork helmet, and solemnly handed it to Lobsang.

'Health and safety at work,' he said. 'Very important.'

'Will it protect me?' said Lobsang, putting it on.

'Not really. But when they find your head, it may be recognizable. When we get into the hall, *don't touch anything*.'

Lobsang had been expecting some vaulted, magnificent structure. People talked about the Procrastinator Hall as if it was some kind of huge cathedral. But what there was, at the end of the passage, was a haze of blue smoke. It was only when his eyes became accustomed to the swirling gloom that he saw the nearest cylinder.

It was a squat pillar of rock, about three yards across and six yards high. It was spinning so fast that it was a blur. Around it the air flickered with slivers of silver-blue light.

'See? They're dumping! Over here! Quick!'

Lobsang ran after Lu-Tze, and saw there were hundreds – no, *thousands* – of the cylinders, some of them reaching all the way to the cavern roof.

There were still monks in here, running to and from the wells with buckets of water, which flashed into steam when they threw it over the smoking stone bearings at the base of the cylinders.

'Idiots,' the sweeper muttered. He cupped his hands and shouted, 'Where-is-the-overseer?'

Lobsang pointed down to the edge of a wooden podium built onto the wall of the hall.

There was a rotting cork hat there, and a pair of ancient sandals. In between was a pile of grey dust.

'Poor fellow,' said Lu-Tze. 'A full fifty thousand years in one jolt, I'd say.' He glared at the scurrying monks again. 'Will you lot stop and come here! I ain't going to ask you twice!'

Several of them swept the sweat out of their eyes and trotted towards the podium, relieved to hear any kind of order, while behind them the Procrastinators screamed.

'Right!' said Lu-Tze, as they were joined by more and more. 'Now listen to me! This is just a surge cascade! You've all heard of them! We can deal with it! We just have to cross-link futures and pasts, fastest ones first—'

'Poor Mr Shoblang already tried that,' said a monk. He nodded at the sad pile.

'Then I want two teams—' Lu-Tze stopped. 'No, we haven't got time! We'll do it by the soles of our feet, like we used to do! One man to a spinner, just smack the bars when I say! Ready to go when I call the numbers!'

Lu-Tze climbed onto the podium and ran his eye over a board covered with wooden bobbins. A red or blue nimbus hovered over each one.

'What a mess,' he said. 'What a *mess*.'

'What do they *mean*?' said Lobsang.

Lu-Tze's hands hovered over the bobbins. 'Okay. The red-tinted ones are winding time out, speeding it up,' he said. 'The blue-tinted ones, they're winding time in, slowing it down. Brightness of the colour, that's how fast they're doing it. Except that now they're all freewheeling because the surge cut them loose, understand?'

'Loose from what?'

'From the load. From the *world*. See up there?' He waved a hand towards two long racks that ran all the way along the cavern wall. Each one held a row of swivelling shutters, one line blue, one line dark red.

107

'The more shutters showing a colour, the more time winding or unwinding?'

'Good lad! Got to keep it balanced! And the way we get through this is we couple the spinners up in twos, so that they wind and unwind one another. Cancel themselves out. Poor old Shoblang was trying to put them back into service, I reckon. Can't be done, not during a cascade. You've got to let it all fall over, and then pick up the pieces when it's nice and quiet.' He glanced at the bobbins and then at the crowd of monks. 'Right. You ... 128 to 17, and then 45 to 89. Off you go. And *you* ... 596 to, let's see ... yes, 402 ...'

'Seven hundred and ninety!' shouted Lobsang, pointing to a bobbin.

'You what?'

'Seven hundred and ninety!'

'Don't be daft. That's still unwinding, lad. Four hundred and two is our man, right here.'

'Seven hundred and ninety is about to start winding time again!'

'It's still bright blue.'

'It's going to wind. I know it. Because' – the novice's finger moved over the lines of bobbins, hesitated, and pointed to a bobbin on the other side of the board – 'it's matching speeds with this one.'

Lu-Tze peered. 'It is written, "Well, I'll go to the foot of our stairs!" ' he said. 'They're forming a natural inversion.' He squinted at Lobsang. 'You're not the reincarnation of someone, are you? That happens a lot in these parts.'

'I don't think so. It's just ... obvious.'

'A moment ago you didn't know anything about these!'

'Yes, yes, but when you see them ... it's obvious.'

'Is it? *Is* it? All right. Then the board's yours, wonder boy!' Lu-Tze stood back.

'Mine? But I—'

'Get on with it! That is an *order*.'

For a moment there was a suggestion of blue light around Lobsang. Lu-Tze wondered how much time he'd folded around himself in that second. Time enough to think, certainly.

Then the boy called out half a dozen pairs of numbers. Lu-Tze turned to the monks.

'Jump to it, boys. Mr Lobsang has the board! You boys just watch those bearings!'

'But he's a novice—' one of the monks began, and stopped and backed away when he saw Lu-Tze's expression. 'All right, Sweeper . . . all right . . .'

A moment later there was the sound of jumpers slamming into place. Lobsang called out another set of numbers.

While the monks dashed to and fro to the butter pits for grease, Lu-Tze watched the nearest column. It was still spinning fast, but he was sure he could see the carvings.

Lobsang ran his eye over the board again and stared up at the rumbling cylinders, and then back to the lines of shutters.

There wasn't anything written down about all this, Lu-Tze knew. You couldn't teach it in a classroom, although they tried. A good spin driver learned it through the soles of his feet, for all the theory that they taught you these days. He'd learn to *feel* the flows, to see the rows of Procrastinators as sinks or fountains of time. Old Shoblang had been so good that he'd been able to pull a couple of hours of wasted time from a classroom of bored pupils without their even noticing, and dump it into a busy workshop a thousand miles away as neat as you pleased.

And then there was that trick he used to do with an apple to amaze the apprentices. He'd put it on a pillar next to them, and then flick time at it off one of the small spindles. In an instant it'd be a collection of small, spindly trees before crumbling to dust. That's what'll happen to you if you get things wrong, he'd say.

Lu-Tze glanced down at the pile of grey dust under the disintegrating hat as he hurried past. Well, maybe it was the way he'd want to go—

A scream of tormented stone made him look up.

'Keep those bearings greased, you lazy devils!' he yelled, running down the rows. 'And watch those rails! Hands off the splines! We're doing fine!'

As he ran he kept his eyes on the columns. They were no longer turning randomly. Now, they had purpose.

'I think you're winning, lad!' he shouted to the figure on the podium.

'Yes, but I can't balance it! There's too much time wound up and nowhere to put it!'

'How much?'

'Almost forty years!'

Lu-Tze glanced at the shutters. Forty years looked about right, but surely—?

'*How* much?' he said.

'Forty! I'm sorry! There's nothing to take it up!'

'No problem! Steal it! Shed load! We can always pull it back later! Dump it!'

'Where?'

'Find a big patch of sea!' The sweeper pointed to a crude map of the world painted on the wall. 'Do you know how to— Can you *see* how to give it the right spin and direction?'

Once again, there was the blueness in the air.

'Yes! I think so!'

'Yes, I imagine you do! In your own time, then!'

Lu-Tze shook his head. Forty years? He was worried about *forty years*? Forty years was nothing! Apprentice drivers had dumped fifty thousand years before now. That was the thing about the sea. It just stayed big and wet. It always had been big and wet, it always would be big and wet. Oh, maybe fishermen would start to dredge up strange whiskery fish that they'd only ever seen before as fossils, but who cared what happened to a bunch of codfish?

The sound changed.

'What are you doing?'

'I've found space on number 422! It can take another forty years! No sense in wasting time! I'm pulling it back *now*!'

There was another change of tone.

'Got it! I'm sure I've *got* it!'

Some of the bigger cylinders were already slowing to a halt. Lobsang was moving pegs around the board now faster than the bewildered Lu-Tze could follow. And, overhead, the shutters were slamming back, one after another, showing age-blackened wood instead of colour.

No one could be that accurate, could they?

'You're down to months now, lad, months!' he shouted. 'Keep it up! No, blimey, you're down to days . . . *days*! Keep an eye on me!'

The sweeper ran towards the end of the hall, to where the Procrastinators were smaller. Time was fine-tuned here, on cylinders of chalk and wood and other short-lived materials. To his amazement, some of them were already slowing.

He raced down an aisle of oak columns a few feet high. But even the Procrastinators that could wind time in hours and minutes were falling silent.

There was a squeaking noise.

Beside him, one final little chalk cylinder at the end of a row rattled around on its bearing like a spinning-top.

Lu-Tze crept towards it, staring at it intently, one hand raised. The squeaking was the only sound now, apart from the occasional *clink* of cooling bearings.

'Nearly there,' he called out. 'Slowing down now . . . wait for it, wait . . . for . . . it . . .'

The chalk Procrastinator, no bigger than a reel of cotton, slowed, spun . . . stopped.

On the racks, the last two shutters closed.

Lu-Tze's hand fell.

'*Now! Kill the board! No one touch a thing!*'

For a moment there was dead silence in the hall. The monks watched, holding their breath.

This was a timeless moment, of perfect balance.

Tick

And in that timeless moment the ghost of Mr Shoblang, to whom the scene was hazy and fuzzy as though seen through a gauze, said, 'This is just *impossible*! Did you see that?'

SEE WHAT? said a dark figure behind him.

Shoblang turned. 'Oh,' he said, and added with sudden certainty, 'You're Death, right?'

YES. I AM SORRY I AM LATE.

The spirit formerly known as Shoblang looked down at the pile of dust that represented his worldly habitation for the previous six hundred years.

'So am I,' he said. He nudged Death in the ribs.

EXCUSE ME?

'I said, "I'm sorry I'm late." Boom, boom.'

I BEG YOUR PARDON?

'Er, you know . . . Sorry I'm *late*. Like . . . dead?'

Death nodded. OH, I SEE. IT WAS THE 'BOOM BOOM' I DID NOT UNDERSTAND.

'Er, that was to show it was a joke,' said Shoblang.

AH, YES. I CAN SEE HOW THAT WOULD BE NECESSARY. IN FACT, MR SHOBLANG, WHILE YOU ARE LATE, YOU ARE ALSO EARLY. BOOM, BOOM.

'Pardon?'

YOU HAVE DIED BEFORE YOUR TIME.

'Well, yes, *I* should think so!'

DO YOU HAVE ANY IDEA WHY? IT'S VERY UNUSUAL.

'All I know is that the spinners went wild and I must've copped a load when one of 'em went overspeed,' said Shoblang. 'But, hey, what about that kid, eh? Look at the way he's making the buggers dance! I wish I'd had him training under me! What am I saying? He could give *me* a few tips!'

Death looked around. TO WHOM DO YOU REFER?

'That boy up on the podium, see him?'

NO, I'M AFRAID I SEE NO ONE THERE.

'What? Look, he's right *there*! Plain as the nose on your fa— Well, obviously not on *your* face . . .'

I SEE THE COLOURED PEGS MOVING . . .

'Well, who do you think is moving them? I mean, you *are* Death, right? I thought you could see everyone!'

Death stared at the dancing bobbins.

EVERYONE . . . THAT I SHOULD SEE, he said. He continued to stare.

'Ahem,' said Shoblang.

OH, YES. WHERE WERE WE?

'Look, if I'm, er, too early, then can't you—'

EVERYTHING THAT HAPPENS STAYS HAPPENED.

'What kind of philosophy is that?'

THE ONLY ONE THAT WORKS. Death took out an hourglass and consulted it. I SEE THAT BECAUSE OF THIS PROBLEM YOU ARE NOT DUE TO REINCARNATE FOR SEVENTY-NINE YEARS. DO YOU HAVE ANYWHERE TO STAY?

'Stay? I'm *dead*. It's not like locking yourself out of your own house!' said Shoblang, who was beginning to fade.

PERHAPS YOU COULD BE BUMPED UP TO AN EARLIER BIRTH?

Shoblang vanished.

In the timeless moment Death turned back to stare at the hall of spinners . . .

Tick

The chalk cylinder started to spin again, squeaking gently.

One by one, the oak Procrastinators began to revolve, picking up the rising load. This time there was no scream of bearings. They twirled slowly, like old ballerinas, this way and that, gradually taking up the strain as millions of humans in the world outside bent time around themselves. The creaking sounded like a tea-clipper rounding Cape Wrath on a gentle breeze.

Then the big stone cylinders groaned as they picked up the time their smaller brethren couldn't handle. A rumbling underlay the creaking now, but it was still gentle, controlled . . .

Lu-Tze lowered his hand gently and straightened up.

'A nice clean pick-up,' he said. 'Well done, everyone.' He turned to the astonished, panting monks and beckoned the most senior towards him.

Lu-Tze pulled a ragged cigarette end out of its lodging behind his ear and said, 'Well now, Rambut Handisides, what d'you think happened just now, eh?'

'Er, well, there was a surge which blew out—'

'Nah, nah, after that,' said Lu-Tze, striking a match on the sole of his sandal. 'See, what I *don't* think happened was that you boys

113

ran around like a lot of headless chickens and a novice got up on the platform and did the sweetest, smoothest bit of rebalancing that I've ever seen. That couldn't have happened, because *that sort of thing does not happen*. Am I right?'

The monks of the Procrastinator floor were not among the temple's great political thinkers. Their job was to tend and grease and strip down and rebuild and follow the directions of the man on the platform. Rambut Handisides' brow wrinkled.

Lu-Tze sighed. 'See, what *I* think happened,' he said helpfully, 'was that you lads rose to the occasion, right, and left myself and the young man there aghast at the practical skills you all showed. The abbot will be impressed and blow happy bubbles. You could be looking at some extra *momo*s in your *thugpa* come dinner-time, if you get my drift?'

Handisides ran this up his mental flagpole and it did indeed send prayers to heaven. He began to smile.

'*However*,' said Lu-Tze, stepping closer and lowering his voice, 'I'll probably be around again soon, this place looks as though it could do with a good sweeping, and if I don't find you boys pin-sharp and prodding buttock inside a week you and I will have a . . . talk.'

The smile vanished. 'Yes, Sweeper.'

'You've got to test them all and see to those bearings.'

'Yes, Sweeper.'

'And someone clear up Mr Shoblang.'

'Yes, Sweeper.'

'Fair play to you, then. Me and young Lobsang here will be going. You've done a lot for his education.'

He took the unresisting Lobsang by the hand and led him out of the hall, past the long lines of turning, humming Procrastinators. A pall of blue smoke still hung under the high ceiling.

'Truly it is written, "You could knock me down with a feather," ' he muttered, as they headed up the sloping passage. 'You spotted that inversion before it happened. I'd have blown us into next week. At *least*.'

'Sorry, Sweeper.'

'Sorry? You don't have to be *sorry*. I don't know what you *are*, son. You're too quick. You're taking to this place like a duck to water. You don't have to learn stuff that takes other people years to get the hang of. Old Shoblang, may he be reincarnated somewhere nice and warm, even he couldn't balance the load down to a second. I mean, a *second*. Over a whole damn *world*!' He shuddered. 'Here's a tip. Don't let it show. People can be funny about that sort of thing.'

'Yes, Sweeper.'

'And another thing,' said Lu-Tze, leading the way out into the light. 'What was all that fuss just before the Procrastinators cut loose? You felt something?'

'I don't know. I just felt . . . everything went wrong for a moment.'

'Ever happened before?'

'No-o. It was a bit like what happened in the Mandala Hall.'

'Well, don't talk about it to anyone else. Most of the high-ups these days probably don't even know how the spinners work. No one cares about them any more. No one notices something that works too well. Of course, in the old days you weren't even allowed to become a monk until you'd spent six months in the hall, greasing and cleaning and fetching. And we were better for it! These days it's all about learning obedience and cosmic harmony. Well, in the old days you learned that in the halls. You learned that if you didn't jump out of the way when someone yelled, "She's dumping!" you got a couple of years where it hurt, and that there's no harmony better than all the spinners turning sweetly.'

The passage rose into the main temple complex. People were still scurrying around as they headed for the Mandala Hall.

'You're sure you can look at it again?' said Lu-Tze.

'Yes, Sweeper.'

'Okay. You know best.'

The balconies overlooking the hall were crowded with monks, but Lu-Tze worked his way forward by polite yet firm use of his broom. The senior monks were clustered at the edge.

Rinpo caught sight of him. 'Ah, Sweeper,' he said. 'Some dust delayed you?'

'Spinners cut free and went overspeed,' muttered Lu-Tze.

'Yes, but you *were* summoned by the abbot,' said the acolyte reproachfully.

'Upon a time,' said Lu-Tze, 'every man jack of us would have legged it down to the hall when the gongs went.'

'Yes, but—'

'*BRRRRbrrrrbrrrr*,' said the abbot, and Lobsang saw now that he was being carried in a sling on the acolyte's back, with an embroidered pixie hood on his head to keep off the chill. 'Lu-Tze always was very keen on the practical approach *BRRRbrrr*.' He blew milky suds into the acolyte's ear. 'I am glad matters have been resolved, Lu-Tze.'

The sweeper bowed, while the abbot started to beat the acolyte gently over the head with a wooden bear.

'History has repeated, Lu-Tze. *DumDumBBBRRRR* . . .'

'Glass clock?' said Lu-Tze.

The senior monks gasped.

'How could you possibly know that?' said the chief acolyte. 'We haven't rerun the Mandala yet!'

'It is written, "I've got a feeling in my water,"' said Lu-Tze. 'And that was the only other time I ever heard of when all the spinners went wild like that. They *all* cut loose. Time-slip. Someone's building a glass clock again.'

'That is quite impossible,' said the acolyte. 'We removed every trace!'

'Hah! It is written, "I'm not as green as I'm cabbage-looking!"' snapped Lu-Tze. 'Something like that you *can't* kill. It leaks back. Stories. Dreams. Paintings on cave walls, whatever—'

Lobsang looked down at the Mandala floor. Monks were clustered around a group of tall cylinders at the far end of the hall. They looked like Procrastinators, but only one small one was spinning, slowly. The others were motionless, showing the mass of symbols that were carved into them from top to bottom.

Pattern storage. The thought arrived in his head. That is where the Mandala's patterns are kept, so that they can be replayed. Today's patterns on the little one, long-term storage on the big ones.

Below him the Mandala rippled, blotches of colour and scraps of pattern drifting across its surface. One of the distant monks called out something, and the small cylinder stopped.

The rolling sand grains were stilled.

'This is how it looked twenty minutes ago,' said Rinpo. 'See the blue-white dot there? And then it spreads—'

'I know what I'm looking at,' said Lu-Tze grimly. 'I was *there* when it happened before, man! Your reverence, get them to run the old Glass Clock sequence! We haven't got a lot of time!'

'I really think we—' the acolyte began, but he was interrupted by a blow from a rubber brick.

'*Wannapottywanna* if Lu-Tze is right, then we must not waste time, gentlemen, and if he is wrong then we have time to spare, is this not so? *Pottynowwannawanna!*'

'Thank you,' said the sweeper. He cupped his hands. 'Oi! You lot! Spindle two, fourth *bhing*, round about the nineteenth *gupa*! And jump to it!'

'I really must respectfully protest, your reverence,' said the acolyte. 'We have practised for just such an emergency as—'

'Yeah, I know all about practising procedures for emergencies,' said Lu-Tze. 'And there's always something missing.'

'Ridiculous! We take great pains to—'

'You always leave out the damn emergency.' Lu-Tze turned back to the hall and the apprehensive workers. 'Ready? Good! Put it on the floor *now*! Or I shall have to come down there! And I don't *want* to have to come down there!'

There was some frantic activity by the men around the cylinders, and a new pattern replaced the one below the balcony. The lines and colours were in different places, but a blue-white circle occupied the centre.

'There,' said Lu-Tze. 'That was less than ten days before the clock struck.'

There was silence from the monks.

Lu-Tze smiled grimly. 'And ten days later—'

'Time stopped,' said Lobsang.

'That's one way of putting it,' said Lu-Tze. He'd gone red in the face.

One of the monks put a hand on his shoulder.

'It's *all right*, Sweeper,' he said soothingly. 'We *know* you couldn't have got there in time.'

'Being in time is supposed to be what we *do*,' said Lu-Tze. 'I was nearly at the damn *door*, Charlie. Too many castles, not enough time . . .'

Behind him the Mandala returned to its slow metering of the present.

'It wasn't your fault,' said the monk.

Lu-Tze shook the hand free and turned to face the abbot over the shoulder of the chief acolyte.

'I want permission to track this one down right now, reverend sir!' he said. He tapped his nose. 'I've got the smell of it! I've been waiting for this all these years! You won't find me wanting this time!'

In the silence the abbot blew a bubble.

'It'll be in Uberwald again,' said Lu-Tze, a hint of pleading in his voice. 'That's where they mess around with the electrick. I know every inch of that place! Give me a couple of men and we can nip this right in the bud!'

'*Babababa* . . . This needs discussion, Lu-Tze, but we thank you for your offer *babababa*,' said the abbot. 'Rinpo, I want all *bdum-bdumbdum* senior field monks in the Room of Silence within five *bababa* minutes! Are the spinners working *bdumbdum* harmoniously?'

One of the monks looked up from a scroll he'd been handed.

'It appears so, your reverence.'

'My congratulations to the board master *BIKKIT!*'

'But Shoblang is dead,' murmured Lu-Tze.

The abbot stopped blowing bubbles. 'That is sad news. And he was a friend of yours, I understand.'

'Shouldn't've happened like that,' the sweeper muttered. 'Shouldn't've happened like that.'

'Compose yourself, Lu-Tze. I will talk to you shortly. *Bikkit!*' The chief acolyte, spurred on by a blow across the ear with a rubber monkey, hurried away.

The press of monks began to thin out as they went about their duties. Lu-Tze and Lobsang were left on the balcony, looking down at the rippling Mandala.

Lu-Tze cleared his throat. 'See them spinners at the end?' he said. 'The little one records the patterns for a day, and then anything interesting is stored in the big ones.'

'I just premembered you were going to say that.'

'Good word. Good word. The lad has talent.' Lu-Tze lowered his voice. 'Anyone watching us?'

Lobsang looked around. 'There's a few people still here.'

Lu-Tze raised his voice again. 'You been taught anything about the Big Crash?'

'Only rumours, Sweeper.'

'Yeah, there were a lot of rumours. "The day time stood still", all that sort of thing.' Lu-Tze sighed. 'Y'know, most of what you get taught is lies. It has to be. Sometimes if you get the truth all at once, you can't understand it. You knew Ankh-Morpork pretty well, did you? Ever go to the opera house?'

'Only for pickpocket practice, Sweeper.'

'Ever *wonder* about it? Ever look at that little theatre just over the road? Called The Dysk, I think.'

'Oh, yes! We got penny tickets and sat on the ground and threw nuts at the stage.'

'And it didn't make you *think*? Big opera house, all plush and gilt and big orchestras, and then there's this little thatched theatre, all bare wood and no seats and one bloke playing a crumhorn for musical accompaniment?'

Lobsang shrugged. 'Well, no. That's just how things are.'

Lu-Tze almost smiled. 'Very flexible things, human minds,' he said. 'It's amazing what they can stretch to fit. We did a fine job there—'

'Lu-Tze?'

One of the lesser acolytes was waiting respectfully.

'The abbot will see you now,' he said.

'Ah, right,' said the sweeper. He nudged Lobsang and whispered, 'We're going to Ankh-Morpork, lad.'

'What? But you said you wanted to be sent to—'

Lu-Tze winked. '''cos it is written, "Them as asks, don't get," see. There's more than one way of choking a *dangdang* than stuffing it with *pling*, lad.'

'Is there?'

'Oh yes, if you've got enough *pling*. Now let's see the abbot, shall we? It'll be time for his feed now. Solids, thank goodness. At least he's done with the wetnurse. It was so embarrassing for him and the young lady, honestly, you didn't know where to put your face and neither did he. I mean, mentally he's nine hundred years old . . .'

'That must make him very wise.'

'Pretty wise, pretty wise. But age and wisdom don't necessarily go together, I've always found,' said Lu-Tze, as they approached the abbot's rooms. 'Some people just become stupid with more authority. Not his reverence, of course.'

The abbot was in his highchair, and had recently flicked a spoonful of nourishing pap all over the chief acolyte, who was smiling like a man whose job depended on looking happy that parsnip-and-gooseberry custard was dribbling down his forehead.

It occurred to Lobsang, not for the first time, that the abbot was a little bit more than purely random in his attacks on the man. The acolyte was, indeed, the kind of mildly objectionable person who engendered an irresistible urge in any right-thinking person to pour goo into his hair and hit him with a rubber yak, and the abbot was old enough to listen to his inner child.

'You sent for me, your reverence,' said Lu-Tze, bowing.

The abbot upturned his bowl down the chief acolyte's robe.

'*Wahahaahaha ah*, yes, Lu-Tze. How old are you now?'

'Eight hundred, your reverence. But that's no age at all!'

'Nevertheless, you have spent a lot of time in the world. I understood you were looking to retire and cultivate your gardens?'

'Yes, but—'

'But,' the abbot smiled angelically, 'like an old warhorse you say "haha!" at the sound of trumpets, yes?'

120

'I don't think so,' said Lu-Tze. 'There's nothing funny about trumpets, really.'

'I meant that you long to be out in the field again. But you *have* been helping to train world operatives for many years, haven't you? These gentlemen?'

A number of burly and muscular monks were sitting on one side of the room. They were kitted out for travel, with rolled sleeping mats on their backs, and dressed in loose black clothing. They nodded sheepishly at Lu-Tze, and their eyes above their half-masks looked embarrassed.

'I did my best,' said Lu-Tze. 'Of course, others trained them. I just tried to undo the damage. I never taught them to be *ninja*s.' He nudged Lobsang. 'That, apprentice, is Agatean for "the Passing Wind",' he said, in a stage whisper.

'I am proposing to send them out immediately *WAH!*' The abbot hit his highchair with his spoon. 'That is my order, Lu-Tze. You are a legend, but you have been a legend for a long time. Why not trust in the future? *Bikkit!*'

'I see,' said Lu-Tze sadly. 'Oh, well, it had to happen some time. Thank you for your consideration, your reverence.'

'*Brrmbrrm* . . . Lu-Tze, I have known you a long time! You will not go within a hundred miles of Uberwald, will you?'

'Not at all, your reverence.'

'That is an order!'

'I understand, of course.'

'You've disobeyed my *baababa* orders before, though. In Omnia, I remember.'

'Tactical decision made by the man on the spot, your reverence. It was more what you might call an *interpretation* of your order,' said Lu-Tze.

'You mean, going where you had distinctly been told not to go and doing what you were absolutely forbidden to do?'

'Yes, your reverence. Sometimes you have to move the seesaw by pushing the other end. When I did what shouldn't be done in a place where I shouldn't have been, I *achieved* what needed to be done in the place where it should have happened.'

121

The abbot gave Lu-Tze a long hard stare, the kind that babies are good at giving.

'Lu-Tze, you are not *nmnmnbooboo* to go to Uberwald or any-where near Uberwald, understand?' he said.

'I do, your reverence. You are right, of course. But, in my dotage, may I travel another path, of wisdom rather than violence? I wish to show this young man . . . the Way.'

There was laughter from the other monks.

'The Way of the Washerwoman?' said Rinpo.

'Mrs Cosmopilite is a dressmaker,' said Lu-Tze calmly.

'Whose wisdom is in sayings like "It won't get better if you pick at it"?' said Rinpo, winking at the rest of the monks.

'Few things get better if you pick at them,' said Lu-Tze, and now his calmness was a lake of tranquillity. 'It may be a mean little Way but, small and unworthy though it is, it is *my* Way.' He turned to the abbot. 'That was how it used to be, your reverence. You recall? Master and pupil go out into the world, where the pupil may pick up practical instruction by precept and example, and then the pupil finds his own Way and at the end of his Way—'

'—he finds himself *bdum*,' said the abbot.

'First, he finds a teacher,' said Lu-Tze.

'He is lucky that you will *bdumbdum* be that teacher.'

'Reverend sir,' said Lu-Tze. 'It is in the nature of Ways that none can be sure who the teacher may be. All I can do is show him a path.'

'Which will be in the direction of *bdum* the city,' said the abbot.

'Yes,' said Lu-Tze. 'And Ankh-Morpork is a *long* way from Uberwald. You won't send me to Uberwald because I am an old man. So, in all respect, I beg you to humour an old man.'

'I have no choice, when you put it like that,' said the abbot.

'Reverend sir—' began Rinpo, who felt that he did.

The spoon was banged on the tray again. 'Lu-Tze is a man of high reputation!' the abbot shouted. 'I trust him implicitly to do the correct action! I just wish I could *blumblum* trust him to do what I *blumblum* want! I have forbidden him to go to Uberwald! Now do you wish me to forbid him *not* to go to Uberwald? *BIKKIT!* I have spoken! And now, will all you gentlemen be so good as to leave? I have urgent business to attend to.'

Lu-Tze bowed and grabbed Lobsang's arm. 'Come on, lad!' he whispered. 'Let's bugger off quick before anyone works it out!'

On the way out they passed a lesser acolyte carrying a small potty with a pattern of bunny rabbits around it.

'It's not easy, reincarnating,' said Lu-Tze, running down the corridor. 'Now we've got to be out of here before someone gets any funny ideas. Grab your bag and bedroll!'

'But no one would countermand the abbot's orders, would they?' said Lobsang, as they skidded round a corner.

'Ha! It'll be his nap in ten minutes and if they give him a new toy when he wakes up he might end up being so busy banging square green pegs into round blue holes that he'll forget what he said,' said Lu-Tze. 'Politics, lad. Too many idiots will start saying what they're sure the abbot would have *meant*. Off you go, now. I'll see you in the Garden of Five Surprises in one minute.'

When Lobsang arrived Lu-Tze was carefully tying one of the bonsai mountains into a bamboo framework. He fastened the last knot and placed it in a bag over one shoulder.

'Won't it get damaged?' said Lobsang.

'It's a mountain. How can it get damaged?' Lu-Tze picked up his broom. 'And we'll just drop in and have a chat with an old mate of mine before we leave, though. Maybe we'll pick up some stuff.'

'What's going on, Sweeper?' said Lobsang, trailing after him.

'Well, it's like this, lad. Me and the abbot and the bloke we're going to see, we go back a long way. Things are a bit different now. The abbot can't just say, "Lu-Tze, you are an old rogue, it was you who put the idea of Uberwald into everyone's heads in the first place, but I see you're onto something so off you go and follow your nose."'

'But I thought he was the supreme ruler!'

'Exactly! And it's very hard to get things done when you're a supreme ruler. There're too many people in the way, mucking things up. This way, the new lads can have fun running around

Uberwald going, "Hai!" and *we*, my lad, will be heading for Ankh-Morpork. The abbot knows that. *Almost* knows that.'

'How do you know the new clock is being built in Ankh-Morpork?' said Lobsang, trailing behind Lu-Tze as he took a mossy, sunken path that led through rhododendron thickets to the monastery wall.

'I *know*. I'll tell you, the day someone pulls the plug out of the bottom of the universe, the chain will lead all the way to Ankh-Morpork and some bugger saying, "I just wanted to see what would happen." All roads lead to Ankh-Morpork.'

'I thought all roads led *away* from Ankh-Morpork.'

'Not the way we're going. Ah, here we are.'

Lu-Tze knocked on the door of a rough but large shed built right up against the wall. At the same moment there was an explosion within and someone – Lobsang corrected himself – *half* of someone tumbled very fast out of the unglazed window beside it and hit the path with bone-cracking force. Only when it stopped rolling did he realize that it was a wooden dummy in a monk's robe.

'Qu's having fun, I see,' said Lu-Tze. He hadn't moved as the dummy had sailed past his ear.

The door burst open and a plump old monk looked out excitedly.

'Did you see that? Did you *see* that?' he said. 'And that was with just one spoonful!' He nodded at them. 'Oh, hello, Lu-Tze. I was expecting you. I've got some things ready.'

'Got what?' said Lobsang.

'Who's the boy?' said Qu, ushering them in.

'The untutored child is called Lobsang,' said Lu-Tze, looking around the shed. There was a smoking circle on the stone floor, with drifts of blackened sand around it. 'New toys, Qu?'

'Exploding mandala,' said Qu happily, bustling forward. 'Just sprinkle the special sand on a simple design anywhere you like, and the first enemy to walk on it— Bang, instant karma! *Don't touch that!'*

Lu-Tze reached across and snatched from Lobsang's inquisitive hands the begging bowl that he had just picked up from a table.

'Remember Rule One,' he said, and hurled the bowl across the room. Hidden blades slid out as it spun, and the bowl buried itself in a beam.

'That would take a man's head right off!' said Lobsang. And then they heard the faint ticking.

'. . . three, four, five . . .' said Qu. 'Everybody duck . . . *Now!*'

Lu-Tze pushed Lobsang to the floor a moment before the bowl exploded. Metal fragments scythed overhead.

'I added just a little something extra since you last saw it,' said Qu proudly, as they got to their feet again. 'A very versatile device. Plus, of course, you can use it to eat rice out of. Oh, and have you seen this?'

He picked up a prayer drum. Both Lu-Tze and Lobsang took a step back.

Qu twirled the drum a few times, and the weighted cords pattered against the skins.

'The cord can be instantly removed for a handy garotte,' he said, 'and the drum itself can be removed – like so – to reveal this useful dagger.'

'Plus, of course, you can use it to pray with?' said Lobsang.

'Well spotted,' said Qu. 'Quick boy. A prayer is always useful in the last resort. In fact we've been working on a very promising mantra incorporating sonic tones that have a particular effect on the human nervous syst—'

'I don't think we need any of this stuff, Qu,' said Lu-Tze.

Qu sighed. 'At least you could let us turn your broom into a secret weapon, Lu-Tze. I've shown you the plans—'

'It is a secret weapon,' said Lu-Tze. 'It's a broom.'

'How about the new yaks we've been breeding? At the touch of a rein their horns will instantly—'

'We want the spinners, Qu.'

The monk suddenly looked guilty. 'Spinners? What spinners?'

Lu-Tze walked across the room and pressed a hand against part of the wall, which slid aside.

'These spinners, Qu. Don't muck me about, we haven't got time.'

Lobsang saw what looked very much like two small

Procrastinators, each one within a metal framework mounted on a board. There was a harness attached to each board.

'You haven't told the abbot about them yet, have you?' said Lu-Tze, unhooking one of the things. 'He'd put a stop to them if you did, you know that.'

'I didn't think *anyone* knew!' said Qu. 'How did *you*—'

Lu-Tze grinned. 'No one notices a sweeper,' he said.

'They're still very experimental!' said Qu, close to panic. 'I *was* going to tell the abbot, of *course*, but I was waiting until I had something to demonstrate! And it would be terrible if they fell into the wrong hands!'

'Then we'll see to it that they don't,' said Lu-Tze, examining the straps. 'How're they powered now?'

'Weights and ratchets were too unreliable,' said Qu. 'I'm afraid I had to resort to . . . clockwork.'

Lu-Tze stiffened, and he glared at the monk. *'Clockwork?'*

'Only as a motive force, only as a motive force!' Qu protested. 'There's really no other choice!'

'Too late now, it'll have to do,' said Lu-Tze, unhooking the other board and passing it across to Lobsang. 'There you go, lad. With a bit of sacking round it it'll look just like a backpack.'

'What *is* it?'

Qu sighed. 'They're portable Procrastinators. *Try* not to break them, please.'

'What will we need them for?'

'I hope you won't have to find out,' said Lu-Tze. 'Thanks, Qu.'

'Are you sure you wouldn't prefer some time bombs?' said Qu hopefully. 'Drop one on the floor and time will slow for—'

'Thanks, but no.'

'The other monks were *fully* equipped,' said Qu.

'But we're travelling light,' said Lu-Tze firmly. 'We'll go out the back way, Qu, okay?'

The back way led to a narrow path and a small gate in the wall. Dismembered wooden dummies and patches of scorched rock indicated that Qu and his assistants often came this way. And then there was another path, beside one of the many icy streamlets.

'Qu means well,' said Lu-Tze, walking fast. 'But if you listen to him you end up clanking when you walk and exploding when you sit down.'

Lobsang ran to keep up. 'It'll take *weeks* to walk to Ankh-Morpork, Sweeper!'

'We'll slice our way there,' said Lu-Tze, and he stopped and turned. 'You think you can do that?'

'I've done it hundreds of times—' Lobsang began.

'In Oi Dong, yes,' said Lu-Tze. 'But there're all kinds of checks and safeguards in the valley. Oh, didn't you know that? Slicing in Oi Dong is *easy*, lad. It's different out there. The air tries to get in the way. Do it wrong and the air is a rock. You have to shape the slice around you so that you move like a fish in water. Know how to do that?'

'We learned a bit of the theory, but—'

'Soto said you stopped time for yourself back in the city. The Stance of the Coyote, it's called. Very hard to do, and I don't reckon they teach it in the Thieves' Guild, eh?'

'I suppose I was lucky, Sweeper.'

'Good. Keep it up. We'll have plenty of time for you to practise before we leave the snow. Get it right before you tread on grass, or kiss your feet goodbye.'

They called it slicing time . . .

There is a way of playing certain musical instruments that is called 'circular breathing', devised to allow people to play the didgeridoo or the bagpipes without actually imploding or being sucked down the tube. 'Slicing time' was very much the same, except time was substituted for air and it was a lot quieter. A trained monk could stretch a second further than an hour . . .

But that wasn't enough. He'd be moving in a rigid world. He'd have to learn to see by echo light and hear by ghost sound and let time leach into his immediate universe. It wasn't hard, once he found the confidence; the sliced world could almost seem normal, apart from the colours . . .

It was like walking in sunsets, although the sun was fixed high in the sky and barely moved. The world ahead shaded towards violet, and the world behind, when Lobsang looked round, was the shade of old blood. And it was lonely. But the worst of it, Lobsang realized, was the silence. There was noise, of a sort, but it was just a deep sizzle at the edge of hearing. His footsteps sounded strange and muffled, and the sound arrived in his ears out of sync with the tread of his feet.

They reached the edge of the valley and stepped out of the perpetual springtime into the real world of the snows. Now the cold crept in, slowly, like a sadist's knife.

Lu-Tze strode on ahead, seemingly oblivious of it.

Of course, that was one of the stories about him. Lu-Tze, it was said, would walk for miles during weather when the clouds themselves would freeze and crash out of the sky. Cold did not affect him, they said.

And yet—

In the stories Lu-Tze had been bigger, stronger . . . not a skinny little bald man who preferred not to fight.

'Sweeper!'

Lu-Tze stopped and turned. His outline blurred slightly, and Lobsang unwrapped himself from time. Colour came back into the world, and while the cold ceased to have the force of a drill it still struck hard.

'Yes, lad?'

'You're going to teach me, right?'

'If there's anything left that you don't know, wonder boy,' said Lu-Tze drily. 'You're slicing well, I can see that.'

'I don't know how you can stand this cold!'

'Ah, you don't know the secret?'

'Is it the Way of Mrs Cosmopilite that gives you such power?'

Lu-Tze hitched up his robe and did a little dance in the snow, revealing skinny legs encased in thick, yellowing tubes.

'Very good, very good,' he said. 'She still sends me these double-knit combinations, silk on the inside, then three layers of wool, reinforced gussets and a couple of handy trapdoors. Very reasonably priced at six dollars a pair because I'm an old customer. For it is written, "Wrap up warm or you'll catch your death." '

'It's just a *trick*?'

Lu-Tze looked surprised. 'What?' he said.

'Well, I mean, it's all tricks, isn't it? Everyone thinks you're a great hero and . . . you don't fight, and they think you possess all kinds of strange knowledge and . . . and it's just . . . *tricking* people. Isn't it? Even the abbot? I thought you were going to teach me . . . things worth knowing . . .'

'I've got her address, if that's what you want. If you mention my name— Oh. I see you don't mean that, right?'

'I don't want to be ungrateful, I just thought—'

'You thought I should use mysterious powers derived from a lifetime of study just to keep my legs warm? Eh?'

'Well—'

'Debase the sacred teachings for the sake of my knees, you think?'

'If you put it like that—'

Then something made Lobsang look down.

He was standing in six inches of snow. Lu-Tze was not. His sandals were standing in two puddles. The ice was melting away around his toes. His pink, warm toes.

'Toes, now, that's another matter,' said the sweeper. 'Mrs Cosmopilite is a wizard with longjohns, but she can't turn a heel worth a damn.' Lobsang looked up into a wink. 'Always remember Rule One, eh?'

Lu-Tze patted the shaken boy on the arm. 'But you're doing well,' he said. 'Let's have a quiet sit down and a brew-up.' He pointed to some rocks, which at least offered some protection from the wind; snow had piled up against them in big white mounds.

'Lu-Tze?'

'Yes, lad?'

'I've got a question. Can you give me a straight answer?'

'I'll try, of course.'

'*What the hell is going on?*'

Lu-Tze brushed the snow off a rock.

'Oh,' he said. 'One of the *difficult* questions.'

Tick

Igor had to admit it. When it came to getting weird things done, sane beat mad hands down.

He'd been used to masters who, despite doing wonderful handstands on the edge of the mental catastrophe curve, couldn't put their own trousers on without a map. Like all Igors, he'd learned how to deal with them. In truth, it wasn't a difficult job (although sometimes you had to work the graveyard shift) and once you got them settled into their routine you could get on with your own work and they wouldn't bother you until the lightning rod needed raising.

It wasn't like that with Jeremy. He was truly a man you could set your watch by. Igor had never seen a life so organized, so slimmed down, so *timed*. He found himself thinking of his new master as the tick-tock man.

One of Igor's former masters had *made* a tick-tock man, all levers and gearwheels and cranks and clockwork. Instead of a brain, it had a long tape punched with holes. Instead of a heart, it had a big spring. Provided everything in the kitchen was very carefully positioned, the thing could sweep the floor and make a passable cup of tea. If everything *wasn't* carefully positioned, or if the ticking, clicking thing hit an unexpected bump, then it'd strip the plaster off the walls and make a furious cup of cat.

Then his master had conceived the idea of making the thing *live*, so that it could punch its own tapes and wind its own spring. Igor, who knew exactly when to follow instructions to the letter, dutifully rigged up the classic rising-table-and-lightning-rod arrangement on the evening of a really good storm. He didn't see exactly what happened thereafter, because he wasn't there when the lightning hit the clockwork. No, Igor was at a dead run halfway down the hill to the village, with all his possessions in a carpet bag. Even so, a white-hot cogwheel had whirred over his head and buried itself in a treetrunk.

Loyalty to a master was very important, but it took second place to loyalty to Igordom. If the world was going to be full of lurching servants, then they were damn well going to be called Igor.

It seemed to this Igor that if you *could* make a tick-tock man live, he'd be like Jeremy. And Jeremy was ticking faster, as the clock neared completion.

Igor didn't much like the clock. He was a *people* person. He preferred things that bled. And as the clock grew, with its shimmering crystal parts that didn't seem entirely all *here*, so Jeremy grew more absorbed and Igor grew more tense. There was definitely something new happening here, and while Igors were avid to learn new things there were limits. Igors did not believe in 'forbidden knowledge' and 'Things Man Was Not Meant to Know', but obviously there were *some* things a man was not meant to know, such as what it felt like to have every single particle of your body sucked into a little hole, and that seemed to be one of the options available in the immediate future.

And then there was Lady LeJean. She gave Igor the willies, and he was a man not usually subject to even the smallest willy. She wasn't a zombie and she wasn't a vampire, because she didn't smell like one. She didn't smell like anything. In Igor's experience, *everything* smelled like *something*.

And there was the other matter.

'Her feet don't touch the ground, thur,' he said.

'Of course they do,' said Jeremy, buffing up part of the mechanism with his sleeve. 'She'll be here again in a minute and seventeen seconds. And I'm sure her feet will be touching the ground.'

'Oh, *thometimeth* they do, thur. But you watch when thee goeth up or down a thtep, thur. Thee doethn't get it egthactly right, thur. You can jutht thee the thadow under her thoeth.'

'Thoeth?'

'On her feet, thur,' sighed Igor. The lisp could be a problem, and in truth any Igor could easily fix it, but it was part of being an Igor. You might as well stop limping.

'Go and get ready by the door,' said Jeremy. 'Floating in the air doesn't make you a bad person.'

Igor shrugged. He was entertaining the idea that it didn't mean you were a person at all, and incidentally he was rather worried that Jeremy seemed to have dressed himself with a little more care this morning.

He'd decided in these circumstances not to broach the subject of his hiring, but he had been working that one out. He'd been hired before her ladyship had engaged Jeremy to do this work? Well, all that showed was that she knew her man. But she'd hired him herself in Bad Schüschein. And he'd got himself onto the mail coach that very day. And it turned out that Lady LeJean had visited Jeremy on that day, too.

The only thing faster than the mail coach between Uberwald and Ankh-Morpork was magic, unless someone had found a way to travel by semaphore. And Lady LeJean hardly looked like a witch.

The shop's clocks were putting up a barrage of noise to signal the passing of seven o'clock when Igor opened the front door. It always Did* to anticipate the knock. That was another part of the Code of the Igors.

He wrenched it open.

'Two pints, sir, lovely and fresh,' said Mr Soak, handing him the bottles. 'And a day like this just says fresh cream, doesn't it?'

Igor glared at him, but took the bottles. 'I prefer it when it'th going green,' he said haughtily. 'Good day to you, Mr Thoak.'

He shut the door.

'It wasn't her?' said Jeremy, when he arrived back in the workshop.

'It wath the milkman, thur.'

'She's twenty-five seconds late!' said Jeremy, looking concerned. 'Do you think anything could have happened to her?'

'Real ladieth are often fathionably late, thur,' said Igor, putting the milk away. It was icy cold under his fingers.

'Well, I'm sure her ladyship is a real lady.'

'I wouldn't know about that, thur,' said Igor, who in fact had the aforesaid very strong doubts in that area. He walked back into the shop and took up position with his hand on the door handle just as the knock came.

Lady LeJean swept past Igor. The two trolls ignored him and took

---

* Not 'Did' anything, just 'Did'. Some things were Done, and some things were Not Done. And the things that were Done, Igors Did.

132

up their positions just inside the workshop. Igor put them down as hired rock, anyone's for two dollars a day plus walking-around money.

Her ladyship was impressed.

The big clock was nearing completion. It wasn't the squat, blocky thing that Igor's grandfather had told him about. Jeremy had, much to Igor's surprise – for there wasn't a scrap of decoration anywhere in the house – gone for the impressive look.

'Your grandfather helped to make the first one,' Jeremy had said. 'So let's build a grandfather clock, eh?' And there it stood – a slim, long-case clock in crystal and spun glass, reflecting the light in worrying ways.

Igor had spent a fortune in the Street of Cunning Artificers. For enough money, you could buy *anything* in Ankh-Morpork, and that included people. He'd made sure that no crystal-cutter or glass-worker had done enough of the work to give them any sort of clue about the finished clock, but he'd worried needlessly about that. Money could buy a lot of uninterest. Besides, who would believe you could measure time with crystals? Only in the workshop did it all come together.

Igor bustled around, polishing things, listening carefully as Jeremy showed off his creation.

'—no *need* for any metal parts,' he was saying. 'We've come up with a way of making the tamed lightning flow across glass, and we've found a workman who can make glass that bends slightly—'

'We', Igor noticed. Well, that was always the way of it. 'We' discovering things meant the master asking for them and Igor thinking them up. Anyway, the flow of lightning was a family passion. With sand and chemicals and a few secrets, you could make lightning sit up and beg.

Lady LeJean reached out with a gloved hand and touched the side of the clock.

'This is the divider mechanism—' Jeremy began, picking up a crystalline array from the workbench.

But her ladyship was still staring up at the clock. 'You've given it a face and hands,' she said. 'Why?'

'Oh, it will function very well in the measurement of traditional time,' said Jeremy. 'Glass gears throughout, of course. In theory it will never need adjusting. It will take its time from the universal tick.'

'Ah. You found it, then?'

'The time it takes the smallest possible thing that *can* happen *to* happen. I know it exists.'

She looked almost impressed. 'But the clock is still unfinished.'

'There is a certain amount of trial and error,' said Jeremy. 'But we will do it. Igor says there will be a big storm on Monday. That should provide the power, he says. And then,' Jeremy's face lit up with a smile, 'I see no reason why every clock in the world shouldn't say precisely the same time!'

Lady LeJean glanced at Igor, who bustled with renewed haste.

'The servant is satisfactory?'

'Oh, he grumbles a bit. But he has got a good heart. And a spare, apparently. He is amazingly skilled in all crafts, too.'

'Yes, Igors generally are,' said the lady distantly. 'They seem to have mastered the art of inheriting talents.' She snapped her fingers and one of the trolls stepped forward and produced a couple of bags.

'Gold and invar,' she said. 'As promised.'

'Hah, but invar will be worthless when we've finished the clock,' said Jeremy.

'We're sorry? You want more gold?'

'No, no! You have been very generous.'

Right, thought Igor, dusting the workbench vigorously.

'Until next time, then,' said Lady LeJean. The trolls were already turning towards the door.

'You'll be here for the start?' said Jeremy, as Igor hurried into the hall to open the front door because, whatever he thought about her ladyship, there was such a thing as tradition.

'Possibly. But we have every confidence in you, Jeremy.'

'Um . . .'

Igor stiffened. He hadn't heard that tone in Jeremy's voice before. In the voice of a master, it was a *bad* tone.

Jeremy took a deep, nervous breath, as if contemplating some

134

minute and difficult piece of clockwork that would, without tremendous care, unwind catastrophically and spray cogwheels across the floor.

'Um . . . I was wondering, um, your ladyship, um . . . perhaps, um, you would like to take dinner with me, um, tonight, um . . .'

Jeremy smiled. Igor had seen a better smile on a corpse.

Lady LeJean's expression flickered. It really did. It seemed to Igor to go from one expression to another as if they were a series of still pictures, with no perceptible movement of the features between each one. It went from her usual blankness to sudden thought-fulness and then all the way to amazement. And then, to Igor's own astonishment, it began to blush.

'Why, Mr Jeremy, I . . . I don't know what to say,' her ladyship stammered, her icy composure turning into a warm puddle. 'I really . . . I don't know . . . perhaps some other time? I do have an important engagement, so glad to have met you, I must be going. Goodbye.'

Igor stood stiffly to attention, as upright as the average Igor could manage, and *almost* shut the door behind her ladyship as she hurried out of the building down the steps.

She ended up, just for a moment, half an inch above the street. It was *only* for a moment, and then she drifted downwards. No one except Igor, glaring balefully through the crack between door and frame, could possibly have noticed.

He darted back into the workshop. Jeremy still stood transfixed, blushing as pinkly as her ladyship had done.

'I'll jutht be nipping out to get that new glathwork for the multiplier, thur,' Igor said quickly. 'It thould be done by now. Yeth?'

Jeremy spun on his heel and marched very quickly over to the workbench.

'You do that, Igor. Thank you,' he said, his voice slightly muffled.

Lady LeJean's party were down the street when Igor slipped out and moved quickly into the shadows.

At the crossroad her ladyship waved one hand vaguely and the trolls headed off by themselves. Igor stayed with her. For all the trademark limp, Igors could move fast when they had to. They often had to, when the mob hit the windmill.*

Out in the open he could see more wrong things. She didn't move quite right. It was as though she was controlling her body, rather than letting it control itself. That's what humans did. Even zombies got the hang of things after a while. The effect was subtle, but Igors had very good eyesight. She moved like someone unused to wearing skin.

The quarry headed down a narrow street, and Igor half hoped that some of the Thieves' Guild were around. He'd very much like to see what happened if one of them gave her the tap on the noggin that was their prelude to negotiations. One had tried it with Igor yesterday, and if the man had been surprised at the metallic clang, he'd been astonished to have his arm grabbed and broken with anatomical exactitude.

In fact, she turned into an alleyway between a couple of the buildings.

Igor hesitated. Letting yourself be outlined in the daylight at the mouth of an alley was item one on the local checklist of death. But, on the other hand, he wasn't actually doing anything wrong, was he? And she didn't look armed.

There was no sound of footsteps in the alley. He waited a moment and stuck his head round the corner.

There was no sign of Lady LeJean. There was also no way out of the alley – it was a dead end, full of rubbish.

But there was a fading grey shape in the air, which vanished even as he stared. It was a hooded robe, grey as fog. It merged into the general gloom and disappeared.

She'd turned into an alleyway, and then she'd turned into . . . something else.

Igor felt his hands twitch.

* Igors were loyal, but they were not stupid. A job was a job. When an employer had no further use for your services, for example because he'd just been staked through the heart by a crowd of angry villagers, it was time to move on before they decided that you ought to be on the next stake. An Igor soon learned a secret way out of any castle and where to stash an overnight bag. In the words of one of the founding Igors: 'We belong dead? Ecthcuthe me? Where doeth it thay "we"?'

136

Individual Igors might have their particular specialities, but they were all expert surgeons and had an inbuilt desire not to see anybody wasted. Up in the mountains, where most of the employment was for woodchoppers and miners, having an Igor living locally was considered very fortunate. There was always the risk of an axe bouncing or a sawblade running wild, and then a man was *glad* to have an Igor around who could lend a hand – or even an entire arm, if you were lucky.

And while they practised their skills freely and generously in the community, the Igors were even more careful to use them amongst themselves. Magnificent eyesight, a stout pair of lungs, a powerful digestive system . . . It was terrible to think of such wonderful workmanship going to the worms. So they made sure it didn't. They kept it in the family.

Igor really *did* have his grandfather's hands. And now they were bunching into fists, all by themselves.

Tick

A very small kettle burned on a fire of wood shavings and dried yak dung.

'It was . . . a long time ago,' said Lu-Tze. 'Exactly when doesn't matter, 'cos of what happened. In fact asking exactly "when" doesn't make any sense any more. It depends where you are. In some places it was hundreds of years ago. Some other places . . . well, maybe it hasn't happened yet. There was this man in Uberwald. Invented a clock. An *amazing* clock. It measured the tick of the universe. Know what that is?'

'No.'

'Me neither. The abbot's your man for that kind of stuff. Lemme see . . . okay . . . think of the smallest amount of time that you can. Really small. So tiny that a second would be like a billion years. Got that? Well, the cosmic quantum tick – that's what the abbot calls it – the cosmic quantum tick is much smaller than that. It's the time it takes to go from *now* to *then*. The time it takes an atom to think of wobbling. It's—'

137

'It's the time it takes for the smallest thing that's possible *to* happen to happen?' said Lobsang.

'Exactly. Well done,' said Lu-Tze. He took a deep breath. 'It's also the time it takes for the whole universe to be destroyed in the past and rebuilt in the future. Don't look at me like that – that's what the *abbot* said.'

'Has it been happening while we've been talking?' said Lobsang.

'Millions of times. An oodleplex of times, probably.'

'How many's that?'

'It's one of the abbot's words. It means more numbers than you can imagine in a yonk.'

'What's a yonk?'

'A very long time.'

'And we don't feel it? The universe is *destroyed* and we don't feel it?'

'They say not. The first time it was explained to me I got a bit jumpy, but it's far too quick for us to notice.'

Lobsang stared at the snow for a while. Then he said, 'All right. Go on.'

'Someone in Uberwald built this clock out of glass. Powered by lightning, as I recall. It somehow got down to a level where it could tick with the universe.'

'Why did he want to do that?'

'Listen, he lived in a big old castle on a crag in Uberwald. People like that don't need a reason apart from "because I can". They have a nightmare and try to make it happen.'

'But, look, you can't make a clock like that, because it's inside the universe, so it'll . . . get rebuilt when the universe does, right?'

Lu-Tze looked impressed, and said so. 'I'm impressed,' he said.

'It'd be like opening a box with the crowbar that's inside.'

'The abbot believes that part of the clock was outside, though.'

'You can't have something *outside* the—'

'Tell that to a man who has been working on the problem for nine lifetimes,' said Lu-Tze. 'You want to hear the rest of the story?'

'Yes, Sweeper.'

'*So* . . . we were spread pretty thin in those days, but there was this young sweeper—'

'You,' said Lobsang. 'This is going to be you, right?'

'Yes, yes,' said Lu-Tze testily. 'I was sent to Uberwald. History hadn't diverged much in those days, and we knew something big was going to happen around Bad Schüschein. I must have spent weeks looking. You know how many remote castles there are along the gorges? You can't *move* for remote castles!'

'That's why you didn't find the right one in time,' said Lobsang. 'I remember what you told the abbot.'

'I was just down in the valley when the lightning struck the tower,' said Lu-Tze. 'You know it is written, "Big events always cast their shadows." But I couldn't detect *where* it was happening until too late. A half-mile sprint uphill faster than a lightning bolt . . . No one could do that. Nearly made it, though – I was actually through the door when it all went to hell!'

'No point in blaming yourself, then.'

'Yes, but you know how it is – you keep thinking "If only I'd got up earlier, or had gone a different way . . ."' said Lu-Tze.

'And the clock struck,' said Lobsang.

'No. It *stuck*. I told you part of it was outside the universe. It wouldn't go with the flow. It was trying to count the tick, not move with it.'

'But the universe is huge! It can't be stopped by a piece of clock work!'

Lu-Tze flicked the end of his cigarette into the fire.

'The abbot says the size wouldn't make any difference at all,' he said. 'Look, it's taken him nine lifetimes to know what he knows, so it's not our fault if we can't understand it, is it? History shattered. It was the only thing that could give. Very strange event. There were cracks left all over the place. The . . . oh, I can't remember the words . . . the fastenings that tell bits of the past which bits of the present they belong to, they were flapping all over the place. Some got lost for ever.' Lu-Tze stared into the dying flames. 'We stitched it up as best we could,' he added. 'Up and down history. Filling up holes with bits of time taken from somewhere else. It's a patchwork, really.'

'Didn't people notice?'

'Why should they? Once we'd done it, it had always been like that. You'd be amazed at what we got away with. F'rinstance—'

'I'm sure they'd spot it somehow.'

Lu-Tze gave Lobsang one of his sidelong glances. 'Funny you should say that. I've always wondered about it. People say things like "Where did the time go?" and "It seems like only yesterday." We had to do it, anyway. And it's healed up very nicely.'

'But people would look in the history books and see—'

'Words, lad. That's all. Anyway, people have been messing around with time ever since there *were* people. Wasting it, killing it, sparing it, making it up. And they *do* it. People's heads were *made* to play with time. Just like we do, except we're better trained and have a few extra skills. And we've spent centuries working to bring it all back in line. You watch the Procrastinators even on a quiet day. Moving time, stretching it here, compressing it there . . . it's a big job. I'm not going to see it smashed a second time. A second time, there won't be enough left to repair.'

He stared at the embers. 'Funny thing,' he said. 'Wen himself had some very curious ideas about time, come the finish. You remember I told you that he reckoned time was alive. He said it acted like a living thing, anyway. Very strange ideas indeed. He said he'd *met* Time, and she was a woman. To him, anyway. Everyone says that was just a very complicated metaphor, and maybe I was simply hit on the head or something, but on that day I looked at the glass clock just as it exploded and—'

He stood up and grabbed his broom.

'Best foot forward, lad. Another two or three seconds and we'll be down in Bong Phut.'

'What were you going to say?' said Lobsang, hurrying to his feet.

'Oh, just an old man rambling,' said Lu-Tze. 'The mind wanders a bit when you get to over seven hundred. Let's get moving.'

'Sweeper?'

'Yes, lad?'

'Why are we carrying spinners on our backs?'

'All in good time, lad. I hope.'

'We're carrying time, right? If time stops, we can keep going? Like . . . divers?'

'Full marks.'

'And—?'

'Another question?'

'Time is a "she"? None of the teachers have mentioned it and I don't recall anything in the scrolls.'

'Don't you think about that. Wen wrote . . . well, the Secret Scroll, it's called. They keep it in a locked room. Only the abbots and the most senior monks ever get to see it.'

Lobsang couldn't let that one pass. 'So how did you—?' he began.

'Well, you wouldn't expect men like that to do the sweeping up in there, would you?' said Lu-Tze. 'Terribly dusty, it got.'

'What was it about?'

'I didn't read much of it. Didn't feel it was right,' said Lu-Tze.

'You? What was it about, then?'

'It was a love poem. And it was a good one . . .'

Lu-Tze's image blurred as he sliced time. Then it faded and vanished. A line of footprints appeared across the snowfield.

Lobsang wrapped time around himself and followed. And a memory came from nowhere at all: *Wen was right.*

Tick

There were lots of places like the warehouse. There always are, in every old city, no matter how valuable the building land is. Sometimes, space just gets lost.

A workshop is built, and then another beside it. Factories and storerooms and sheds and temporary lean-tos crawl towards one another, meet and merge. Spaces between outside walls are roofed with tar paper. Odd-shaped bits of ground are colonized by nailing up a bit of wall and cutting a doorway. Old doorways are masked by piles of lumber or new tool racks. The old men who know what was where move on and die, just like the flies who punctuate the thick cobwebs on the grubby windows. Young men, in this noisome world of whirring lathes and paint shops and cluttered workbenches, don't have time to explore.

And so there were spaces like this, a small warehouse with a crusted skylight that no fewer than four factory owners thought was owned by one of the other three, when they thought about it at all. In fact each of them owned one wall, and certainly no one recalled who roofed the space. Beyond the walls on all four sides men and dwarfs bent iron, sawed planks, made string and turned screws. But in here was a silence known only to rats.

The air moved, for the first time in years. Dust balls rolled across the floor. Little motes sparkled and spun in the light that forced its way down from the roof. In the surrounding area, invisible and subtle, matter began to move. It came from workmen's sandwiches and gutter dirt and pigeon feathers, an atom here, a molecule there, and streamed unheeded into the centre of the space.

It spiralled. Eventually it became, after passing through some strange, ancient and horrible shapes, Lady LeJean.

She staggered, but managed to stay upright.

Other Auditors also appeared and, as they did so, it seemed that they had never really *not* been there. The dead greyness of the light merely took on shapes; they emerged like ships from a fog. You stared at the fog, and suddenly part of the fog was hull that had been there all along, and now there was nothing for it but to race for the lifeboats . . .

Lady LeJean said: 'I cannot keep doing this. It is too painful.'

One said, *Ah, can you tell us what pain is like? We have often wondered.*

'No. No, I don't think I can. It is . . . a body thing. It is not pleasant. From now on, I will retain the body.'

One said, *That could be dangerous.*

Lady LeJean shrugged. 'We have been through that before. It's only a matter of appearance,' she said. 'And it is remarkable how much easier it is to deal with humans in this form.'

One said, *You shrugged. And you are talking with your mouth. A hole for food and air.*

'Yes. It is remarkable, isn't it?' Lady LeJean's body found an old crate, pulled it over and sat on it. She hardly had to think about muscle movements at all.

One said, *You aren't* eating, *are you?*

'As yet, no.'

One said, *As yet? That raises the whole dreadful subject of . . . orifices.*

One said, *And how did you* learn *to shrug?*

'It comes with the body,' said her ladyship. 'We never realized this, did we? Most of the things it does it appears to do automatically. Standing upright takes no effort whatsoever. The whole business gets easier every time.'

The body shifted position slightly, and crossed its legs. Amazing, she thought. It did it to be comfortable. I didn't have to think about it at all. We never guessed.

One said, *There will be questions.*

The Auditors *hated* questions. They hated them almost as much as they hated decisions, and they hated decisions almost as much as they hated the idea of the individual personality. But what they hated most was things moving around randomly.

'Believe me, everything will be fine,' said Lady LeJean. 'We will not be breaking any of the rules, after all. All that will happen is that time will stop. Everything thereafter will be neat. Alive, but not moving. Tidy.'

One said, *And we can get the filing finished.*

'Exactly,' said Lady LeJean. 'And he *wants* to do it. That is the strange thing. He hardly thinks about the consequences.'

One said, *Splendid.*

There was one of those pauses when no one is quite ready to speak. And then:

One said, *Tell us . . . What is it like?*

'What is what like?'

One said, *Being insane. Being human.*

'Strange. Disorganized. Several levels of thinking go on at once. There are . . . things we have no word for. For example, the idea of eating seems now to have an attraction. The body tells me this.'

One said, *Attraction? As in gravity?*

'Ye-es. One is drawn towards food.'

One said, *Food in large masses?*

'Even in small amounts.'

One said, *But eating is simply a function. What is the . . . attraction of performing a function? Surely the knowledge that it is necessary for continued survival is sufficient?*

'I cannot say,' said Lady LeJean.

One Auditor said, *You persist in using a personal pronoun.*

And one added, *And you have not died! To be an individual is to live, and to live is to die!*

'Yes. I know. But it is essential for humans to use the personal pronoun. It divides the universe into two parts. The darkness behind the eyes, where the little voice is, and everything else. It is . . . a horrible feeling. It is like being . . . questioned, all the time.'

One said, *What is the little voice?*

'Sometimes thinking is like talking to another person, but that person is also you.'

She could tell this disturbed the other Auditors. 'I do not wish to continue in this way any longer than necessary,' she added. And realized that she had lied.

One said, *We do not blame you.*

Lady LeJean nodded.

The Auditors could see into human minds. They could see the pop and sizzle of the thoughts. But they could not read them. They could see the energies flow from node to node, they could see the brain glittering like a Hogswatch decoration. What they couldn't see was what was *happening*.

So they'd built one.

It was the logical thing to do. They'd used human agents before, because early on they'd worked out that there were many, many humans who would do *anything* for sufficient gold. This was puzzling, because gold did not seem to the Auditors to hold any significant value for a human body – it *needed* iron and copper and zinc, but only the most minute traces of gold. Therefore, they'd reasoned, this was further evidence that the humans who required it were flawed, and this was why attempts to make use of them were doomed. But *why* were they flawed?

Building a human being was easy; the Auditors knew *exactly* how to move matter around. The trouble was that the result didn't do anything but lie there and, eventually, decompose. This was annoying, since human beings, without any special training or education, seemed to be able to make working replicas quite easily.

Then they learned that they could make a human body which worked if an Auditor was inside it.

There were, of course, huge risks. Death was one of them. The Auditors avoided death by never going so far as to get a life. They strove to be as indistinguishable as hydrogen atoms, and with none of the latter's *joie de vivre*. Some luckless Auditor might be risking death by 'operating' the body. But lengthy consultation decided that if the *driver* took care, and liaised at all times with the rest of the Auditors, this risk was minimal and worth taking, considering the goal.

They built a woman. It was a logical choice. After all, while men wielded more obvious power than women, they often did so at the expense of personal danger, and no Auditor liked the prospect of personal danger. Beautiful women often achieved great things, on the other hand, merely by smiling at powerful men.

The whole subject of 'beauty' caused the Auditors a lot of difficulty. It made no sense at a molecular level. But research turned up the fact that the woman in the picture *Woman Holding Ferret* by Leonard of Quirm was considered the epitome of beauty, and so they'd based Lady LeJean on that. They had made changes, of course. The face in the picture was asymmetrical and full of minor flaws, which they had carefully removed.

The result would have been successful beyond the Auditors' wildest dreams, had they ever dreamed. Now that they had their stalking horse, their *reliable* human, anything was possible. They were learning fast, or at least collecting data, which they considered to be the same as learning.

So was Lady LeJean. She had been a human for two weeks, two astonishing, shocking weeks. Whoever would have guessed that a brain operated like this? Or that colours had a meaning that went way, way beyond spectral analysis? How could she even *begin* to describe the blueness of blue? Or how much thinking the brain did all by itself? It was terrifying. Half the time her thoughts seemed not to be her own.

She had been quite surprised to find that she did not want to tell the other Auditors this. She did not want to tell them a lot of things. And she didn't *have* to!

She had *power*. Oh, over Jeremy, that was not in question and was now, she had to admit, rather worrying. It was causing her body to do things by itself, like blush. But she had power over the other Auditors, too. She made them nervous.

Of course, she wanted the project to work. It was their goal. A tidy and predictable universe, where everything stayed in its place. If Auditors dreamed, this would be another dream.

Except . . . except . . .

The young man had smiled at her in a nervous, worrying way, and the universe was turning out to be a lot more chaotic than even the Auditors had ever suspected.

A lot of the chaos was happening inside Lady LeJean's head.

Tick

Lu-Tze and Lobsang passed through Bong Phut and Long Nap like ghosts in twilight. People and animals were blueish statues and were not, said Lu-Tze, to be touched in any circumstances.

Lu-Tze restocked his travel bag with food from some of the houses, making sure to leave little copper tokens in their place.

'It means we're obliged to them,' he said, filling Lobsang's bag as well. 'The next monk through here might have to give someone a minute or two.'

'A minute or two isn't much.'

'For a dying woman to say goodbye to her children, it's a lifetime,' said Lu-Tze. 'Is it not written, "Every second counts"? Let's go.'

'I'm *tired*, Sweeper.'

'I did say every second counts.'

'But everybody has to sleep!'

'Yes, but not yet,' Lu-Tze insisted. 'We can rest in the caves down at Songset. Can't fold time while you're asleep, see?'

'Can't we use the spinners?'

'In theory, yes.'

'In theory? They could wind out time for us. We'd only sleep for a few seconds—'

'They're for emergencies only,' said Lu-Tze bluntly.

'How do you define an emergency, Sweeper?'

'An emergency is when I decide it's time to use a clockwork spinner designed by Qu, wonder boy. A lifebelt's for saving your life. That's when I'll trust an uncalibrated, unblessed spinner powered by springs. When I *have* to. I know Qu says—'

Lobsang blinked and shook his head. Lu-Tze grabbed his arm.

'You felt something again?'

'Ugh . . . like having a tooth out in my brain,' said Lobsang, rubbing his head. He pointed. 'It came from over there.'

'A *pain* came from over there?' said Lu-Tze. He glared at the boy. 'Like last time? But we've never found a way of detecting which *way*—'

He stopped and rummaged in his sack. Then he used the sack to sweep snow off a flat boulder.

'We'll see what—'

Glass house.

This time Lobsang could concentrate on the tones that filled the air. Wet finger on a wineglass? Well, you could start there. But the finger would have to be the finger of a god on the glass of some celestial sphere. And the wonderful, complex, shifting tones did not simply fill the air, they were the air.

The moving blur beyond the walls was getting closer now. It was just beyond the closest wall, then it found the open doorway . . . and vanished.

Something was behind Lobsang.

He turned. There was nothing there that he could see, but he felt movement and, for just a moment, something warm brushed his cheek . . .

'—the sand says,' said Lu-Tze, tipping the contents of a small bag onto the rock.

The coloured grains bounced and spread. They did not have the sensitivity of the Mandala itself, but there was a blue bloom in the chaos.

He gave Lobsang a sharp look.

'It's been *proved* that no one can do what you just did,' he said. 'We've never found *any* way of detecting where a disturbance in time is actually being caused.'

'Er, sorry.' Lobsang raised a hand to his cheek. It was damp. 'Er, what did I do?'

'It takes a huge—' Lu-Tze stopped. 'Ankh-Morpork's that way,' he said. 'Did you *know* that?'

'No! Anyway, *you* said you had a feeling things would happen in Ankh-Morpork!'

'Yes, but I've had a lifetime of experience and cynicism!' Lu-Tze scooped the sand back into its bag. 'You're just *gifted*. Come on.'

Four more seconds, sliced thinly, took them below the snowline, into scree slopes that slid under their feet and then through alder forests not much taller than themselves. And it was there they met the hunters, gathered round in a wide circle.

The men did not pay them much attention. Monks were commonplace in these parts. The leader, or at least the one who was shouting, and this *is* usually the leader, looked up and waved them past.

Lu-Tze stopped, though, and looked amiably at the thing in the centre of the circle. It looked back at him.

'Good catch,' he said. 'What're you going to do now, boys?'

'Is it any business of yours?' said the leader.

'No, no, just asking,' said Lu-Tze. 'You boys up from the lowlands, yes?'

'Yeah. You'd be amazed at what you can get for catching one of these.'

'Yes,' said Lu-Tze. 'You *would* be amazed.'

Lobsang looked at the hunters. There were more than a dozen of them, all heavily armed and watching Lu-Tze carefully.

'Nine hundred dollars for a good pelt and another thousand for the feet,' said their leader.

'That much, eh?' said Lu-Tze. 'That's a lot of money for a pair of feet.'

'That's 'cos they're big feet,' said the hunter. 'And you know what they say about men with big feet, eh?'

'They need bigger shoes?'

148

'Yeah, right,' said the hunter, grinning. 'Load of nonsense, really, but there's rich old boys with young wives over on the Counterweight Continent who'll pay a fortune for a powdered yeti foot.'

'And there was me thinking they're a protected species,' said Lu-Tze, leaning his broom against a tree.

'They're only a kind of troll. Who's going to protect them out here?' said the hunter. Behind him, the local guides, who *did* know Rule One, turned and ran.

'Me,' said Lu-Tze.

'Oh?' said the hunter, and this time the grin was nasty. 'You don't even have a weapon.' He turned to look at the fleeing guides. 'You're one of the weird monks from up in the valleys, aren't you?'

'That's right,' said Lu-Tze. 'Small, smiling, weird monk. Totally unarmed.'

'And there's fifteen of us,' said the hunter. '*Well* armed, as you can see.'

'It's very important that you are all heavily armed,' said Lu-Tze, pulling his sleeves out of the way. 'It makes it fairer.'

He rubbed his hands together. No one seemed inclined to retreat.

'Er, any of you boys heard of any rules?' he said, after a while.

'Rules?' said one of the hunters. 'What rules?'

'Oh, you know,' said Lu-Tze. 'Rules like . . . Rule Two, say, or Rule Twenty-seven. Any kind of rules of that sort of description.'

The leading hunter frowned. 'What in damnation are you talking about, mister?'

'Er, not so much a "mister" as a small, rather knowing, elderly, entirely unarmed, weird monk,' said Lu-Tze. 'I'm just wondering if there is anything about this situation that makes you, you know . . . slightly nervous?'

'You mean, us being well armed and outnumbering you, and you backing away like that?' said one of the hunters.

'Ah. Yes,' said Lu-Tze. 'Perhaps we're up against a cultural thing here. I know, how about . . . this?' He stood on one leg, wobbling a little, and raised both hands. 'Ai! Hai-eee! Ho? Ye-hi? No? Anyone?'

There was a certain amount of bewilderment amongst the hunters.

'Is it a book?' said one who was slightly intellectual. 'How many words?'

'What I'm trying to find out here,' said Lu-Tze, 'is whether you have any idea what happens when a lot of big armed men try to attack a small, elderly, *unarmed* monk?'

'To the best of my knowledge,' said the intellectual of the group, 'he turns out to be a very unlucky monk.'

Lu-Tze shrugged. 'Oh, well,' he said, 'then we'll just have to try it the hard way.'

A blur in the air hit the intellectual on the back of the neck. The leader stirred to step forward, and learned too late that his boot-laces were tied together. Men reached for knives that were no longer in sheaths, for swords that were inexplicably leaning against a tree on the far side of the clearing. Legs were swept from underneath them, invisible elbows connected with soft parts of their bodies. Blows rained out of empty air. Those who fell down learned to stay that way. A raised head *hurt*.

The group was reduced to men lying humbly on the ground, groaning gently. It was then that they heard a low, rhythmic sound.

The yeti was clapping. It had to be a slow handclap, because of the creature's long arms. But when the hands met, they'd come a long way and were glad to see one another. They echoed around the mountains.

Lu-Tze reached down and raised the leader's chin.

'If you have enjoyed this afternoon, please tell your friends,' he said. 'Tell them to remember Rule One.'

He let the chin go, and walked across to the yeti and bowed.

'Shall I release you, sir, or would you like to do it yourself?' he said.

The yeti stood up, looked down at the cruel iron trap around one leg, and concentrated for a moment.

At the *end* of the moment, the yeti was a little way from the trap, which was still set and almost hidden in leaves.

'Well done,' said Lu-Tze. 'Methodical. And very smooth. Headed down to the lowlands?'

The yeti had to bend double to bring its long face close to Lu-Tze.

'Yaas,' it said.

'What do you want to do with these people?'

The yeti looked round at the cowering hunters.

'It bein' daark soon,' he said. 'No guides noaw.'

'They've got torches,' said Lu-Tze.

'Ha. Ha,' said the yeti, and it said it, rather than laughed. 'Dat's *good*. Torches show up aat night.'

'Hah! Yes. Can you give us a lift? It's really important.'

'You and daat whizzin' kid I seein' there?'

A patch of grey air at the edge of the clearing became Lobsang, out of breath. He dropped the broken branch he'd been holding.

'The lad is called Lobsang. I'm training him up,' said Lu-Tze.

'Looks like you gotta hurry before you runnin' out of things he don't knoow,' said the yeti. 'Ha. Ha.'

'Sweeper, what were you—' Lobsang began, hurrying forward.

Lu-Tze put his finger to his lips. 'Not in front of our fallen friends,' he said. 'I'm looking for Rule One to become a lot better respected in these parts as a result of this day's work.'

'But I had to do all the—'

'We must be going,' said Lu-Tze, waving him into silence. 'I reckon we can snooze quite happily while our friend here carries us.'

Lobsang glanced up at the yeti, and then back at Lu-Tze. And then back to the yeti. It was *tall*. In some ways it was like the trolls he'd met in the city, but rolled out thin. It was more than twice as high as he was, and most of the extra height was skinny legs and arms. The body was a ball of fur, and the feet were indeed huge.

'If he could've got out of the trap at any—' he began.

'*You* are the apprentice, right?' said Lu-Tze. '*Me*, I'm the master? I'm sure I wrote that down somewhere . . .'

'But you said you weren't going to say any of those know-it-all—'

'Remember Rule One! Oh, and pick up one of those swords. We'll need it in a minute. Okay, yer honour . . .'

The yeti picked them up gently and firmly, cradled them in the crook of each arm, and strode away through the snow and trees.

'Snug, eh?' said Lu-Tze after a while. 'Their wool is spun out of rock in some way, but it's pretty comfy.'

There was no answer from the other arm.

'I spent some time with the yetis,' said Lu-Tze. 'Amazing people. They taught me a thing or two. Valuable stuff. For is it not written, "We live and learn"?'

Silence, a kind of sullen, *deliberate* silence, reigned.

'I'd think myself lucky if I was a boy your age actually being carried by an actual yeti. A lot of people back in the valley have never even seen one. Mind you, they don't come that close to settlements any more. Not since that rumour about their feet got around.'

Lu-Tze got the feeling that he was taking part in a dialogue of one.

'Something you want to say, is there?' he said.

'Well, as a matter of fact, yes, there *is*, actually,' said Lobsang. 'You let me do all the work back there! You weren't going to do *anything*!'

'I was making sure I had their full attention,' said Lu-Tze smoothly.

'Why?'

'So that *you* didn't have their full attention. I had every confidence in you, of course. A good master gives the pupil an opportunity to demonstrate his skills.'

'And what would you have done if I hadn't been here, pray?'

'Yes, probably,' said Lu-Tze.

'What?'

'But I expect I would have found some way to use their stupidity against them,' said Lu-Tze. 'There generally is one. Is there a problem here?'

'Well, I just . . . I thought . . . well, I just thought you'd be teaching me more, that's all.'

152

'I'm teaching you things all the time,' said Lu-Tze. 'You might not be learning them, of course.'

'Oh, I *see*,' said Lobsang. 'Very smug. Are you going to *try* to teach me about this yeti, then, and why you made me bring a sword?'

'You'll need the sword to learn about yetis,' said Lu-Tze.

'How?'

'In a few minutes we'll find a nice place to stop and you can cut his head off. Is that all right by you, sir?'

'Yaas. Sure,' said the yeti.

In the Second Scroll of Wen the Eternally Surprised a story is written concerning one day when the apprentice Clodpool, in a rebellious mood, approached Wen and spake thusly:

'Master, what is the difference between a humanistic, monastic system of belief in which wisdom is sought by means of an apparently nonsensical system of questions and answers, and a lot of mystic gibberish made up on the spur of the moment?'

Wen considered this for some time, and at last said: 'A fish!'

And Clodpool went away, satisfied.

Tick

The Code of the Igors was very strict.

Never Contradict: it was no part of an Igor's job to say things like 'No, thur, that'th an artery.' The marthter was always right.

Never Complain: an Igor would never say 'But that'th a thouthand mileth away!'

Never Make Personal Remarks: no Igor would dream of saying anything like 'I thould have thomething done about that laugh, if I wath you.'

And never, ever Ask Questions. Admittedly, Igor knew, that meant never ask BIG questions. 'Would thur like a cup of tea around now?' was fine, but 'What do you need a hundred virginth for?' or 'Where do you ecthpect me to find a brain at thith time of night?' was not. An Igor stood for loyal, dependable, discreet service with a smile, or at least a sort of lopsided grin, or possibly just a curved scar in the right place.*

And, therefore, Igor was getting worried. Things were wrong, and when an Igor thinks that, they are *really* wrong. Great difficulty lay in getting this across to Jeremy without breaking the Code, though. Igor was increasingly ill at ease with someone so clearly stark, staring sane. Nevertheless, he tried.

'Her ladythip will be along *again* thith morning,' he said, as they watched yet another crystal grow in its solution. And I know you know that, he thought, because you've smoothed your hair down with soap and put on a clean shirt.

'Yes,' said Jeremy. 'I wish we had better progress to report. However, I'm sure we're nearly there now.'

'Yeth, that'th very thtrange, ithn't it?' said Igor, seizing the opening.

'Strange, you say?'

'Call me Mithter Thilly, thur, but it theemth to me that we're alwayth on the point of thuctheth when her ladythip payth uth a vithit, but when thee'th gone we ecthperienth new difficultieth.'

'What are you suggesting, Igor?'

'Me, thur? I'm not a thuggethtive perthon, thur. But latht time part of the divider array had cracked.'

'You know I think that was because of dimensional instability!'

'*Yeth*, thur.'

'Why are you giving me that funny look, Igor?'

Igor shrugged. That is, one shoulder was momentarily as high as the other one. 'Goeth with the fathe, thur.'

'She'd hardly pay us so handsomely and then sabotage the project, would she? Why would she do that?'

Igor hesitated. He had his back right up against the Code now.

'I am thtill wondering if thee ith all thee theemth, thur.'

---

* And it has to be said that there was nothing intrinsically evil about Igors themselves. They just didn't pass judgement on other people. Admittedly, that was because if you worked for werewolves and vampires and people who looked on surgery as modern art rather than science, passing judgement would mean you'd never have time to get anything *done*.

'Sorry? I didn't catch that.'

'I wonder if we can trutht her, thur,' said Igor patiently.

'Oh, go and calibrate the complexity resonator, will you?'

Grumbling, Igor obeyed.

The second time Igor'd followed their benefactor she'd gone to a hotel. Next day she'd headed for a large house in Kings Way, where she'd been met by an oily man who'd made a great play of presenting her with a key. Igor had followed the oleaginous man back to his office in a nearby street where – because there are few things that are kept from a man with a face full of stitches – he'd learned that she'd just bought the lease for a very large bar of gold.

After that, Igor had resorted to an ancient Ankh-Morpork tradition and paid someone to follow her ladyship. There was enough gold in the workshop, heavens knew, and the master took no interest in it.

Lady LeJean went to the opera. Lady LeJean went to art galleries. Lady LeJean was living life to the fullest. Except that Lady LeJean, as far as Igor could determine, never visited restaurants and had no food delivered to the house.

Lady LeJean was up to something. Igor could spot this easily. Lady LeJean also did not appear in *Twurp's Peerage* or the *Almanack de Gothic* or any of the other reference books Igor had checked as a matter of course, which meant that she had something to hide. Of course, he had worked for masters who occasionally had a great deal to hide, sometimes in deep holes at midnight. But this situation was morally different for two reasons. Her ladyship wasn't his master, Jeremy was, and that was where his loyalty lay. And Igor had *decided* it was morally different.

Now he reached the glass clock.

It looked almost complete. Jeremy had designed a mechanism to go behind the face and Igor had got it made up, all in glass. It had nothing whatsoever to do with the *other* mechanism, which flickered away down behind the pendulum and took up a disconcertingly small amount of room now that it was assembled; quite a few of its parts were no longer sharing the same set of dimensions as the rest of it. But the clock had a face, and a face needed hands, and so the glass pendulum swung and the glass hands moved and told normal, everyday time. The 'tick' had a slightly bell-like quality, as though someone were flicking a wineglass with a fingernail.

Igor looked at his hand-me-down hands. They were beginning to worry him. Now that the glass clock *looked* like a clock, they began to shake every time Igor came near it.

Tick

No one noticed Susan in the library of the Guild of Historians, leafing her way through a pile of books. Occasionally she made a note.

She didn't know if her other gift was from Death, but she'd always told the children that they had a lazy eye and a business eye. There were two ways of looking at the world. The lazy eye just saw the surface. The business eye saw through into the reality beneath.

She turned a page.

Seen through her business eye, history was very strange indeed. The scars stood out. The history of the country of Ephebe was puzzling, for example. Either its famous philosophers lived for a very long time, or they inherited their names, or extra bits had been stitched into history there. The history of Omnia was a *mess*. Two centuries had been folded into one, by the look of it, and it was only because of the mind-set of the Omnians, whose religion in any case mixed the past and future with the present, that it could possibly have passed unnoticed.

And what about Koom Valley? Everyone knew that there had been a famous battle there, between dwarfs and trolls and mercenaries on both sides, but how many battles had there actually *been*? Historians talked about the valley being in just the right place in disputed territory to become more or less the preferred local pitch for all confrontations, but you could just as easily believe – at least you could if you had a grandfather called Death – that a patch that just happened to fit had been welded into history several times, so that different generations went round through the whole stupid disaster

156

again and again, shouting 'Remember Koom Valley!' as they did so.*

There were anomalies everywhere.

And no one had noticed.

You had to hand it to human beings. They had one of the strangest powers in the universe. Even her grandfather had remarked upon it. No other species anywhere in the world had invented *boredom*. Perhaps it was boredom, not intelligence, that had propelled them up the evolutionary ladder. Trolls and dwarfs had it, too, that strange ability to look at the universe and think 'Oh, the same as yesterday, how dull. I wonder what happens if I bang this rock on that head?'

And along with this had come an associated power, to make things *normal*. The world changed mightily, and within a few days humans considered it was *normal*. They had the most amazing ability to shut out and forget what didn't fit. They told themselves little stories to explain away the inexplicable, to make things *normal*.

Historians were especially good at it. If it suddenly looked as though hardly anything had happened in the fourteenth century, they'd weigh in with twenty different theories. Not one of these would be that maybe most of the time had been cut out and pasted into the nineteenth century, where the Crash had not left enough coherent time for everything that needed to happen, because it only takes a week to invent the horse collar.

The History Monks had done their job well, but their biggest ally was the human ability to think narratively. And humans had risen to the occasion. They'd say things like 'Thursday already? What happened to the week?' and 'Time seems to go a lot faster these days,' and 'It seems like only yesterday . . .'

But some things remained.

The Monks had carefully wiped out the time when the Glass Clock had struck. It had been surgically removed from history. Almost . . .

* Every society needs a cry like that, but only in a very few do they come out with the complete, unvarnished version, which is 'Remember-the-Atrocity-Committed-Against-Us-Last-Time-That-Will-Excuse-the-Atrocity-That-We're-About-to-Commit-Today! And So On! Hurrah!'

Susan picked up *Grim Fairy Tales* again. Her parents hadn't bought her books like this when she was a child. They'd tried to bring her up *normally*; they knew that it is not entirely a good idea for humans to be too close to Death. They taught her that facts were more important than fancy. And then she'd grown up and found out that the real fantasies weren't the Pale Rider or the Tooth Fairy or bogeymen – *they* were all solid facts. The big fantasy was that the world was the place where the toast didn't care if it came butter side down or not, where logic was sensible, and where things could be made not to have happened.

Something like the Glass Clock had been too big to hide. It had leaked out via the dark, hidden labyrinths of the human mind, and had become a folk tale. People had tried to coat it with sugar and magic swords, but its true nature still lurked like a rake in an over-grown lawn, ready to rise up at the incautious foot.

Now someone was treading on it again, and the point, the key point, was that the chin it was rising to meet belonged to . . .

. . . someone like me.

She sat and stared at nothing for a while. Around her, historians climbed library ladders, fumbled books onto their lecterns and generally rebuilt the image of the past to suit the eyesight of today. One of them was in fact looking for his glasses.

Time had a son, she thought, someone who walks in the world.

There was a man who devoted himself to the study of time so wholeheartedly that, for him, time became real. He learned the ways of time and Time noticed him, Death had said. There was something there like love.

And Time had a son.

How? Susan had the kind of mind that would sour a narrative with a question like that. Time and a mortal man. How could they ever . . . ? Well, how *could* they?

Then she thought: my grandfather is Death. He adopted my mother. My father was his apprentice for a while. That's all that happened. They were both human, and I turned up in the normal way. There is *no* way I should be able to walk through walls and live outside time and be a little bit immortal, but I am, and so this is not an area where logic and, let's face it, basic biology have any part to play.

In any case, time is constantly creating the future. The future contains things that didn't exist in the past. A small baby should be easy for something . . . *someone* who rebuilds the universe once every instant.

Susan sighed. And you had to remember that Time probably wasn't time, in the same way that Death wasn't exactly the same as death and War wasn't exactly the same as war. She'd met War, a big fat man with an inappropriate sense of humour and a habit of losing the thread, and he certainly didn't personally attend every minor fracas. She disliked Pestilence, who gave her funny looks, and Famine was just wasted and weird. None of them *ran* their . . . call it their discipline. They *personified* it.

Given that she'd met the Tooth Fairy, the Soul Cake Duck and Old Man Trouble, it amazed Susan that she had grown up to be mostly human, nearly normal.

As she stared at her notes, her hair unwound itself from its tight bun and took up its ground-state position, which was the hair of someone who had just touched something highly electrical. It spread out around her head like a cloud, with one black streak of nearly normal hair.

Grandfather might be an ultimate destroyer of worlds and the final truth of the universe, but that wasn't to say he didn't take an interest in the little people. Perhaps Time did, too.

She smiled.

Time waited for no man, they said.

Perhaps she'd waited for one, once.

Susan was aware that someone *was* looking at her, turned and saw the Death of Rats peering through the lens of the glasses belonging to the mildly distracted man searching for them on the other side of the room. Up on a long-disregarded bust of a former historian the raven preened itself.

'Well?' she said.

SQUEAK!

'Oh, he is, is he?'

The doors of the library were nuzzled open and a white horse walked in. There is a terrible habit amongst horsy people to call a white horse 'grey', but even one of that bowlegged fraternity would have had to admit that this horse, at least, was white – not as white as snow, which is a dead white, but at least as white as milk, which is alive. His bridle and reins were black, and so was the saddle, but all of them were in a sense just for show. If the horse of Death was inclined to let you ride him, then you'd stay on, saddle or no. And there was no upper limit to the number of people he could carry. After all, plagues sometimes happened suddenly.

The historians paid him no attention. Horses did not walk into libraries.

Susan mounted. There were plenty of times when she wished she'd been born completely human and wholly normal, but the reality was that she'd give it all up tomorrow—

—apart from Binky.

A moment later, four hoofprints glowed like plasma in the air above the library, and then faded away.

Tick

The crunch-crunch of the yeti's feet over the snow and the eternal wind of the mountains were the only sounds.

Then Lobsang said, 'By "cut off his head", you actually mean . . . ?'

'Sever the head from the body,' said Lu-Tze.

'And,' said Lobsang, still in the tones of one carefully exploring every corner of the haunted cave, 'he doesn't mind?'

'Waal, it's a nuisance,' said the yeti. 'A bit of a paarty trick. But it's okaay, if it helps. The sweeper haas alwaays been a goood friend to us. We owe him faavours.'

'I've tried teaching 'em the Way,' said Lu-Tze proudly.

'Yaas. Ver' usefuul. "A washed pot never boils," ' said the yeti.

Curiosity vied with annoyance in Lobsang's head, and won.

'What have I missed here?' he said. 'You don't die?'

'I doon't die? Wit my head cut off? For laughing! Ho. Ho,' said

160

the yeti. 'Of course I die. But this is not such a sizeaable traansaaction.'

'It took us *years* to work out what the yetis were up to,' said Lu-Tze. 'Their loops played hob with the Mandala until the abbot worked out how to allow for them. They've been extinct three times.'

'Three times, eh?' said Lobsang. 'That's a lot of times to go extinct. I mean, most species only manage it once, don't they?'

The yeti was entering taller forest now, of ancient pines.

'This'd be a good place,' said Lu-Tze. 'Put us down, sir.'

'And we'll chop your head off,' said Lobsang weakly. 'What am I saying? *I'm* not going to chop anyone's head off!'

'You heard him say it doesn't worry him,' said Lu-Tze, as they were gently lowered to the ground.

'That's not the point!' said Lobsang hotly.

'It's *his* head,' Lu-Tze pointed out.

'But *I* mind!'

'Oh, well, in that case,' said Lu-Tze, 'is it not written, "If you want a thing done properly you've got to do it yourself"?'

'Yaas, it is,' said the yeti.

Lu-Tze took the sword out of Lobsang's hand. He held it carefully, like someone unused to weapons. The yeti obligingly knelt.

'You're up to date?' said Lu-Tze.

'Yaas.'

'I cannot believe you're really doing this!' said Lobsang.

'Interesting,' said Lu-Tze. 'Mrs Cosmopilite says, "Seeing is believing," and, strangely enough, the Great Wen said, "I have seen, and I believe"!'

He brought the sword down and cut off the yeti's head.

Tick

There was a sound rather like a cabbage being sliced in half, and then a head rolled into the basket to cheers and cries of 'Oh, I say, well done!' from the crowd. The city of Quirm was a nice, peaceful, law-abiding place and the city council kept it that way with a penal policy that combined the maximum of deterrence with the minimum of re-offending.

GRIPPER 'THE BUTCHER' SMARTZ?

The late Gripper rubbed his neck.

'I demand a retrial!' he said.

THIS MAY NOT BE A GOOD TIME, said Death.

'It couldn't possibly have been murder because the . . .' The soul of Gripper Smartz fumbled in its spectral pockets for a ghostly piece of paper, unfolded it and continued, in a voice of those to whom the written word is an uphill struggle, '. . . because the bal-ance of my mind was d . . . dess-turbed.'

REALLY, said Death. He found it best to let the recently departed get things off their chest.

'Yes, 'cos I really, really *wanted* to kill him, right? And you can't tell me that's a normal frame of mind, right? He was a dwarf, anyway, so I don't think that should count as manslaughter.'

I UNDERSTAND THAT WAS THE SEVENTH DWARF YOU KILLED, said Death.

'I'm very prone to being dess-turbed,' said Gripper. 'Really, it's *me* who's the victim here. All I needed was a bit of understanding, someone to see *my* point of view for five minutes . . .'

WHAT *WAS* YOUR POINT OF VIEW?

'All dwarfs need a damn good kicking, in my opinion. 'Ere, you're Death, right?'

YES INDEED.

'I'm a big fan! I've always wanted to meet you, y'know? I've got a tattoo of you on my arm, look here. Done it *myself*.'

The benighted Gripper turned at the sound of hooves. A young woman in black, entirely unregarded by the crowd, who were gathered around the food stalls and souvenir stands and the guillo-tine, was leading a large white stallion towards them.

'And you've even got valet parking!' said Gripper. 'Now that's what I call *style*!' and with that he faded.

WHAT A CURIOUS PERSON, said Death. AH, SUSAN. THANK YOU FOR COMING. OUR SEARCH NARROWS.

'Our search?'

YOUR SEARCH, IN FACT.

'It's just mine now, is it?'

I HAVE SOMETHING ELSE TO ATTEND TO.

'More important than the end of the world?'

IT *IS* THE END OF THE WORLD. THE RULES SAY THAT THE HORSEMEN SHALL RIDE OUT.

'That old legend? But you don't *have* to do that!'

IT IS ONE OF MY FUNCTIONS. I HAVE TO OBEY THE RULES.

'Why? *They*'re breaking the rules!'

BENDING THEM. THEY HAVE FOUND A LOOPHOLE. I DO NOT HAVE THAT KIND OF IMAGINATION.

It was like Jason and the Battle for the Stationery Cupboard, Susan told herself. You soon learned that 'No one is to open the door of the Stationery Cupboard' was a prohibition that a seven-year-old simply would not understand. You had to *think*, and rephrase it in more immediate terms, like, 'No one, Jason, no matter what, no, not even if they thought they heard someone shouting for help, no one – are you paying attention, Jason? – is to open the door of the Stationery Cupboard, or accidentally fall on the door handle so that it opens, or threaten to steal Richenda's teddy bear unless she opens the door of the Stationery Cupboard, or be standing nearby when a mysterious wind comes out of nowhere and blows the door open all by itself, honestly, it really did, or in any way open, cause to open, ask anyone else to open, jump up and down on the loose floorboard to open or in any other way seek to obtain entry to the Stationery Cupboard, *Jason*!'

'A loophole,' said Susan.

YES.

'Well, why can't you find one too?'

I AM THE GRIM REAPER. I DO NOT THINK PEOPLE WISH ME TO GET . . . CREATIVE. THEY WOULD WISH ME TO DO THE TASK ASSIGNED TO ME AT THIS TIME, BY CUSTOM AND PRACTICE.

'And that's just . . . riding out?'

YES.

'Where to?'

EVERYWHERE, I THINK. IN THE MEANTIME, YOU WILL NEED THIS.

Death handed her a lifetimer.

It was one of the *special* ones, slightly bigger than normal. She took it reluctantly. It looked like an hourglass, but all those little glittering shapes tumbling through the pinch were seconds.

'You know I don't like doing the . . . the whole scythe thing,' she said. 'It's not— Hey, this is really heavy!'

HE IS LU-TZE, A HISTORY MONK. EIGHT HUNDRED YEARS OLD. HE HAS AN APPRENTICE. I HAVE LEARNED THIS. BUT I CANNOT FEEL HIM, I CANNOT SEE HIM. HE IS THE ONE. BINKY WILL TAKE YOU TO THE MONK, YOU WILL FIND THE CHILD.

'And then what?'

I SUSPECT HE WILL NEED SOMEONE. WHEN YOU HAVE FOUND HIM, LET BINKY GO. I SHALL NEED HIM.

Susan's lips moved as a memory collided with a thought.

'To ride out on?' she said. 'Are you *really* talking about the *Apocalypse*? Are you *serious*? No one believes in that sort of thing any more!'

I DO.

Susan's jaw dropped. 'You're really going to do that? Knowing everything you know?'

Death patted Binky on the muzzle.

YES, he said.

Susan gave her grandfather a sideways look.

'Hold on, there's a trick, isn't there . . . ? You're planning something and you're not even going to tell me, right? You're not really going to just wait for the world to end and *celebrate* it, are you?'

WE WILL RIDE OUT.

'No!'

YOU WILL NOT TELL THE RIVERS NOT TO FLOW. YOU WILL NOT TELL THE SUN NOT TO SHINE. YOU WILL NOT TELL ME WHAT I SHOULD AND SHOULD NOT DO.

'But it's so—' Susan's expression changed, and Death flinched. 'I thought you *cared*!'

TAKE THIS ALSO.

Without wanting to, Susan took a smaller lifetimer from her grandfather.

SHE MAY TALK TO YOU.

'And who is *this*?'

THE MIDWIFE, said Death. NOW . . . FIND THE SON.

He faded.

Susan looked down at the lifetimers in her hands. He's done it to you *again*! she screamed at herself. You don't have to do this and you can put this thing down and you can go back to the classroom and you can be normal again and you just *know* that you won't, and so does he—

SQUEAK?

The Death of Rats was sitting between Binky's ears, grasping a lock of the white mane and giving the general impression of someone anxious to be going. Susan raised a hand to slap him off, and then stopped herself. Instead, she pushed the heavy lifetimers into the rat's paws.

'Make yourself useful,' she said, grasping the reins. 'Why do I *do* this?'

SQUEAK.

'I have *not* got a nice nature!'

Tick

There was not, surprisingly, a great deal of blood. The head rolled into the snow, and the body slowly toppled forward.

'Now you've killed—' Lobsang began.

'Just a second,' said Lu-Tze. 'Any moment now . . .'

The headless body vanished. The kneeling yeti turned his head to Lu-Tze, blinked and said, 'Thaat stung a biit.'

'Sorry.'

Lu-Tze turned to Lobsang. 'Now, hold on to that memory!' he commanded. 'It'll try to vanish, but you've had training. You've got to go on remembering that you saw something that now *did not happen*, understand? Remember that time's a lot less unbending than people think, if you get your head right! Just a little lesson! Seeing is believing!'

'How did it *do* that?'

'Good question. They can save their life up to a certain point and go back to it if they get killed,' said Lu-Tze. '*How* it's done . . . well, the abbot spent the best part of a decade working that one out. Not that anyone else can understand it. There's a lot of quantum involved.' He took a pull of his permanent foul cigarette. 'Gotta be *good* working-out, if no one else can understand it.'*

'How is der abboott these daays?' said the yeti, getting to its feet again and picking up the pilgrims.

'Teething.'

'Ah. Reincarnation's alwaays a problem,' said the yeti, falling into its long, ground-eating lope.

'Teeth are the worst, he says. Always coming or going.'

'How fast are *we* going?' said Lobsang.

The yeti's stride was more like a continuous series of leaps from one foot to the other; there was so much spring in the long legs that each landing was a mere faint rocking sensation. It was almost restful.

'I reckon we're doing thirty miles an hour or so, clock time,' said Lu-Tze. 'Get some rest. We'll be above Copperhead in the morning. It's all downhill from there.'

'Coming back from the dead . . .' Lobsang murmured.

'It's more like not actually ever *going* in the first place,' said Lu-Tze. 'I've studied them a bit, but . . . well, unless it's built in you'd have to *learn* how to do it, and would you want to bet on getting it right first time? Tricky one. You'd have to be desperate. I hope I'm never that desperate.'

Tick

* The yeti of the Ramtops, where the Discworld's magical field is so intense that it is part of the very landscape, are one of the few creatures to utilize control of personal time for genetic advantage. The result is a kind of physical premonition – you find out what is going to happen next by allowing it to happen. Faced with danger, or any kind of task that involves risk of death, a yeti will *save* its life up to that point and then proceed with all due caution, yet in the comfortable knowledge that, should everything go pancake-shaped, it will wake up at the point where it saved itself with, and this is the important part, *knowledge of the events which have just happened but which will not now happen because it's not going to be such a damn fool next time*. This is not quite the paradox it appears because, after it has taken place, it hasn't happened. All that actually remains is a memory in the yeti's head, which merely turns out to be a remarkably accurate premonition. The little eddies in time caused by all this are just lost in the noise of all the kinks, dips and knots put in time by every other living creature.

Susan recognized the country of Lancre from the air, a little bowl of woods and fields perched like a nest on the edge of the Ramtop mountains. And she found the cottage, too, which was not the corkscrew-chimneyed compost-heap kind of witch's house popularized by *Grim Fairy Tales* and other books, but a spanking new one with gleaming thatch and a manicured front lawn.

There were more ornaments – gnomes, toadstools, pink bunnies, big-eyed deer – around a tiny pond than any sensible gardener should have allowed. Susan spotted one brightly painted gnome fishi— No, that wasn't a rod he was holding, was it? Surely a nice old lady wouldn't put something like *that* in her garden, would she? Would she?

Susan was bright enough to go round to the back, because witches were allergic to front doors. The door was opened by a small, fat, rosy-cheeked woman whose little currant eyes said, yep, that's my gnome all right, and be thankful he's only widdling in the pond.

'Mrs Ogg? The midwife?'

There was a pause before Mrs Ogg said, 'The very same.'

'You don't know me, but—' said Susan, and realized that Mrs Ogg was looking past her at Binky, who was standing by the gate. The woman was a witch, after all.

'Maybe I do know you,' said Mrs Ogg. 'O'course, if you just *stole* that horse, you just don't *know* how much trouble you're in.'

'I borrowed it. The owner is . . . my grandfather.'

Another pause, and it was disconcerting how those friendly little eyes could bore into yours like an auger.

'You'd better come in,' said Mrs Ogg.

The inside of the cottage was as clean and new as the outside. Things gleamed, and there were a lot of them to gleam. The place was a shrine to bad but enthusiastically painted china ornaments, which occupied every flat surface. What space was left was full of framed pictures. Two harassed-looking women were polishing and dusting.

'I got comp'ny,' said Mrs Ogg sternly, and the women left with such alacrity that the word 'fled' might have been appropriate.

'My daughters-in-law,' said Mrs Ogg, sitting down in a plump armchair which, over the years, had shaped itself to fit her. 'They like to help a poor old lady who's all alone in the world.'

Susan took in the pictures. If they were all family members, Mrs Ogg was head of an army. Mrs Ogg, unashamedly caught out in a flagrant lie, went on: 'Sit down, girl, and say what's on your mind. There's tea brewing.'

'I want to know something.'

'Most people do,' said Mrs Ogg. 'And they can go on wantin'.'

'I want to know about . . . a birth,' said Susan, persevering.

'Oh, yes? Well, I done hundreds of confinements. Thousands, prob'ly.'

'I imagine this one was difficult.'

'A lot of them are,' said Mrs Ogg.

'You'd remember this one. I don't know how it started, but I'd imagine that a stranger came knocking.'

'Oh?' Mrs Ogg's face became a wall. The black eyes stared out at Susan as if she was an invading army.

'You're not helping me, Mrs Ogg.'

'That's right. I ain't,' said Mrs Ogg. 'I think I know about you, miss, but I don't care who you are, you see. You can go and get the other one, if you like. Don't think I ain't seen him, neither. I've been at plenty of deathbeds, too. But deathbeds is public, mostly, and birthbeds ain't. Not if the lady don't want them to be. So you get the other one, and I'll spit in his eye.'

'This is very important, Mrs Ogg.'

'You're right there,' said Mrs Ogg firmly.

'I can't say how long ago it was. It may have been last week, even. Time, that's the key.'

And there it was. Mrs Ogg was not a poker player, at least against someone like Susan. There was the tiniest flicker of the eyes.

Mrs Ogg's chair was rammed back in her effort to rise, but Susan got to the mantelpiece first and snatched what was there, hidden in plain view amongst the ornaments.

'You give that here!' shouted Mrs Ogg, as Susan held it out of her reach. She could feel the power in the thing. It seemed to pulse in her hand.

'Have you any idea what this *is*, Mrs Ogg?' she said, opening her hand to reveal the little glass bulbs.

'Yes, it's an eggtimer that don't work!' Mrs Ogg sat down hard in her overstuffed chair, so that her little legs rose off the floor for a moment.

'It looks to me like a day, Mrs Ogg. A day's worth of time.'

Mrs Ogg glanced at Susan, and then at the little hourglass in her hand.

'I *reckoned* there was something odd about it,' she said. 'The sand don't go through when you tip it up, see?'

'That's because you don't need it to yet, Mrs Ogg.'

Nanny Ogg appeared to relax. Once again Susan reminded herself that she was dealing with a witch. They tended to keep up.

'I kept it 'cos it was a gift,' said the old lady. 'And it looks so pretty, too. What do them letters round the edge say?'

Susan read the words etched on the metal base of the lifetimer: *Tempus Redux*. '"Time Returned",' she said.

'Ah, that'd be it,' said Mrs Ogg. 'The man did say I'd be repaid for my time.'

'The man . . . ?' said Susan gently.

Nanny Ogg glanced up, her eyes ablaze.

'Don't you try to take advantage of me just 'cos I'm moment'r'ly a bit flustered,' she snapped. 'There's no way round Nanny Ogg!'

Susan looked at the woman, and this time not with the lazy eye. And there was, indeed, no way round Mrs Ogg. But there was another way, with Mrs Ogg. It went straight through the heart.

'A child needs to know his parents, Mrs Ogg,' she said. 'Now more than ever. He needs to know who he really is. It's going to be hard for him, and I want to help him.'

'Why?'

'Because I wish someone had helped me,' said Susan.

'Yes, but there's rules to midwifery,' said Nanny Ogg. 'You don't say what was said or what you saw. Not if the lady don't want you to.'

The witch wriggled awkwardly in her chair, her face going red. She wants to tell me, Susan knew. She's desperate to. But I've got to play it right, so she can square it with herself.

'I'm not asking for names, Mrs Ogg, because I expect you don't know them,' she went on.

'That's true.'

'But the child—'

'Look, miss, I'm not supposed to tell a living soul about—'

'If it helps, I'm not entirely certain that I am one,' said Susan. She watched Mrs Ogg for a while. 'But I understand. There have to be rules, don't there? Thank you for your time.'

Susan stood up and put the preserved day back on the mantel-piece. Then she walked out of the cottage, shutting the door behind her. Binky was waiting by the gate. She mounted up, and it wasn't until then that she heard the door open.

'That's what *he* said,' said Mrs Ogg. 'When he gave me the eggtimer. "Thank you for your time, Mrs Ogg," he said. You'd better come back in, my girl.'

Tick

Death found Pestilence in a hospice in Llamedos. Pestilence liked hospitals. There was always something for him to do.

Currently he was trying to remove the 'Now Wash Your Hands' sign over a cracked basin. He looked up.

'Oh, it's you,' he said. 'Soap? I'll give 'em soap!'

I SENT OUT THE CALL, said Death.

'Oh. Yes. Right. Yes,' said Pestilence, clearly embarrassed.

YOU'VE STILL GOT YOUR HORSE?

'Of course, but . . .'

YOU HAD A FINE HORSE.

'Look, Death . . . it's . . . look, it's not that I don't see your point, but— Excuse me . . .' Pestilence stepped aside as a white-robed nun, completely ignorant of the two Horsemen, passed between them. But he took the opportunity to breathe in her face.

'Just a mild flu,' he said, catching Death's expression.

SO WE CAN COUNT ON YOU, CAN WE?

'To ride out . . .'

YES.

170

'For the Big One . . .'

IT'S EXPECTED OF US.

'How many of the others have you got?'

YOU ARE THE FIRST.

'Er . . .'

Death sighed. Of course, there had been plenty of diseases, long before humans had been around. But humans had definitely created Pestilence. They had a genius for crowding together, for poking around in jungles, for siting the midden so handily next to the well. Pestilence was, therefore, part human, with all that this entailed. He was frightened.

I SEE, he said.

'The way you put it—'

YOU ARE AFRAID?

'I'll . . . think about it.'

YES. I AM SURE YOU WILL.

Tick

Quite a lot of brandy splashed into Mrs Ogg's mug. She waved the bottle vaguely at Susan, with an enquiring look.

'No, thank you.'

'Fair enough. Fair enough.' Nanny Ogg put the bottle aside and took a draught of the brandy as though it were beer.

'A man came knocking,' she said. 'Three times he came, in my life. Last time was, oh, maybe ten days ago. Same man every time. He wanted a midwife—'

'Ten days ago?' said Susan. 'But the boy's at least sixt—' She stopped.

'Ah, you've got it,' said Mrs Ogg. 'I could see you was bright. Time didn't matter to him. He wanted the *best* midwife. And it was, like, he'd found out about me but got the date wrong, just like you or me could knock on the wrong door. Can you understand what I mean?'

'More than you think,' said Susan.

'The third time' – another gulp at the brandy – 'he was in a bit of a state,' said Mrs Ogg. 'That's how I knew he was just a man, despite everything that happened after. It was because he was panicking, to tell you the truth. Pregnant fathers often panic. He was going on about me coming right away and how there was no time. He had all the time in the world, he just wasn't thinking properly, 'cos husbands never do when the time comes. They panic 'cos it ain't their world any more.'

'And what happened next?' said Susan.

'He took me in his, well, it was like one of them old chariots, he took me to . . .' Mrs Ogg hesitated. 'I've seen a lot of strange things in my life, I'll have you know,' she said, as if preparing the ground for a revelation.

'I can believe it.'

'It was a castle made of glass.' Mrs Ogg gave Susan a look that dared her to disbelieve. Susan decided to hurry things up.

'Mrs Ogg, one of my earliest memories is of helping to feed the Pale Horse. You know? The one outside? The horse of Death? His name is Binky. So please don't keep stopping. There is practically no limit to the things I find normal.'

'There was a woman . . . well, *eventually* there was a woman,' said the witch. 'Can you imagine someone exploding into a million pieces? Yes, I expect you can. Well, imagine it happening the other way. There's a mist and it's all flying together and then, whoosh, there's a woman. Then, whoosh, back into a mist again. And all the time, this noise . . .' Mrs Ogg ran her finger round the edge of the brandy glass, making it hum.

'A woman kept . . . incarnating and then disappearing again? Why?'

'Because she was frightened, of course! First time, see?' Mrs Ogg grinned. 'I person'ly never had any problems in that area, but I've been at a lot of births when it's all new to the girl and she'll be frightened as hell and when push comes to shove, if you take my meaning, old midwifery term, she'll be yellin' and swearin' at the father and I reckon that she'd give anything to be somewhere else. Well, this lady *could* be somewhere else. We'd have been in a real pickle if it wasn't for the man, as it turned out.'

'The man who brought you?'

'He was kind of foreign, you know? Like the Hub people. Bald as a coot. I remember thinking "You look like a young man, mister, but you look like you've been a young man for a long, long time if I'm any judge." Normally I wouldn't have any man there, but he sat and talked to her in his foreign lingo and sang her songs and little poems and soothed her and back she came, out of thin air, and I was ready and it was one, two, *done*. And then she was gone. Except that she was still there, I think. In the air.'

'What did she look like?' said Susan.

Mrs Ogg gave her a Look. 'You've got to remember the view I got where I was sitting,' she said. 'The kind of description I might give you ain't a thing anyone'd put on a poster, if you get my meaning. And no woman looks at her best at a time like that. She was young, she had dark hair . . .' Mrs Ogg refilled her brandy glass and this meant the pause went on for some time. 'And she was old, too, if you're after the truth of it. Not old like me. I mean *old*.'

She stared at the fire. 'Old like darkness and stars,' she said, to the flames.

'The boy was left outside the Thieves' Guild,' said Susan, to break the silence. 'I suppose they thought that with gifts like that he'd be all right.'

'The boy? Hah. Tell me, miss . . . why are we talking about *he*?'

Tick

Lady LeJean was being strong.

She'd never realized how much humans were controlled by their bodies. The thing nagged night and day. It was always too hot, too cold, too empty, too full, too tired . . .

The key was discipline, she was sure. Auditors were immortal. If she couldn't tell her body what to do, she didn't deserve to have one. Bodies were a major human weakness.

Senses, too. The Auditors had hundreds of senses, since every possible phenomenon had to be witnessed and recorded. She could find only five available now. Five ought to be easy to deal with. But they were wired directly into the rest of the body! They didn't just submit information, they made demands!

She'd walked past a stall selling roasted meats and her mouth had started to drool! The sense of smell wanted the body to eat without consulting the brain! But that wasn't the worst of it! The brain *itself* did its own thinking!

That was the hardest part. The bag of soggy tissue behind the eyes worked away independently of its owner. It took in information from the senses, and checked it all against memory, and presented options. Sometimes the hidden parts of it even fought for control of the mouth! Humans weren't individuals, they were, each one, a committee!

Some of the other members of the committee were dark and red and entirely uncivilized. They had joined the brain before civilization; some of them had got aboard even before humanity. And the bit that did the joined-up thinking had to fight, in the darkness of the brain, to get the casting vote!

After little more than a couple of weeks as a human, the entity that was Lady LeJean was having real trouble.

Food, for example. Auditors did not eat. They recognized that feeble life forms had to consume one another to obtain energy and body-building material. The process was astonishingly inefficient, however, and her ladyship had tried assembling nutrients directly out of the air. This worked, but the process felt . . . What was the word? Oh, yes . . . *creepy*.

Besides, part of the brain didn't believe it was getting fed and insisted that it was hungry. Its incessant nagging interfered with her thought processes and so, despite everything, she'd had to face up to the whole, well, the whole *orifices* business.

The Auditors had known about these for a long time. The human body appeared to have up to eight of them. One didn't seem to work and the rest appeared to be multi-functional, although surprisingly there seemed to be only one thing that could be done by the ears.

Yesterday she'd tried a piece of dry toast.

It had been the single worst experience of her existence.

It had been the single most *intense* experience of her existence.

It had been something else, too. As far as she could understand the language, it had been *enjoyable*.

It seemed that the human sense of taste was quite different from the sense as employed by an Auditor. That was precise, measured, analytical. But the human sense of taste was like being hit in the mouth by the whole world. It had been half an hour of watching fireworks in her head before she remembered to swallow.

How did humans survive this?

She'd been fascinated by the art galleries. It was clear that some humans could present reality in a way that made it even more real, that spoke to the viewer, that seared the mind . . . but what could possibly transcend the knowledge that the genius of an artist had to poke alien substances into his face? Could it be that humans had got *used* to it? And that was only the *start* . . .

The sooner the clock was finished, the better. A species as crazy as this couldn't be allowed to survive. She was visiting the clockmaker and his ugly assistant every day now, giving them as much help as she dared, but they always seemed one vital step away from completion—

Amazing! She could even lie to *herself*! Because another voice in her head, which was part of the dark committee, said, 'You're *not* helping, are you? You're stealing parts and twisting parts . . . and you go back every day because of the way he looks at you, don't you . . . ?'

Parts of the internal committee that were so old they didn't have voices, only direct control of the body, tried to interfere at this point. She tried in vain to put them out of her mind.

And now she had to face the other Auditors. They would be punctual.

She pulled herself together. Water had taken to running out of her eyes lately for no reason at all. She did the best she could with her hair, and made her way to the large drawing room.

Greyness was already filling the air. In this space, there was not room for too many Auditors, but that did not really matter. One could speak for all.

Lady LeJean found the corners of her mouth turned up automatically as nine of them appeared. Nine was three threes, and the Auditors *liked* threes. Two would keep an eye on the other one. *Each* two would keep an eye on *each* other one. They don't trust themselves, said one of the voices in her head. Another voice cut in: It's *we*, *we* don't trust ourselves. And she thought: Oh, yes. We, not they. I must remember I'm a we.

An Auditor said, *Why is there no further progress?*

The corners of the mouth turned down again.

'There have been minor problems of precision and alignment,' said Lady LeJean. She found that her hands were rubbing themselves together slowly, and wondered why. She hadn't *told* them to.

Auditors had never needed body language, so they didn't understand it.

One said, *What is the nature of—?*

But another one cut in with, *Why are you dwelling in this building?* The voice was tinted with suspicion.

'The body requires one to do things that cannot be done on the street,' said Lady LeJean, and, because she'd got to know something about Ankh-Morpork, she added, 'at least, on many streets. Also, I believe the servant of the clockmaker is suspicious. I have allowed the body to yield to gravity, since that is what it was designed for. It is as well to give the appearance of humanity.'

One, and it was the same one, said, *And what is the meaning of these?*

It had noticed the paints and the easel. Lady LeJean wished fervently that she'd remembered to put them away.

The one said, *You are making an image with pigments?*

'Yes. Very badly, I am afraid.'

One said, *For what reason?*

'I wished to see how humans do it.'

One said, *That is simple: the eye receives the input, the hand applies the pigment.*

'That's what I thought, but it appears to be much more complex than that—'

The one who had raised the question of the painting drifted towards one of the chairs and said, *And what is* this?

'It is a cat. It arrived. It does not appear to wish to depart.'

The cat, a feral ginger tom, flicked a serrated ear and curled up in a tighter ball. Anything that could survive in Ankh-Morpork's alleys, with their abandoned swamp dragons, dog packs and furriers' agents, was not about to open even one eye for a bunch of floating nightdresses.

The one who was now getting on Lady LeJean's nerves said: *And the reason for its presence?*

'It appears to tolerate the company of hu— of apparent humans, asking nothing in return but food, water, shelter and comfort,' said Lady LeJean. 'This interests me. Our purpose *is* to learn, and thus I have, as you can see, begun.' She hoped it sounded better to them than it did to her.

One said, *When will the clock problems you spoke of be resolved?*

'Oh, soon. Very soon. Yes.'

The one that was beginning to terrify Lady LeJean said, *We wonder: is it possible that you are slowing the work in some way?*

Lady LeJean felt a prickling on her forehead. Why was it doing that?

'No. Why should I slow the work? There would be no logic to it!'

One said, *Hmm.*

And an Auditor did not say 'Hmm' by accident. 'Hmm' had a very precise meaning.

It went on: *You are making moisture on your head.*

'Yes. It's a body thing.'

One said, *Yes.* And that, too, had a very specific and *ominous* meaning.

One said, *We wonder if too long in a solid body weakens resolve. Also, we find it hard to see your thoughts.*

'Body again, I am afraid. The brain is a very imprecise in-strument.' Lady LeJean got control of her hands at last.

One said, *Yes.*

Another said, *When water fills a jug, it takes the shape of the jug. But the water is not the jug, nor is the jug the water.*

'Of course,' said Lady LeJean. And, inside, a thought that she

177

hadn't known she was thinking, a thought that turned up out of the darkness behind the eyes, said: We are surely the most stupid creatures in the universe.

One said, *It is not good to act alone.*

She said, 'Of course.' And once again a thought emerged from the darkness: I'm in trouble now.

One said, *And therefore you will have companions. No blame attaches. One should never be alone. Together, resolve is strengthened.*

Motes began to twinkle in the air.

Lady LeJean's body backed away automatically and, when she saw what was forming, she backed it away further. She had seen humans in all states of life and death, but seeing a body being spun out of raw matter was curiously disquieting when you were currently inhabiting a similar one. It was one of those times when the stomach did the thinking, and thought it wanted to throw up.

Six figures took shape, blinked and opened their eyes. Three of the figures were male, three were female. They were dressed in human-sized equivalents of the Auditors' robes.

The remaining Auditors drew back, but one said, *They will accompany you to the clockmaker, and matters will be resolved today. They will not eat or breathe.*

Hah! thought one of the little voices that made up Lady LeJean's thinking.

One of the figures whimpered.

'The body *will* breathe,' said her ladyship. 'You will not persuade it that air is not required.'

She was aware of the choking noises.

'You are thinking, yes, we can exchange necessary materials with the outside world, and this is true,' she went on. 'But the body *does not know that*. It thinks it is dying. Let it breathe.'

There was a series of gasps.

'And you will feel better shortly,' said her ladyship, and was enthralled to hear the inner voice think: These are your jailers, and you are already stronger than them.

One of the figures felt its face with a clumsy hand and, panting, said, 'Whom do you speak to with your mouth?'

178

'You,' said Lady LeJean.

'Us?'

'This will take some explaining—'

'No,' said the Auditor. 'Danger lies that way. We believe the body imposes a method of thought on the brain. No blame attaches. It is a . . . malfunction. We will accompany you to the clockmaker. We will do this now.'

'Not in those clothes,' said Lady LeJean. 'You will frighten him. It may lead to irrational actions.'

There was a moment of silence. The Auditors-made-flesh looked hopelessly at one another.

'You have to talk with your mouth,' Lady LeJean prompted. 'The minds stay inside the head.'

One said, 'What is wrong with these clothes? It is a simple shape found in many human cultures.'

Lady LeJean walked to the window. 'See the people down there?' she said. 'You must dress in appropriate city fashions.'

Reluctantly the Auditors did so, and, while they retained the greyness, they did give themselves clothes that would pass unnoticed in the street. Up to a point, anyway.

'Only those of female appearance should wear dresses,' Lady LeJean pointed out.

A hovering grey shape said, *Warning. Danger. The one calling itself Lady LeJean may give unsafe advice. Warning.*

'Understood,' said one of the incarnate ones. 'We know the way. We will lead.'

It walked into the door.

The Auditors clustered around the door for a while, and then one of them glared at Lady LeJean, who smiled.

'Doorknob,' she said.

The Auditor turned back to the door, stared at the brass knob, and then looked the door up and down. It dissolved into dust.

'Doorknob was simpler,' said Lady LeJean.

Tick

179

There were big mountains around the Hub. But the ones towering above the temple didn't all have names, because there were simply too many of them. Only gods have enough time to name all the pebbles on a beach, but gods don't have the patience.

Copperhead was small enough to be big enough to have a name. Lobsang awoke and saw its crooked peak, towering above the lesser local mountains, outlined against the sunrise.

Sometimes the gods have no taste at all. They allow sunrises and sunsets in ridiculous pink and blue hues that any professional artist would dismiss as the work of some enthusiastic amateur who'd never looked at a real sunset. This was one of those sunrises. It was the kind of sunrise a man looks at and says, 'No *real* sunrise could paint the sky Surgical Appliance Pink.'

Nevertheless, it was beautiful.*

Lobsang was half covered in a pile of dry bracken. There was no sign of the yeti.

It was springtime here. There was still snow, but with the occasional patch of bare soil and a hint of green. He stared around, and saw leaves in bud.

Lu-Tze was standing some way off, gazing up into a tree. He didn't turn his head as Lobsang approached.

'Where's the yeti?'

'He wouldn't go further than this. Can't ask a yeti to leave snow,' whispered Lu-Tze.

'Oh,' whispered Lobsang. 'Er, why are we whispering?'

'Look at the bird.'

It was perched on a branch by a fork in the tree, next to what looked like a birdhouse, and nibbling at a piece of roughly round wood it held in one claw.

'Must be an old nest they're repairing,' said Lu-Tze. 'Can't have got that advanced this early in the season.'

'Looks like some kind of old box to me,' said Lobsang. He squinted to see better. 'Is it an old . . . clock?' he added.

'Look at what the bird is nibbling,' suggested Lu-Tze.

* But not tasteful.

'Well, it looks like . . . a crude gearwheel? But why—'

'Well spotted. That, lad, is a clock cuckoo. A young one, by the look of it, trying to build a nest that'll attract a mate. Not much chance of that . . . See? It's got the numerals all wrong and it's stuck the hands on crooked.'

'A bird that *builds* clocks? I thought a cuckoo clock was a clock with a mechanical cuckoo that came out when—'

'And where do you think people got such a strange idea from?'

'But that's some kind of miracle!'

'Why?' said Lu-Tze. 'They barely go for more than half an hour, they keep lousy time and the poor dumb males go frantic trying to keep them wound.'

'But even to—'

'Everything happens somewhere, I suppose,' said Lu-Tze. 'Not worth making too much of a fuss. Got any food left?'

'No. We finished it last night,' said Lobsang. He added, hopefully, 'Er . . . I heard tell that really advanced monks can live on the, er, life force in the actual air itself . . .'

'Only on the planet Sausage, I expect,' said Lu-Tze. 'No, we'll skirt Copperhead and find something in the valleys on the other side. Let's go, there's not much time.'

But time enough to watch a bird, thought Lobsang as he let the world around him become blue and fade, and the thought was comforting.

It was easier going without the snow on the ground, provided he avoided the strange resistance offered by bushes and long grass. Lu-Tze walked on ahead, looking oddly colourful and unreal against the faded landscape.

They went past the entrance to dwarf mines, but saw no one above ground. Lobsang was glad of that. The statues he had seen in the villages yesterday weren't dead, he knew, but merely frozen at a different speed of time. Lu-Tze had forbidden him to go near anyone, but he needn't have bothered. Walking around the living statues was invasive, somehow. It made it worse when you realized that they *were* moving, but very, very slowly . . .

The sun had barely moved from the horizon when they came

down through warmer woods on the Rim side of the mountain. Here the landscape had a more domesticated air. It was woodland rather than forest. The game trail they'd been following crossed a creek at a point where there were cart tracks, old but still not overgrown.

Lobsang looked behind him after he'd walked across the ford, and watched the water very slowly reclaim the shape of his footprints in the stream.

He'd been trained in time-slicing on the snowfields above the valley, like the rest of the novices. That was so they couldn't come to any harm, the monks had said, although no one actually explained what harm they *might* come to. Outside the monastery, this was the first time Lobsang had sliced in a living landscape.

It was marvellous! Birds hung in the sky. Early morning bumblebees hovered over the opening flowers. The world was a crystal made of living things.

Lobsang slowed near a group of deer cropping the grass, and watched as the nearer eye of one of them swivelled, with geological slowness, to watch him. He saw the skin move as the muscles underneath started to bunch for flight . . .

'Time for a smoko,' said Lu-Tze.

The world around Lobsang speeded up. The deer fled, along with the magic of the moment.

'What's a smoko?' said Lobsang. He was annoyed. The quiet slow world had been fun.

'You ever been to Fourecks?'

'No. There's a barman at the Bunch of Grapes from there, though.'

Lu-Tze lit one of his skinny cigarettes.

'Don't mean much,' he said. 'The barman *everywhere* is from there. Strange country. Big time source right in the middle, very useful. Time and space all tangled up. Probably all that beer. Nice place, though. Now, you see that country down there?'

On one side of the clearing the ground fell away steeply, showing treetops and, beyond, a small patchwork of fields tucked into a fold in the mountains. In the distance was a gorge, and Lobsang thought he could make out a bridge across it.

'Doesn't look much like a country,' he said. 'Looks more like a shelf.'

'That's witch country,' said Lu-Tze. 'And we're going to borrow a broomstick. Quickest way to Ankh-Morpork. Only way to travel.'

'Isn't that, er, interfering with history? I mean, I was told that sort of thing is all right up in the valleys, but down here in the world . . .'

'No, it's absolutely forbidden,' said Lu-Tze. ' 'cos it's Interfering With History. Got to be careful of your witch, of course. Some of them are pretty canny.' He caught Lobsang's expression. 'Look, that's why there's rules, understand? So that you *think* before you break 'em.'

'But—'

Lu-Tze sighed, and pinched out the end of his cigarette. 'We're being watched,' he said.

Lobsang spun round. There were only trees, and insects buzzing in the early-morning air.

'Up there,' said Lu-Tze.

There was a raven perched on the broken crown of a pine tree, shattered in some winter storm. It looked at them looking at it.

'Caw?' it said.

'It's just a raven,' said Lobsang. 'There's lots of them in the valley.'

'It was watching us when we stopped.'

'There's ravens all over the mountains, Sweeper.'

'And when we met the yeti,' Lu-Tze persisted.

'That settles it, then. It's coincidence. One raven couldn't move that fast.'

'Maybe it's a special raven,' said Lu-Tze. 'Anyway, it's not one of our mountain ravens. It's a lowland raven. Mountain ravens croak. They don't caw. Why's it so interested in us?'

'It's a bit . . . weird, thinking you're being followed by a bird,' said Lobsang.

'When you get to my age you notice things in the sky,' said Lu-Tze. He shrugged and gave a grin. 'You start worrying they might be vultures.'

183

They faded into time, and vanished.

The raven ruffled its feathers.

'Croak?' it said. 'Damn.'

Tick

Lobsang felt around under the thatched eaves of the cottage, and his hand closed on the bristles of a broomstick that had been thrust among the reeds.

'This is rather like stealing,' he said, as Lu-Tze helped him down.

'No, it's not,' said the sweeper, taking the broomstick and holding it up so he could look along its length. 'And I'll tell you why. If we sort things out, we'll drop it off on our way back and she'll never know it's gone . . . and if we don't sort things out, well, she'll *still* never know it's gone. Honestly, they don't take much care of their sticks, witches. Look at the bristles on this one. I wouldn't use it to clean a pond! Oh, well . . . back into clock time, lad. I'd hate to fly one of these things while I was slicing.'

He straddled the stick and gripped the handle. It rose a little way.

'Good suspension, at least,' he said. 'You can have the comfy seat on the back. Hold tight to my own broom and make sure you wrap your robe around you. These things are pretty breezy.'

Lobsang pulled himself aboard and the stick rose. As it drew level with the lower branches around the clearing, it brought Lu-Tze to eye level with a raven.

It shifted uneasily and turned its head this way and that, trying to fix both eyes on him.

'Are you going to caw or croak, I wonder,' said Lu-Tze, apparently to himself.

'Croak,' said the raven.

'So you're not the raven we saw on the other side of the mountain, then.'

'Me? Gosh, no,' said the raven. 'That's croaking territory over there.'

'Just checking.'

The broom rose higher, and set off above the trees in a Hubwards direction.

The raven ruffled its feathers and blinked.

'Damn!' it said. It shuffled around the tree to where the Death of Rats was sitting.

SQUEAK?

'Look, if you want me to do this undercover work you've got to get me a book on ornithology, okay?' said Quoth. 'Let's go, or I'll never keep up.'

Tick

Death found Famine in a new restaurant in Genua. He had a booth all to himself and was eating Duck and Dirty Rice.

'Oh,' said Famine. 'It's you.'

YES. WE MUST RIDE. YOU MUST HAVE GOT MY MESSAGE.

'Pull up a chair,' Famine hissed. 'They do a very good alligator sausage here.'

I SAID, WE MUST RIDE.

'Why?'

Death sat down and explained. Famine listened, although he never stopped eating.

'I see,' he said at last. 'Thank you, but I think I shall sit this one out.'

SIT IT OUT? YOU'RE A HORSEMAN!

'Yes, of course. But what is my role here?'

I BEG YOUR PARDON?

'No famine appears to be involved, does it? A shortage of food *per se*? As such?'

WELL, NO. NOT AS SUCH, OBVIOUSLY, BUT—

'So I would, as it were, be turning up just to wave. No, thank you.'

YOU USED TO RIDE OUT EVERY TIME, said Death accusingly.

Famine waved a bone airily. 'We had proper apocalypses in those days,' he said, and sucked at the bone. 'You could sink your teeth into them.'

NEVERTHELESS, THIS IS THE END OF THE WORLD.

Famine pushed his plate aside and opened the menu. 'There are other worlds,' he said. 'You're too sentimental, Death. I've always said so.'

Death drew himself up. Humans had created Famine, too. Oh, there had always been droughts and locusts, but for a really good famine, for fertile land to be turned into a dustbowl by stupidity and avarice, you needed humans. Famine was arrogant.

I AM SORRY, he said, TO HAVE TRESPASSED ON YOUR TIME.

He went outside, into the crowded street, all alone.

Tick

The stick swooped down towards the plains, and levelled off a few hundred feet above the ground.

'We're on our way now!' shouted Lu-Tze, pointing ahead.

Lobsang looked down at a slim wooden tower hung with complicated boxes. There was another one in the far distance, a toothpick in the morning mist.

'Semaphore towers!' Lu-Tze shouted. 'Ever seen them?'

'Only in the city!' Lobsang shouted above the slipstream.

'It's the Grand Trunk!' the sweeper shouted back. 'Runs like an arrow all the way to the city! All we have to do is follow it!'

Lobsang clung on. There was no snow beneath them and it looked as though spring was well advanced. And therefore it was unfair that here, that much nearer the sun, the air was frigid and was being driven into his flesh by the wind of their travel.

'It's very cold up here!'

'Yes! Did I tell you about the double-knit combinations?'

'Yes!'

'I've got a spare pair in my sack. You can have them when we stop!'

'Your own personal pair?'

'Yes! Second-best but well darned!'

'No, thank you!'

'They've been washed!'

'Lu-Tze?'

186

'Yes?'

'*Why* can't we slice when we're on this thing?'

The tower was well past them. The next one was pencil-sized already. The black-and-white shutters on the boxes were twinkling in the sunlight.

'Do you know what happens if you slice time on a magically powered vehicle travelling at more than seventy miles an hour?'

'No!'

'Me neither! And I don't want to find out!'

Tick

Igor opened the door before the second knock. An Igor might be filling coffins with earth in the cellar, or up on the roof adjusting the lightning conductor, but a caller never had to knock twice.

'Ladythip,' he muttered, nodding his head. He looked blankly at the six figures behind her.

'We have called to inspect progress,' said Lady LeJean.

'And thethe ladieth and gentlemen, ladythip?'

'My associatcs,' said hcr ladyship, matching Igor's blank stare.

'If you will be tho kind ath to thtep inthide, I will thee if the marthter ith in,' said Igor, observing the convention that a true butler never knows the whereabouts of anyone in the house until they decide they want it to be known.

He backed through the door into the workshop and then lurched into the kitchen, where Jeremy was calmly pouring a spoonful of medicine down the sink.

'That woman ith here,' he said, 'and thee hath brought *lawyerth*.'

Jeremy held out a hand, palm downwards, and examined it critically.

'You see, Igor?' he said. 'Here we are, almost at the completion of our great work, and I remain absolutely calm. You could build a house on my hand, it is so steady.'

'*Lawyerth*, thur,' said Igor, giving the word some extra spin.

'And?'

'Well, we have had a lot of money,' said Igor, with the conviction of a man who has informally secreted a small but sensible amount of gold in his own bag.

'And we have finished the clock,' said Jeremy, still watching his hand.

'We've been *nearly* finithed for *dayth*,' said Igor darkly. 'If it wathn't for *her*, I reckon we could've caught that thunderthtorm two dayth ago.'

'When's the next one?'

Igor screwed up his face and banged his temple a couple of times with the palm of his hand.

'Unthettled conditionth with a low approaching from the Rim,' he said. 'Can't promith anything with the thloppy weather you get here. Hah, back home the thunderthtormth come running ath thoon ath they thee you put up the iron pole. Tho what do you want me to do about the lawyerth?'

'Show them in, of course. We have nothing to hide.'

'Are you thure, thur?' said Igor, whose carpet bag could not in fact be lifted with one hand.

'Please *do* it, Igor.'

Jeremy smoothed down his hair while the grumbling Igor disappeared into the shop and returned with the guests.

'Lady LeJean, thur. And thome other . . . people,' said Igor.

'It's good to see you, your ladyship,' said Jeremy, smiling glassily. He vaguely remembered something he had read. 'Won't you introduce me to your friends?'

Lady LeJean gave him a nervous look. Oh, yes . . . humans always needed to know names. And he was smiling again. It made it so hard to *think*.

'Mr Jeremy, these are my . . . associates,' she said. 'Mr Black. Mr Green. Miss Brown. Miss White. Miss . . . Yellow. And Mr Blue.'

Jeremy held out his hand. 'I am pleased to meet you,' he said.

Six pairs of eyes looked uncomprehendingly at the hand.

'The custom here is to shake hands,' said her ladyship.

In unison, the Auditors extended a hand and wiggled it slowly in the air.

'The hand of the other person,' said her ladyship. She gave Jeremy a thin-lipped smile. 'They are foreigners,' she said.

And she recognized the panic in their eyes, even if they didn't. We can count the number and types of atom in this room, they were thinking. How can there be anything in here we cannot understand?

Jeremy managed to catch one wavering hand in his. 'And you are Mr—?'

The Auditor turned worried eyes on Lady LeJean.

'Mr Black,' she said.

'I understood that *we* were Mr Black,' said another male-shaped Auditor.

'No, you are Mr Green.'

'Nevertheless, we would prefer Mr Black. We are the senior, and black is a more significant shade. We do not wish to be Mr Green.'

'The translation of your names is not, I think, important,' said Lady LeJean. She gave Jeremy another smile. 'They are my accountants,' she added, some reading on her part having suggested that this might excuse most oddities.

'You see, Igor?' said Jeremy. 'They are simply accountants.'

Igor grimaced. Where his baggage was concerned, accountants were probably worse news than lawyers.

'Grey would be acceptable,' said Mr Green.

'Nevertheless, you are Mr Green. We are Mr Black. It is a matter of status.'

'If that is the case,' said Miss White, 'white is higher status than black. Black is absence of colour.'

'The point is valid,' said Mr Black. 'Therefore we are now Mr White. You are Miss Red.'

'You previously indicated that you were Mr Black.'

'New information indicates a change of position. This does not indicate incorrectness of said previous position.'

It's happening already, thought Lady LeJean. It's in the darkness where your eyes can't see. The universe becomes two halves, and you live in the half behind the eyes. Once you have a body, you have a 'me'.

I have seen galaxies die. I have watched atoms dance. But until I had the dark behind the eyes, I didn't know the death from the dance. And we were wrong. When you pour water into a jug, it becomes jug-shaped *and it is not the same water any more*. An hour ago they never dreamed of having names, and now they are arguing about them . . .

And they can't hear what I think!

She wanted more *time*. The habits of a billion years don't yield entirely to a mouthful of bread, and she could see that a crazy life form like humanity should not be allowed to exist. Yes, indeed. Certainly. Of course.

But she wanted more time.

They should be studied. Yes, studied.

There should be . . . reports. Yes. Reports. Full reports. Long, long, full reports.

Caution. That was it. That was the word! Auditors *loved* that word. Always put off until tomorrow something that, tomorrow, you could put off until, let's say, next year.

It has to be said that Lady LeJean was not herself at this point. She didn't quite have a herself to be. The other six Auditors . . . in *time*, yes, they'd think the same way. But there wasn't *time*. If only she could persuade them to *eat* something. That would . . . yes, that would bring them to their senses. There seemed to be no food around, though.

She *could* see a very large hammer on the bench.

'How is progress, Mr Jeremy?' she said, walking over to the clock. Igor moved very fast, and stood almost protectively next to the glass pillar.

Jeremy hurried forward. 'We have carefully aligned all the systems—'

'Again,' Igor growled.

'Yes, again—'

'Theveral timeth, in fact,' Igor added.

'And now we simply await the right weather conditions.'

'But I thought you stored lightning?'

Her ladyship indicated the greenish glass cylinders bubbling and

190

hissing along the wall of the workshop. Just by the bench with, yes, the hammer on it. And no one could read her thoughts! The *power*!

'There will easily be enough to keep the mechanism working, but to start the clock will require what Igor calls a *jump*,' said Jeremy.

Igor held up two crocodile clips the size of his head.

''th right,' he said. 'But you hardly ever get the right kind of thunderthtormth down here. Thould've built thith in Uberwald, I keep thaying.'

'What is the nature of this delay?' said – possibly – Mr White.

'We need a thunderstorm, sir. For the lightning,' said Jeremy. Lady LeJean stepped back, a little closer to the bench.

'Well? Arrange one,' said Mr White.

'Hah, well, if we were in Uberwald, of courthe—'

'It is merely a matter of pressures and potentials,' said Mr White. 'Can you not simply create one?'

Igor gave him a look of disbelief mixed with respect.

'You're not from Uberwald, are you?' he said. Then he gasped, and banged the side of his head.

'Hey, I felt *that* one,' he said. 'Whoopth! How did you do that? Prethure dropping like a *thtone*!'

Sparks glittered along his black fingernails. He beamed.

'I'll jutht go and raithe the lightning rod,' he said, hurrying to a pulley system on the wall.

Lady LeJean turned on the others. This time she wished they *could* read her thoughts. She didn't know enough pronounceable human swearwords.

'That is *against the rules*!' she hissed.

'Mere expediency,' said Mr White. 'If you had not been . . . lax, this would have been concluded by now!'

'I counselled further study!'

'Unnecessary!'

'Is there a problem?' said Jeremy, in the diffident voice he used for conversations not involving clocks.

'The clock should not be started yet!' said Lady LeJean, not taking her eyes off the other Auditors.

'But you *asked* me . . . We've been . . . It's all set up!'

191

'There may be . . . problems! I think we should see another week of testing!'

But there weren't problems, she knew. Jeremy had built the thing as if he'd built a dozen like it before. It had been all Lady LeJean could do to spin things out this long, especially with the Igor watching her like a hawk.

'What is your "name", young person?' said Mr White to Jeremy.

The clockmaker backed away. 'Jeremy,' he said, 'and I . . . I don't understand, Mr, er, White. A clock tells the time. A clock isn't *dangerous*. How can a clock be a problem? It's a *perfect* clock!'

'Then start it!'

'But her ladyship—'

The door knocker thundered.

'Igor?' said Jeremy.

'Yeth, thur?' said Igor, from the hallway.

'How did the servant person get there?' said Mr White, still watching her ladyship.

'It's a, a sort of trick they, they have,' said Jeremy. 'I'm, I'm sure it's only—'

'It'th Dr Hopkinth, thur,' said Igor, entering from the hall. 'I told him you were buthy, but—'

—but Dr Hopkins, although apparently as mild-mannered as milk, was also a Guild official and had survived as such for several years. Ducking under Igor's arm was no problem at all for a man who could handle a meeting of clockmakers, no two of whom exactly ticked in time with the rest of humanity.

'I just happened to have business this way,' he began, smiling brightly, 'and it was no trouble to drop in at the apothecary to pick up— Oh, you have company?'

Igor grimaced, but there was the Code to think of.

'Thall I make thome tea, thur?' he said, as all the Auditors glared at the doctor.

'What is this tea?' Mr White demanded.

'It is protocol!' snapped Lady LeJean.

Mr White hesitated. Protocol was important.

'Er, er, er, yes,' said Jeremy. 'Tea, Igor, please. Please.'

'My word, I see you have finished your clock!' said Dr Hopkins, apparently oblivious of an atmosphere that could have floated iron. 'What a magnificent piece of work!'

The Auditors stared at one another as the doctor ambled past them and looked up at the glass face.

'Well done indeed, Jeremy!' he said, removing his glasses and polishing them enthusiastically. 'And what is this pretty blue glow?'

'It's, it's the crystal ring,' said Jeremy. 'It, it—'

'It spins light,' said Lady LeJean. 'And then it makes a hole in the universe.'

'Really?' said Dr Hopkins, putting his glasses back on. 'What an original idea! Does a cuckoo come out?'

Tick

Of the very worst words that can be heard by anyone high in the air, the pair known as 'Oh-oh' possibly combine the maximum of bowel-knotting terror with the minimum wastage of breath.

When Lu-Tze uttered them, Lobsang didn't need a translation. He'd been watching the clouds for some time. They were getting blacker, and thicker, and darker.

'The handle's tingling!' shouted Lu-Tze.

'That's because there's a storm right above us!' screamed Lobsang. 'The sky was as clear as a bell a few minutes ago!'

Ankh-Morpork was much closer now. Lobsang could make out some of the taller buildings, and see the river snaking across the plain. But the storm was coming up all around the city.

'I'm going to have to land this thing while I can!' Lu-Tze said. 'Hold on . . .'

The stick dropped until it was a few feet above the cabbage fields. The plants were a rushing green blur inches below Lobsang's sandals.

Lobsang heard another word that, while not the *worst* you can hear while airborne, is not at all good when it's said by the person steering.

'Er . . .'

'Do you know how to *stop* this?' yelled Lobsang.

'Not in so many words,' shouted Lu-Tze. 'Hold on, I'm going to try something . . .'

The stick tilted up but kept moving in the same direction. The bristles dipped into the cabbages.

It took the width of a field to slow down, at the end of a furrow with the smell that only squashed cabbage leaves can yield.

'How fine can you slice time?' the sweeper said, scrambling over the battered plants.

'I'm pretty good—' Lobsang began.

'Get better quick!'

Lu-Tze faded to blue as he ran towards the city. Lobsang caught him up within a hundred yards but the sweeper was still fading, still slicing time thinner and thinner. The apprentice gritted his teeth and followed, straining every muscle.

The old man might be a fraud when it came to fighting, but there was no kidding here. The world went from blue to indigo to an inky, unnatural darkness, like the shadow of an eclipse.

This was deep time. You couldn't stay there long, he knew. Even if you could tolerate the ghastly chill, there were parts of the body that just weren't designed for this. Go too far down, too, and you'd die if you came back too quickly . . .

He hadn't seen it, of course, no apprentice had, but there were some quite graphic drawings in the classrooms. A man's life could become very, very painful if his blood began to move through time faster than his bones. It would also be very short.

'I can't . . . keep this up . . .' he panted, running after Lu-Tze in the violet gloom.

'You can,' gasped the sweeper. 'You're fast, right?'

'I'm not . . . trained . . . for *this*!'

The city was getting closer.

'No one's trained for this!' growled Lu-Tze. 'You do it, and you find out that you're good at it!'

'What happens if you find out you're no good?' said Lobsang. The going felt easier now. He no longer had the feeling that his skin was trying to drag itself off him.

194

'Dead men don't find things out,' said Lu-Tze. He turned his head to his apprentice and his evil grin was a yellow-toothed curve in the shadows. 'Getting the hang?' he added.

'I'm . . . I'm on top of it . . .'

'Right! Then now that we've warmed up . . .'

To Lobsang's horror, the sweeper faded further into the dark.

He called up reserves he knew he didn't have. He screamed at his liver to stay with him, thought that he felt his brain creak, and plunged on.

The shape of Lu-Tze lightened as Lobsang drew level with him in time.

'Still here? One last effort, lad!'

'I can't!'

'You bloody well can!'

Lobsang gulped freezing air and fell onwards—

—where the light was suddenly a calm, pale blue and Lu-Tze was trotting gently between the frozen carts and unmoving people around the city's gate.

'See? Nothing to it,' said the sweeper. 'Just *maintain*, that's all. Nice and steady.'

It was like balancing on a wire. It was fine if you didn't think about it.

'But all the scrolls say you go to blue and violet and into the black and then you hit the Wall,' said Lobsang.

'Ah, well, *scrolls*,' said Lu-Tze, and left it there, as if the tone of voice said it all. 'This is Zimmerman's Valley, lad. It helps if you know it's here. The abbot said it's something to do with . . . what was it? . . . Oh, yeah, boundary conditions. Something like . . . the foam on the tide. We're right on the edge, boy!'

'But I can breathe easily!'

'Yeah. Shouldn't happen. Keep moving about, though, otherwise you'll exhaust all the good air around your body field. Good old Zimmerman, eh? One of the best, he was. And he reckoned there was another dip even closer to the Wall, too.'

'Did he ever find it?'

'Don't think so.'

'Why?'

'The way he exploded gave me a hint. Don't worry! You can maintain the slice easily here. You don't have to think about it. You've got *other* things to think about! Keep an eye on those clouds!'

Lobsang looked up. Even in this blue-on-blue landscape, the clouds over the city looked ominous.

'It's what happened back in Uberwald,' said Lu-Tze. 'The clock needs a lot of power. The storm blew up out of nowhere.'

'But the city's huge! How can we find a clock here?'

'First, we're going to head for the centre,' said Lu-Tze.

'Why?'

'Because with luck we won't have to run so far when the lightning strikes, of course.'

'Sweeper, no one can outrun lightning!'

Lu-Tze spun round and grabbed Lobsang by the robe, dragging him closer.

'Then tell me where to run, speedy boy!' he shouted. 'There's more to you than meets the third eye, lad! No apprentice should be able to find Zimmerman's Valley! It takes hundreds of years of training! And no one should be able to make the spinners sit up and dance to his tune the very first time he sees them! Think I'm daft, do you? Orphan boy, strange power . . . what the hell are you? The Mandala *knew* you! Well, I'm just a mortal human, and what I know is, I'll be damned if I'll see the world shattered a second time! So *help me*! Whatever it is you've got, I need it now! Use it!'

He let go, and stood back. A vein in his bald head was throbbing.

'But I don't know what I can do to–'

'*Find out what you can do!*'

Tick

Protocol. Rules. Precedent. *Ways of doing things.* That's how we've always worked, thought Lady LeJean. *This* and *this* must follow *that*. It has always been our strength. I wonder if it can be a weakness?

196

If looks could have killed, Dr Hopkins would have been a smear on the wall. The Auditors watched his every move like cats watching a new species of mouse.

Lady LeJean had been incarnate much longer than the others. Time can change a body, especially when you've never had one before. She wouldn't have stared and fumed. She would have clubbed the doctor to the ground. What was one more human?

She realized, with some amazement, that the thought there was a *human* thought.

But the other six were still wet behind the ears. They hadn't yet realized the dimensions of duplicity that you needed to survive as a human being. They clearly found it hard to think inside the little dark world behind the eyes, too. Auditors reached decisions in concert with thousands, *millions* of other Auditors.

Sooner or later they'd learn to be their own thinkers, though. It might take a while, because they'd try to learn from one another first.

At the moment they were watching Igor's tea tray with great suspicion.

'Drinking tea *is* protocol,' said Lady LeJean. 'I must insist.'

'Is this correct?' Mr White barked at Dr Hopkins.

'Oh, yes,' said the doctor. 'With a ginger biscuit, usually,' he added hopefully.

'A ginger biscuit,' repeated Mr White. 'A biscuit of red-brown colouring?'

'Yeth, thur,' said Igor. He nodded to the plate on his tray.

'I would like to try a ginger biscuit,' volunteered Miss Red.

Oh yes, thought Lady LeJean, *please* try the ginger biscuits.

'We do not eat or drink!' snapped Mr White. He gave Lady LeJean a look of deep suspicion. 'It could cause incorrect ways of thinking.'

'But it is the custom,' said Lady LeJean. 'To ignore protocol is to draw attention.'

Mr White hesitated. But he was a quick adaptor.

'It is against our religion!' he said. 'Correct!'

It was an amazing leap. It was *inventive*. And he'd come up with it all alone. Lady LeJean was impressed. The Auditors had tried to understand religion, because so much that made no sense whatsoever was done in its name. But it could also excuse practically any kind of eccentricity. Genocide, for example. By comparison, a lack of tea drinking was easy.

'Yes, indeed!' said Mr White, turning to the other Auditors. 'Is that not true?'

'Yes, that is not true. Indeed!' said Mr Green desperately.

'Oh?' said Dr Hopkins. 'I did not know there was any religion that forbade tea.'

'Indeed!' said Mr White. Lady LeJean could almost feel his mind racing. 'It is a . . . yes, it is a drink of the . . . correct . . . it is a drink of the . . . extremely bad negatively regarded gods. It is a . . . correct . . . it is a commandment of our religion to . . . yes . . . to shun ginger biscuits also.' There was sweat on his forehead. For an Auditor, this was genius-level creativity. 'Also,' he went on slowly, as if reading the words off some page invisible to everyone else, 'our religion . . . correct! . . . our religion demands that the clock be started now! For . . . who may know when the hour may be?'

Despite herself, Lady LeJean nearly applauded.

'Who indeed?' said Dr Hopkins.

'I, I absolutely agree,' said Jeremy, who had been staring at Lady LeJean. 'I don't understand who you . . . why there's all this fuss . . . I don't understand why . . . oh, dear . . . I'm having a headache . . .'

Dr Hopkins spilled his tea because of the speed with which he got up and reached into his coat pocket.

'AhitsohappensIwaspassingtheapothecaryonmywayhere—' he began, all in one breath.

'I feel it's not the time to start the clock,' said Lady LeJean, edging herself along the desk. The hammer was still invitingly there.

'I'm seeing those little flashes of light, Dr Hopkins,' said Jeremy urgently, staring into the middle distance.

'Not the flashes of light! Not the flashes of light!' said Dr Hopkins. He grabbed a teaspoon off Igor's tray, stared at it, threw it over his shoulder, tipped the tea out of a cup, opened the bottle of blue medicine by smashing the top off on the edge of the bench, and poured a cupful, spilling quite a lot of it in his hurry.

The hammer was inches away from her ladyship's hand. She didn't dare look round, but she could *sense* it there. While the Auditors stared at the trembling Jeremy, she let her fingers walk across the bench. She wouldn't even have to move. A brisk over-arm throw should do it.

She saw Dr Hopkins try to put the cup to Jeremy's lips. The boy put his hands over his face and elbowed the cup out of the way, spilling the medicine across the floor.

Then Lady LeJean's fingers were grasping the handle. She brought her hand round and hurled the hammer directly at the clock.

Tick

The war was going badly for the weaker side. Their positioning was wrong, their tactics ragged, their strategy hopeless. The Red army advanced across the whole front, dismembering the scurrying remnant of the collapsing Black battalions.

There was room for only *one* anthill on this lawn . . .

Death found War down among the grass blades. He admired attention to detail. War was in full armour, too, but the human heads he normally had tied to his saddle had been replaced by ant heads, feelers and all.

DO THEY NOTICE YOU, DO YOU THINK? he said.

'I doubt it,' said War.

NEVERTHELESS, IF THEY DID, I'M SURE THEY WOULD APPRECIATE IT.

'Ha! Only decent theatre of war around these days,' said War. 'That's what I like about ants. The buggers don't learn, what?'

IT HAS BEEN RATHER PEACEFUL OF LATE, I AGREE, said Death.

'Peaceful?' said War. 'Ha! I may as well change m'name to "Police Action", or "Negotiated Settlement"! Remember the old days? Warriors used to froth at the mouth! Arms and legs bouncing in all directions! Great times, eh?' He leaned across and slapped Death on the back. 'I'll bag 'em and you tag 'em, what?'

This looked hopeful, Death thought.

TALKING OF THE OLD DAYS, he said carefully, I'M SURE YOU REMEMBER THE TRADITION OF RIDING OUT?

War gave him a puzzled look. 'Mind's a blank on that one, old boy.'

I SENT OUT THE CALL.

'Can't say it rings a bell . . .'

APOCALYPSE? said Death. END OF THE WORLD?

War continued to stare. 'Definitely knocking, old chap, but no one's home. And talking of home . . .' War looked around at the twitching remains of the recent slaughter. 'Spot of lunch?'

Around them the forest of grass grew shorter and smaller until it was, indeed, no more than grass, and became the lawn outside a house.

It was an ancient long-house. Where else would War live? But Death saw ivy growing over the roof. He remembered when War would never have allowed anything like that, and a little worm of worry began to gnaw.

War hung up his helmet as he entered, and once he would have kept it on. And the benches around the fire pit would have been crowded with warriors, and the air would have been thick with beer and sweat.

'Brought an old friend back, dear,' he said.

Mrs War was preparing something on the modern black iron kitchen range which, Death saw, had been installed in the fire pit, with shiny pipes extending up to the hole in the roof. She gave Death the kind of nod a wife gives a man whom her husband has, despite previous warnings, unexpectedly brought back from the pub.

'We're having rabbit,' she said, and added in the voice of one who has been put upon and will extract payment later, 'I'm *sure* I can make it stretch to three.'

War's big red face wrinkled. 'Do I like rabbit?'

'Yes, dear.'

'I thought I liked beef.'

'No, dear. Beef gives you wind.'

'Oh.' War sighed. 'Any chance of onions?'

'You don't like onions, dear.'

'I don't?'

'Because of your stomach, dear.'

'Oh.'

War smiled awkwardly at Death. 'It's rabbit,' he said. 'Erm . . . dear, do I ride out for Apocalypses?'

Mrs War took the lid off a saucepan and prodded viciously at something inside.

'No, dear,' she said firmly. 'You always come down with a cold.'

'I thought I rather, er, sort of *liked* that kind of thing . . . ?'

'No, dear. You don't.'

Despite himself, Death was fascinated. He had never come across the idea of keeping your memory inside someone else's head.

'Perhaps I would like a beer?' War ventured.

'You don't like beer, dear.'

'I don't?'

'No, it brings on your trouble.'

'Ah. Uh, how do I feel about brandy?'

'You don't like brandy, dear. You like your special oat drink with the vitamins.'

'Oh, yes,' said War mournfully. 'I'd forgotten I liked that.' He looked sheepishly at Death. 'It's quite nice,' he said.

COULD I HAVE A WORD WITH YOU, said Death, IN PRIVATE?

War looked puzzled. 'Do I like wo—'

IN *PRIVATE*, PLEASE, Death thundered.

Mrs War turned and gave Death a disdainful look.

'I understand, I *quite* understand,' she said haughtily. 'But don't you dare say anything to bring on his acid, that's all I shall say.'

Mrs War had been a Valkyrie once, Death remembered. It was another reason to be extremely careful on the battlefield.

'You've never been tempted by the prospect of marriage, old man?' said War, when she'd gone.

NO. ABSOLUTELY NOT. IN NO WAY.

'Why not?'

Death was nonplussed. It was like asking a brick wall what it thought of dentistry. As a question, it made no sense.

I HAVE BEEN TO SEE THE OTHER TWO, he said, ignoring it. FAMINE DOESN'T CARE AND PESTILENCE IS FRIGHTENED.

'The two of us, against the Auditors?' said War.

RIGHT IS ON OUR SIDE.

'Speaking as War,' said War, 'I'd hate to tell you what happens to very small armies that have Right on their side.'

I HAVE SEEN YOU FIGHT.

'My old right arm isn't what it was . . .' War murmured.

YOU ARE IMMORTAL. YOU ARE NOT ILL, said Death, but he could see the worried, slightly hunted look in War's eyes and knew that there was only one way this was going to go.

To be human was to change, Death realized. The Horsemen . . . were horse*men*. Men had wished upon them a certain shape, a certain form. And, just like the gods, and the Tooth Fairy, and the Hogfather, their shape had changed them. They would never *be* human, but they had caught aspects of humanity as though they were some kind of disease.

Because the point was that nothing, *nothing*, had one aspect and one aspect alone. Men would envisage a being called Famine, but once they gave him arms and legs and eyes, that meant he had to have a brain. That meant he'd think. And a brain can't think about plagues of locusts *all* the time.

Emergent behaviour again. Complications always crept in. Everything changed.

THANK GOODNESS, thought Death, THAT I AM COMPLETELY UNCHANGED AND EXACTLY THE SAME AS I EVER WAS.

And then there was one.

Tick

The hammer stopped, halfway across the room. Mr White walked over and picked it out of the air.

'Really, your ladyship,' he said. 'You think we don't watch you? You, the Igor, make the clock ready!'

Igor looked from him to Lady LeJean and back. 'I only take orderth from Marthter Jeremy, thank you,' he said.

'The world will end if you start that clock!' said Lady LeJean.

'What a foolish idea,' said Mr White. 'We laugh at it.'

'Hahaha,' said the other Auditors obediently.

'I *don't* need medicine!' Jeremy shouted, pushing Dr Hopkins out of the way. 'And I don't need people to tell me what to do. Shut up!'

In the silence, thunder grumbled in the clouds.

'Thank you,' said Jeremy, more calmly. 'Now, I hope I am a rational man, and I shall approach this rationally. A clock is a measuring device. I have built the perfect clock, my lady. I mean ladies. And gentlemen. It will revolutionize timekeeping.'

He reached up and moved the hands of the clock to almost one o'clock. Then he reached down, gripped the pendulum, and set it swinging.

The world continued to exist.

'You see? The universe doesn't stop even for *my* clock,' Jeremy went on. He folded his hands and sat down. 'Watch,' he said calmly.

The clock ticked gently. Then something rattled in the machinery around it, and the big green glass tubes of acid began to sizzle.

'Well, nothing seems to have happened,' said Dr Hopkins. 'That's a blessing.'

Sparks crackled around the lightning rod positioned above the clock.

'This is just making a path for the lightning,' said Jeremy happily. 'We send a little lightning up, and a lot more comes back—'

Things were moving inside the clock. There was a sound best represented as *fizzle*, and greenish-blue light filled the case.

'Ah, the cascade has initialized,' said Jeremy. 'As a little exercise, the, ah, more *traditional* pendulum clock has been slaved to the Big Clock, you'll see, so that every second it will be readjusted to the correct time.' He smiled, and one cheek twitched. 'Some day all clocks will be like this,' he said, and added, 'While I normally hate such an imprecise term as "any second now", nevertheless I—'

Tick

There was a fight going on in the square. In the strange colours involved in the time-slicing state known as Zimmerman's Valley, it was picked out in shades of light blue.

By the look of it, a couple of watchmen were trying to take on a gang. One man was airborne, and hung there without support. Another had fired a crossbow directly at one of the watchmen; the arrow was nailed unmoving in the air.

Lobsang examined it curiously.

'You're going to touch it, aren't you?' said a voice behind Lobsang. 'You're just going to reach out and touch it, despite everything I've told you. Pay attention to the damn sky!'

Lu-Tze was smoking nervously. When it got a few inches away from his body, the smoke went rigid in the air.

'Are you *sure* you can't feel where it is?' he snapped.

'It's all round us, Sweeper. We're so close, it . . . it's like trying to see the wood when you're standing under the trees!'

'Well, this is the Street of Cunning Artificers and that's the Guild of Clockmakers over there,' said Lu-Tze. 'I don't dare go inside if it's this close, not until we're certain.'

'What about the University?'

'Wizards aren't mad enough to try it!'

'You're going to try and race the lightning?'

'It's do-able, if we start from here in the Valley. Lightning ain't as quick as people think.'

'Are we waiting to see a little pointy bit of lightning coming out of a cloud?'

'Hah! Kids today, where *do* they get their education? The first stroke is from the ground to the air, lad. That makes a nice hole in the air for the main lightning to come down. Look for the glow. We've got to be giving the road plenty of sandal by the time it reaches the clouds. You holding up okay?'

'I could go on like this all day,' said Lobsang.

'Don't try it.' Lu-Tze scanned the sky again. 'Maybe I was wrong. Maybe it's just a storm. Sooner or later you get—'

He stopped. One look at Lobsang's face was enough.

'O-kay,' said the sweeper slowly. 'Just give me a direction. Point if you can't speak.'

Lobsang dropped to his knees, hands rising to his head. 'I don't know . . . don't know . . .'

Silvery light rose over the city, a few streets away. Lu-Tze grabbed the boy's elbow.

'Come on, lad. On your feet. Faster than lightning, eh? Okay?'

'Yeah . . . yeah, okay . . .'

'You can do it, right?'

Lobsang blinked. He could see the glass house again, stretching away as a pale outline overlaid the city.

'Clock,' he said thickly.

'Run, boy, run!' shouted Lu-Tze. 'And don't stop for *anything*.'

Lobsang plunged forward, and found it hard. Time moved aside for him, sluggishly at first, as his legs pumped. With every step he pushed himself faster and faster, the landscape changing colours again as the world slowed even further.

There was another stitch in time, the sweeper had said. Another valley, even closer to the null point. Insofar as he could think at all, Lobsang hoped he would reach it soon. His body felt as though it would fly apart; he could feel his bones *creaking*.

The glow ahead was halfway to the iron-heavy clouds now, but he'd reached a crossroads and he could see it was rising from a house halfway down the street.

He turned to look for the sweeper, and saw the man yards behind him, mouth open, a statue falling forward.

Lobsang turned, concentrated, let time speed up.

He reached Lu-Tze and caught him before he hit the ground. There was blood coming from the old man's ears.

'I can't do it, lad,' the sweeper mumbled. 'Get on! Get on!'

'I can do it! It's like running downhill!'

'Not for me it ain't!'

'I can't just leave you here like this!'

'Save us from heroes! Get that bloody clock!'

Lobsang hesitated. The downstroke was already emerging from the clouds, a drifting, glowing *spike*.

He ran. The lightning was falling towards a shop, a few buildings away. He could see a big clock hanging over its window.

He pushed against the flow of time ever further, and it yielded. But the lightning had reached the iron pole atop the building.

The window was closer than the door. He lowered his head and jumped through it, the glass shattering around him and then freezing in mid-air, clocks pinwheeling off the display and stopping as if caught in invisible amber.

There was another door ahead of him. He grabbed the knob and pulled, feeling the terrible resistance of a slab of wood urged to move at an appreciable fraction of the speed of light.

It was barely open a few inches when he saw, beyond, the slow ooze of lightning run down the rod and into the heart of the big clock.

The clock struck one.

Time stopped.

Ti—

Mr Soak the dairyman was washing bottles at the sink when the air dimmed and the water solidified.

He stared at it for a moment and then, with the manner of a man trying an experiment, held the bottle over the stone floor and let it go.

It remained hanging in the air.

'Dammit,' he said. 'Another idiot with a clock, eh?'

What he did then was not usual dairy practice. He walked into the centre of the room and made a few passes in the air with his hands.

The air brightened. The water splashed. The bottle smashed – although, when Ronnie turned round and waved a hand at it, the glass slivers ran together again.

Then Ronnie Soak sighed and went into the cream-settling room. Large wide bowls stretched away into the distance and, if Ronnie had ever allowed another to notice this, the distance contained far more distance than is ever found in a normal building.

'Show me,' he said.

The surface of the nearest bowl of milk became a mirror, and then began to show pictures . . .

Ronnie went back into the dairy, took his peaked cap off its hook by the door, and crossed the courtyard to the stable. The sky overhead was a sullen, unmoving grey as he emerged, leading his horse.

The horse was black, glistening with condition, and there was this about it that was odd: it shone as though it was illuminated by a red light. Redness spangled off its shoulders and flanks, even under the greyness.

And even when it was harnessed to the cart it didn't look like any kind of horse that should be hitched to any kind of wagon, but people never noticed this and, again, Ronnie took care to make sure that they didn't.

The cart gleamed with white paint, picked out here and there with a fresh green.

The wording on the side declared, proudly:

RONALD SOAK, Hygienic Dairyman.
ಐ Established ಐ

Perhaps it was odd that people never asked, 'Established *when*, exactly?' If they ever had, the answer would have had to be quite complicated.

Ronnie opened the gates to the yard and, milk crates rattling, set out into the timeless moment. It was terrible, he thought, the way things conspired against the small businessman.

Lobsang Ludd awoke to a little clicking, spinning sound.

He was in darkness, but it yielded reluctantly to his hand. It felt like velvet, and it was. He'd rolled under one of the display cabinets.

There was a vibration in the small of his back. He reached around gingerly, and realized that the portable Procrastinator was revolving in its cage.

So . . .

How did it go, now? He was living on borrowed time. He'd got maybe an hour, perhaps a lot less. But he could slice it, so . . .

No. Something told him that trying that would be a really terminal idea with time stored in a device made by Qu. The mere thought made him feel that his skin was inches from a universe full of razorblades.

So . . . one hour, perhaps a lot less. But you could rewind a spinner, right?

No. The handle was at the back. You could rewind *someone else's* spinner. Thank you, Qu, and your experimental models.

Could you take it off, then? No. The harness was part of it. Without it, different parts of your body would be travelling at different speeds. The effect would probably be rather like freezing a human body solid, and then pushing it down a flight of stone stairs.

Open the box with the crowbar that you will find inside . . .

There was a green-blue glow through the crack in the door. He took a step towards it, and heard the spinner suddenly pick up speed. That meant it was shedding more time, and that was *bad* when you had an hour, perhaps a lot less.

He took a step away from the door and the Procrastinator settled back into its routine clicking.

So . . .

Lu-Tze was out in the street and *he* had a spinner and that should have cut in automatically too. In this timeless world, he was going to be the only person who could turn a handle.

The glass that he had broken in his leap through the window had opened around the hole like a great sparkling flower. He reached out to touch a piece. It moved as though alive, cut his finger, and then dropped towards the ground, stopping only when it fell out of the field around his body.

Don't touch people, Lu-Tze had said. Don't touch arrows. Don't

208

touch things that were moving, that was the rule. But the glass—

—but the glass, in normal time, had been flying through the air. It'd still have that energy, wouldn't it?

He eased himself carefully around the glass, and opened the front door of the shop.

The wood moved very slowly, fighting against the enormous speed.

Lu-Tze was not in the street. But there was something new, hovering in the air just a few inches above the ground right where the old man had been. It had not been there before.

Someone with their *own* portable time had been here, and dropped this and moved on before it reached the ground.

It was a small glass jar, coloured blue by temporal effects. Now, how much energy could it have? Lobsang cupped his hand and gingerly brought it underneath and up, and there was a tingle and a sudden feeling of weight as the spinner's field claimed it.

Now its true colours came back. The jar was a milky pink or, rather, clear glass that looked pink because of the contents. The paper lid was covered with badly printed pictures of unbelievably flawless strawberries, surrounding some ornate lettering which read:

Ronald Soak, Hygienic Dairyman.

STRAWBERRY YOGHURT

'Fresh As The Morning Dew'

Soak? He *knew* the name! The man had delivered milk to the Guild! Good fresh milk, too, not the watery, green-tinted stuff the other dairies supplied. Very reliable, everyone said. But, reliable or not, he was just a milkman. All right, just a *very good* milkman, and if time had stopped, then why—

Lobsang looked around desperately. The people and carts that thronged the street were still there. No one had moved. No one *could* move.

But something *was* running along the gutter. It looked like a rat in a black robe, running along on its hind legs. It looked up at Lobsang, and he saw that it had a skull rather than a head. As skulls went, it was quite a cheerful one.

The word SQUEAK manifested itself inside his brain without bothering to go via his ears. Then the rat hopped onto the pavement and scampered down an alley.

Lobsang followed it.

A moment later someone behind him grabbed him by the neck. He went to break the lock, and realized how much he'd relied on slicing when he was fought. Besides, the person behind him had a very strong grip indeed.

'I just want to make sure you don't do anything silly,' it said. It was a female voice. 'What is this thing on your back?'

'Who are—?'

'The protocol in these matters,' said the voice, 'is that the person with the killer neck-grip asks the questions.'

'Er, it's a Procrastinator. Er, it stores time. Who—'

'Oh dear, there you go again. What is your name?'

'Lobsang. Lobsang Ludd. Look, could you wind me up, please? It's urgent.'

'Certainly. Lobsang Ludd, you are thoughtless and impulsive and deserve to die a stupid and pointless death.'

'What?'

'And you are also rather slow on the uptake. You are referring to this handle?'

'Yes. I'm running out of time. *Now* can I ask who you are?'

'Miss Susan. Hold still.'

He heard, behind him, the incredibly welcome sound of the Procrastinator's clockwork being rewound.

'Miss Susan?' he said.

'That's what most people I know call me. Now, I'm going to let you go. I will add that trying anything stupid will be counterproductive. Besides, I'm the only person in the world right now who might be inclined to twiddle your handle again.'

The pressure was released. Lobsang turned slowly.

Miss Susan was a slightly built young woman, dressed severely all in black. Her hair stood out around her head like an aura, white-blond with one black streak. But the most striking thing about her was . . . was everything, Lobsang realized, everything from her expression to the way she stood. Some people fade into the background. Miss Susan faded into the foreground. She stood out. Everything she stood in front of became nothing more than background.

'Finished?' she said. 'Seen everything?'

'Sorry. Have *you* seen an old man? Dressed a bit like me? With one of these on his back?'

'No. Now it's my turn. Have you got rhythm?'

'What?'

Susan rolled her eyes. 'All right. Do you have music?'

'Not on me, no!'

'And you certainly haven't got a girl,' said Susan. 'I saw Old Man Trouble go past a few minutes ago. It'd be a good idea if you don't bump into him, then.'

'And is *he* likely to have taken my friend?'

'I doubt it. And Old Man Trouble is more an "it" than a "he". Anyway, there's far worse than him around right now. Even the bogeymen have gone to ground.'

'Look, time has stopped, right?' said Lobsang.

'Yes.'

'So how can you be here talking to me?'

'I'm not what you might call a creature of time,' said Susan. 'I work in it, but I don't have to live there. There are a few of us about.'

'Like this Old Man Trouble you mentioned?'

'Right. And the Hogfather, the Tooth Fairy, the Sandman, people like that.'

'I thought they were mythical?'

'So?' Susan glanced out of the mouth of the alley again.

'And you're not?'

'I take it you didn't stop the clock,' said Miss Susan, looking up and down the street.

'No. I was . . . too late. Perhaps I shouldn't have gone back to help Lu-Tze.'

'I'm sorry? You were dashing to prevent the end of the world but you stopped to help some old man? You . . . *hero!*'

'Oh, I wouldn't say that I was a—' And then Lobsang stopped. She hadn't said 'You hero' in the tone of voice of 'You star'; it had been the tone in which people say 'You idiot.'

'I see a lot of your sort,' Susan went on. 'Heroes have a very strange grasp of elementary maths, you know. If you'd smashed the clock *before* it struck, everything would have been fine. Now the world has stopped and we've been invaded and we're probably all going to die, just because you stopped to help someone. I mean, very worthy and all that, but very, very . . . human.'

She used the word as if she meant it to mean 'silly'.

'You mean you need cool calculating bastards to save the world, do you?' said Lobsang.

'The cool calculation does help, I must admit,' said Susan. 'Now, shall we go and look at this clock?'

'Why? The damage is done now. If we smash it, it'll only make things worse. Besides, uh, the spinner started to run wild and I, er, I felt—'

'Cautious,' said Susan. 'Good. Caution is sensible. But there's something I want to check.'

Lobsang tried to pull himself together. This strange woman had the air of someone who knew exactly what she was doing – who knew exactly what *everyone* was doing – and, besides, what alternative did he have? Then he remembered the yoghurt pot.

'Does this mean anything?' he said. 'I'm certain it was dropped in the street after time stopped.'

She took the pot and examined it. 'Oh,' she said casually. 'Ronnie's been around, has he?'

'Ronnie?'

'Oh, we all know Ronnie.'

'What's that supposed to mean?'

'Let's just say if *he* found your friend then your friend is going to be okay. Probably okay. More okay than he would be if just about

212

anything else found him, at least. Look, this is not a time when you should be worrying about one person. Cold calculation, right?'

She stepped out into the street. Lobsang followed. Susan walked as if she owned the street. She scanned every alley and doorway, but not like a potential victim apprehensive of attackers. It seemed to Lobsang that she was disappointed to find nothing dangerous in the shadows.

She reached the shop, stepped inside, and paused for a moment to regard the floating flower of broken glass. Her expression suggested that she considered it to be a perfectly normal kind of thing to find, and had seen far more interesting things. Then she walked on and stopped at the inner door. There was still a glow from the crack, but it was dimmer now.

'Settling down,' she said. 'Shouldn't be too bad . . . but there's two people in here.'

'Who?'

'Wait, I'll open the door. And be careful.'

The door moved very slowly. Lobsang stepped into the workshop after the girl. The spinner began to speed up.

The clock glowed in the middle of the floor, painful to look at.

But he stared nevertheless. 'It's . . . it's just as I imagined it,' he said. 'It's the way to—'

'Don't go near it,' said Susan. 'It's uncertain death, believe me. *Do* pay attention.'

Lobsang blinked. The last couple of thoughts didn't seem to have belonged to him.

'What did you say?'

'I said it's uncertain death.'

'Is that worse than certain death?'

'Much. Watch.' Susan picked up a hammer that was lying on the floor and poked it gently towards the clock. It vibrated in her hand when she brought it closer, and she swore under her breath as it was dragged from her fingers and vanished. Just before it did there was a brief, contracting ring around the clock that might have been something like a hammer would be if you rolled it very flat and bent it into a circle.

'Have you any idea why that happened?' she said.

'No.'

'Nor have I. Now imagine that you were the hammer. Uncertain death, see?'

Lobsang looked at the two frozen people. One was medium-sized and had all the right number of appendages to qualify as a member of the human race, and so therefore probably had to be given the benefit of the doubt. It was staring at the clock. So was the other figure, which was that of a middle-aged, sheep-faced man still holding a cup of tea and, as far as Lobsang could make out, a biscuit.

'The one who wouldn't win a beauty contest even if he was the only entrant is an Igor,' said Susan. 'The other one is Dr Hopkins of the Clockmakers' Guild here.'

'So we know who built the clock, at least,' said Lobsang.

'I don't think so. Mr Hopkins's workshop is several streets away. And he makes novelty watches for a rather strange kind of discerning customer. It's his speciality.'

'Then the . . . Igor must've built it?'

'Good grief, no! Igors are professional servants. They never work for themselves.'

'You seem to know a lot,' said Lobsang, as Susan circled the clock like a wrestler trying to spy out a hold.

'Yes,' she said, without turning her head. 'I do. The first clock broke. This one's holding. Whoever designed it was a genius.'

'An evil genius?'

'It's hard to say. I can't see any signs.'

'What kind of signs?'

'Well, "Hahaha!!!!!" painted on the side would be a definite clue, don't you think?' she said, rolling her eyes.

'I'm in your way, am I?' said Lobsang.

'No, not at all,' said Susan, turning her attention to the workbench. 'Well, there's nothing here. I suppose he could have set a timer. A sort of alarm clock—'

She stopped. She picked up a length of rubber hosepipe that was coiled on a hook by the glass jars and looked hard at it. Then she tossed it into a corner and stared at it as if she had never seen anything like it before.

'Don't say a word,' she said quietly. 'They have some very acute senses. Just ease back among those big glass vats behind you and try to look inconspicuous. And do it Now.'

The last word had odd harmonics to it and Lobsang felt his legs begin to move almost without his conscious control.

The door moved a little and a man came in.

What was strange about the face, Lobsang thought afterwards, was how unmemorable it was. He'd never seen a face so lacking in anything to mention. It had a nose and mouth and eyes, and they were all quite flawless, but somehow they didn't make up a *face*. They were just parts that made no proper whole. If they became anything at all it was the face of a statue, good looking but without anything looking *out* of it.

Slowly, like someone who had to *think* about his muscles, the man turned to look at Lobsang.

Lobsang felt himself bunch up to slice time. The spinner groaned a warning on his back.

'That's about enough, I think,' said Susan, stepping forward. The man was spun around. An elbow was jabbed into his stomach and then the palm of her hand caught him so hard under his chin that he was lifted off the floor and slammed against the wall.

As he fell, Susan hit him on the head with a wrench.

'We might as well be going,' she said, as if she'd just shuffled some paper that had been untidy. 'Nothing more for us here.'

'You *killed* him!'

'Certainly. He's not a human being. I have . . . a sense about these things. It's sort of inherited. Besides, go and pick up the hose. Go on.'

Since she was still holding the wrench, Lobsang did so. Or tried to do so. The coil she'd flung into the corner was knotted and tangled like rubber spaghetti.

'Malignancy, my grandfather calls it,' said Susan. 'The local hostility of things towards non-things always increases when there's an Auditor about. They can't help it. The hosepipe test is very reliable in the field, according to a rat I know.'

Rat, thought Lobsang, but he *said*: 'What's an Auditor?'

'And they have no sense of colour. They don't understand it. Look how he's dressed. Grey suit, grey shirt, grey shoes, grey cravat, grey *everything*.'

'Er . . . er . . . perhaps it was just someone trying to be very cool?'

'You think so? No loss there, then,' said Susan. 'Anyway, you're wrong. Watch.'

The body was disintegrating. It was a fast and quite un-gory process, a sort of dry evaporation. It simply became floating dust, which expanded away and vanished. But the last few handfuls formed, just for a few seconds, a familiar shape. That too vanished, with the merest whisper of a scream.

'That was a *dhlang*!' he said. 'An evil spirit! The peasants down in the valleys hang up charms against them! But I thought they were just a superstition!'

'No, they're a substition,' said Susan. 'I mean they're real, but hardly anyone really believes in them. Mostly everyone believes in things that aren't real. Something very strange is going on. These things are all over the place, and they've got *bodies*. That's not right. We've got to find the person who built the clock—'

'And, er, what are *you*, Miss Susan?'

'Me? I'm . . . a schoolteacher.'

She followed his gaze to the wrench that she still held in her hand, and shrugged.

'It can get pretty rough at break time, can it?' said Lobsang.

There was an overpowering smell of milk.

Lu-Tze sat bolt upright.

It was a large room, and he had been placed on a table in the middle of it. By the feel of the surface, it was sheeted with metal. There were churns stacked along the wall, and big metal bowls ranged beside a sink the size of a bath.

216

Under the milk smell were many others – disinfectant, well-scrubbed wood and a distant odour of horses.

Footsteps approached. Lu-Tze lay back hurriedly and shut his eyes.

He heard someone enter the room. They were whistling under their breath, and they had to be a man, because no woman in Lu-Tze's long experience had ever whistled in that warbling, hissing way. The whistling approached the slab, stayed still for a moment, then turned away and headed for the sink. It was replaced by the sound of a pump handle being operated.

Lu-Tze half opened one eye.

The man standing at the sink was quite short, so that the standard-issue blue-and-white striped apron he wore almost reached the floor. He appeared to be washing bottles.

Lu-Tze swung his legs off the slab, moving with a stealthiness that made the average *ninja* sound like a brass band, and let his sandals gently touch the floor.

'Feeling better?' said the man, without turning his head.

'Oh, er, yes. Fine,' said Lu-Tze.

'I thought, here's a little bald monk sort of a fellow,' said the man, holding a bottle up to the light to inspect it. 'With a wind-up thing on his back, and down on his luck. Fancy a cup of tea? Kettle's on. I've got yak butter.'

'Yak? Am I still in Ankh-Morpork?' Lu-Tze looked down at a rack of ladles beside him. The man still hadn't looked round.

'Hmm. Interestin' question,' said the bottle-washer. 'You could say you're *sort* of in Ankh-Morpork. No to yak milk? I can get cow's milk, or goat, sheep, camel, llama, horse, cat, dog, dolphin, whale or alligator if you prefer.'

'What? Alligators don't give milk!' said Lu-Tze, grasping the biggest ladle. It made no noise as it came off its hook.

'I didn't say it was easy.'

The sweeper got a good grip. 'What is this place, friend?' he said.

'You are in . . . the dairy.'

The man at the sink said the last word as if it was as portentous as 'castle of dread', placed another bottle on the draining board, and, still with his back to Lu-Tze, held up a hand. All the fingers were folded except for the middle digit, which was extended.

'You know what this is, monk?' he said.

'It's not a friendly gesture, friend.' The ladle felt good and heavy. Lu-Tze had used much worse weapons than this.

'Oh, a superficial interpretation. You are an old man, monk. I can see the centuries on you. Tell me what this is, and know what I am.'

The coldness in the dairy got a little colder.

'It's your middle finger,' said Lu-Tze.

'Pah!' said the man.

'Pah?'

'Yes, pah! You have a brain. Use it.'

'Look, it was good of you to—'

'You know the secret wisdoms that everyone seeks, monk.' The bottle-washer paused. 'No, I even suspect that you know the explicit wisdoms, the ones hidden in plain view, which practically no one looks for. Who am I?'

Lu-Tze stared at the solitary finger. The walls of the dairy faded. The cold grew deeper.

His mind raced, and the librarian of memory took over.

This wasn't a normal place, that wasn't a normal man. A finger. One finger. One of the five digits on a— One of five. One of *Five*. Faint echoes of an ancient legend signalled his attention.

One from five is four.

And one left over.

Lu-Tze very carefully hung the ladle back on its hook.

'One from Five,' he said. 'The Fifth of Four.'

'There we are. I could see you were educated.'

'You were . . . you were the one who left before they became famous?'

'Yes.'

'But . . . this is a dairy, and you're washing bottles!'

'Well? I had to do something with my time.'

'But . . . you were the Fifth Horseman of the Apocalypse!' said Lu-Tze.

'And I bet you can't remember my name.'

Lu-Tze hesitated. 'No,' he said. 'I don't think I ever heard it.'

The Fifth Horseman turned round. His eyes were black. Completely black. Shiny, and black, and without any whites at all.

'My name,' said the Fifth Horseman, 'is . . .'

'Yes?'

'My name is Ronnie.'

Timelessness grew like ice. Waves froze on the sea. Birds were pinned to the air. The world went still.

But not quiet. There was a sound like a finger running around the rim of a very large glass.

'Come *on*,' said Susan.

'Can't you hear it?' said Lobsang, stopping.

'But it's no use to us—'

She pushed Lobsang back into the shadows. The robed grey shape of an Auditor appeared in the air halfway down the street, and began to spin. The air around it filled with dust, which became a whirling cylinder, which became, slightly unsteady on its feet, something that looked human.

It rocked backwards and forwards for a moment. It raised its hands slowly and looked at them, turning them this way and that. Then it marched away, purposefully. Further along the street it was joined by another one, emerging from an alley.

'This really isn't like them,' said Susan, as the pair turned a corner. 'They're up to something. Let's follow them.'

'What about Lu-Tze?'

'What about him? How old did you say he was?'

'He says he's eight hundred years old.'

'Hard to kill, then. Ronnie's safe enough if you're alert and don't argue. Come on.'

She set off along the streets.

The Auditors were joined by others, weaving between the silent carts and motionless people and along the street towards, as it turned out, Sator Square, one of the biggest open spaces in the city. It was market day. Silent, motionless figures thronged the stalls. But, amongst them, there were scurrying grey shapes.

219

'There's hundreds of them,' said Susan. 'All human-shaped, and it looks like they're having a meeting.'

Mr White was losing patience. Until now he had never been aware that he had any, because if anything he had been *all* patience. But now he could feel it evaporating. It was a strange, hot sensation in his head. And how could a thought be *hot*?

The mass of incarnated Auditors watched him nervously.

'I am Mr White!' he said, to the luckless new Auditor that had been brought before him, and shuddered with the astonishment of using that singular word and surviving. 'You *cannot* be Mr White also. It would be a matter of confusion.'

'But we are running out of colours,' said Mr Violet, intervening.

'That cannot be the case,' said Mr White. 'There is an infinite number of colours.'

'But there are not that many names,' said Miss Taupe.

'That is not possible. A colour must have a name.'

'We can find only one hundred and three names for green before the colour becomes noticeably either blue or yellow,' said Miss Crimson.

'But the shades are endless!'

'Nevertheless, the names are not.'

'This is a problem that must be solved. Add it to the list, Miss Brown. We must name every possible shade.'

One of the female Auditors looked startled. 'I cannot remember all the things,' she said. 'Nor do I understand why you are giving orders.'

'Apart from the renegade, I have the greatest seniority as an incarnate.'

'Only by a matter of seconds,' said Miss Brown.

'That is immaterial. Seniority is seniority. This is a fact.'

It was a fact. Auditors respected facts. And it was also a fact, Mr White knew, that there were now more than seven hundred Auditors walking rather awkwardly around the city.

Mr White had put a stop to the relentless increase in incarnations as more and more of his fellows rushed into the trouble spot. It was too dangerous. The renegade had demonstrated, he pointed out, that the human shape forced the mind to think in a certain troublesome way. The utmost caution was necessary. This was a fact. Only those with a proven ability to survive the process should be allowed to incarnate and complete the work. This was a fact.

Auditors respected facts. At least until now. Miss Brown took a step back.

'Nevertheless,' she said, 'being here is dangerous. It is my view that we should discarnate.'

Mr White found his body replying by itself. It let out a breath of air.

'And leave things unknown?' he said. 'Things that are unknown are dangerous. We are learning much.'

'What we are learning makes no sense,' said Miss Brown.

'The more we learn, the more sense it will make. There is nothing we cannot understand,' said Mr White.

'I do not understand why it is that I now perceive a desire to bring my hand in sharp contact with your face,' said Miss Brown.

'Exactly my point,' said Mr White. 'You do not understand it, and therefore it is dangerous. Perform the act, and we will know more.'

She hit him.

He raised his hand to his cheek.

'Unbidden thoughts of avoidance of repetition are engendered,' he said. 'Also heat. Remarkably, the body does indeed appear to do some thinking on its own behalf.'

'For my part,' said Miss Brown, 'the unbidden thoughts are of satisfaction coupled with apprehension.'

'Already we learn more about humans,' said Mr White.

'To what end?' said Miss Brown, whose sensations of apprehension were increasing at the sight of the contorted expression on Mr White's face. 'For our purposes, they are no longer a factor. Time has ended. They are fossils. The skin under one of your eyes is twitching.'

'You are guilty of inappropriate thought,' said Mr White. 'They exist. Therefore we must study them in every detail. I wish to try a further experiment. My eye is functioning perfectly.'

He took an axe from a market stall. Miss Brown took another step back.

'Unbidden thoughts of apprehension increase markedly,' she said.

'Yet this is a mere lump of metal on a piece of wood,' said Mr White, hefting the axe. 'We, who have seen the hearts of stars. We, who have watched worlds burn. We, who have seen space tormented. What is there about this axe that could cause concern to *us*?'

He swung. It was a clumsy blow and the human neck is a lot tougher than people believe, but Miss Brown's neck exploded into coloured motes and she collapsed.

Mr White looked around at the nearest Auditors, who all stepped back.

'Is there anyone else who wishes to try the experiment?' he said.

There was a chorus of hasty refusals.

'Good,' said Mr White. 'Already we are learning a great deal!'

'He chopped her head off!'

'Don't shout! And keep *your* head down!' Susan hissed.

'But he—'

'I think she knows! Anyway, it's an it. And so's it.'

'What's going on?'

Susan drew back into the shadows. 'I'm not . . . *entirely* sure,' she said, 'but I think they've tried to make themselves human bodies. Pretty good copies, too. And now . . . they're acting human.'

'Do you call *that* acting human?'

Susan gave Lobsang a sad look. 'You don't get out much, do you? My grandfather says that if an intelligent creature takes a human shape, it starts to *think* human. Form defines function.'

'That was the action of an intelligent creature?' said Lobsang, still shocked.

222

'Not only doesn't get out much, also doesn't read history,' said Susan glumly. 'Do you know about the curse of the werewolves?'

'Isn't being a werewolf curse enough?'

'They don't think so. But if they stay wolf-shaped for too long, they stay a wolf,' said Susan. 'A wolf is a very strong . . . form, you see? Even though the mind is human, the wolf creeps in through the nose and the ears and the paws. Know about witches?'

'We, er, stole the broomstick of one of them to get here,' said Lobsang.

'Really? Bit of luck for you that the world's ended, then,' said Susan. 'Anyway, some of the best witches have this trick they call Borrowing. They can get into the mind of an animal. Very useful. But the trick is to know when to pull out. Be a duck for too long and a duck you'll stay. A bright duck, maybe, with some odd memories, but still a duck.'

'The poet Hoha once dreamed he was a butterfly, and then he awoke and said, "Am I a man who dreamed he was a butterfly, or am I a butterfly dreaming he is a man?" ' said Lobsang, trying to join in.

'Really?' said Susan briskly. 'And which was he?'

'What? Well . . . who knows?'

'How did he write his poems?' said Susan.

'With a brush, of course.'

'He didn't flap around making information-rich patterns in the air or laying eggs on cabbage leaves?'

'No one ever mentioned it.'

'Then he was probably a man,' said Susan. 'Interesting, but it doesn't move us on a lot. Except you could say that the Auditors are dreaming that they're human, and the dream is real. And they've got no imagination. Just like my grandfather, really. They can create a perfect copy of anything, but they can't make anything that's *new*. So what I *think* is happening is that they're finding out what being human really means.'

'Which is?'

'That you're not as much in control as you think.' She took another careful look at the crowd in the square. 'Do you know anything about the person who built the clock?'

'Me? No. Well, not really . . .'

'Then how did you find the place?'

'Lu-Tze thought this was where the clock was being built.'

'Really? Not a bad guess. You even got the right house.'

'I, er, it was me that found the house. It, er, I knew that was where I should be. Does that sound silly?'

'Oh, yes. With twinkly bells and bluebirds on it. But it might be true. *I* always know where I should be, too. And where should you be now?'

'Just a minute,' said Lobsang. 'Who *are* you? Time has stopped, the world is given over to . . . fairy tales and monsters, and there's a *schoolteacher* walking around?'

'Best kind of person to have,' said Susan. 'We don't like silliness. Anyway, I told you. I've inherited certain talents.'

'Like living outside time?'

'That's one of them.'

'It's a weird talent for a schoolteacher!'

'Good for marking, though,' said Susan calmly.

'Are you actually human?'

'Hah! As human as you are. I won't say I haven't got a few skeletons in the family closet, though.'

There was something about the way she said it . . .

'That wasn't just a figure of speech, was it?' said Lobsang flatly.

'No, not really,' said Susan. 'That thing on your back. What happens when it stops spinning?'

'I'll run out of time, of course.'

'Ah. So the fact that it slowed down and stopped back there when that Auditor practised its axemanship isn't a factor, then?'

'It's not turning?' Panicking, Lobsang tried to reach round to the small of his back, spinning himself in the effort.

'It looks as though you have a hidden talent,' said Susan, leaning against the wall and grinning.

'Please! Wind me up again!'

'All right. You are a—'

'*That wasn't very funny the first time!*'

'That's all right, I don't have much of a sense of humour.'

She grabbed his arms as he wrestled with the straps of the spinner.

'You don't *need* it, understand?' she said. 'It's just a dead weight! Trust me! *Don't* give in! You're making your own time. Don't wonder how.'

He stared at her in terror. 'What's happening?'

'It's okay, it's *okay*,' said Susan, as patiently as she could. 'This sort of thing always comes as a shock. When it happened to me there wasn't anyone around, so consider yourself lucky.'

'What happened to you?'

'I found out who my grandfather *was*. And don't ask. Now, concentrate. Where ought you to be?'

'Uh, uh . . .' Lobsang looked around. 'Uh . . . over *that* way, I think.'

'I wouldn't dream of asking you how you know,' said Susan. 'And it's away from that mob.'

She smiled. 'Look on the bright side,' she added. 'We're young, we've got all the time in the world . . .' She swung the wrench onto her shoulder. 'Let's go clubbing.'

If there had been such a thing as time, it would have been a few minutes after Susan and Lobsang left that a small robed figure, about six inches high, strutted into the workshop. It was followed by a raven, which perched on the door and regarded the glowing clock with considerable suspicion.

'Looks dangerous to me,' it said.

SQUEAK? said the Death of Rats, advancing on the clock.

'No, don't you go trying to be a hero,' said Quoth.

The rat walked up to the base of the clock, stared up at it with a the-bigger-they-are-the-harder-they-fall expression, and then whacked it with its scythe.

Or, at least, tried to. There was a flash as the blade made contact. For a moment the Death of Rats was a ring-shaped, black-and-white blur around the clock, and then it vanished.

'Told yer,' said the raven, preening its feathers. 'I bet you feel like Mister Silly now, right?'

'. . . and then I thought, what's a job that really needs someone with my talents?' said Ronnie. 'To me, time is just another direction. And then I thought, everyone wants fresh milk, yes? And *everyone* wants it delivered early in the morning.'

'Got to be better than the window-cleaning,' said Lu-Tze.

'I only went into that after they invented windows,' said Ronnie. 'It was the jobbing gardening before that. More rancid yak butter in that?'

'Please,' said Lu-Tze, holding out his cup.

Lu-Tze was eight hundred years old, and that was why he was having a rest. A hero would have leapt up and rushed out into the silent city and then—

And there you had it. Then a hero would have had to wonder what to do next. Eight hundred years had taught Lu-Tze that what happens stays happened. It might stay happened in a different set of dimensions, if you wanted to get technical, but you couldn't make it un-happen. The clock had struck, and time had stopped. Later, a solution would present itself. In the meantime, a cup of tea and conversation with his serendipitous rescuer might speed that time. After all, Ronnie was not your average milkman.

Lu-Tze had long considered that everything happens for a reason, except possibly football.

'It's the real stuff you got there, Ronnie,' he said, taking a sip. 'The butter we're getting these days, you wouldn't grease a cart with it.'

'It's the breed,' said Ronnie. 'I go and get this from the highland herds six hundred years ago.'

'Cheers,' said Lu-Tze, raising his cup. 'Funny, though. I mean, if you said to people there were originally *five* Horsemen of the Apocalypse, and then one of them left and is a milkman, well, they'd be a bit surprised. They'd wonder about why you . . .'

For a moment Ronnie's eyes blazed silver.

'Creative differences,' he growled. 'The whole ego thing. Some people might say . . . No, I don't like to talk about it. I wish them all the luck in the world, of course.'

'Of course,' said Lu-Tze, keeping his expression opaque.

'And I've watched their careers with great interest.'

'I'm sure.'

'Do you know I even got written out of the official history?' said Ronnie. He held up a hand and a book appeared in it. It looked brand new.

'This was *before*,' he said sourly. 'Book of Om, Prophecies of Tobrun. Ever meet him? Tall man, beard, tendency to giggle at nothing?'

'Before my time, Ronnie.'

Ronnie handed the book over. 'First edition. Try Chapter 2, verse 7,' he said.

And Lu-Tze read: ' "And the Angel clothèd all in white opened the Iron Book, and a *fifth* rider appeared in a chariot of burning ice, and there was a snapping of laws and a breaking of bonds and the multitude cried 'Oh God, we're in trouble now!' " '

'That was me,' said Ronnie proudly.

Lu-Tze's eyes strayed to verse 8: ' "And I saw, sort of like rabbits, in many colours but basically a plaid pattern, kind of spinning around, and there was a sound as of like big syrupy things." '

'That verse got cut for the next edition,' said Ronnie. 'Very open to visions of all sorts, old Tobrun. The fathers of Omnianism could pick and mix what they wanted. Of course, in those days every-thing was new. Death was Death, *of course*, but the rest were really just Localized Crop Failure, Scuffles and Spots.'

'And you—?' Lu-Tze ventured.

'The public wasn't interested in me any more,' said Ronnie. 'Or so I was told. Back in those days we were only playing to very small crowds. One plague of locusts, some tribe's waterhole drying up, a volcano exploding . . . We were glad of any gig going. There wasn't room for five.' He sniffed. 'So I was told.'

Lu-Tze put down his cup. 'Well, Ronnie, it's been very nice talk-ing to you, but time's . . . time's not rushing, you see.'

'Yeah. Heard about that. The streets are full of the Law.' Ronnie's eyes blazed again.

'Law?'

'*Dhlang*. The Auditors. They've had the glass clock built again.'

'You *know* that?'

'Look, I might not be one of the Fearsome Four, but I do keep my eyes and ears open,' said Ronnie.

'But that's the end of the world!'

'No, it's not,' said Ronnie calmly. 'Everything's still here.'

'But it's not going anywhere!'

'Oh, well, that's not my problem, is it?' said Ronnie. 'I do milk and dairy products.'

Lu-Tze looked around the sparkling dairy, at the glistening bottles, at the gleaming churns. What a job for a timeless person. The milk would always be fresh.

He looked back at the bottles, and an unbidden thought rose in his mind.

The Horsemen were people-shaped, and people are vain. Knowing how to use other people's vanity was a martial art all in itself, and Lu-Tze had been doing it for a long time.

'I bet I can work out who you were,' he said. 'I bet I can work out your real name.'

'Hah. Not a chance, monk,' said Ronnie.

'Not a monk, just a sweeper,' said Lu-Tze calmly. 'Just a sweeper. You called them the Law, Ronnie. There's got to be a law, right? They make the rules, Ronnie. And you've got to have rules, isn't that true?'

'I do milk and milk products,' said Ronnie, but a muscle twitched under his eye. 'Also eggs by arrangement. It's a good steady business. I'm thinking of taking on more staff for the shop.'

'Why?' said Lu-Tze. 'There won't be anything for them to do.'

'And expand the cheese side,' said Ronnie, not looking at the sweeper. 'Big market for cheese. And I thought maybe I could get a c-mail address, people could send in orders, it could be a big market.'

'All the rules have won, Ronnie. Nothing moves any more. Nothing is unexpected because nothing happens.'

Ronnie sat staring at nothing.

'I can see you've found your niche, then, Ronnie,' said Lu-Tze soothingly. 'And you keep this place like a new pin, there's no doubt about it. I expect the rest of the lads'd be really pleased to know that you're, you know, getting on all right. Just one thing, uh . . . Why did you rescue me?'

'What? Well, it was my charitable duty—'

'You're the Fifth Horseman, Mr Soak. Charitable duty?' Except, Lu-Tze thought, you've been human-shaped a long time. You *want* me to find out . . . You *want* me to. Thousands of years of a life like this. It's curled you in on yourself. You'll fight me all the way, but you want me to drag your name out of you.

Ronnie's eyes glowed. 'I look after my own, Sweeper.'

'I'm one of yours, am I?'

'You have . . . certain worthwhile points.'

They stared at one another.

'I'll take you back to where I found you,' said Ronnie Soak. 'That's all. I don't do that other stuff any more.'

The Auditor lay on its back, mouth open. Occasionally it made a weak little noise, like the whimper of a gnat.

'Try again, Mr—'

'Dark Avocado, Mr White.'

'Is that a real colour?'

'Yes, Mr White!' said Mr Dark Avocado, who wasn't entirely sure that it was.

'Try again, then, Mr Dark Avocado.'

Mr Dark Avocado, with great reluctance, reached down towards the supine figure's mouth. His fingers were a few inches away when, apparently of its own volition, the figure's left hand moved in a blur and gripped them. There was a crackle of bone.

'I feel extreme pain, Mr White.'

'What is in its mouth, Mr Dark Avocado?'

'It appears to be cooked fermented grain product, Mr White. The extreme pain is continuing.'

'A foodstuff?'

'Yes, Mr White. The sensations of pain are really quite noticeable at this point.'

'Did I not give an order that there should be no eating or drinking or unnecessary experimentation with sensory apparatus?'

'Indeed you did, Mr White. The sensation known as extreme pain, which I mentioned previously, is now really quite acute. What shall I do now?'

The concept of 'orders' was yet another new and intensely unfamiliar one for any Auditor. They were used to decisions by committee, reached only when the possibilities of doing nothing whatsoever about the matter in question had been exhausted. Decisions made by everyone were decisions made by no one, which therefore precluded any possibility of blame.

But the *bodies* understood orders. This was clearly something that made humans human, and so the Auditors went along with it in a spirit of investigation. There was no choice, in any case. All kinds of sensations arose when they were given instructions by a man holding an edged weapon. It was surprising how smoothly the impulse to consult and discuss metamorphosed into a pressing desire to do what the weapon said.

'Can you not persuade him to let go of your hand?'

'He appears to be unconscious, Mr White. His eyes are bloodshot. He is making a little sighing noise. Yet the body seems determined that the bread should not be removed. Could I raise again the issue of the unbearable pain?'

Mr White signalled to two other Auditors. With considerable effort, they pried Mr Dark Avocado's fingers loose.

'This is something we will have to learn more about,' said Mr White. 'The renegade spoke of it. Mr Dark Avocado?'

'Yes, Mr White?'

'Do the sensations of pain persist?'

'My hand feels both hot and cold, Mr White.'

'How strange,' said Mr White. 'I see that we will need to investigate pain in greater depth.' Mr Dark Avocado found that a little voice in the back of his head screamed at the thought of this, while Mr White went on: 'What other foodstuffs are there?'

'We know the names of three thousand, seven hundred and nineteen foods,' said Mr Indigo-Violet, stepping forward. He had become the expert on such matters, and this was another new thing for the Auditors. They had never had experts before. What one knew, all knew. Knowing something that others did not know marked one as, in a small way, an individual. Individuals could die. But it also gave you power and value, which meant that you might *not* die quite so easily. It was a lot to deal with, and like some of the other Auditors he was already assembling a number of facial tics and twitches as his mind tried to cope.

'Name one,' said Mr White.

'Cheese,' said Mr Indigo-Violet smartly. 'It is rotted bovine lactation.'

'We will find some cheese,' said Mr White.

Three Auditors went past.

Susan peered out of a doorway. 'Are you *sure* we're going the right way?' she said. 'We're leaving the city centre.'

'This is the way I should be going,' said Lobsang.

'All right, but I don't like these narrow streets. I don't like *hiding*. I'm not a hiding kind of person.'

'Yes, I've noticed.'

'What's that place ahead?'

'That's the back of the Royal Art Museum. Broad Way's on the other side,' said Lobsang. 'And that's the way we need to go.'

'You know your way around for a man from the mountains.'

'I grew up here. I know five different ways to break into the museum, too. I used to be a thief.'

'I used to be able to walk through the walls,' said Susan. 'Can't seem to do it with time stopped. I think the power gets cancelled out somehow.'

'You could really walk through a solid wall?'

'Yes. It's a family tradition,' Susan snapped. 'Come on, let's go through the museum. At least no one moves about much in there at the best of times.'

Ankh-Morpork had not had a king for many centuries, but palaces tend to survive. A city might not need a king, but it can always use big rooms and some handy large walls, long after the monarchy is but a memory and the building is renamed the Glorious Memorial to the People's Industry.

Besides, although the last king of the city was no oil painting himself – especially when he'd been beheaded, after which no one looks their best, not even a short king – it was generally agreed that he had amassed some pretty good works of art. Even the common people of the city had a keen eye for works like Caravati's *Three Large Pink Women and One Piece of Gauze* or Mauvaise's *Man with Big Figleaf* and, besides, a city with a history the length of Ankh-Morpork's accumulated all kinds of artistic debris, and in order to prevent congestion in the streets it needed some sort of civic attic in which to store it. And thus, at little more cost than a few miles of plush red rope and a few old men in uniform to give directions to *Three Large Pink Women and One Piece of Gauze*, the Royal Art Museum was born.

Lobsang and Susan hurried through the silent halls. As with Fidgett's, it was hard to know if time had stopped here. Its passage was barely perceptible in any case. The monks at Oi Dong considered it a valuable resource.

Susan stopped and turned to look up at a huge, gilt-framed picture that occupied one whole wall of a lengthy corridor, and said, quietly: 'Oh . . .'

'What is it?'

'*The Battle of Ar-Gash*, by Blitzt,' said Susan.

Lobsang looked at the flaking, uncleaned paint and the yellow-brown varnish. The colours had faded to a dozen shades of mud, but something violent and evil shone through.

'Is that meant to be Hell?' he said.

'No, it was an ancient city in Klatch, thousands of years ago,' said Susan. 'But Grandfather did say that men made it Hell. Blitzt went mad when he painted it.'

'Er, he did good stormclouds, though,' said Lobsang, swallowing. 'Wonderful, er, light . . .'

'Look at what's coming out of the clouds,' said Susan.

Lobsang squinted into the crusted cumulus and fossilized lightning.

'Oh, yes. The Four Horsemen. You often get them in—'

'Count again,' said Susan.

Lobsang stared. 'There's two—'

'Don't be silly, there's fi—' she began, and then followed his gaze. He hadn't been interested in the art.

A couple of Auditors were hurrying away from them, towards the Porcelain Room.

'They're running away from us!' said Lobsang.

Susan grabbed his hand. 'Not exactly,' she said. 'They always consult! There have to be three of them to do that! And they'll be back, so come *on*!'

She grabbed his hand and towed him into the next gallery.

There were grey figures at the far end. The pair ran on, past dust-encrusted tapestries, and into another huge, ancient room.

'Ye gods, there's a picture of three huge pink women with only—' Lobsang began, as he was dragged past.

'Pay attention, will you? The way to the main door was back there! This place is *full* of Auditors!'

'But it's just an old art gallery! There's nothing for them here, is there?'

They slid to a stop on the marble slabs. A wide staircase led up to the next floor.

'We'll be trapped up there,' said Lobsang.

'There're balconies all round,' said Susan. 'Come on!' She dragged him up the stairs and through an archway. And stopped.

The galleries were several storeys high. On the first floor, visitors could look down on to the floor below. And, in the room below, the Auditors were very busy.

'What the hell are they doing *now*?' whispered Lobsang.

'I think,' said Susan grimly, 'that they are appreciating Art.'

Miss Tangerine was annoyed. Her body kept making strange demands of her, and the work with which she had been entrusted was going so very badly.

The frame of what once had been Sir Robert Cuspidor's *Waggon Stuck In River* was leaning against a wall in front of her. It was empty. The bare canvas was neatly rolled beside it. In front of the frame, carefully heaped in order of size, were piles of pigment.

Several dozen Auditors were breaking these down into their component molecules.

'Still nothing?' she said, striding along the line.

'No, Miss Tangerine. Only known molecules and atoms so far,' said an Auditor, its voice shaking slightly.

'Well, is it something to do with the proportions? The balance of molecules? The basic geometry?'

'We are continuing to—'

'Get on with it!'

The other Auditors in the gallery, clustered industriously in front of what had once been a painting and in fact still was, insofar as every single molecule was still present in the room, glanced up and then bent again to their tasks.

Miss Tangerine was getting even angrier because she couldn't work out why she was angry. One reason was probably that, when he gave her this task, Mr White had *looked* at her in a funny way. Being looked at was an unfamiliar experience for an Auditor in any case – no Auditor bothered to look at another Auditor very often because all Auditors looked the same – and neither were they used to the idea that you could say things with your face. Or even have a face. Or have a body that reacted in strange ways to the expression on another face belonging to, in this case, Mr White. When he looked at her like that she felt a terrible urge to claw his face off.

Which made absolutely no sense at all. No Auditor should feel like that about another Auditor. No Auditor should feel like that about *anything*. No Auditor should *feel*.

She *felt* livid. They'd all lost so many powers. It was ridiculous to have to communicate by flapping bits of your skin, and as for the tongue . . . *Yuerkkk* . . .

As far as she knew, in the whole life of the universe, no Auditor had ever experienced the sensation of *yuerkkk*. This wretched body was full of opportunities for *yuerkkk*. She could leave it at any time and yet, and yet . . . part of her didn't want to. There was this horrible desire, second by second, to hang on.

And she *felt* hungry. And that also made no sense. The stomach

234

was a bag for digesting food. It wasn't supposed to issue *commands*. The Auditors could survive quite well by exchanging molecules with their surroundings and making use of any local source of energy. That was a fact.

Try telling that to the stomach. She could feel it. It was sitting there, grumbling. She was being *harassed* by her internal organs. Why the . . . why the . . why had they copied internal organs? *Yuerkkk.*

It was all too much. She wanted to . . . she wanted to . . . express herself by shouting some, some, some terrible words . . .

'Discord! Confusion!'

The other Auditors looked around in terror.

But the words didn't work for Miss Tangerine. They just didn't have the same force that they used to. There had to be something worse. Ah, yes . . .

'Organs!' she shouted, pleased to have found it at last. 'And what are all you . . . organs looking at?' she added. 'Get on with it!'

'They're taking everything apart,' whispered Lobsang.

'That's the Auditors for you,' said Susan. 'They think that's how you find out about things. You know, I *loathe* them. I really do.'

Lobsang glanced sideways at her. The monastery was not a single-sex institution. That is to say, it *was*, but corporately it had never thought of itself like that because the possibility of females working there had never crossed even minds capable of thinking of sixteen dimensions. But the Thieves' Guild had recognized that girls were at least as good as boys in all areas of thieving – he had, for example, fond memories of his class-mate Steff, who could steal the small change out of your back pocket and climb better than an Assassin. He was at home around girls. But Susan scared the life out of him. It was as if some secret place inside her boiled with wrath, and with the Auditors she let it out.

He remembered her hitting that one with the wrench. There had been just a faint frown of concentration, as if she was making certain the job was done properly.

'Shall we go?' he ventured.

'Look at them,' continued Susan. 'Only an Auditor would take a picture apart to see what made it a work of art.'

'There's a big pile of white dust over there,' said Lobsang.

'*Man with Huge Figleaf*,' said Susan absently, her eyes still intent on the grey figures. 'They'd dismantle a clock to search for the tick.'

'How do you know it's *Man with Huge Figleaf*?'

'I just happen to remember where it is, that's all.'

'You, er, you appreciate art?' Lobsang ventured.

'I know what I like,' said Susan, still staring at the busy grey figures. 'And right now I'd like quite a lot of weaponry.'

'We'd better move—'

'The *bastards* get into your head if you let them,' said Susan, not moving. 'When you find yourself thinking "There ought to be a law" or "I don't make the rules, after all" or—'

'I really think we should leave,' said Lobsang carefully. 'And I think this because there are some of them coming up the stairs.'

Her head jerked around. 'What are you standing about for, then?' she said.

They ran through the next arch and into a gallery of pottery, turning to look only when they reached the far end. Three Auditors were following them. They weren't running, but there was something about their synchronized step that had a horrible we'll-keep-on-coming quality.

'All right, let's go this way—'

'No, let's go *this* way,' said Lobsang.

'That's not the way we need to go!' Susan snapped.

'No, but the sign up there says "Arms and Armour"!'

'So? Are you any good with weapons?'

'*No!*' said Lobsang proudly, and then realized she'd taken this the wrong way. 'You see, I've been taught to fight without—'

'Maybe there's a sword I can use,' Susan growled, and strode forward.

By the time the Auditors entered the gallery there were more than three of them. The grey crowd paused.

Susan had found a sword, part of a display of Agatean armour. It had been blunted by disuse, but anger flared along the blade.

'Should we keep running?' said Lobsang.

'No. They always catch up. I don't know if we can kill them here, but we can make them wish we could. You still haven't got a weapon?'

'No, because, you see, I've been trained to—'

'Just keep out of my way, then, okay?'

The Auditors advanced cautiously, which struck Lobsang as odd.

'We can't kill them?' said Lobsang.

'It depends on how alive they've let themselves become.'

'But they *look* scared,' he said.

'They're human-shaped,' said Susan over her shoulder. 'Human bodies. Perfect copies. Human bodies have had thousands and thousands of years of not wanting to be cut in half. That sort of leaks into the brain, don't you think?'

And then the Auditors were circling and moving in. Of course they would all attack at once. No one would want to be first.

Three made a grab at Lobsang.

He'd enjoyed the fighting, back in the training dojos. Of course, everyone was padded, and no one was actually trying to kill you, and that helped. But Lobsang had done well because he was good at slicing. He could always find that extra edge. And if you had that edge, you didn't need quite so much skill.

There was no edge here. There was no time to slice.

He adopted a mixture of *sna-fu* and *okidoki* and anything that worked, because you were dead if you treated a real fight like the dojo. The grey men were no contest, in any case. They just attempted to grab and hug. A granny would have been able to fend them off.

He sent two reeling and turned to the third, which was trying to grab him around the neck. He broke the hold, spun around ready to chop, and hesitated.

'Oh, good grief!' said a voice.

Susan's blade whirled past Lobsang's face.

The head in front of him was parted from its former body in a

237

shower not of blood but of coloured, floating dust. The body evaporated, became very briefly a grey-robed shape in the air, and vanished.

Lobsang heard a couple of thumps behind him, and then Susan grabbed his shoulder.

'You're not supposed to *hesitate*, you know!' she said.

'But it was a woman!'

'It was *not*! But it *was* the last one. Now let's go, before the rest get here.' She nodded at a second group of Auditors that were watching them very carefully from the end of the hall.

'They weren't much of a contest anyway,' said Lobsang, getting his breath. 'What are *those* doing?'

'Learning. Can you fight better than that?'

'Of course!'

'Good, because next time they'll be as good as you just were. Where to now?'

'Er, this way!'

The next gallery was full of stuffed animals. There'd been a vogue for it a few centuries before. These weren't the sad old hunting-trophy bears or geriatric tigers whose claws had faced a man armed with nothing more than five crossbows, twenty loaders and a hundred beaters. Some of *these* animals were arranged in groups. Quite small groups, of quite small animals.

There were frogs, seated around a tiny dining table. There were dogs, dressed in hunting jackets, in pursuit of a fox wearing a cap with feathers in it. There was a monkey playing a banjo.

'Oh, no, it's an entire band,' said Susan in tones of horrified astonishment. 'And just *look* at the little kittens dancing . . .'

'Horrible!'

'I wonder what happened when the man who did this met my grandfather.'

'Would he have met your grandfather?'

'Oh, yes,' said Susan. 'Oh, yes. And my grandfather is rather fond of cats.'

Lobsang paused at the foot of a staircase, half hidden behind a luckless elephant. A red rope, now hard as a bar, suggested that this wasn't part of the public museum. There was an added hint in the shape of a notice saying: 'Absolutely No Admittance'.

'I should be up there,' he said.

'Let's not hang around, then, eh?' said Susan, leaping over the rope.

The narrow stairs led up onto a large, bare landing. Boxes were stacked here and there.

'The attics,' said Susan. 'Hold on . . . What's that sign for?'

' "Keep left",' Lobsang read. 'Well, if they have to move heavy items around—'

'*Look* at the sign, will you?' said Susan. 'Don't see what you expect to see, see what's in front of you!'

Lobsang looked.

'What a stupid sign,' he said.

'Hmm. Interesting, certainly,' said Susan. 'Which way do *you*

think we should go? I don't think it'll take them too long to decide to follow us.'

'We're so close! Any passage might do!' said Lobsang.

'Any passage it is, then.' Susan headed for a narrow gap between packing cases.

Lobsang followed. 'What do you mean, decide?' he said, as they entered the gloom.

'The sign on the stairs said there was no admittance.'

'You mean they'll disobey it?' He stopped.

'Eventually. But they'll have a terrible feeling that they ought not to. They obey rules. They *are* the rules, in a way.'

'But you *can't* obey the Keep Left/Right sign, no matter what you do . . . oh, I see . . .'

'Isn't learning fun? Oh, and here's another one.'

DO NOT FEED THE ELEPHANT.

'Now that,' said Susan, 'is good. You can't obey it . . .'

'. . . because there's no elephant,' said Lobsang. 'I think I'm getting the hang of this . . .'

'It's an Auditor trap,' said Susan, peering at a packing case.

'Here's another good one,' said Lobsang.

IGNORE THIS SIGN.
By order

'Nice touch,' Susan agreed, 'but I'm wondering . . . who put up the signs?'

There were voices somewhere behind them. They were low, but then one was suddenly raised.

'—says Left but points Right! It has no sense!'

'The fault is yours! We disobeyed the first sign! Woe to them that stray onto the pathway of irregularity!'

'Don't you give me that, you organic thing! I raise my voice at you, you—'

There was a soft sound, a choking noise, and a scream that dopplered into nothing.

'Are they *fighting* one another?' said Lobsang.

'We can only hope so. Let's move,' said Susan. They crept on, weaving through the maze of spaces between the crates, and past a sign saying:

DUCK

'Ah . . . now we're getting metaphysical,' said Susan.

'Why duck?' said Lobsang.

'Why indeed?'

Somewhere amongst the cases a voice reached the end of its tether.

'What organic damn elephant? Where is the elephant?'

'There is no elephant!'

'How can there be a sign, then?'

'It is a—'

. . . and once again the little choke, and the vanishing scream. And then . . . running footsteps.

Susan and Lobsang backed into the shadows, and then Susan said, 'What *have* I put my foot in?'

She reached down and picked up the soft, sticky mess. And as she rose, she saw the Auditor come round the corner.

It was wild-eyed and frantic. It focused on the pair of them with difficulty, as if trying to remember who and what they were. But it was holding a sword, and holding it correctly.

A figure rose up behind it. One hand grabbed it by the hair and jerked its head back. The other was thrust over its open mouth.

The Auditor struggled for a moment, and then went rigid. And then disintegrated, tiny particles spinning away and disappearing into nothing.

For a moment the last few handfuls tried to form, in the air, the shape of a small cowled figure. Then it too was dragged apart, with a faint scream that was heard via the hairs on the back of the neck.

Susan glared at the figure in front of her. 'You're a . . . you can't be a . . . what *are* you?' she demanded.

The figure was silent. This might have been because thick cloth covered its nose and mouth. Heavy gloves encased its hands. And this was odd, because most of the rest of it was wearing a sequinned evening gown. And a mink stole. And a knapsack. And a huge picture hat with enough feathers to make three rare species totally extinct.

The figure rummaged in the knapsack, and then thrust out a piece of dark brown paper, as if proffering holy writ. Lobsang took it with care.

241

'It says here "Higgs & Meakins Luxury Assortment",' he said. 'Caramel Crunch, Hazelnut Surprise . . . They're chocolates?'

Susan opened her hand and looked at the crushed Strawberry Whirl she had picked up. She gave the figure a careful look.

'How did you know that would work?' she said.

'Please! You have nothing to fear from me,' said the muffled voice through the bandages. 'I'm down to the ones with the nuts in now, and they don't melt very quickly.'

'Sorry?' said Lobsang. 'You just killed an Auditor with a *chocolate*?'

'My last Orange Creme, yes. We are exposed here. Come with me.'

'An Auditor . . .' Susan breathed. 'You're an Auditor too. Aren't you? Why should I trust you?'

'There isn't anyone else.'

'But you are one of *them*,' said Susan. 'I can tell, even under all that . . that stuff!'

'I *was* one of them,' said Lady LeJean. 'Now I rather think I'm one of me.'

People were living in the attic. There was a whole family up there. Susan wondered if their presence was official or unofficial or one of those in-between states that were so common in Ankh-Morpork, where there was always a chronic housing shortage. So much of the city's life took place on the street because there was no room for it inside. Whole families were raised in shifts, so that the bed could be used for twenty-four hours a day. By the look of it, the caretakers and men who knew the way to Caravati's *Three Large Pink Women and One Piece of Gauze* had moved their families in to the rambling attics.

The rescuer had simply moved in on top of them. A family, or at least one shift of it, was seated on benches around a table, frozen in timelessness. Lady LeJean removed her hat, hung it on the mother and shook out her hair. Then she unwrapped the heavy bandages from her nose and mouth.

'We are relatively safe here,' she said. 'They are mostly in the main streets. Good . . . day. My name is Myria LeJean. I know who you are, Susan Sto Helit. I do not know the young man, which surprises me. I take it you are here to destroy the clock?'

'To stop it,' said Lobsang.

'Hold on, hold *on*,' said Susan. 'This makes no sense. Auditors hate everything about life. And you *are* an Auditor, aren't you?'

'I have no idea what I am,' sighed Lady LeJean. 'But right now I know that I am everything an Auditor should not be. We . . . they . . . we have to be stopped!'

'With chocolate?' said Susan.

'The sense of taste is new to us. Alien. We have no defences.'

'But . . . chocolate?'

'A dry biscuit almost killed me,' said her ladyship. 'Susan, can you imagine what it is like to experience taste for the first time? We built our bodies well. Oh, yes. Lots of tastebuds. Water is like wine. But chocolate . . . Even the mind stops. There is nothing but the taste.' She sighed. 'I imagine it is a wonderful way to die.'

'It doesn't seem to affect you,' said Susan suspiciously.

'The bandages and the gloves,' said Lady LeJean. 'Even then it is all I can do not to give in. Oh, where are my manners? Do sit down. Pull up a small child.'

Lobsang and Susan exchanged a glance. Lady LeJean noticed it.

'I said something wrong?' she said.

'We don't use people as furniture,' said Susan.

'But surely they will not be aware of it?' said her ladyship.

'*We* will,' said Lobsang. 'That's the point, really.'

'Ah. I have so much to learn. There is . . . there is so much *context* to being human, I am afraid. You, sir, can you stop the clock?'

'I don't know how to,' said Lobsang. 'But I . . . I think I *should* know. I'll try.'

'Would the clockmaker know? He is here.'

'*Where?*' said Susan.

'Just down the passage,' said Lady LeJean.

'You carried him here?'

'He was barely able to walk. He was hurt badly in the fight.'

'What?' said Lobsang. 'How could he walk at all? We're outside time!'

Susan took a deep breath. 'He carries his own time, just like you,' she said. 'He's your brother.'

And it was a lie. But he wasn't ready for the truth. By the look on his face, he wasn't even ready for the lie.

'Twins,' said Mrs Ogg. She picked up the brandy glass, looked at it, and put it down. 'There wasn't one. There was twins. Two boys. But . . .'

She turned on Susan a glare like a thermic lance. 'You'll be thinking, this is an old biddy of a midwife,' she said. 'You'll be thinking, what does she know?'

Susan paid her the courtesy of not lying. 'Part of me was,' she admitted.

'Good answer! Part *of us thinks all kinds of things,' said Mrs Ogg. 'Part of me is thinking, who's this haughty little miss who talks to me as if I was a kiddie of five? But most of me is thinking, she's got a heap of troubles of her own and has seen plenty of things a human shouldn't have to see. Mind you, part of me says, so have I. Seeing things a human shouldn't have to see makes us human. Well, miss . . . if you've any sense,* part *of you is thinking, there's a witch in front of me who's seen my granddad many times, when she's sat by a sickbed that's suddenly become a deathbed, and if she's ready to spit in his eye when the time comes then she could probably bother me considerably right now if she puts her mind to it. Understand? Let's all keep our parts to ourselves,' and suddenly she gave Susan a wink, 'as the High Priest said to the actress.'*

'I absolutely agree,' said Susan. 'Completely.'

'Right,' said Mrs Ogg. 'So . . . twins . . . well, it was her first time, and human wasn't exactly a familiar shape with her, I mean, you can't do what comes naturally when you ain't exactly natural and . . . twins ain't quite *the right word . . .'*

'A brother,' said Lobsang. 'The clockmaker?'

'Yes,' said Susan.

'But I was a foundling!'

'So was he.'

'I want to see him now!'

'That might not be a good idea,' said Susan.

'I am not interested in your opinion, thank you.' Lobsang turned to Lady LeJean. 'Down that passage?'

'Yes. But he's asleep. I think the clock upset his mind, and also he was hit in the fight. He says things in his sleep.'

'Says what?'

'The last thing I heard him say before I came to find you was, "We're so close. Any passage might do,"' said her ladyship. She looked from one to the other. 'Have I said the wrong thing?'

Susan put her hand over her eyes. Oh dear . . .

'*I* said that,' said Lobsang. 'Just after we came up the stairs.' He glared at Susan. 'Twins, right? I've heard about this sort of thing! What one thinks the other thinks too?'

Susan sighed. Sometimes, she thought, I really am a coward. 'Something like that, yes,' she said.

'I'm going to see him, then, even if he can't see me!'

Damn, thought Susan, and hurried after Lobsang as he headed along the passage. The Auditor trailed behind them, looking concerned.

Jeremy was lying on a bed, although it was no softer than anything else in the timeless world. Lobsang stopped, and stared.

'He looks . . . quite like me,' he said.

'Oh, yes,' said Susan.

'Thinner, perhaps.'

'Could be, yes.'

'Different . . . lines on his face.'

'You've led different lives,' said Susan.

'How did you know about him and me?'

'My grandfather takes, er, an interest in this sort of thing. I found out some more by myself, too,' she said.

'Why should we interest anyone? We're not special.'

'This is going to be quite hard to explain.' Susan looked round at Lady LeJean. 'How safe are we here?'

'The signs upset them,' said her ladyship. 'They tend to keep away. I . . . shall we say? . . . took care of the ones who followed you.'

245

'Then you'd better sit down, Mr Lobsang,' said Susan. 'It might help if I told you about me.'

'Well?'

'My grandfather is Death.'

'That's a strange thing to say. Death is just the end of life. It's not a . . . a person—'

'PAY ATTENTION TO ME WHEN I AM TALKING TO YOU . . .'

A wind whipped around the room, and the light changed. Shadows formed on Susan's face. A faint blue light outlined her.

Lobsang swallowed.

The light faded. The shadows vanished.

'There is a process called death, and there is a person called Death,' said Susan. 'That is how it works. And I am Death's grand-daughter. Am I going too fast for you?'

'Er, no, although right up until just now you looked human,' said Lobsang.

'My parents were human. There's more than one kind of genetics.' Susan paused. 'You look human, too. Human is a very popular look in these parts. You'd be amazed.'

'Except that I *am* human.'

Susan gave a little smile that, on anyone less obviously in full control of themselves, might have seemed slightly nervous.

'Yes,' she said. 'And, then again, no.'

'No?'

'Take War, now,' said Susan, backing away from the point. 'Big man, hearty laugh, tends to fart after meals. As human as the next man, you say. But the next man is Death. He's human-shaped, too. And that's because humans invented the idea of . . . of . . . of *ideas*, and they think in human shapes—'

'Get back to the "and, then again, no", will you?'

'Your mother is Time.'

'No one knows who my mother is!'

'I could take you to the midwife,' said Susan. 'Your father found the best there's ever been. She delivered you. Your mother was Time.'

Lobsang sat with his mouth open.

'It was easier for me,' said Susan. 'When I was very small my parents used to let me visit my grandfather. I thought every grandfather had a long black robe and rode a pale horse. And then they decided that maybe that wasn't the right environment for a child. They were worried about how I was going to grow up!' She laughed mirthlessly. 'I had a very strange education, you know? Maths, logic, that sort of thing. And then, when I was a bit younger than you, a rat turned up in my room and suddenly everything I thought I knew was wrong.'

'I'm a human! I do human things! I'd *know* if—'

'You had to live in the world. Otherwise, how could you learn to be human?' said Susan, as kindly as she could.

'And my brother? What about *him*?'

Here it comes, Susan thought. 'He's not your brother,' she said. 'I lied a bit. I'm sorry.'

'But you said—'

'I had to lead up to it,' said Susan. 'It's one of those things you have to get hold of a bit at a time, I'm afraid. He's not your brother. He's you.'

'Then who am I?'

Susan sighed. 'You. Both of you . . . are you.'

'And there I was, and there she was,' said Mrs Ogg, 'and out the baby came, no problem there, but that's always a tryin' moment for the new mum, and there was . . .' she paused, her eyes peering through the windows of memory, 'like . . . like a feelin' that the world had stuttered, and I was holdin' the baby and I looked down and there was me deliverin' a baby, and I looked at me, and I looked at me, and I remember saying, "This is a fine to-do, Mrs Ogg," and she, who was me, said, "You never said a truer word, Mrs Ogg," and then it all went strange and there I was, just one of me, holdin' two babies.'

'Twins,' Susan said.

'You could call them twins, yes, I s'pose you could,' said Mrs Ogg. 'But I always thought that twins is two little souls born once, not one born twice.'

Susan waited. Mrs Ogg looked in the mood to talk.

'So I said to the man, I said, "What now?" and he said, "Is that any

business of yours?" and I said he could be damn sure it was my business and he could look me in the eye and I'd speak my mind to anyone. But I was thinking, you're in trouble now, Mrs Ogg, 'cos it'd all gone myffic.'

'Mythic?' said schoolteacher Susan.

'Yep. With extra myff. And you can get into big trouble, with myffic. But the man just smiled and said that he must be brought up human until he's of age and I thought, yep, it's gone myffic all right. I could see he hadn't got a clue about what to do next and it was all going to be down to me.'

Mrs Ogg took a suck at her pipe and her eyes twinkled at Susan through the smoke. 'I don't know how much experience you have with this sort of thing, my girl, but sometimes when the high and mighty make big plans they don't always think about the fine detail, right?'

Yes. I'm a fine detail, Susan thought. One day Death took it into his skull to adopt a motherless child, and I'm a fine detail. She nodded.

'I thought, how does this go, in a myffic kind of way?' Mrs Ogg went on. 'I mean, technic'ly I could see we're in that area where the prince gets brought up as a swineherd until he manifests his destiny, but there's not that many swineherding jobs around these days, and poking hogs with a stick is not all it's cracked up to be, believe you me. So I said, well, I'd heard the Guilds down in the big cities took in foundlings out of charity, and looked after them well enough, and there's many well set-up men and women who started life that way. There's no shame in it, plus, if the destiny doesn't manifest as per schedule, he'd have set his hands to a good trade, which would be a consolation. Whereas swineherding's just swineherding. You're giving me a stern look, miss.'

'Well, yes. It was rather a chilly decision, wasn't it?'

'Someone has to make 'em,' said Mrs Ogg sharply. 'Besides, I've been around for some time and I've noticed that them as has it in them to shine will shine through six layers of muck, whereas those who ain't shiny won't shine however much you buff 'em. You may think otherwise, but it was me standing there.'

She investigated the bowl of her pipe with a matchstick.

Eventually she went on: 'And that was it. I would have stayed, of course, because there wasn't so much as a crib in the place, but the man took me aside and said thank you and that it was time to go. And why would I

248

argue? There was love there. It was in the air. But I won't say that I don't sometimes wonder how it all turned out. I really do.'

There were differences, Susan had to admit. Two different lives had indeed burned their unique tracks on the faces. And the selves had been born a second or so apart, and a lot of the universe can change in a second.

Think of identical twins, she told herself. But they are two different selves occupying bodies that, at least, start out identical. They don't start out as identical *selves*.

'He looks *quite* like me,' said Lobsang, and Susan blinked. She leaned closer to the unconscious form of Jeremy.

'Say that again,' she said.

'I said, he looks quite like me,' said Lobsang.

Susan glanced at Lady LeJean, who said, 'I saw it too, Susan.'

'Who saw what?' said Lobsang. 'What are you hiding from me?'

'His lips move when you speak,' said Susan. 'They try to form the same words.'

'He can pick up my thoughts?'

'It's more complicated than that, I think.' Susan picked up a limp hand and gently pinched the web of skin between thumb and forefinger.

Lobsang winced, and glanced at his own hand. A patch of white skin was reddening again.

'Not just thoughts,' said Susan. 'This close, you feel his pain. Your speech controls his lips.'

Lobsang stared down at Jeremy.

'Then what will happen,' he said slowly, 'when he comes round?'

'I'm wondering the same thing,' said Susan. 'Perhaps you shouldn't be here.'

'But this is where I have to be!'

'We at least should not stay here,' said Lady LeJean. 'I know my kind. They will have been discussing what to do. The signs will not hold them for ever. And I have run out of soft centres.'

'What are you supposed to *do* when you are where you're supposed to *be*?' said Susan.

Lobsang reached down and touched Jeremy's hand with his fingertip.

The world went white.

Susan wondered later if this was what it would be like at the heart of a star. It wouldn't be yellow, you wouldn't see fire, there would just be the searing whiteness of every overloaded sense screaming all at once.

It faded, gradually, into a mist. The walls of the room appeared, but she could see through them. There were other walls beyond, and other rooms, transparent as ice and visible only at the corners and where the light caught them. In each one another Susan was turning to look at her.

The rooms went on for ever.

Susan was sensible. It was, she knew, a major character flaw. It did not make you popular, or cheerful, and – this seemed to her to be the most unfair bit – it didn't even make you *right*. But it did make you definite, and she was definite that what was happening around her was not, in any accepted sense, real.

That was not in itself a problem. Most of the things humans busied themselves with weren't real, either. But sometimes the mind of the most sensible person encountered something so big, so complex, so alien to all understanding, that it told itself little stories about it instead. Then, when it felt it understood the story, it felt it understood the huge incomprehensible thing. And this, Susan knew, was her mind telling itself a story.

There was a sound like great heavy metal doors slamming, one after another, getting louder and faster . . .

The universe reached a decision.

The other glass rooms vanished. The walls clouded. Colour rose, pastel at first, then darkening as timeless reality flowed back.

The bed was empty. Lobsang had gone. But the air was full of slivers of blue light, turning and swirling like ribbons in a storm.

Susan remembered to breathe again. 'Oh,' she said aloud. 'Destiny.'

She turned. The bedraggled Lady LeJean was still staring at the empty bed.

'Is there another way out of here?'

'There's an elevator at the end of the corridor, Susan, but what happened to—?'

'Not Susan,' said Susan sharply. 'It's *Miss* Susan. I'm only Susan to my friends, and you are not one of them. I don't trust you at all.'

'I don't trust me either,' said Lady LeJean meekly. 'Does that help?'

'Show me this elevator, will you?'

It turned out to be nothing more than a large box the size of a small room, which hung from a web of ropes and pulleys in the ceiling. It had been installed recently, by the look of it, to move the large works of art around. Sliding doors occupied most of one wall.

'There are capstans in the cellar for winching it up,' said Lady LeJean. 'Downward journeys are slowed safely because of a mechanism by which the weight of the descending elevator causes water to be pumped up into rainwater cisterns on the roof, which in turn can be released back into a hollow counterweight that assists in the elevation of heavier items of—'

'Thank you,' said Susan quickly. 'But what it really needs in order to descend is *time*.' Under her breath she added, 'Can you help?'

The ribbons of blue light orbited her, like puppies anxious to play, and then drifted towards the elevator.

'However,' she added, 'I believe Time is on our side now.'

Miss Tangerine was amazed at how fast a body learned.

Until now, Auditors had learned by counting. Sooner or later, everything came down to numbers. If you knew all the numbers, you knew everything. Often the 'later' was a *lot* later, but that did not matter because for an Auditor time was just another number. But a brain, a few soggy pounds of gristle, counted numbers so fast that they stopped being numbers at all. She'd been astonished at how easily it could direct a hand to catch a ball in the air, calculating future positions of hand and ball without her even being aware of it.

The senses seemed to operate and present her with conclusions before *she* had time to think.

At the moment she was trying to explain to other Auditors that not feeding an elephant when there was no elephant not to feed was not in fact impossible. Miss Tangerine was one of the faster-learning Auditors and had already formulated a group of things, events and situations that she categorized as 'bloody stupid'. Things that were 'bloody stupid' could be dismissed.

Some of the others were having difficulty understanding this, but now she stopped in mid-harangue when she heard the rumble of the elevator.

'Do we have anyone upstairs?' she demanded.

The Auditors around her shook their heads. 'IGNORE THIS NOTICE' had produced too much confusion.

'Then someone is coming down!' said Miss Tangerine. 'They are out of place! They must be stopped!'

'We must discuss—' an Auditor began.

'Do what I say, you organic organ!'

'It's a matter of personalities,' said Lady LeJean, as Susan pushed open a door in the roof and stepped out onto the leads.

'Yes?' said Susan, looking around at the silent city. 'I thought you didn't have them.'

'They will have them now,' said Lady LeJean, climbing out behind her. 'And personalities define themselves in terms of other personalities.'

Susan, prowling along the parapet, considered this strange sentence.

'You mean there will be flaming rows?' she said.

'Yes. We have never had egos before.'

'Well, *you* seem to be managing.'

'Only by becoming completely and utterly insane,' said her ladyship.

Susan turned. Lady LeJean's hat and dress had become even

more tattered, and she was shedding sequins. And then there was the matter of the face. An exquisite mask on a bone structure like fine china had been made up by a clown. Probably a blind clown. And one who was wearing boxing gloves. In a fog. Lady LeJean looked at the world through panda eyes and her lipstick touched her mouth only by accident.

'You don't *look* insane,' lied Susan. 'As such.'

'Thank you. But sanity is defined by the majority, I am afraid. Do you know the saying "The whole is greater than the sum of the parts"?'

'Of course.' Susan scanned the rooftops for a way down. She did not need this. The . . . thing seemed to want to talk. Or, rather, to chatter aimlessly.

'It is an insane statement. It is a nonsense. But now I believe that it is true.'

'Good. That elevator should be getting down about . . . now.'

Slivers of blue light, like trout slipping through a stream, danced around the elevator door.

The Auditors gathered. They had been learning. Many of them had acquired weapons. And a number of them had taken care not to communicate to the others that gripping something offensive in the hand seemed a very *natural* thing to do. It spoke to something right down in the back of the brain.

It was therefore unfortunate that when a couple of them pulled open the elevator door it was to reveal, slightly melting in the middle of the floor, a cherry liqueur chocolate.

The scent *wafted*.

There was only one survivor and, when Miss Tangerine ate the chocolate, there wasn't even that.

'One of life's little certainties,' said Susan, standing on the edge of the museum's parapet, 'is that there is generally a last chocolate hidden in all those empty wrappers.'

Then she reached down and grabbed the top of a drainpipe.

She wasn't certain how this would work. If she fell . . . but would she fall? There was no *time* to fall. She had her own personal time. In theory, if anything so definite as a theory existed in a case like this, that meant she could just drift down to the ground. But the time to test a theory like that was when you had no other choice. A theory was just an idea, but a drainpipe was a fact.

The blue light flickered around her hands.

'Lobsang?' she said quietly. 'It *is* you, isn't it?'

That name is as good as any for us. The voice was as faint as a breath.

'This may seem a stupid question, but where are you?'

We are just a memory. And I am weak.

'Oh.' Susan slid a little further.

But I will grow strong. Get to the clock.

'What's the point? There was nothing we could do!'

Times have changed.

Susan reached the ground. Lady LeJean followed, moving clumsily. Her evening dress had acquired several more tears.

'Can I offer a fashion tip?' said Susan.

'It would be welcomed,' said her ladyship politely.

'Long cerise bloomers with that dress? Not a good idea.'

'No? They are very colourful, and quite warm. What should I have chosen instead?'

'With that cut? Practically nothing.'

'That would have been acceptable?'

'Er . . .' Susan blanched at unfolding the complex laws of lingerie to someone who wasn't even, she felt, anybody. 'To anyone likely to find out, yes,' she finished. 'It would take too long to explain.'

Lady LeJean sighed. 'All of it does,' she said. 'Even clothing. Skin-substitutes to preserve body heat? So simple. So easy to say. But there are so many rules and exceptions, impossible to understand.'

Susan looked along Broad Way. It was thick with silent traffic, but there was no sign of an Auditor.

'We'll run into more of them,' she said aloud.

'Yes. There will be hundreds, at least,' said Lady LeJean.

'Why?'

'Because we have always wondered what life is like.'

'Then let's get up into Zephire Street,' said Susan.

'What is there for us?'

'Wienrich and Boettcher.'

'Who are they?'

'I think the original Herr Wienrich and Frau Boettcher died a long time ago. But the shop still does very good business,' said Susan, darting across the street. 'We need ammunition.'

Lady LeJean caught up. 'Oh. They make chocolate?' she said.

'Does a bear poo in the woods?' said Susan, and realized her mistake straight away.*

Too late. Lady LeJean looked thoughtful for a moment.

'Yes,' she said at last. 'Yes, I believe that most varieties do indeed excrete as you suggest, at least in the temperate zones, but there are several that—'

'I meant to say that, yes, they make chocolate,' said Susan.

Vanity, vanity, thought Lu-Tze, as the milk cart rattled through the silent city. Ronnie would have been like a god, and people of that stripe don't like hiding. Not *really* hiding. They like to leave a little clue, some emerald tablet somewhere, some code in some tomb under the desert, something to say to the keen researcher: I was here, and I was great.

What else had the first people been afraid of? Night, maybe. Cold. Bears. Winter. Stars. The endless sky. Spiders. Snakes. One another. People had been afraid of so many things.

He reached into his pack for the battered copy of the Way, and opened it at random.

Koan 97: 'Do unto otters as you would have them do unto you.' Hmm. No real help there. Besides, he'd occasionally been unsure that he'd written that one down properly, although it certainly had worked. He'd always left aquatic mammals well alone, and they had done the same to him.

He tried again.

---

* Teaching small children for any length of time can do this to a vocabulary.

Koan 124: 'It's amazing what you see if you keep your eyes open.'

'What's the book, monk?' said Ronnie.

'Oh, just . . . a little book,' said Lu-Tze. He looked around.

The cart was passing a funeral parlour. The owner had invested in a large plate-glass window, even though the professional under-taker does not, in truth, have that much to sell that looks good in a window and they usually make do with dark, sombre drapes and perhaps a tasteful urn.

And the name of the Fifth Horseman.

'Hah!' said Lu-Tze quietly.

'Something funny, monk?'

'Obvious, when you think about it,' said Lu-Tze, as much to him-self as to Ronnie. Then he turned in his seat and stuck out his hand.

'Pleased to meet you,' he said. 'Let me guess your name.'

And said it.

Susan had been unusually inexact. To call Wienrich and Boettcher 'chocolate makers' was like calling Leonard of Quirm 'a decent painter who also tinkered with things', or Death 'not someone you'd want to meet every day'. It was accurate, but it didn't tell the whole story.

For one thing, they didn't make, they *created*. There's an important difference.* And, while their select little shop sold the results, it didn't do anything so crass as to fill the window with them. That would suggest . . . well, over-eagerness. Generally, W&B had a display of silk and velvet drapes with, on a small stand, perhaps one of their special pralines or no more than three of their renowned frosted caramels. There was no price tag. If you had to ask the price of W&B's chocolates, you couldn't afford them. And if you'd tasted one, and still couldn't afford them, you'd save and scrimp and rob and sell elderly members of your family for just one more of those mouthfuls that fell in love with your tongue and turned your soul to whipped cream.

---

* Up to ten dollars a pound, usually.

There was a discreet drain in the pavement in case people standing in front of the window drooled too much.

Wienrich and Boettcher were, naturally, foreigners, and according to Ankh-Morpork's Guild of Confectioners they did not understand the peculiarities of the city's tastebuds.

Ankh-Morpork people, said the Guild, were hearty, no-nonsense folk who did not *want* chocolate that was stuffed with cocoa liquor, and were certainly not like effete la-di-dah foreigners who wanted cream in everything. In fact they actually *preferred* chocolate made mostly from milk, sugar, suet, hooves, lips, miscellaneous squeezings, rat droppings, plaster, flies, tallow, bits of tree, hair, lint, spiders and powdered cocoa husks. This meant that according to the food standards of the great chocolate centres in Borogravia and Quirm, Ankh-Morpork chocolate was formally classed as 'cheese' and only escaped, through being the wrong colour, being defined as 'tile grout'.

Susan allowed herself one of their cheaper boxes per month. And she could easily stop at the first layer if she wanted to.

'You needn't come in,' she said, as she opened the shop door. Rigid customers lined the counter.

'Please call me Myria.'

'I don't think I—'

'Please?' said Lady LeJean meekly. 'A name is important.'

Suddenly, in spite of everything, Susan felt a brief pang of sympathy for the creature.

'Oh, very *well*. Myria, you needn't come in.'

'I can stand it.'

'But I thought chocolate was a raging temptation?' said Susan, being firm with herself.

'It is.'

They stared up at the shelves behind the counter.

'Myria . . . Myria,' said Susan, speaking only some of her thoughts aloud. 'From the Ephebian word *myrios*, meaning "innumerable". And LeJean as a crude pun of "legion" . . . Oh dear.'

'We thought a name should say what a thing is,' said her ladyship. 'And there is safety in numbers. I am sorry.'

'Well, these are their basic assortments,' said Susan, dismissing the shop display with a wave of her hand. 'Let's try the back room— Are you all right?'

'I am fine, I am fine . . .' murmured Lady LeJean, swaying.

'You're not going to pig out on me, are you?'

'We . . . I . . . know about will-power. The body craves the chocolate but the mind does not. At least, so I tell myself. And it must be true! The mind can overrule the body! Otherwise, what is it for?'

'I've often wondered,' said Susan, pushing open another door. 'Ah. The magician's cave . . .'

'Magic? They use magic here?'

'Nearly right.'

Lady LeJean leaned on the door frame for support when she saw the tables.

'Oh,' she said. 'Uh . . . I can detect . . . sugar, milk, butter, cream, vanilla, hazelnuts, almonds, walnuts, raisins, orange peel, various liqueurs, citrus pectin, strawberries, raspberries, essence of violets, cherries, pineapples, pistachios, oranges, limes, lemons, coffee, cocoa—'

'Nothing there to be frightened of, right?' said Susan, surveying the workshop for useful weaponry. 'Cocoa is just a rather bitter bean, after all.'

'Yes, but . . .' Lady LeJean clenched her fists, shut her eyes and bared her teeth, 'put them all together and they make—'

'Steady, steady . . .'

'The will can overrule the emotions, the will can overrule the instincts—' the Auditor intoned.

'Good, good, now just work your way up to the bit where it says chocolate, okay?'

'That's the hard one!'

In fact it seemed to Susan, as she walked past the vats and counters, that chocolate lost some of its attraction when you saw it like this. It was the difference between seeing the little heaps of pigment and seeing the whole picture. She selected a syringe that seemed designed to do something intensely personal to female elephants, athough she decided that here it was probably used for doing the wiggly bits of decoration.

And over *here* was a small vat of cocoa liquor.

She stared around at the trays and trays of fondant cremes, marzipans and caramels. Oh, and here was an entire table of Soul Cake eggs. But they weren't the hollow-shelled, cardboard tasting presents for children, oh, no – these were the confectionery equivalent of fine, intricate jewellery.

Out of the corner of her eye she saw movement. One of the statue-like workers bent over her tray of Praline Dreams was shifting almost imperceptibly.

Time was flowing into the room. Pale blue light glinted in the air.

She turned and saw a vaguely human figure hovering beside her. It was featureless and as transparent as mist, but in her head it said, *I'm stronger. You are my anchor, my link to this world. Can you guess how hard it is to find it again in so many? Get me to the clock . . .*

Susan turned and thrust the icing syringe into the arms of the groaning Myria. 'Grab that. And make some kind of . . . of sling or something. I want you to be carrying as many of those chocolate eggs as possible. And the cremes. And the liqueurs. Understand? You can do it!'

Oh, gods, there was no alternative. The poor thing needed some kind of morale boost. '*Please*, Myria? And that's a stupid name! You're not many, you're one. Okay? Just be . . . yourself. Unity . . . that'd be a *good* name.'

The new Unity raised a mascara-streaked face. 'Yes, it is, it's a good name . . .'

Susan snatched as much merchandise as she could carry, aware of some rustling behind her, and turned to find Unity standing to attention holding, by the look of it, a bench-worth of assorted confectionery in . . .

. . . a sort of big cerise sack.

'Oh. Good. Intelligent use of the materials to hand,' said Susan weakly. Then the teacher within her cut in and added, 'I hope you brought enough for *everybody*.'

*

259

'You were the first,' said Lu-Tze. 'You basically *created* the whole business. Innovative, you were.'

'That was then,' said Ronnie Soak. 'It's all changed now.'

'Not like it used to be,' agreed Lu-Tze.

'Take Death,' said Ronnie Soak. 'Impressive, I'll grant you, and who doesn't look good in black? But, after all, Death . . . What's death?'

'Just a big sleep,' said Lu-Tze.

'Just a big sleep,' said Ronnie Soak. 'As for the others . . . War? If war's so bad, why do people keep doing it?'

'Practically a hobby,' said Lu-Tze. He began to roll himself a cigarette.

'Practically a hobby,' said Ronnie Soak. 'As for Famine and Pestilence, well . . .'

'Enough said,' said Lu-Tze sympathetically.

'Exactly. I mean, Famine's a fearful thing, obviously—'

'—in an agricultural community, but you've got to move with the times,' said Lu-Tze, putting the roll-up in his mouth.

'That's it,' said Ronnie. 'You've got to move with the times. I mean, does your average city person fear famine?'

'No, he thinks food grows in shops,' said Lu-Tze. He was beginning to enjoy this. He had eight hundred years' worth of experience in steering the thoughts of his superiors, and most of them had been *intelligent*. He decided to strike out a little.

'Fire, now: city folk really fear fire,' he said. '*That*'s new. Your primitive villager, he reckoned fire was a good thing, didn't he? Kept the wolves away. If it burned down his hut, well, logs and turf are cheap enough. But now he lives in a street of crowded wooden houses and everyone's cooking in their rooms, well—'

Ronnie glared.

'Fire? *Fire?* Just a demi-god! Some little tea-leaf pinches the flame from the gods and suddenly he's immortal? You call that training and experience?' A spark leapt from Ronnie's fingers and ignited the end of Lu-Tze's cigarette. 'And as for gods—'

'Johnny-come-latelys, the pack of 'em,' said Lu-Tze quickly.

'Right! People started worshipping them because they were afraid of me,' said Ronnie. 'Did you know that?'

'No, really?' said Lu-Tze innocently.

But now Ronnie sagged. 'That was then, of course,' he said. 'It's different now. I'm not what I used to be.'

'No, no, obviously not, no,' said Lu-Tze soothingly. 'But it's all a matter of how you look at it, am I correct? Now, supposing a man— that is to say a—'

'Anthropomorphic personification,' said Ronnie Soak. 'But I've always preferred the term "avatar".'

Lu-Tze's brow wrinkled. 'You fly around a lot?' he said.

'That would be aviator.'

'Sorry. Well, supposing an avatar, thank you, who was perhaps a bit ahead of his time thousands of years ago, well, supposing he took a good look around now, he might just find the world is ready for him again.'

Lu-Tze waited. 'My abbot, now, he reckons you are the bees' knees,' he said, for a little reinforcement.

'Does he?' said Ronnie Soak suspiciously.

'Bee's knees, cat's pyjamas and dog's . . . elbows,' Lu-Tze finished. 'He's written scrolls and scrolls about you. Says you are hugely important in understanding how the universe works.'

'Yeah, but . . . he's just one man,' said Ronnie Soak, with all the sullen reluctance of someone cuddling a lifetime's huge snit like a favourite soft toy.

'Technically, yes,' said Lu-Tze. 'But he's an abbot. And brainy? He thinks such big thoughts he needs a second lifetime just to finish them off! Let a lot of peasants fear famine, I say, but someone like you should aim for *quality*. And you look at the cities, now. Back in the old days there were just heaps of mud bricks with names like Ur and Uh and Ugg. These days there's *millions* of people living in cities. Very, very complicated cities. Just you think about what they really, *really* fear. And fear . . . Well, fear *is* belief. Hmm?'

There was another long pause.

'Well, all right, but . . .' Ronnie began.

'Of course, they won't be living in 'em very long, because by the time the grey people have finished taking them to pieces to see how they work there won't be any belief *left*.'

261

'My customers do depend on me . . .' Ronnie Soak mumbled.

'What customers? That's Soak speaking,' said Lu-Tze. 'That's not the voice of Kaos.'

'Hah!' said Kaos bitterly. 'You haven't told me yet how you worked that one out.'

Because I've got more than three brain cells and you're vain and you painted your actual name back to front on your cart whether you knew it or not and a dark window is a mirror and K and S are still recognizable in a reflection even when they're back to front, thought Lu-Tze. But that wasn't a good way forward.

'It was just obvious,' he said. 'You sort of shine through. It's like putting a sheet over an elephant. You might not be able to *see* it, but you're sure the elephant's still there.'

Kaos looked wretched. 'I don't know,' he said. 'It's been a long time—'

'Oh? And I thought you said you were Number One?' said Lu-Tze, deciding on a new approach. 'Sorry! Still, I suppose it's not your fault you've lost a few skills over the centuries, what with one thing and—'

'Lost skills?' snapped Kaos, waving a finger under the sweeper's nose. 'I could certainly take *you* to the cleaner's, you little maggot!'

'What with? A dangerous yoghurt?' said Lu-Tze, climbing off the cart.

Kaos leapt down after him. 'Where do you get off, talking to me like that?' he demanded.

Lu-Tze glanced up. 'Corner of Merchant and Broad Way,' he said. 'So what?'

Kaos roared. He tore off his striped apron and his white cap. He seemed to grow in size. Darkness evaporated off him like smoke.

Lu-Tze folded his hands and grinned. 'Remember Rule One,' he said.

'Rules? Rules? I'm Kaos!'

'Who was the first?' said Lu-Tze.

'Yes!'

'Creator and Destroyer?'

'Damn right!'

'Apparently complicated, apparently patternless behaviour that nevertheless has a simple, deterministic explanation and is a key to new levels of understanding of the multidimensional universe?'

'You'd better believe it— What?'

'Got to move with the times, mister, got to keep up!' shouted Lu-Tze excitedly, hopping from foot to foot. 'You're what people think you are! And they've changed you! I hope you're good at sums!'

'You can't tell *me* what to *be*!' Kaos roared. 'I'm Kaos!'

'You don't think so? Well, your big comeback ain't gonna happen now that the Auditors have taken over! The *rules*, mister! That's what they are! They're the cold dead *rules*!'

Silver lightning flickered in the walking cloud that had once been Ronnie. Then cloud, cart and horse vanished.

'Well, could have been worse, I suppose,' said Lu-Tze to himself. 'Not a very bright lad, really. Possibly a bit too old-fashioned.'

He turned round and found a crowd of Auditors watching him. There were dozens of them.

He sighed and grinned his sheepish little grin. He'd had just about enough for one day.

'Well, I expect *you* have heard of Rule One, right?' he said.

That seemed to give them pause. One said, 'We know millions of rules, human.'

'Billions. Trillions,' said another.

'Well, you can't attack *me*,' said Lu-Tze, ''cos of Rule One.'

The nearest Auditors went into a huddle.

'It must involve gravitation.'

'No, quantum effects. Obviously.'

'Logically there cannot be a Rule One because at that point there would be no concept of plurality.'

'But if there is not a Rule One, can there be any other rules? If there is no Rule One, where is Rule Two?'

'There are millions of rules! They cannot fail to be numbered!'

Wonderful, thought Lu-Tze. All I have to do is wait until their heads melt.

But an Auditor stepped forward. It looked more wild-eyed than the others, and was much more unkempt. It was also carrying an axe.

'We do not have to discuss this!' it snapped. 'We must think: This is nonsense, we will not discuss it!'

'But what is Rule—' an Auditor began.

'You will call me Mr White!'

'Mr White, what *is* Rule One?'

'I am not glad you asked that question!' screamed Mr White, and swung the axe. The body of the other Auditor crumbled in around the blade, dissolving into floating motes that dispersed in a fine cloud.

'Anyone *else* got any questions?' said Mr White, raising the axe again.

One or two Auditors, not yet entirely in tune with current developments, opened their mouths to speak. And shut them again.

Lu-Tze took a few steps back. He prided himself on an incredibly well-honed ability to talk his way in or out of anything, but that rather depended on a passably sane entity being involved at the other end of the dialogue.

Mr White turned to Lu-Tze. 'What are you doing out of your place, organic?'

But Lu-Tze was overhearing another, whispered conversation. It was coming from the other side of a nearby wall, and it went like this:

'*Who cares about the damn wording!*'

'*Accuracy is important, Susan. There is a precise description on the little map inside the lid. Look.*'

'*And you think that will impress anyone?*'

'*Please. Things should be done properly.*'

'*Oh, give it to me, then!*'

Mr White advanced on Lu-Tze, axe raised. 'It is forbidden to—' he began.

'*Eat . . . Oh, good grief . . . Eat . . . "a delicious fondant sugar creme infused with delightfully rich and creamy raspberry filling wrapped in mysterious dark chocolate" . . . you grey bastards!*'

264

A shower of small objects pattered down on the street. Several of them broke open.

Lu-Tze heard a whine or, rather, the silence caused by the absence of a whine he'd grown used to.

'Oh, no, I'm winding dow . . .'

Trailing smoke, but looking more like a milkman again, albeit one that'd just delivered to a blazing house, Ronnie Soak stormed into his dairy.

'Who does he think he is?' he muttered, gripping the spotless edge of a counter so hard that the metal bent. 'Hah, oh yes, they just toss you aside, but when they want you to make a comeback—'

Under his fingers the metal went white hot and then dripped.

'I've got customers. I've got customers. People depend on me. It might not be a glamorous job, but people will always need milk—'

He clapped a hand to his forehead. Where the molten metal touched his skin the metal evaporated.

The headache was really *bad*.

He could remember the time when there was only him. It was *hard* to remember, because . . . there *was* nothing, no colour, no sound, no pressure, no time, no spin, no light, no life . . .

Just Kaos.

And the thought arose: Do I want that again? The perfect order that goes with changelessness?

More thoughts were following that one, like little silvery eels in his mind. He was, after all, a Horseman, and had been ever since the time the people in mud cities on baking plains put together some hazy idea of Something that had existed before anyone else. And a Horseman picks up the noises of the world. The mud-city people and the skin-tent people, they'd known instinctively that the world swirled perilously through a complex and uncaring multiverse, that life was lived a mirror's thickness from the cold of space and the gulfs of night. They knew that everything they called reality, the web of rules that made life happen, was a bubble on the tide. They *feared* old Kaos. But now—

He opened his eyes and looked down at his dark, smoking hands. To the world in general, he said, 'Who am I now?'

Lu-Tze *heard* his voice speed up from nothing: '—wn . . .'

'No, you're wound up again,' said a young woman in front of him. She stood back, giving him a critical look. Lu-Tze, for the first time in eight hundred years, felt that he'd been caught doing something wrong. It was that kind of expression – searching, rummaging around inside his head.

'You'll be Lu-Tze, then,' said Susan. 'I'm Susan Sto Helit. No time for explanations. You've been out for . . . well, not for long. We have to get Lobsang to the glass clock. Are you any good? Lobsang thinks you're a bit of a fraud.'

'Only a bit? I'm surprised.' Lu-Tze looked around. 'What happened here?'

The street was empty, except for the ever-present statues. But scraps of silver paper and coloured wrappers littered the ground, and across the wall behind him was a long splash of what looked very much like chocolate icing.

'Some of them got away,' said Susan, picking up what Lu-Tze could only hope was a giant icing syringe. 'Mostly they fought with one another. Would *you* try to tear someone apart just for a coffee creme?'

Lu-Tze looked into those eyes. After eight hundred years you learn how to read people. And Susan was a story that went back a very long way. She probably even knew about Rule One, and didn't care. This was someone to treat with respect. But you couldn't let even someone like her have it all their own way.

'The kind with a coffee bean on the top, or the ordinary kind?' he said.

'The kind without the coffee bean, I think,' said Susan, holding his gaze.

'Nnn–o. No. No, I don't think I would,' said Lu-Tze.

'But they are learning,' said a woman's voice behind the sweeper. 'Some resisted. We *can* learn. That's how humans became humans.'

266

Lu-Tze regarded the speaker. She looked like a society lady who had just had a really bad day in a threshing machine.

'Can I just be clear here?' he said, staring from one woman to the other. 'You've been fighting the grey people with *chocolate*?'

'Yes,' said Susan, peering round the corner. 'It's the sensory explosion. They lose control of their morphic field. Can you throw at all? Good. Unity, give him as many chocolate eggs as he can carry. The secret is to get them to land hard so that there's lots of shrapnel—'

'And where *is* Lobsang?' said Lu-Tze.

'Him? You could say he's with us in spirit.'

There were blue sparkles in the air.

'Growing pains, I think,' Susan added.

Centuries of experience once again came to Lu-Tze's aid.

'He always looked like a lad who needed to find himself,' he said.

'Yes,' said Susan. 'And it came as a bit of a shock. Let's go.'

Death looked down at the world. Timelessness had reached the Rim now, and was expanding into the universe at the speed of light. The Discworld was a sculpture in crystal.

Not *an* apocalypse. There had always been plenty of those – small apocalypses, not the full shilling at all, fake apocalypses: apocryphal apocalypses. Most of them had been back in the old days, when the world as in 'end of the world' was often objectively no wider than a few villages and a clearing in the forest.

And those little worlds had ended. But there had always been *somewhere else*. There had been the horizon, to start with. The fleeing refugees would find that the world was bigger than they'd thought. A few villages in a clearing? Hah, how could they have been so stupid! *Now* they knew it was a whole island! Of course, there was that horizon again . . .

The world had run out of horizons.

As Death watched, the sun stopped in its orbit and its light became duller, redder.

He sighed, and nudged Binky. The horse stepped forward, in a direction that could not be found on any map.

And the sky was full of grey shapes. There was a ripple in the ranks of Auditors as the Pale Horse trotted forward.

One drifted towards Death and hung in the air a few feet away.

It said, *Should you not be riding out?*

DO YOU SPEAK FOR ALL?

You know the custom, said the voice in Death's mind. *Among us, one speaks for all.*

WHAT IS BEING DONE IS WRONG.

It is not your business.

NEVERTHELESS, WE ARE ALL ANSWERABLE.

The universe will last for ever, said the voice. *Everything preserved, ordered, understood, lawful, filed . . . changeless. A perfect world. Finished.*

NO.

It will all end one day in any case.

BUT THIS IS TOO SOON. THERE IS *UNFINISHED* BUSINESS.

And that is—?

EVERYTHING.

And, with a flash of light, a figure clothèd all in white appeared, holding a book in one hand.

It looked from Death to the endlessly massing ranks of the Auditors, and said: 'Sorry? Is this the right place?'

Two Auditors were measuring the number of atoms in a paving slab.

They looked up at a movement.

'Good afternoon,' said Lu-Tze. 'May I draw your attention to the notice my assistant is holding up?'

Susan held up the sign. It read: Mouths Must Be Open. By Order.

And Lu-Tze unfolded his hands. There was a caramel in each one, and he was a good shot.

The mouths shut. The faces went impassive. Then there was a sound somewhere between a purr and a wail, which disappeared into the ultrasonic. And then . . . the Auditors dissolved, gently, first going fuzzy around the edges and, as the process accelerated, swiftly becoming a spreading cloud.

'Hand-to-mouth fighting,' said Lu-Tze. 'Why doesn't it happen to humans?'

'It nearly does,' said Susan, and when they stared at her she blinked and said, 'To stupid, indulgent humans, anyway.'

'*You* don't have to concentrate to stay the same shape,' said Unity. 'And that was the last of the caramels, by the way.'

'No, there's six in one of W&B's Gold Selections,' said Susan. 'Three have got white chocolate cream in dark chocolate and three have got whipped cream in milk chocolate. They're the ones in the silver wrapp— Look, I just happen to *know* things, all right? Let's keep going, okay? Without mentioning chocolate.'

You have no power over us, said the Auditor. *We are not alive.*

BUT YOU ARE DEMONSTRATING ARROGANCE, PRIDE AND STUPIDITY. THESE ARE EMOTIONS. I WOULD SAY THEY ARE SIGNS OF LIFE.

'Excuse me?' said the shining figure in white.

But you are all alone *here!*

'Excuse *me*?'

YES? said Death. WHAT IS IT?

'This is *the* Apocalypse, yes?' said the shining figure petulantly.

WE ARE *TALKING*.

'Yes, right, but *is* it the Apocalypse? The actual end of the actual whole world?'

No, said the Auditor.

YES, said Death. IT IS.

'Great!' said the figure.

What? said the Auditor.

WHAT? said Death.

The figure looked embarrassed. 'Well, not great, *obviously*. Obviously not *great*, as such. But it's what I'm here for. It's what I'm *for*, really.' It held up the book. 'Er, I've got the place marked ready. Wow! It's been, you know, so long . . .'

Death glanced at the book. The cover and all the pages were made of iron. Realization dawned.

YOU ARE THE ANGEL CLOTHED ALL IN WHITE OF THE IRON BOOK FROM THE PROPHECIES OF TOBRUN, AM I CORRECT?

'That's right!' The pages clanged as the angel hurriedly thumbed through them. 'And it's clothèd, by the way, if you don't mind.

Clo-*theddd*. Just a detail, I know, but I like to get it right.'

What is happening here? the Auditor growled.

I DON'T KNOW HOW TO TELL YOU THIS, said Death, ignoring the interruption. BUT YOU ARE NOT OFFICIAL.

The pages stopped clanking. 'What do you mean?' said the angel suspiciously.

THE BOOK OF TOBRUN HAS NOT BEEN CONSIDERED OFFICIAL CHURCH DOGMA FOR A HUNDRED YEARS. THE PROPHET BRUTHA REVEALED THAT THE WHOLE CHAPTER WAS A METAPHOR FOR A POWER STRUGGLE WITHIN THE EARLY CHURCH. IT IS NOT INCLUDED IN THE REVISED VERSION OF THE BOOK OF OM, AS DETERMINED BY THE CONVOCATION OF EE.

'Not at all?'

I'M SORRY.

'I've been thrown out? Just like the damn rabbits and the big syrupy things?'

YES.

'Even the bit where I blow the trumpet?'

OH, YES.

'You sure?'

ALWAYS.

'But you are Death and this is the Apocalypse, right?' said the angel, looking wretched. 'So therefore—'

UNFORTUNATELY, HOWEVER, YOU ARE NO LONGER A FORMAL PART OF THE PROCEEDINGS.

Out of the corner of his mind, Death was observing the Auditor. Auditors always listened when people spoke. The more people spoke, the closer to consensus every decision came, and the less responsibility anyone had. But the Auditor was showing signs of impatience and annoyance . . .

Emotions. And emotions made you *alive*. Death knew how to deal with the living.

The angel looked around at the universe. 'Then what am *I* supposed to *do*?' he wailed. 'This is what I've been waiting for! For thousands of years!' He stared at the iron book. 'Thousands of dull, boring, wasted years . . .' he mumbled.

Have you quite finished? said the Auditor.

270

'One big scene. That's all I had. That was my *purpose*. You wait, you practise – and then you're just edited out because brimstone is no longer a fashionable colour?' Anger was infusing the bitterness in the angel's voice. 'No one told *me*, of course . . .'

He glared at the rusted pages. 'It ought to be Pestilence next,' he muttered.

'Am I late, then?' said a voice in the night.

A horse walked forward. It gleamed unhealthily, like a gangrenous wound just before the barber-surgeon would be called in with his hacksaw for a quick trim.

I THOUGHT YOU WEREN'T COMING, said Death.

'I didn't want to,' Pestilence oozed, 'but humans do get such interesting diseases. I'd rather like to see how weasles turn out, too.' One crusted eye winked at Death.

'You mean measles?' said the angel.

'Weasles, I'm afraid,' said Pestilence. 'People are getting really careless with this bio-artificing. We're talking boils that really *bite*.'

Two of you will not suffice! snarled the Auditor in their heads.

A horse walked out of the darkness. Some toast racks had more flesh.

'I've been thinking,' said a voice. 'Maybe there are things worth putting up a fight for.'

'And they are—?' said Pestilence, looking round.

'Salad-cream sandwiches. You just can't beat them. That tang of permitted emulsifiers? Marvellous.'

'Hah! You're Famine, then?' said the Angel of the Iron Book. It fumbled with the heavy pages again.

What, what, what is this nonsense of 'salad cream'?* shouted the Auditor.

Anger, thought Death. A *powerful* emotion.

'Do I like salad cream?' said a voice in the dark.

A second, female voice replied: 'No, dear, it gives you hives.'

The horse of War was huge and red and the heads of dead

---

* If you live in a country where the tradition calls for mayonnaise, just don't ask. Just don't.

warriors hung from the saddle horn. And Mrs War was hanging on to War, grimly.

'All four. Bingo!' said the Angel of the Iron Book. 'So much for the Convocation of Ee!'

War had a woolly scarf round his neck. He looked sheepishly at the other Horsemen.

'He's not to strain himself,' said Mrs War sharply. 'And you're not to let him do anything dangerous. He's not as strong as he thinks. And he gets confused.'

So, the gang is all here, said the Auditor.

Smugness, Death noticed. And self-satisfaction.

There was a clanging as of metal pages. The Angel of the Iron Book was looking puzzled.

'Actually, I don't think that's entirely correct,' it said.

No one paid it any attention.

Off you go on your little pantomime, said the Auditor.

And now irony and sarcasm, thought Death. They must be picking it up from the ones down in the world. All the little things that go to make up a . . . *personality.*

He looked along the row of Horsemen. They caught his eye, and there were almost imperceptible nods from Famine and Pestilence.

War turned in the saddle and spoke to his wife. 'Right now, dear, I'm not confused at all. Could you get down, please?'

'Remember what happened when—' Mrs War began.

'*Right now*, please, my dear,' said War, and this time his voice, which was still calm and polite, had echoes of steel and bronze.

'Er . . . oh.' Mrs War was suddenly flustered. 'That was just how you used to talk when—' She stopped, blushed happily for a moment, and slid off the horse.

War nodded at Death.

And now you must all go and bring terror and destruction and so on and so forth, said the Auditor. *Correct?*

Death nodded. Floating in the air above him, the Angel of the Iron Book slammed the pages back and forth in an effort to find his place.

EXACTLY. ONLY, WHILE IT IS TRUE WE HAVE TO RIDE OUT, Death added, drawing his sword, IT DOESN'T SAY ANYWHERE AGAINST *WHOM*.

Your meaning? hissed the Auditor, but now there was a flicker of fear. Things were happening that it didn't understand.

Death grinned. In order to fear, you had to be a *me*. Don't let anything happen to *me*. That was the song of fear.

'He means,' said War, 'that he asked us all to think about whose side we're really on.'

Four swords were drawn, blazing along their edges like flame. Four horses charged.

The Angel of the Iron Book looked down at Mrs War.

'Excuse me,' he said, 'but do you have a pencil?'

Susan peered round the corner into Artificers Street, and groaned.

'It's full of them . . . and I think they've gone mad.'

Unity took a look. 'No. They have not gone mad. They are being Auditors. They are taking measurements, assessing and standardizing where necessary.'

'They're taking up the paving slabs now!'

'Yes. I suspect it is because they are the wrong size. We do not like irregularities.'

'What the hell is the wrong size for a slab of rock?'

'Any size that is not the average size. I'm sorry.'

The air around Susan flashed blue. She was very briefly aware of a human shape, transparent, spinning gently, which vanished again.

But a voice in her ear, *in* her ear said: *Nearly strong enough. Can you get to the end of the street?*

'Yes. Are you sure? You couldn't do anything to the clock before!'

Before, I was not me.

A movement in the air made Susan look up. The lightning bolt that had stood rigid over the dead city had gone. The clouds were rolling like ink poured into water. There were flashes within them, sulphurous yellows and reds.

The Four Horsemen are fighting the other Auditors, Lobsang supplied.

'Are they winning?'

Lobsang did not answer.

'I said—'

It's hard for me to say. I can see ... everything. Everything that could be ...

Kaos listened to history.

There were new words. Wizards and philosophers had found Chaos, which is Kaos with his hair combed and a tie on, and had found in the epitome of disorder a new order undreamed of. *There are different kinds of rules. From the simple comes the complex, and from the complex comes a different kind of simplicity. Chaos is order in a mask ...*

Chaos. Not dark, ancient Kaos, left behind by the evolving universe, but new, shiny Chaos, dancing in the heart of everything. The idea was strangely attractive. And it was a reason to go on living.

Ronnie Soak adjusted his cap. Oh, yes ... there was one last thing.

The milk was always lovely and fresh. Everyone remarked on that. Of course, being *everywhere* at seven in the morning was no trouble to him. If even the Hogfather could climb down every chimney in the world in one night, doing a milk round for most of a city in one second was hardly a major achievement.

Keeping things cool *was*, however. But there he had been lucky.

Mr Soak walked into the ice room, where his breath turned to fog in the frigid air. Churns were stacked across the floor, sparkling on the outside. Vats of butter and cream were piled on shelves that glistened with ice. Rack after rack of eggs were just visible through the frost. He'd been planning to add the ice-cream business in the summer. It was such an obvious step. Besides, he needed to use up the cold.

A stove was burning in the middle of the floor. Mr Soak always bought good coal from the dwarfs, and the iron plates were glowing red. The room, one felt, ought to be an oven, but there was a gentle sizzling on the stove as frost battled with the heat. With the stove roaring, the room was merely an ice-box. Without the stove . . .

Ronnie opened the door of a white-rimed cupboard and smashed at the ice within with his fist. Then he reached inside.

What emerged, crackling with blue flame, was a sword.

It was a work of art, the sword. It had imaginary velocity, negative energy and positive cold, cold so cold that it met heat coming the other way and took on something of its nature. *Burning* cold. There had never been anything as cold as this since before the universe began. In fact, it seemed to Chaos, *everything* since then had been merely lukewarm.

'Well, I'm back,' he said.

The Fifth Horseman rode out, and a faint smell of cheese followed him.

Unity looked at the other two, and at the blue glow that still hovered around the group. They had taken cover behind a fruit barrow.

'If I may make a suggestion,' she said, 'it is that w— that Auditors are not good with surprises. The impulse is always to consult. And the assumption is always that there will be a plan.'

'So?' said Susan.

'I suggest total madness. I suggest you and . . . and the . . . young man run for the shop, and I will attract the attention of the Auditors. I believe this old man should assist me because he will die soon in any case.'

There was silence.

'Accurate yet unnecessary,' said Lu-Tze.

'That was not good etiquette?' she said.

'It could have been better. However, is it not written, "When you have got to go, you have got to go"?' said Lu-Tze. 'And also that, "You should always wear clean underwear because you never know if you will be knocked down by a cart"?'

'Will it help?' said Unity, looking very puzzled.

'That is one of the great mysteries of the Way,' said Lu-Tze, nodding sagely. 'What chocolate do we have left?'

'We're down to the nougat now,' said Unity. 'And I believe nougat is a terrible thing to cover with chocolate, where it can ambush the unsuspecting. Susan?'

Susan was peering up the street. 'Mmm?'

'Do you have any chocolate left?'

Susan shook her head. 'Mmm-mmm.'

'I believe you were carrying the cherry cremes?'

'Mmm?'

Susan swallowed, and then gave a cough that expressed, in a remarkably concise way, embarrassment *and* annoyance.

'I just had one!' she snapped. 'I need the sugar.'

'I'm sure no one said you did have more than one,' said Unity meekly.

'We haven't been counting at *all*,' said Lu-Tze.

'If you have a handkerchief,' said Unity, still diplomatically, 'I could wipe away the chocolate around your mouth which must have inadvertently got there during the last engagement.'

Susan glared and used the back of her hand.

'It's just the sugar,' she said. 'That's all. It's fuel. And do stop going on about it! Look, we can't just let you die to get—'

Yes, we can, said Lobsang.

'Why?' said Susan, shocked.

Because I have seen everything.

'Would you like to tell everyone?' said Susan, reverting to Classroom Sarcasm. 'We'd all like to know how this ends!'

You misunderstand the meaning of 'everything'.

Lu-Tze rummaged in his sack of ammunition and produced two chocolate eggs and a paper bag. Unity went white at the sight of the bag.

'I didn't know we had any of those!' she said.

'Good, are they?'

'Coffee beans coated in chocolate,' breathed Susan. 'They should be outlawed!'

The two women watched in horror as Lu-Tze put one in his mouth. He gave them a surprised look.

'Quite nice, but I prefer liquorice,' he said.

'You mean you don't want another one?' said Susan.

'No, thank you.'

'Are you *sure*?'

'Yes. I'd quite like liquorice, though, if you have any . . .'

'Have you had some special monk training?'

'Well, not in chocolate combat, no,' said Lu-Tze. 'But is it not written, "If you have another one you won't have an appetite for your dinner"?'

'You really mean you will *not* eat a second chocolate coffee bean?'

'No, thank you.'

Susan looked across at Unity, who was trembling. 'You *do* have tastebuds, don't you?' she said, but she felt a pressure on her arm pulling her away.

'You two get behind that cart over there and run when you get the signal,' said Lu-Tze. 'Go now!'

'What signal?'

We'll know, said the voice of Lobsang.

Lu-Tze watched them hurry away. Then he picked up his broom in one hand and stepped out into the view of a street full of grey people.

'Excuse me?' he said. 'Could I have your attention, please?'

'What is he doing?' said Susan, crouching behind the cart.

They're all going towards him, said Lobsang. *Some of them have weapons.*

'They'll be the ones giving the orders,' said Susan.

Are you sure?

'Yes. They've learned from humans. Auditors aren't used to taking orders. They need persuading.'

He's telling them about Rule One, and that means he's got a plan. I think it's working. Yes!

'What's he done? What's he done?'

Come on! He'll be fine!

Susan leapt up. 'Good!'

Yes, they've cut his head off . . .

*

Fear, anger, envy . . . Emotions bring you alive, which is a brief period just before you die. The grey shapes fled in front of the swords.

But there were billions of them. And they had their own ways of fighting. Passive, subtle ways.

'This is stupid!' Pestilence shouted. 'They can't even catch a common cold!'

'No soul to damn, no arse to kick!' said War, hacking at grey shreds that rolled away from his blade.

'They have a kind of hunger,' said Famine. 'I just can't find a way to get at it!'

The horses were reined in. The wall of greyness hovered in the distance, and began to close in again.

THEY ARE FIGHTING BACK, said Death. CAN YOU NOT FEEL IT?

'I just feel we're too damn stupid,' said War.

AND WHERE DOES THAT FEELING COME FROM?'

'Are you saying they're affecting our minds?' said Pestilence. 'We're Horsemen! How can they do that to *us*?'

WE HAVE BECOME TOO HUMAN.

'Us? Human? Don't make me lau—'

LOOK AT THE SWORD IN YOUR HAND, said Death. DON'T YOU NOTICE ANYTHING?

'It's a sword. Sword-shaped. Well?'

LOOK AT THE HAND. FOUR FINGERS AND A THUMB. A *HUMAN* HAND. HUMANS GAVE YOU THAT SHAPE. AND THAT IS THE WAY IN. *LISTEN!* DO YOU NOT FEEL SMALL IN A BIG UNIVERSE? THAT IS WHAT THEY ARE SINGING. IT IS BIG AND YOU ARE SMALL AND AROUND YOU THERE IS NOTHING BUT THE COLD OF SPACE AND YOU ARE SO VERY ALONE.

The other three Horsemen looked unsettled, nervous.

'That's coming from them?' said War.

YES. IT IS THE FEAR AND HATRED THAT MATTER HAS FOR LIFE AND THEY ARE THE BEARERS OF THAT HATRED.

'Then what can we do?' said Pestilence. 'There're too many of them!'

DID YOU THINK THAT THOUGHT, OR DID THEY? Death snapped.

'They're coming closer again,' said War.

THEN WE WILL DO WHAT WE CAN.

'Four swords against an army? That'll never work!'

YOU THOUGHT IT MIGHT A FEW MOMENTS AGO. WHO IS TALKING FOR YOU NOW? HUMANS HAVE ALWAYS FACED *US* AND THEY HAVE NOT SUR-RENDERED.

'Well, *yes*,' said Pestilence. 'But with *us* they could always hope for a remission.'

'Or a sudden truce,' said War.

'Or—' Famine began, and hesitated, and said finally, 'A shower of fish?' He looked at their expressions. 'That actually happened once,' he added defiantly.

IN ORDER TO HAVE A CHANGE OF FORTUNE AT THE LAST MINUTE YOU HAVE TO TAKE YOUR FORTUNE TO THE LAST MINUTE, said Death. WE MUST DO WHAT WE CAN.

'And if that doesn't work?' said Pestilence.

Death gathered up Binky's reins. The Auditors were much closer now. He could make out their individual, identical shapes. Remove one, and there were always a dozen more.

THEN WE DID WHAT WE COULD, he said, UNTIL WE COULD NOT.

On his cloud, the Angel Clothèd all in White wrestled with the Iron Book.

'What are they talking about?' said Mrs War.

'I don't know, I can't hear! And these two pages are stuck together!' said the angel. It scrabbled ineffectively at them for a moment.

'This is all because he wouldn't wear his vest,' said Mrs War firmly. 'It's just the sort of thing I—'

She had to stop because the angel had wrenched the halo from its head and was dragging it down the fused edge of the pages, with sparks and a sound like a cat slipping down a blackboard.

The pages clanged apart.

'Right, let's see . . .' It scanned the newly revealed text. 'Done that . . . done that . . . oh . . .' It stopped and turned a pale face to Mrs War.

'Oh, boy,' it said, 'we're in trouble now.'

A comet sprang up from the world below, growing visibly larger as the angel spoke. It flamed across the sky, burning fragments detaching and dropping away and revealing, as it closed with the Horsemen, a chariot on fire.

It was a blue flame. Chaos burned with cold.

The figure standing in the chariot wore a full-face helmet dominated by two eye holes that looked slightly like the wings of a butterfly and rather more like the eyes of some strange, alien creature. The burning horse, barely sweating, trotted to a halt; the other horses, regardless of their riders, moved aside to make room.

'Oh, no,' said Famine, waving a hand in disgust. 'Not him, too? I said what'd happen if he came back, didn't I? Remember that time he threw the minstrel out of the hotel window in Zok? Didn't I say—'

SHUT UP, said Death. He nodded. HELLO, RONNIE. GOOD TO SEE YOU. I WONDERED IF YOU WOULD COME.

A hand trailing cold steam came up and removed the helmet.

'Hello, boys,' said Chaos pleasantly.

'Uh . . . long time no see,' said Pestilence.

War coughed. 'Heard you were doing well,' he said.

'Yes, indeed,' said Ronnie, in a careful tone of voice. 'There's a real future in the retail milk and milk derivatives business.'

Death glanced at the Auditors. They'd stopped moving in but were circling, watchfully.

'Well, the world will always need cheese,' said War desperately. 'Haha.'

'Looks like there's some trouble here,' said Ronnie.

'We can handl—' Famine began.

WE CAN'T, said Death. YOU CAN SEE HOW IT IS, RONNIE. TIMES HAVE CHANGED. WOULD YOU CARE TO SIT IN FOR THIS ONE?

'Hey, we haven't discussed—' Famine began, but stopped when War glared at him.

Ronnie Soak put on his helmet, and Chaos drew his sword. It glinted and, like the glass clock, looked like the intrusion into the world of something a great deal more complex.

'Some old man told me you live and learn,' he said. 'Well. I have lived, and now I've learned that the edge of a sword is infinitely

280

long. I've also learned how to make damn good yoghurt, although this is not a skill I intend to employ today. Shall we go get 'em, boys?'

Far down, in the street, a few of the Auditors moved forward.

'What *is* Rule One?' said one of them.

'It does not matter. I am Rule One!' An Auditor with a big axe waved them back. 'Obedience is necessary!'

The Auditors wavered, watching the cleaver. They'd learned about pain. They'd never felt pain before, not in billions of years. Those who had felt it had no desire at all to feel it again.

'Very well,' said Mr White. 'Now get back to—'

A chocolate egg spun out of nowhere and smashed on the stones. The crowd of Auditors rippled forward, but Mr White slashed the axe through the air a few times.

'Stand back! Stand back!' he screamed. 'You three! Find out who threw that! It came from behind that stall! No one is to touch the brown material!'

He stooped carefully and picked up a large fragment of chocolate, on which could just be made out the shape of a smiling duck in yellow icing. Hand shaking and sweat beading his forehead, he raised it aloft and flourished the cleaver triumphantly. There was a collective sigh from the crowd.

'You see?' he shouted. 'The body can be overcome! You see? We *can* find a way to live! If you are good, there may be brown material! If you disobey, there *will* be the sharp edge! Ah . . .' He lowered his arms as a struggling Unity was dragged towards him.

'The pathfinder,' he said, 'the renegade . . .'

He walked towards the captive. 'What will it be?' he said. 'The cleaver or the brown material?'

'It's called chocolate,' snapped Unity. 'I do not eat it.'

'We shall see,' Mr White said. 'Your associate seemed to prefer the axe!'

He pointed to the body of Lu-Tze.

To the empty patch of cobbles where Lu-Tze had been.

A hand tapped him on the shoulder.

'Why is it,' said a voice by his ear, 'that *no one* ever believes in Rule One?'

Above him the sky began to burn blue.

Susan sped up the street to the clock shop.

She glanced sideways, and Lobsang was there, running beside her. He looked . . . human, except that not many humans had a blue glow around them.

'There will be grey men around the clock!' he shouted.

'Trying to find what makes it tick?'

'Hah! Yes!'

'What are you going to do?'

'Smash it!'

'That'll destroy history!'

'So?'

He reached out and took her hand. She felt a shock run up her arm.

'You won't need to open the door! You won't need to stop! Head straight for the clock!' he said.

'But—'

'Don't talk to me! I've got to remember!'

'Remember what?'

'Everything!'

Mr White was already raising the axe as he turned round. But you just can't trust a body. It thinks for itself. When it is surprised, it does a number of things even before the brain has been informed.

The mouth opens, for example.

'Ah, good,' said Lu-Tze, raising his cupped hand. 'Eat this!'

The door was no more substantial than mist. There *were* Auditors in the workshop, but Susan moved through them like a ghost.

The clock glowed. And, as she ran towards it, it moved away. The floor unrolled in front of her, dragging her back. The clock accelerated towards some distant event horizon. At the same time it grew bigger but became more insubstantial, as if the same amount of clockness was trying to spread itself across more space.

Other things were happening. She blinked, but there was no flicker of darkness.

'Ah,' she said to herself, 'so I'm not seeing with my eyes. And what else? What's happening to *me*? My hand . . . looks normal, but does that mean it is? Am I getting smaller or bigger? Does—?'

'Are you *always* like this?' said the voice of Lobsang.

'Like what? I can feel your hand and I can hear your voice – at least, I *think* I can hear it, but maybe it's just in my head – but I can't feel myself running—'

'So . . . so *analytical*?'

'Of course. What am I supposed to be thinking? "Oh, my paws and whiskers"? Anyway, it's quite straightforward. It's all metaphorical. My senses are telling me stories because they can't cope with what is *really* happening—'

'Don't let go of my hand.'

'It's all right, I won't let you go.'

'I *meant*, don't let go of my hand because otherwise every part of your body will be compressed into a space much, much smaller than an atom.'

'Oh.'

'And don't try to imagine what this *really* looks like from outside. Here comes the cloooccckkkkkkkk—'

Mr White's mouth closed. His expression of surprise became one of horror, and then one of shock, and then one of terrible, wonderful bliss.

He began to unravel. He came apart like a big and complex jigsaw puzzle made of tiny pieces, crumbling gently at the extremities and then vanishing into the air. The last piece to evaporate was the lips, and then they too were gone.

A half-chewed chocolate-coated coffee bean dropped onto the street. Lu-Tze reached down quickly, picked up the axe and flourished it at the other Auditors. They leaned back out of the way, mesmerized by authority.

'Who does this belong to now?' he demanded. 'Come on, whose is it?'

'It is mine! I am Miss Taupe!' shouted a woman in grey.

'I am Mr Orange and it belongs to me! No one is even sure that taupe is a proper colour!' screamed Mr Orange.

An Auditor in the crowd said, rather more thoughtfully, 'Is it the case, then, that hierarchy is negotiable?'

'Certainly not!' Mr Orange was jumping up and down.

'You have to decide it amongst yourselves,' said Lu-Tze. He tossed the axe into the air. A hundred pairs of eyes watched it fall.

Mr Orange got there first, but Miss Taupe trod on his fingers. After that, it became very busy and confusing and, to judge by the sounds from within the growing scrum, also very, very painful.

Lu-Tze took the arm of the astonished Unity.

'Shall we be going?' he said. 'Oh, don't worry about me. I was just desperate enough to try something I'd learned from a yeti. It did sting a bit . . .'

There was a scream from somewhere in the mob.

'Democracy at work,' said Lu-Tze happily. He glanced up. The flames above the world were dying out, and he wondered who'd won.

There was bright blue light ahead and dark red light behind, and it amazed Susan how she could see both kinds without opening her eyes and turning her head. Eyes open or shut, she couldn't see herself. All that told her that she was something else besides mere point of view was a slight pressure on what she remembered as her fingers.

And the sound of someone laughing, close to her.

A voice said, 'The sweeper said everyone has to find a teacher and then find their Way.'

'And?' said Susan.

'This *is* my Way. It's the way home.'

And then, with a noise that was unromantically very similar to the kind Jason would make by putting a wooden ruler on the edge of his desk and twanging it, the journey ended.

It might not even have begun. The glass clock was in front of her, full size, glittering. There was no blue glow inside. It was just a clock, entirely transparent, and ticking.

Susan looked down the length of her arm, and up *his* arm to Lobsang. He let go of her hand.

'We're here,' he said.

'*With* the clock?' said Susan. She could feel herself gasping to get her breath back.

'This is only a part of the clock,' said Lobsang. 'The *other* part.'

'The bit outside the universe?'

'Yes. The clock has many dimensions. Do not be afraid.'

'I don't think I have ever been afraid of anything in my life,' said Susan, still gulping air. 'Not really *afraid*. I get angry. I'm getting angry now, in fact. Are you Lobsang or are you Jeremy?'

'Yes.'

'Yes, I walked into that. Are you Lobsang *and* are you Jeremy?'

'Much closer. Yes. I will always remember both of them. But I would prefer you to call me Lobsang. Lobsang has the better memories. I never liked the name Jeremy even when I *was* Jeremy.'

'You really *are* both of them?'

'I am . . . everything about them that was worth being, I hope. They were very different and they were both me, born just an instant apart, and neither of them was very happy by himself. It makes you wonder if there is anything to astrology after all.'

'Oh, there is,' said Susan. 'Delusion, wishful thinking and gullibility.'

'Don't you *ever* let go?'

'I haven't yet.'

'Why?'

'I suppose . . . because in this world, after everyone panics, there's always got to be someone to tip the wee out of the shoe.'

The clock ticked. The pendulum swung. But the hands did not move.

'Interesting,' said Lobsang. 'You're not a follower of the Way of Mrs Cosmopilite, are you?'

'I don't even know what it is,' said Susan.

'Have you got your breath back now?'

285

'Yes.'

'Let's turn around, then.'

Personal time moved on again, and a voice behind them said, 'Is this yours?'

Behind them there were glass steps. At the top of the steps was a man dressed like a History Monk, shaven-headed, besandalled. The eyes gave away a lot more. A young man who'd been alive for a very long time, Mrs Ogg had said, and she had been right.

He was holding a struggling Death of Rats by the scruff of his robe.

'Er, he's his own,' said Susan, as Lobsang bowed.

'Then please take him away with you. We cannot have him running around here. Hello, my son.'

Lobsang walked towards him and they embraced, briefly and formally.

'Father,' said Lobsang, straightening up. 'This is Susan. She has been . . . very helpful.'

'Of course she has,' said the monk, smiling at Susan. 'She is helpfulness personified.' He put the Death of Rats on the floor and prodded him forward.

'Yes, I'm very dependable,' said Susan.

'And interestingly sarcastic, too,' the monk added. 'I am Wen. Thank you for joining us. And for helping our son find himself.'

Susan looked from the father to the son. The words and the movements were stilted and chilly, but there was a communication going on that she wasn't party to, and it was happening a lot faster than speech.

'Aren't we supposed to be saving the world?' she said. 'I don't want to rush anybody, of course.'

'There's something I must do first,' said Lobsang. 'I must meet my mother.'

'Have we got ti—?' Susan began, and then added, 'We have, haven't we? All the time in the world.'

'Oh, no. Far more time than that,' said Wen. 'Besides, there's always time to save the world.'

Time appeared. Again there was the impression that a figure that was in the air, unfocused, was resolving itself into a million specks of matter that poured together and filled a shape in space, slowly at first and then . . . someone was there.

She was a tall woman, quite young, dark-haired, wearing a long red-and-black dress. By the look on her face, Susan thought, she had been weeping. But she was smiling now.

Wen took Susan by the arm, and gently pulled her aside.

'They'll want to talk,' he said. 'Shall we walk?'

The room vanished. Now there was a garden, with peacocks and fountains, and a stone seat, upholstered with moss.

Lawns unrolled towards woodlands that had the manicured look of an estate that had been maintained for hundreds of years so that nothing grew here that was not wanted, or in the wrong place. Long-tailed birds, their plumage like living jewels, flashed from treetop to treetop. Deeper in the woods, other birds called.

As Susan watched, a kingfisher alighted on the edge of a fountain. It glanced at her and flew away, its wingbeats sounding like a snapping of tiny fans.

'Look,' said Susan, 'I don't . . . I'm not . . . Look, I *understand* this sort of thing. Really. I'm not stupid. My grandfather has a garden where everything is black. But Lobsang built the clock! Well, part of him did. So he's saving the world and destroying it, all at once?'

'Family trait,' said Wen. 'It is what Time does at every instant.'

He gave Susan the look of a teacher confronted with a keen but stupid pupil.

'Think like this,' he said at last. 'Think of *everything*. It's an everyday word. But "everything" means . . . everything. It's a much bigger word than "universe". And everything contains all possible things that can happen at all possible times in all possible worlds. Don't look for complete solutions in any one of them. Sooner or later, everything causes everything else.'

'Are you saying one little world is not important, then?' said Susan.

Wen waved a hand, and two glasses of wine appeared on the stone.

'Everything is as important as everything else,' he said.

287

Susan grimaced. 'You know, that's why I've never liked philosophers,' she said. 'They make it all sound grand and simple, and then you step out into a world that's full of *complications*. I mean, look around. I bet this garden needs regular weeding, and the fountains have to be unblocked, and the peacocks shed feathers and dig up the lawn . . . and if they *don't* do that, then this is just a fake.'

'No, everything is real,' said Wen. 'At least, it is as real as anything else. But this is a perfect moment.' He smiled at Susan again. 'Against one perfect moment, the centuries beat in vain.'

'I'd prefer a more specific philosophy,' said Susan. She tried the wine. It was perfect.

'Certainly. I expected that you would. I see you cling to logic as a limpet clings to a rock in a storm. Let me see . . . Defend the small spaces, don't run with scissors, and remember that there is often an unexpected chocolate,' said Wen. He smiled. 'And never resist a perfect moment.'

A breeze made the fountains splash over the sides of their bowls, just for a second. Wen stood up.

'And now, I believe my wife and son have finished their meeting,' he said.

The garden faded. The stone seat melted like mist as soon as Susan got up, although until then it had felt as solid as, well, rock. The wineglass vanished from her hand, leaving only a memory of its pressure on her fingers and the taste lingering in her mouth.

Lobsang was standing in front of the clock. Time herself was not visible, but the song that wove through the rooms now had a different tone.

'She's happier,' said Lobsang. 'She's free now.'

Susan looked around. Wen had vanished along with the garden. There was nothing but the endless glass rooms.

'Don't you want to talk to your father?' she said.

'Later. There will be plenty of time,' said Lobsang. 'I shall see to it.'

The way he said it, so carefully dropping the words into place, made her turn.

'You're going to take over?' she said. '*You* are Time now?'

'Yes.'

'But you're mostly human!'

'So?' Lobsang's smile took after his father. It was the gentle and, to Susan, the infuriating smile of a god.

'What's in all these rooms?' she demanded. 'Do you know?'

'One perfect moment. In each one. An oodleplex of oodleplexes.'

'I'm not certain there's such a thing as a genuinely perfect moment,' said Susan. 'Can we go home now?'

Lobsang wrapped the edge of his robe around his fist and smashed it against the glass front panel of the clock. It shattered, and dropped to the ground.

'When we get to the other side,' he said, 'don't stop and don't look back. There will be a lot of flying glass.'

'I'll try to dive behind one of the benches,' said Susan.

'They probably won't be there.'

SQUEAK?

The Death of Rats had scurried up the side of the clock and was peering cheerfully over the top.

'What do we do about *that*?' said Lobsang.

'*That* looks after itself,' said Susan. 'I never worry about it.'

Lobsang nodded. 'Take my hand,' he said. She reached out.

With his free hand Lobsang grasped the pendulum and stopped the clock.

A blue-green hole opened in the world.

The return journey was a lot swifter but, when the world existed again, she was falling into water. It was brown, muddy and stank of dead plants. Susan surfaced, fighting against the drag of her skirts, and trod water while she tried to get her bearings.

The sun was nailed to the sky, the air was heavy and humid, and a pair of nostrils was watching her from a few feet away.

Susan had been brought up to be practical and that meant swimming lessons. The Quirm College for Young Ladies had been very advanced in that respect, and its teachers took the view that a girl who couldn't swim two lengths of the pool with her clothes on wasn't making an effort. To their credit, she'd left knowing four swimming strokes and several life-saving techniques, and was entirely at home in the water. She also knew what to do if you were sharing the same stretch of water with a hippopotamus, which was to find another stretch of water. Hippos only look big and cuddly from a distance. Close up, they just look big.

Susan summoned up all the inherited powers of the deathly voice plus the terrible authority of the schoolroom, and yelled, GO AWAY!

The creature floundered madly in its effort to turn round, and Susan struck out for the shore. It was an unsure shore, the water becoming land in a tangle of sandbanks, sucking black muck, rotted tree roots and swamp. Insects swirled around and—

—the cobbles were muddy underfoot, and there was the sound of horsemen in the mist—

—and ice, piled up against dead trees—

—and Lobsang, taking her arm.

'Found you,' he said.

'You just shattered history,' said Susan. 'You *broke* it!'

The hippo had come as a shock. She'd never realized one mouth could hold so much bad breath, or be so big and deep.

'I know. I had to. There was no other way. Can you find Lu-Tze? I know Death can locate any living thing, and since you—'

'All right, all right, I know,' said Susan darkly. She held out her hand and concentrated. An image of Lu-Tze's extremely heavy life-timer appeared, and gathered weight.

'He's only a few hundred yards over there,' she said, pointing to a frozen drift.

'And I know *when* he is,' said Lobsang. 'Only sixty thousand years away. So . . .'

Lu-Tze, when they found him, was looking calmly up at an enormous mammoth. Under its huge hairy brow its eyes were squinting with the effort both of seeing him and of getting all three of its brain cells lined up so that it could decide whether to trample on him or gouge him out of the frost-bound landscape. One brain cell was saying 'gouge', one was going for 'trample' but the third had wandered off and was thinking about as much sex as possible.

At the far end of its trunk, Lu-Tze was saying, 'So, you've never *heard* of Rule One, then?'

Lobsang stepped out of the air beside him. 'We must go, Sweeper!'

The appearance of Lobsang did not seem to surprise Lu-Tze at all, although he did seem annoyed at the interruption.

'No rush, wonder boy,' he said. 'I've got this perfectly under control—'

'Where's the lady?' said Susan.

'Over by that snowdrift,' said Lu-Tze, indicating with his thumb while still trying to outstare a pair of eyes five feet apart. 'When this turned up she screamed and twisted her ankle. Look, you can see I've made it nervous—'

Susan waded into the drift and hauled Unity upright. 'Come on, we're leaving,' she said brusquely.

'I saw his head cut off!' Unity babbled. 'And then suddenly we were here!'

'Yes, that kind of thing happens,' said Susan.

Unity stared at her, wild-eyed.

'Life is full of surprises,' said Susan, but the sight of the creature's distress made her hesitate. All right, the thing was one of *them*, one that was merely wearing— Well, at least had started out merely wearing a body as a kind of coat, but now . . . After all, you could say that about *everyone*, couldn't you?

Susan had even wondered if the human soul without the anchor of a body would end up, eventually, as something like an Auditor. Which, to be fair, meant that Unity, who was getting more firmly wrapped in flesh by the minute, was something like a human. And that was a pretty good definition of Lobsang and, if it came to it, Susan as well. Who knew where humanity began and where it finished?

'Come along,' she said. 'We've got to stick together, right?'

Like shards of glass, spinning through the air, fragments of history drifted and collided and intersected in the dark.

There was a lighthouse, though. The valley of Oi Dong held on to the ever-repeating day. In the hall almost all of the giant cylinders stood silent, all time run out. Some had split. Some had melted. Some had exploded. Some had simply vanished. But one still turned.

Big Thanda, the oldest and largest, ground slowly on its basalt bearing, winding time out at one end and back on the other, ensuring as Wen had decreed that the perfect day would never end.

Rambut Handisides was all alone in the hall, sitting beside the turning stone in the light of a butter lamp and occasionally throwing a handful of grease onto the base.

A clink of stone made him peer into the darkness. It was heavy with the smoke of fried rock.

There the sound was again and, then, the scratch and flare of a match.

'Lu-Tze?' he said. 'Is that you?'

'I hope so, Rambut, but who knows, these days?' Lu-Tze stepped into the light and sat down. 'Keeping you busy, are they?'

Handisides sprang to his feet. 'It's been terrible, Sweeper! Everyone's up in the Mandala Hall! It's worse than the Great Crash! There's bits of history everywhere and we've lost half the spinners! We'll never be able to put it all—'

'Now, now, you look like a man who's had a busy day,' said Lu-Tze kindly. 'Not got a lot of sleep, eh? Tell you what, I'll take care of this. You go and get a bit of shut-eye, okay?'

'We thought you were lost out in the world, and—' the monk burbled.

'And now I'm back,' smiled Lu-Tze, patting him on the shoulder. 'There's still that little alcove round the corner where you repair the smaller spinners? And there's still those unofficial bunks for when it's the night shift and you only need a couple of lads to keep their eye on things?'

Handisides nodded, and looked guilty. Lu-Tze wasn't supposed to know about the bunks.

'You get along, then,' said Lu-Tze. He watched the man's retreating back and added, quietly, 'and if you wake up you might turn out to be the luckiest idiot that ever there was. Well, wonder boy? What next?'

'We put everything back,' said Lobsang, emerging from the shadows.

'You know how long that took us last time?'

'Yes,' said Lobsang, looking around the stricken hall and heading towards the podium, 'I do. I don't think it will take me as long.'

'I wish you sounded more certain,' said Susan.

'I'm . . . pretty certain,' said Lobsang, running his fingers over the bobbins on the board.

Lu-Tze waved a cautionary hand at Susan. Lobsang's mind was already on the way to somewhere else, and now she wondered how large a space it was occupying. His eyes were closed.

'The . . . spinners that are left . . . Can you move the jumpers?' he said.

'I can show the ladies how to,' said Lu-Tze.

'Are there not monks who know how to do this?' said Unity.

'It would take too long. I am an apprentice to a sweeper. They would run around asking questions,' said Lobsang. 'You will not.'

'He's got a point right enough,' said Lu-Tze. 'People will start saying "What is the meaning of this?" and "Bikkit!", and we'll never get anything done.'

Lobsang looked down at the bobbins and then across at Susan.

'Imagine . . . that there is a jigsaw, all in pieces. But . . . I am very good at spotting edges and shapes. *Very* good. And all the pieces are moving. But because they were once linked, they have by their very nature a memory of that link. Their shape *is* the memory. Once a few are in the right position, the rest will be easier. Oh, and imagine that all the bits are scattered across the whole of eventuality, and mixing randomly with pieces from other histories. Can you grasp all that?'

'Yes. I think so.'

'Good. Everything I have just said is nonsense. It bears no resemblance to the truth of the matter in any way at all. But it is a lie that you can . . . understand, I think. And then, afterwards—'

'You're going to go, aren't you,' said Susan. It was not a question.

'I will not have enough power to stay,' said Lobsang.

'You need power to stay human?' said Susan. She hadn't been aware of the rise of her heart, but now it was sinking.

'Yes. Even trying to *think* in a mere four dimensions is a terrible effort. I'm sorry. Even to hold in my mind the concept of something called "now" is hard. You thought I was mostly human. I'm mostly not.' He sighed. 'If only I could tell you what everything looks like to me . . . it's so beautiful.'

Lobsang stared into the air above the little wooden bobbins. Things twinkled. There were complex curves and spirals, brilliant against the blackness.

It was like looking at a clock in pieces, with every wheel and spring carefully laid out in the dark in front of him. Dismantled, controllable, every part of it understood . . . but a number of small but important things had gone *ping* into the corners of a very large room. If you were really good, then you could work out where they'd landed.

'You've only got about a third of the spinners,' came the voice of Lu-Tze. 'The rest are smashed.'

Lobsang couldn't see him. There was only the glittering show before his eyes.

'That . . . is true, but *once* they were whole,' he said. He raised his hands and lowered them onto the bobbins.

Susan looked around at the sudden grinding noise and saw row after row of columns rising out of the dust and debris. They stood like lines of soldiers, rubble cascading from them.

'Good trick!' Lu-Tze shouted to Susan's ear, above the thunder. 'Feeding time into the spinners themselves! Theoretically possible, but we never managed to do it!'

'Do you know what he's actually going to *do*?' Susan shouted back.

'Yeah! Snatch the extra time out of bits of history that are too far ahead and shove it into the bits that have fallen behind!'

'Sounds simple!'

'Just one problem!'

'What?'

'Can't do it! Losses!' Lu-Tze snapped his fingers, trying to explain time dynamics to a non-initiate. 'Friction! Divergence! All sorts of stuff! You can't *create* time on the spinners, you can only move it around—'

There was a sudden bright blue glow around Lobsang. It flickered over the board, and then snapped across the air to form arcs of light leading to all the Procrastinators. It crawled between the carved symbols and clung to them in a thickening layer, like cotton winding on a reel.

Lu-Tze looked at the whirling light and the shadow within it, almost lost against the glow.

'—at least,' he added, 'until now.'

The spinners wound up to their working speed and then went faster, under the lash of the light. It poured across the cavern in a solid, unending stream.

Flames licked around the bottom of the nearest cylinder. The base was glowing, and the noise from its stone bearing was joining a rising, cavern-filling scream of stone in distress.

Lu-Tze shook his head. 'You, Susan, buckets of water from the wells! You, Miss Unity, you follow her with the grease pails!'

'And what are you going to do?' said Susan, grabbing two buckets.

'I'm going to worry like hell and that's not an easy job, believe me!'

Steam built up then, and there was a smell of burning butter. There was no time for anything but to run from the wells to the nearest spitting bearing and back, and there was not enough time even for that.

The spinners turned back and forth. There was no need for the jumpers now. The crystal rods that had survived the crash hung uselessly from their hooks as time arced overhead from one Procrastinator to another, showing up as red or blue glows in the air. It was a sight to frighten the *knopta*s off any trained spinner-driver, Lu-Tze knew. It looked like a cascade running wild, but there was some control in there, some huge pattern being woven.

Bearings squealed. Butter bubbled. The bases of some spinners were smoking. But things held. They're *being* held, Lu-Tze thought.

He looked up at the registers. The boards slammed back and forth, sending lines of red or blue or bare wood across the wall of the cavern. There was a pall of white smoke around them as their own wooden bearings gently charred.

Past and future were streaming through the air. The sweeper could feel them.

On the podium, Lobsang was wrapped in the glow. The bobbins were not being moved any more. What was going on now was on some other level, which didn't need the intervention of crude mechanisms.

Lion tamer, Lu-Tze thought. He starts off needing chairs and whips but one day, if he's really good, he can go into the cage and do the show using nothing more than eye and voice. But only if he's really good, and you'll *know* if he's really good because he'll come out of the cage again—

He stopped his prowl along the thundering lines because there was a change in the sound.

One of the biggest spinners was slowing down. It stopped as Lu-Tze watched, and didn't start again.

Lu-Tze raced around the cavern until he found Susan and Unity. Three more spinners stopped before he reached them.

'He's doing it! He's doing it! Come away!' he shouted. With a jolt that shook the floor, another spinner stopped.

The three ran towards the end of the cavern, where the smaller Procrastinators were still whirling, but the halt was already speeding down the rows. Spinner after spinner slammed to a standstill, the domino effect overtaking the humans until, when they reached the little chalk spinners, they were in time to see the last ones rattle gently to a halt.

There was silence, except for the sizzle of grease and the click of cooling rock.

'Is it all over?' said Unity, wiping the sweat from her face with her dress and leaving a trail of sequins.

Lu-Tze and Susan looked at the glow at the other end of the hall, and then at one another.

'I . . . don't . . . think . . . so,' said Susan.

Lu-Tze nodded. 'I think it's just—' he began.

Bars of green light leapt from spinner to spinner and hung in the air as rigid as steel. They flickered on and off between the columns, filling the air with thunderclaps. Patterns of switching snapped back and forth across the cavern.

The tempo increased. The thunderclaps became one long roll of overpowering sound. The bars brightened, expanded and then the air was all one brilliant light—

Which vanished. The sound ceased so abruptly that the silence clanged.

The trio got to their feet, slowly.

'What was *that*?' said Unity.

'I think he made some changes,' said Lu-Tze.

The spinners were silent. The air was hot. Smoke and steam filled the roof of the cavern.

Then, responding to the routine of humanity's eternal wrestle with time, the spinners began to pick up the load.

It came gently, like a breeze. And the spinners took the strain, from the smallest to the largest, settling once again into their gentle, ponderous pirouette.

'Perfect,' said Lu-Tze. 'Almost as good as it was, I'll bet.'

'Only almost?' said Susan, wiping the butter off her face.

'Well, he's partly human,' said the sweeper. They turned to the podium, and it was empty. Susan was not surprised. He'd be weak now, of course. Of course, something like this would take it out of anyone. Of course, he'd need to rest. Of course.

'He's gone,' she said flatly.

'Who knows?' said Lu-Tze. 'For is it not written, "You never know what's going to turn up" ?'

The reassuring rumble of the Procrastinators now filled the cave. Lu-Tze could feel the time flows in the air. It was invigorating, like the smell of the sea. I ought to spend more time down here, he thought.

'He broke history *and* repaired it,' said Susan. 'Cause and cure. That makes no sense!'

'Not in four dimensions,' said Unity. 'In eighteen, it's all perfectly clear.'

'And now, may I suggest you ladies leave by the back way?' said Lu-Tze. 'People are going to come running down here in a minute and it's all going to get very excitable. Probably best if you aren't around.'

'What will you do?' said Susan.

'Lie,' said Lu-Tze happily. 'It's amazing how often that works.'

—ick

Susan and Unity stepped out of a door in the rock. A path led through rhododendron groves out of the valley. The sun was touching the horizon and the air was warm, although there were snowfields quite close by.

At the lip of the valley the water from the stream plunged over a cliff in a fall so long that it landed as a sort of rain. Susan pulled herself onto a rock, and settled down to wait.

'It is a long way to Ankh-Morpork,' said Unity.

'We'll have a lift,' said Susan. The first stars were already coming out.

'The stars are very pretty,' said Unity.

'Do you *really* think so?'

'I am learning to. Humans believe they are.'

'The thing is, I mean, there's times when you look at the universe and you think, "What about me?" and you can just hear the universe replying, "Well, what about you?"'

Unity appeared to consider this. 'Well, what *about* you?' she said.

Susan sighed. 'Exactly.' She sighed again. 'You can't think about just one person while you're saving the world. You have to be a cold, calculating bastard.'

'That sounded as if you were quoting somebody,' said Unity. 'Who said that?'

'Some total idiot,' said Susan. She tried to think of other things, and added, 'We didn't get all of them. There's still Auditors down there somewhere.'

'That will not matter,' said Unity calmly. 'Look at the sun.'

'Well?'

'It is *setting*.'

'And . . .?'

'That means time is flowing through the world. The body exacts its toll, Susan. Soon my— my former colleagues, bewildered and fleeing, will become tired. They will have to sleep.'

'I follow you, but—'

'I am insane. I know this. But the first time it happened to me I found such horror that I cannot express it. Can you imagine what it is like? For an intellect a billion years old, in a body which is an ape on the back of a rat that grew out of a lizard? Can you imagine what comes out of the dark places, uncontrolled?'

'What are you telling me?'

'They will die in their dreams.'

Susan thought about this. Millions and millions of years of thinking precise, logical thoughts – and then humanity's murky past drops all its terrors on you in one go. She could almost feel sorry for them. Almost.

'But you didn't,' she said.

'No. I think I must be . . . different. It is a terrible thing to be different, Susan. Did you have romantic hopes in connection with the boy?'

The question came out of nowhere and there was no defence. Unity's face showed nothing but a kind of nervous concern.

'No,' said Susan. Unfortunately, Unity did not seem to have mastered some of the subtleties of human conversation, such as when a tone of voice means 'Stop this line of inquiry right now or may huge rats eat you by day and by night.'

'I confess to strange feelings regarding his . . . self that was the clockmaker. Sometimes, when he smiled, he was normal. I wanted to help him, because he seemed so closed in and sad.'

. 'You don't have to *confess* to things like that,' Susan snapped. 'How do you even know the word *romantic*, anyway?' she added.

'I found some books of poetry.' Unity actually looked embarrassed.

'Really? I've never trusted it,' said Susan. Huge, giant, *hungry* rats.

'I found it most curious. How can words on a page have a power like that? There is no doubt that being human is incredibly difficult and cannot be mastered in one lifetime,' said Unity sadly.

Susan felt a stab of guilt. It wasn't Unity's fault, after all. People learn things as they grow up, things that never get written down. And Unity had never grown up.

'What are you going to do now?' she said.

'I do have a rather human ambition,' said Unity.

'Well, if I can help in any way . . .'

It was, she realized later, one of those phrases like 'How are you?' People were supposed to understand that it wasn't a real question. But Unity hadn't learned that, either.

'Thank you. You can indeed help.'

'Uh, fine, if—'

'I wish to die.'

And, galloping out of the sunset, some riders were approaching.

Tick

Small fires burned in the rubble, brightening the night. Most of the houses had been completely destroyed, although, Soto considered, the word 'shredded' was much more accurate.

He was sitting by the side of the street, watching carefully, with his begging bowl in front of him. There were of course far more interesting and complex ways for a History Monk to avoid being noticed, but he'd adopted the begging bowl method ever since Lu-Tze had shown him that people never see anyone who wants them to give him money.

He'd watched the rescuers drag the bodies out of the house. Initially they'd thought that one of them had been hideously mutilated in the explosion, until it had sat up and explained that it was an Igor and in very good shape for an Igor, at that. The other he'd recognized as Dr Hopkins of the Guild of Clockmakers, who was miraculously unharmed.

Soto did not believe in miracles, however. He was also suspicious about the fact that the ruined house was full of oranges, that Dr Hopkins was babbling about getting sunlight out of them, and that his sparkling little abacus was telling him that something enormous had happened.

He decided to make a report and see what the boys at Oi Dong said.

Soto picked up the bowl and set off through the network of alleys back to his base. He didn't bother much about concealment now; Lu-Tze's time in the city had been a process of accelerated education for many citizens of the lurking variety. The people of Ankh-Morpork knew all about Rule One.

At least, they had known until now. Three figures lurched out of the dark, and one of them swung a heavy cleaver which would have connected with Soto's head if he hadn't ducked.

He was used to this sort of thing, of course. There was always the occasional slow learner, but they presented no peril that a neat slice couldn't handle.

He straightened up, ready to ease his way out of there, and a thick lock of black hair fell onto his shoulder, slithered down his robe and flopped onto the ground. It made barely a sound, but the expression on his face as Soto looked down and then up at his attackers made them draw back.

He could see, through the blood-red rage, that they all wore stained grey clothes and looked even crazier than the usual alley people; they looked like accountants gone mad.

One of them reached out towards the begging bowl.

Everyone has a conditional clause in their life, some little unspoken addition to the rules like 'except when I really need to' or 'unless no one is looking' or, indeed, 'unless the first one was nougat'. Soto had for centuries embraced a belief in the sanctity of all life and the ultimate uselessness of violence, but his personal conditional clause was 'but not the hair. No one touches the hair, okay?'

Even so, everyone ought to have a *chance*.

The attackers recoiled as he threw the bowl against the wall, where the hidden blades buried themselves in the woodwork.

Then it began to tick.

Soto ran back down the alley, skidded round the corner and *then* shouted, 'Duck!'

Unfortunately for the Auditors, alas, he was just a tiny, tiny fraction of a second too late—

Tick

Lu-Tze was in his Garden of Five Surprises when the air sparkled and fragmented and swirled into a shape in front of him.

He looked up from his ministrations to the yodelling stick insect, who'd been off its food.

Lobsang stood on the path. The boy was wearing a black robe dotted with stars, which blew and rattled its rags around him on this windless morning as if he was standing in the centre of a gale. Which, Lu-Tze supposed, he more or less was.

'Back again, wonder boy?' said the sweeper.

'In a way, I never leave,' said Lobsang. 'Things have gone well with you?'

'Don't you know?'

'I could. But part of me has to do this the traditional way.'

'Well, the abbot is mighty suspicious and there's some amazing rumours flying around the place. I didn't say much. What do I know about anything? I'm just a sweeper.'

With that, Lu-Tze turned his attention to the sick insect. He'd counted to four under his breath before Lobsang said: 'Please? I have to know. I believe that the fifth surprise is you. Am I right?'

Lu-Tze cocked his head. A low noise, which he'd heard for so long he no longer consciously heard it, had changed its tone.

'The spinners are all winding out,' he said. 'They know you're here, lad.'

'I shall not be here long, Sweeper. Please?'

'You just want to know my little surprise?'

'Yes. I know nearly everything else,' said Lobsang.

'But you are Time. What I tell you in the future you'll know now, right?'

'But I'm partly human. I want to *stay* partly human. That means doings things the right way round. Please?'

Lu-Tze sighed and looked for a while down the avenue of cherry blossom.

'When the pupil can beat the master, there is nothing the master cannot tell him,' he said. 'Remember?'

'Yes.'

'Very well. The Iron Dojo should be free.'

Lobsang looked surprised. 'Uh, the Iron Dojo . . . Isn't that the one with all the sharp spikes in the walls?'

'And the ceiling, yes. The one that's like being inside a giant porcupine turned inside out.'

Lobsang looked horrified. 'But that's not for practice! The rules say—'

'That's the one,' said Lu-Tze. 'And *I* say we use it.'

'Oh.'

'Good. No argument,' said Lu-Tze. 'This way, lad.'

Blossom cascaded from the trees as they passed. They entered the monastery, and took the same route they'd taken once before.

This brought them into the Hall of the Mandala, and the sand rose like a dog welcoming its master and spiralled in the air far below Lobsang's sandals. Lu-Tze heard the shouts of the attendants behind him.

News like this spread throughout the valley like ink in water. Hundreds of monks, apprentices and sweepers were trailing the pair as they crossed the inner courtyards, like the tail of a comet.

Above them, all the time, petals of cherry blossom fell like snow.

At last Lu-Tze reached the high, round metal door of the Iron Dojo. The clasp of the door was fifteen feet up. No one who did not belong there was supposed to open the door of the dojo.

The sweeper nodded at his former apprentice.

'You do it,' he said. 'I can't.'

Lobsang glanced at him, and then looked up at the high clasp. Then he pressed a hand against the iron.

Rust spread under his fingers. Red stains spread out across the ancient metal. The door began to creak, and then to crumble. Lu-Tze prodded it with an experimental finger, and a slab of biscuit-strong metal fell out and collapsed on the flagstones.

'Very impress—' he began. A squeaky rubber elephant bounced off his head.

'Bikkit!'

The crowd parted. The chief acolyte ran forward, carrying the abbot.

'What is the *wanna bikkit BIKKIT* meaning of this? Who is *wozza funny man* this person, Sweeper? The spinners are dancing in their hall!'

Lu-Tze bowed.

'He is Time, reverend one, as you have suspected,' he said. Still bent in the bow, he looked up and sideways at Lobsang.

'Bow!' he hissed.

Lobsang looked puzzled. '*I* should bow even now?' he said.

'Bow, you little *stonga*, or I shall teach you such discipline! Show deserved respect! You are *still* my apprentice until I give you leave!'

Shocked, Lobsang bowed.

'And why do you visit us in our timeless valley?' said the abbot.

'Tell the abbot!' Lu-Tze snapped.

'I . . . I wish to learn the Fifth Surprise,' said Lobsang.

'—reverend one—' said Lu-Tze.

'—reverend one,' Lobsang finished.

'You visit us just to learn of our clever sweeper's fancies?' said the abbot.

'Yes, er, reverend one.'

'Of all the things Time could be doing, you wish to see an old man's trick? *Bikkit!*'

'Yes, reverend one.' The monks stared at Lobsang. His robe still fluttered this way and that in the teeth of the intangible gale, the stars glinting when they caught the light.

The abbot smiled a cherubic smile. 'So should we all,' he said. 'None of us has ever seen it, I believe. None of us has ever been able to wheedle it out of him. But . . . this is the Iron Dojo. It has rules! Two may walk in, but only one can walk out! This is no practice dojo! *Wanna 'lephant!* Do you understand?'

'But I don't want—' Lobsang began, and the sweeper jerked an elbow into his ribs.

'You say "Yes, reverend one," ' he growled.

'But I never intended—'

This time the back of his head was slapped.

'This is no time to step back!' Lu-Tze said. 'You're too late, wonder boy!' He nodded to the abbot. 'My apprentice understands, reverend one.'

'Your *apprentice*, Sweeper?'

'Oh, yes, reverend one,' said Lu-Tze. 'My apprentice. Until I say otherwise.'

'Really? *Bikkit!* Then he may enter. You too, Lu-Tze.'

'But I only meant to—' Lobsang protested.

'Inside!' Lu-Tze roared. 'Will you shame me? Shall people think I have taught you nothing?'

The inside of the Iron Dojo was, indeed, a darkened dome full of spikes. They were needle thin and there were tens of thousands of them covering the nightmare walls.

'Who would build something like this?' said Lobsang, looking up at the glistening points that covered even the ceiling.

'It teaches the virtues of stealth and discipline,' said Lu-Tze, cracking his knuckles. 'Impetuosity and speed can be as dangerous to the attacker as to the attacked, as perhaps you will learn. One condition: we are all human here? Agreed?'

'Of course, Sweeper. We are all human here.'

'And shall we agree: no tricks?'

'No tricks,' said Lobsang. 'But—'

'Are we fighting, or are we talking?'

'But, look, if only one can walk out, that means I'll have to kill you—' Lobsang began.

'Or vice versa, of course,' said Lu-Tze. 'That is the rule, yes. Shall we get on?'

'But I didn't know that!'

'In life, as in breakfast cereal, it is always best to read the instructions on the box,' said Lu-Tze. 'This is the Iron Dojo, wonder boy!'

He stepped back and bowed.

Lobsang shrugged, and bowed in return.

Lu-Tze took a few steps back. He closed his eyes for a moment, and then went through a series of simple moves, limbering up. Lobsang winced to hear the crackle of joints.

Around Lobsang there was a series of snapping noises, and for a moment he thought of the old sweeper's bones. But tiny hatches all over the curved wall were swinging open. He could hear whispers as people jostled for position. And by the sound of it, there were a great many people.

He extended his hands, and let himself rise gently in the air.

'I thought we said no tricks?' said Lu-Tze.

'Yes, Sweeper,' said Lobsang, poised in mid-air. 'And then *I* thought: never forget Rule One.'

'Aha! Well done. You've learned something!'

Lobsang drifted closer. 'You cannot believe the things that I have seen since last I saw you,' he said. 'Words cannot describe them. I have seen worlds nesting within worlds, like those dolls they carve in Uberwald. I have heard the music of the years. I know more than I can ever understand. But I do not know the Fifth Surprise. It is a trick, a conundrum . . . a test.'

'Everything is a test,' said Lu-Tze.

'Then show me the Fifth Surprise and I promise not to harm you.'

'You promise not to harm me?'

'I promise not to harm you,' Lobsang repeated solemnly.

'Fine. You only had to ask,' said Lu-Tze, smiling broadly.

'What? I asked before and you refused!'

'You only had to ask at the right time, wonder boy.'

'And is it the right time now?'

'It is written, "There's no time like the present," ' said Lu-Tze. 'Behold, the Fifth Surprise!'

He reached into his robe.

Lobsang floated closer.

The sweeper produced a cheap carnival mask. It was one of those that consisted of a fake pair of spectacles, glued above a big pink nose, and finished with a heavy black moustache.

He put it on and waggled his ears once or twice.

'Boo,' he said.

'What?' said Lobsang, bewildered.

'Boo,' Lu-Tze repeated. 'I never said it was a particularly *imaginative* surprise, did I?'

He waggled his ears again, and then waggled his eyebrows.

'Good, eh?' he said, and grinned.

Lobsang laughed. Lu-Tze grinned wider. Lobsang laughed louder, and lowered himself to the mat.

The blows came out of nowhere. They caught him in the stomach, on the back of his neck, in the small of his back and swept his legs from under him. He landed on his stomach, with Lu-Tze pinning him down in the Straddle of the Fish. The only way to get out of that was to dislocate your own shoulders.

There was a sort of collective sigh from the hidden watchers.

'*Déjà-fu!*'

'What?' said Lobsang, into the mat. 'You said none of the monks knew *déjà-fu*!'

'I never taught it to 'em, that's why!' said Lu-Tze. 'Promise not to harm me, would you? Thank you so very much! Submit?'

'You never told me *you* knew it!' Lu-Tze's knees, rammed into the secret pressure points, were turning Lobsang's arms into powerless lumps of flesh.

'I may be old but I'm not daft!' Lu-Tze shouted. 'You don't think I'd give away a trick like *that*, do you?'

'That's not fair—'

Lu-Tze leaned down until his mouth was an inch from Lobsang's ear.

'Didn't say "fair" on the box, lad. But you can win, you know. You could turn me into dust, just like that. How could I stop Time?'

'I can't do that!'

'You mean you won't, and we both know it. Submit?'

Lobsang could feel parts of his body trying to shut themselves down. His shoulders were on fire. I can discarnate, he thought. Yes,

307

I can, I could turn him to dust with a thought. And lose. I'd walk out and he'd be dead and I'd have lost.

'Nothing to worry about, lad,' said Lu-Tze, calmly now. 'You just forgot Rule Nineteen. Submit?'

'Rule *Nineteen*?' said Lobsang, almost pushing himself off the mat until terrible pain forced him down again. 'What the hell is Rule Nineteen? Yes, yes, submit, submit!'

'"Remember Never to Forget Rule One",' said Lu-Tze. He released his grip. 'And always ask yourself: how come it was created in the first place, eh?'

Lu-Tze got to his feet, and went on: 'But you have performed well, all things considered, and therefore as your master I have no hesitation in recommending you for the yellow robe. Besides,' he lowered his voice to a whisper, 'everyone peeking in here has seen me beat Time and that's the sort of thing that'll look really good on my curriculum vitae, if you catch my meaning. Def'nitely give the ol' Rule One a fillip. Let me give you a hand up.'

He reached down.

Lobsang was about to take the hand when he hesitated. Lu-Tze grinned again, and gently pulled him upright.

'But only one of us can leave, Sweeper,' said Lobsang, rubbing his shoulders.

'Really?' said Lu-Tze. 'But playing the game changes the rules. I say the hell with it.'

The remains of the door were pushed aside by the hands of many monks. There was the sound of someone being hit with a rubber yak. '*Bikkit!*'

'. . . and the abbot, I believe, is ready to present you with the robe,' said Lu-Tze. 'Don't make any comment if he dribbles on it, please.'

They left the dojo and, followed now by every soul in Oi Dong, headed for the long terrace.

It was, Lu-Tze reminisced later, an unusual ceremony. The abbot did not appear overawed, because babies generally aren't and will throw up over *anyone*. Besides, Lobsang might have been master of the gulfs of time, but the abbot was master of the valley, and therefore respect was a line that travelled in both directions.

But the handing over of the robe had caused a difficult moment.

Lobsang had refused it. It had been left to the chief acolyte to ask why, while the whispered current of surprise washed through the crowd.

'I am not worthy, sir.'

'Lu-Tze has declared that you have completed your apprenticeship, my lo— Lobsang Ludd.'

Lobsang bowed. 'Then I will take the broom and the robe of a sweeper, sir.'

This time the current was a tsunami. It crashed over the audience. Heads turned. There were gasps of shock, and one or two nervous laughs. And, from the lines of sweepers who had been allowed to pause in their tasks to watch the event, there was a watchful, intent silence.

The chief acolyte licked his suddenly dehydrated lips.

'But . . . but . . . you are the incarnation of Time . . .'

'In this valley, sir,' said Lobsang firmly, 'I am as worthy as a sweeper.'

The chief acolyte looked around, but there was no help anywhere. The other senior members of the monastery had no wish to share in the huge pink cloud of embarrassment. The abbot merely blew bubbles, and grinned the inward knowing grin of all babies everywhere.

'Do we have any . . . uh . . . do we present sweepers with . . . do we by any chance . . . ?' the acolyte mumbled.

Lu-Tze stepped up behind him. 'Can I be of any help, your acolytility?' he said, with a sort of mad keen subservience that was quite alien to his normal attitude.

'Lu-Tze? Ah . . . er . . . yes . . . er . . .'

'I could fetch a nearly new robe, sir, and the lad can have my old broom if you'll sign a chitty for me to get a new one from stores, sir,' said Lu-Tze, sweating helpfulness at every pore.

The chief acolyte, drowning well out of his depth, seized on this like a passing lifebelt.

309

'Oh, would you be so good, Lu-Tze? It is so kind of you . . .'

Lu-Tze vanished in a blur of helpful speed that, once again, quite surprised those who thought they knew him.

He reappeared with his broom and a robe made white and thin with frequent bashings on the stones by the river. He solemnly handed them over to the chief acolyte.

'Er, uh, thank you, er, *is* there a special ceremony for the, for the, er, for . . . er . . .' the man burbled.

'Very simple one, sir,' said Lu-Tze, still radiating eagerness. 'Wording is quite loose, sir, but generally we say, "This is your robe, look after it, it belongs to the monastery," sir, and then with the broom we say something like "Here's your broom, treat it well, it is your friend, you will be fined if you lose it, remember they do not grow on trees," sir.'

'Er, um, uh,' the chief acolyte murmured. 'And does the abbot—?'

'Oh no, the abbot would not make a presentation to a sweeper,' said Lobsang quickly.

'Lu-Tze, who does the, er, does, uh, does the . . .'

'It's generally done by a senior sweeper, your acolytility.'

'Oh? And, er, by some happy chance, er, do *you* happen to be—?'

Lu-Tze bobbed a bow. 'Oh, *yes*, sir.'

To the chief acolyte, still floundering in the flood of the turning tide, this was as welcome as the imminent prospect of dry land. He beamed manically.

'I wonder, I wonder, I wonder, then, if you would be so kind, er, then, er, to—'

'Happy to, sir.' Lu-Tze swung round. 'Right now, sir?'

'Oh, please, yes!'

'Right you are. Step forward, Lobsang Ludd!'

'Yes, Sweeper!'

Lu-Tze held out the worn robe and the elderly broom. 'Broom! Robe! Do not lose them, we are not made of money!' he announced.

'I thank you for them,' said Lobsang. 'I am honoured.'

Lobsang bowed. Lu-Tze bowed. With their heads close together and at the same height, Lu-Tze hissed, 'Very surprising.'

'Thank you.'

'Nicely mythic, the whole thing, definitely one for the scrolls, but bordering on smug. Do not try it again.'

'Right.'

They both stood up. 'And, er, what happens now?' said the chief acolyte. He was a broken man, and he knew it. Nothing was going to be the same after this.

'Nothing, really,' said Lu-Tze. 'Sweepers get on with sweeping. You take that side, lad, and I'll take this.'

'But he is Time!' said the chief acolyte. 'The son of Wen! There is so much we have to ask!'

'There is so much I will not tell,' said Lobsang, smiling. The abbot leaned forward and dribbled into the chief acolyte's ear.

IIc gavc up. 'Of course, it is not up to us to question you,' he said, backing away.

'No,' said Lobsang. 'It is not. I suggest you all get on with your very important work, because this plaza is going to need all my attention.'

There were frantic hand signals amongst the senior monks and, gradually, reluctantly, the monastery staff moved away.

'They'll be watching us from every place they can hide,' mumbled Lu-Tze, when the sweepers were alone.

'Oh, yes,' said Lobsang.

'So, how are you, then?'

'Very well. And my mother is happy, and she will retire with my father.'

'What? A cottage in the country, that sort of thing?'

'Not quite. Similar, though.'

There was no sound for a while but the brushing of two brooms.

Then Lobsang said, 'I'm aware, Lu-Tze, that it is usual for an apprentice to give a small gift or token to his master when he finishes his apprenticeship.'

'Possibly,' said Lu-Tze, straightening up. 'But I don't need anything. I've got my mat, my bowl and my Way.'

'Every man has something he desires,' said Lobsang.

'Hah! Got you there, then, wonder boy. I'm eight hundred years old. I've run through all my desires long ago.'

'Oh dear. That is a shame. I hoped I could find *something*.' Now Lobsang straightened up and swung his broom onto his shoulder. 'In any case, I must leave,' he said. 'There is so much still to do.'

'I'm sure there is,' said Lu-Tze. 'I'm sure there is. There's the whole stretch under the trees, for one thing. And while we're on the subject, wonder boy, did you let that witch have her broomstick back?'

Lobsang nodded. 'Let us just say . . . I put things back. It's a lot newer than it was, too.'

'Hah!' said Lu-Tze, sweeping up a few more petals. 'Just like that. Just like that. So easily does a thief of time repay his debts!'

Lobsang must have caught the rebuke in the tone. He stared down at his feet. 'Well, perhaps not *all* of them, I admit,' he said.

'Oh?' said Lu-Tze, still apparently fascinated by the end of his own broom.

'But when you have to save a world you cannot think of one person, you see, because one person is a part of that world,' Lobsang went on.

'Really?' said the sweeper. 'You think so? You've been talking to some very strange people, my lad.'

'But now I have time,' said Lobsang earnestly. 'And I hope she'll understand.'

'It's amazing what a lady will understand, if you find the right way of putting it,' said Lu-Tze. 'Best of luck, lad. You didn't do so bad, on the whole. And is it not written, "There's no time like the present"?'

Lobsang smiled at him, and vanished.

Lu-Tze went back to his sweeping. After a while, he smiled at a memory. An apprentice gives a gift to the master, eh? As if Lu-Tze could want anything that Time could give him . . .

And he stopped, and looked up, and laughed out loud.

Overhead, swelling as he watched, the cherries were ripening.

Tick

312

In some place that had not existed before, and only existed now for this very purpose, stood a large, gleaming vat.

'Ten thousand gallons of delicate fondant sugar cream infused with essence of violet and stirred into dark chocolate,' said Chaos. 'There are also strata of hazelnut praline in rich butter cream, and areas of soft caramel for that special touch of delight.'

SO . . . YOU'RE SAYING THAT THIS VAT COULD EXIST SOMEWHERE IN A TRULY INFINITE EVERYWHERE, AND THEREFORE IT CAN EXIST HERE? said Death.

'Indeed,' said Chaos.

BUT IT NO LONGER EXISTS IN THE PLACE WHERE IT SHOULD EXIST.

'No. It should, *now*, exist here. The maths is easy,' said Chaos.

AH? WELL, MATHS, said Death dismissively. GENERALLY I NEVER GET MUCH FURTHER THAN SUBTRACTION.

'In any case, chocolate is hardly a rare commodity,' said Chaos. 'There are planets covered in the stuff.'

REALLY?

'Indeed.'

IT MIGHT BE BEST, said Death, IF NEWS LIKE THAT DID NOT GET ABOUT.

He walked back to where Unity was waiting in the darkness.

YOU DO NOT NEED TO DO THIS, he said.

'What else is there?' said Unity. 'I have betrayed my own kind. And I am hideously insane. I can never be at home anywhere. And staying here would be an agony.'

She stared into the chocolate abyss. A dusting of sugar sparkled on its surface.

Then she slipped out of her dress. To her amazement she felt embarrassed about doing so, but still drew herself up haughtily.

'Spoon,' she commanded, and held out her right hand imperiously. Chaos gave a silver ladle a final, theatrical polish and passed it to her.

'Goodbye,' said Unity. 'Do pass on my best wishes to your granddaughter.'

She walked a few steps back, turned, broke into a run, and took off into a perfect swallow dive.

The chocolate closed over her with barely a sound. Then the two watchers waited until the fat, lazy ripples had died away.

'Now there was a lady with *style*,' said Chaos. 'What a waste.'

YES. I THOUGHT SO.

'Well, it's been fun . . . up to that point, anyway. And now I must be off,' said Chaos.

YOU'RE CONTINUING WITH THE MILK ROUND?

'People rely on me.'

Death looked impressed. IT'S GOING TO BE . . . INTERESTING TO HAVE YOU BACK, he said.

'Yeah. It is,' said Chaos. 'You're not coming?'

I'M GOING TO WAIT HERE FOR A WHILE.

'Why?'

JUST IN CASE.

'Ah.'

YES.

It was some minutes later that Death reached into his robe and pulled out a lifetimer that was small and light enough to have been designed for a doll. He turned round.

'But . . . I *died*,' said the shade of Unity.

YES, said Death. THIS IS THE NEXT PART . . .

Tick

Emma Robertson sat in the classroom with wrinkled brow, chewing on her pencil. Then, rather slowly but with the air of one imparting great secrets, she set to work.

> We went to Lanker where there are witches they are kind they grow
> erbs. We met this which she was very jole and sang us a snog abot a
> hedghog it had dificut words. Jason try to kick her cat it chase him up
> a tre. I know a lot about wiches now they do not have warts they do not
> eat you they are just like your grane except your grane does not know
> difult words.

At her high desk Susan relaxed. There was nothing like a classroom of bent heads. A good teacher used whatever materials there were to hand, and taking the class to visit Mrs Ogg was an education in herself. Two educations.

A classroom going well had its own smell: a hint of pencil shavings, poster paints, long-dead stick insect, glue and, of course, the faint aroma of Billy.

There had been an uneasy meeting with her grandfather. She'd raged that he hadn't told her things. And he'd said of course he hadn't. If you told humans what the future held, it wouldn't. That made sense. Of course it made sense. It was good logic. The trouble was that Susan was only *mostly* logical. And so, now, things were back in that uneasy, rather cool state where they spent most of their time, in the tiny little family that *ran* on dysfunctionality.

Maybe, she thought, that was a normal family state. When push came to shove – thank you, Mrs Ogg, she'd always remember that phrase now – they'd rely on each other automatically, without a thought. Apart from that, they kept out of one another's way.

She hadn't seen the Death of Rats lately. It was too much to hope that he was dead. In any case, it hadn't slowed him down so far.

That made her think wistfully about the contents of her desk. Susan was very strict about eating in class and took the view that, if there were rules, then they applied to everyone, even her. Otherwise they were merely tyranny. But maybe rules were there to make you think before you broke them.

There was still half a box of Higgs & Meakins' cheapest assortment tucked in there amongst the books and papers.

Opening the lid carefully and slipping her hand in was easy, and so was the maintenance of a suitably teachery face while she did so. Questing fingers found a chocolate in the nest of empty paper cups, and told her that it was a damn nougat. But she was resolute. Life was tough. Sometimes you got nougat.

Then she briskly picked up the keys and walked to the Stationery Cupboard with what she hoped was the purposeful step of someone about to check on the supply of pencils. After all, you never knew, with pencils. They needed watching.

The door clicked behind her, leaving only the dim light through the transom. She put the chocolate in her mouth and shut her eyes.

A faint, cardboardy sound made her open them. The lids were gently lifting on the boxes of stars.

They spilled out and whirled up into the shadows of the cupboard, brilliant against the darkness, a galaxy in miniature, gently spinning.

Susan watched them for a while, and then said, 'All right, you have my full attention, whoever you are.'

At least, that was what she meant to say. The peculiar stickiness of the nougat caused it to come out as: 'Allite, you ot my fo' a'nen'on, oover ooah.' Damn!

The stars spiralled around her head, and the cupboard's interior darkened into interstellar black.

'If iss is oo, Def o' Raffs—' she began.

'It's me,' said Lobsang.

Tick

Even with nougat, you can have a perfect moment.